THE
CASTOFF
CHILDREN

THE
CASTOFF
CHILDREN

L.M. Browning

HOMEBOUND PUBLICATIONS

Ensuring the mainstream isn't the only stream.

Copyright © 2016 by L.M. Browning
All Rights Reserved
Printed in the United States of America
as well as the United Kingdom and Australia.
First Edition Trade Paperback

Paperback ISBN 978-1-938846-98-4
Front Cover Image © Ruta Saulyte-Laurinaviciene
Cover and Interior Designed by Leslie M. Browning

www.lmbrowning.com
www.homeboundpublications.com

10 9 8 7 6 5 4 3 2 1

Homebound Publications greatly values the natural
environment and invests in environmental conservation. Our
books are printed on paper with chain of custody certification
from the Forest Stewardship Council, Sustainable Forestry
Initiative, and the Program for the Endorsement of Forest
Certification. In addition, each year Homebound Publications donates
1% of our net profit to a humanitarian or ecological charity.

To my mother, Marianne:
We wrote this together and we lived this together.

———

WHEN THE WINTER HAS BEEN LONG you can forget there is a spring. The harsh cold seeps into you and the feeling of warmth is forgotten.

———————————

PROLOGUE

THE FACE OF THE FULL MOON WAS HIDDEN. A funnel of powdery snow spun like a dervish between the high brick walls of the deserted alley. The winter wind howled high and low through the dark channels of the city. Tucked away in a forgotten place were twelve castoff children, taking comfort in the only thing left to them: each other.

"Duncan," the voice of a young boy sounded, "tell us again, the story about the whale." The boy, Asa, looked up at the young man holding him.

"It's time to sleep." Duncan patted the boy's back. Asa laid his head down against Duncan's chest.

"Joseph, how deep is the snow gonna be?" Asa squirmed, unable to sleep. He turned to the shadowy figure next to him.

"The papers say the people down south got a couple of feet," replied Joseph.

"How much is that?" Asa perked up.

"About as much as you are," Duncan laughed.

Marie let out a sigh. "Hush now, let's try to sleep," she gently chimed in. She gave Duncan a soft nudge in the dark.

"Yes, sleep," Duncan quickly reinforced. "In the morning we will—"

There was a bang and the clap of breaking wood. The front doors lay splintered on the ground. Heavy boots thundered through the entry way. A flood of a half dozen men came bursting into the great room. The children scattered like spooked mice bolting towards the doors racing out into the snowy night.

PART ONE

CHAPTER 1
THE COLDNESS

THE BOY WAS A PICTURE OF NEGLECT. His baggy, thread-bare clothes hung off his rail-thin body. The once-thick cottons were reduced to thin cheesecloth wrappings, which gave no warmth or softness. Wound around his feet were old scraps of faded drapes that most likely hung in the windows of the well-to-do townhouses along Beacon Street before he found them in a trash bin. The outermost layer of his makeshift shoes were made of burlap potato sacks unloaded from the cargo ships moored along the southern harbor.

Tall for fourteen, Joseph had neither the look of the man he had once called *Father* nor the woman he had once called *Mother*. His plump, young face had been gouged out—prematurely lined—by the hand of hardship. Malnutrition and stress had thinned the boy's dark brown hair. Overgrown chunks draped along the sides of his face and rogue strands hung down into his chestnut-brown eyes.

This winter had aged him more than any other. It was the worst in memory. All day he had heard people talk about the storms, and his heart hardened with each snippet of conversation he caught. To the people of Boston, two massive

1

Nor'easters in five days was a record—something to be commented about on street corners after having a mug-up of coffee, while enjoying a pipe and the morning edition of *The Boston Post*. But to Joseph and all those on the streets, it was far from a joking matter.

*   *   *   *   *

T HE NOONDAY SUN WAS DESCENDING, taking with it what little warmth there was to be had. The hustle and bustle of the streets was starting to pick up as the next storm silently approached in the distance.

For hours he walked along the narrow paths in the hardening slush carved out by the carriage wheels along Beacon Street as he made his way towards the North End, where he would hole up during the storm.

The fires in each hearth burned bright tonight as the cold deepened. Each chimney poured out heavy smoke. Framed in frosted windows set aglow by the fire burning within the house, Joseph stared in on the perfect scene: red-faced, bright-eyed people, eating forkfuls of food from steaming plates, drinking and laughing.

Turning away from the happy scene, Joseph shuffled back into the street. He hungrily rummaged through a trash bin, found nothing and continued on.

The approaching night pressed in on him as the bells tolled 3 p.m.. On nights such as these he always used to say, "Hope burns warmer and brighter than even the fattest Yule log," as he and his friends sat huddled around the light of their hopes. Tonight, however, he was alone and hope was flickering.

What we want is so very simple, he thought to himself…
so simple. Why then must it be so hard? An image formed in
his imagination: a woman with a kind face putting a plate in
front of him and the warmth of a father's pride beaming upon
him from the head of the dinner table. Joseph ached for the
heavy warmth of a wool blanket, a thick pair of knitted socks,
a mug of hot tea, a warm bowl of soup, and the company of his
friends. The image we carry in our mind of how it *should be*
always makes the reality in front of us that much harder to bear.

Unable to go on but unable to stop, he just kept walking—
dragging his numb feet forward—until finally his body
stopped of its own accord. He saw something. It took a
moment for what was happening to catch up with his tired
mind—something his eyes had passed over had brought him
to a stop. He saw another child lying in a snow bank—a child
he knew very well.

Joseph's weak heart jolted to life. Breaking out of his frozen
shock, Joseph took off running—hobbling over to the child as
fast as his stiffening legs would take him across the icy ground.
Once there, he knelt beside the still figure.

"Ben!"

The tiny figure did not move—not even a stir at the sound
of a friend's voice.

Joseph's excitement rolled over to terror.

"Ben, Ben, I found you. …Ben?"

Joseph pulled Ben into his arms. A momentary relief
washed over him. Yet as the reality sunk into him, relief
became panic. Ben was sick. A storm was coming. *What do I
do?* he asked himself in alarm. Joseph held Ben tight trying to
warm the fragile boy with an embrace, but he had little body
heat to give.

Ben's hands and feet were frozen. His shoes, which were nothing more than old dress shoes made of cracked leather, had begun to rip away from the soles. The thin socks that he wore were soaked by the wet streets he had trod during the day and frozen hard by the cold night air. Between the dirt and dried blood smeared across his face, Ben looked like a small soldier after a prolonged battle.

"Ben…Teddy, I'm here. It's Joseph,"

When Joseph had first found Ben, all those years ago, he had been sitting in the same place for days on end—the place where his mother had left him and told him to stay and wait for her, with no intention of ever returning to him.

Uprooted from his home, forsaken by those he loved and depended upon, all Ben had left from before that traumatizing day was his small teddy bear—a tiny, worn bear with a brown corduroy body that had been squeezed so tightly throughout the years it was balding and misshapen. The bear had two buttons for eyes: one green and one pale blue. Thankfully, Anna was good at sewing and, despite limited material to work with, had managed to keep the precious bear intact—sewing and re-sewing the tearing seams, closing holes, re-stitching the detail of the bear's little smile and triangular nose.

Ben carried the bear everywhere. Even now as Joseph hugged the freezing boy he could feel the bulge of it underneath Ben's coat. It was because of his affinity for the stuffed animal that all of the others in the group had over time taken to calling Ben *Teddy*.

A firm resolve settled in Joseph's heart. Not even feeling his own fatigue, Joseph stood up, picked Ben up and marched on. He went to the nearby houses but no help came. When finally Joseph had finished traveling the length of Hanover Street, he entered the slums of the North End where he came to his only option.

The doors to a tenement building were flung open. One of the double doors broken off its hinges was left propped up against the side of the brick building. Joseph stared at the building apprehensively, before finally assenting to pass into the dark mouth of the hallway. He wished there was some other place where he could find help, but there was not.

Before the Revolutionary War, such buildings were mansions of well-heeled families, many of which had alliances with England and departed after the redcoats were defeated. The mansions fell into decay and were taken over by landlords, who rented the rooms one by one to the flood of Irish immigrants arriving in ships that docked in the harbor. The once affluent neighborhood darkened further as the dockyards grew more popular, bringing sailors with their pent-up thirst for strong drink, women, and gambling. All but the poorest and those with the vilest tastes remained, making it a place of last resort.

With the broken doors letting the snow sweep in, the air in the stairwell was as cold as the air outside. Joseph spotted two figures ahead, lying on the first landing of the stairwell. His breath caught in his chest. He pulled himself against the wall in an attempt to blend in and waited. Thankfully, the men did not stir, empty bottles lay lax in their callused hands.

Joseph passed by the drunken men as he continued to climb the steps. Teeth clenched tight, under his breath he prayed for one thing alone: To find some quiet corner in which to rest. His eyes were wide—whites clearly visible in the dark.

Don't wake up. Don't wake up. He willed through gritted teeth.

He felt like he was trying to creep past sleeping beasts. Men with scarred faces and broken teeth, who reeked of liquor and smoke, growled gibberish and slurred threats at him as he walked by with his head down.

Finally he came at last to the top floor where he proceeded down a narrow, dark hallway. Each time he came to a door, he glanced in looking for a safe place to lay Ben down until finally he found one at the far end.

The room was dark. The offensive, acidic smell of urine and vomit caused Joseph's nose to curl.

"At least we're out of the snow, he whispered to the hardly conscious Ben.

Suddenly from out of a shadowed corner, a forbidding figure appeared.

"Hey! You! Whatcha doin' here boy?"

A thin, twitchy young man moved forward. His hair was matted, his eyes sunken.

"Ummm. Nothin'. Leavin'." Joseph muttered as he turned around.

"Oh no you're not." The man moved quickly to block the boys' exit.

Joseph's breathing quickened. He tried to push past the man.

"No. No. No. No. No." He rocked back and forth. "Can't let you go. Can't. Can't," the deranged man mumbled.

"Yes you can. We need to go." Joseph assured.

Their eyes met in the shadows. The air in the room seized

taut. The ratty man grabbed Ben and pulled him from Joseph's arms. The sickly boy hit the floor with a muffled thud. Joseph charged. The man was pushed back but reached out a boney hand. A wiry fist closed around the collar of Joseph's shirt. Joseph ran forward, letting the thinning shirt tear away from him. Wrapping his arms around Ben, he hoisted the boy over his shoulder and made for the door.

"Not so fast," the ghostly man shouted as he clamored to his feet.

Joseph kept moving. The man grabbed hold of Ben's coat, but it too was ripped away from the boy as Joseph ran from the room, barreled down the stairs and disappeared into the snowy night. Snow and ice was launched into the air as he sped into the street, still clutching Ben tight against his chest.

* * * * *

IT WAS NEAR DUSK. The streets were crowded. Frantic people buzzed around, going from shop to shop filling their baskets with supplies as the next storm loomed. Wood sold by the bundle, lamp oil by the liter and coal by the bucketful. The panic was so thick it was almost tangible. Everyone was wrapped in concern for themselves, taking no notice of two young boys moving down the street—a small one who was paler than the snow itself and the other older one struggling to carry him—both without coats, shivering in a cold sweat.

Minutes drew out like hours. The eerie stillness that always precedes a great storm fell over the city. The crowds thinned along Hanover Street the further down the lane Joseph got. In the mounting silence, Joseph could feel the brute winter breathing down his neck. Ben still could not walk. Eyes focused and his jaw set, Joseph forced himself forward. His eyes watered as the wind picked up small shards of ice from the ground and blasted his bare face. His teeth chattered. The wet air expelled from his deep, ragged breaths turned to crystalline vapor immediately. He looked down at Ben in his arms who was drifting in and out of consciousness. The dark blue circles around his eyes had deepened, making him look like a pale skeleton—a ghost of a child.

Joseph turned his gaze upward toward the sky just ahead of him. The churning front approached—gray mixing with pearly white, charcoal black clouds were descending, colliding and expanding—the storm was amassing. *It'll be here soon,* Joseph thought to himself.

"We'll be all right, Teddy," Joseph repeated over and over again. Ben did not answer. His head lay limp, rocking lightly on Joseph's arm with each heavy step taken. "We'll be all right," Joseph repeated again, this time trying to comfort himself.

Nowhere else to go, they marched into the throat of the inescapable storm. "I'm taking us somewhere warm, Ben. Just stay with me," Joseph's voice trailed off. His eyes scanned each inch of the street. Taking in the iced air with each deep breath was like being stabbed in the side with a fiery knife.

He pushed on, but then it came: the impact against the icy ground. His knees buckled and the rest of his body gave way. "Dammit!" He cried out. The strike rang up his bones, causing him to shout out loud, sending a pained cry down the now-deserted street. Upon impact, Joseph spilled Ben out onto the street. He lay spread-eagle on the ice with Ben lying sprawled off to the side a little ways from him like a ragdoll—unmoving.

He drifted off for a time while laying there—ten or twenty minutes—he did not know. No help came. Joseph's cry of pain as he hit the ice had echoed through an indifferent city.

He rolled over onto all fours, braced his weight upon his palms and pushed himself up.

Joseph stood, oriented himself and then finally managed to take a few shaky steps toward Ben, who had not awakened from the sudden impact of the fall.

Joseph had planned to find them some shelter, but that was not going to happen.

He grabbed both of Ben's arms and pulled the boy along, walking backwards against the cutting wind. Turning down a side alleyway, Joseph made his way to the very back, putting Ben to rest in an empty corner against one of the high brick walls.

Holding Ben to his chest, Joseph shook as he stared out into the darkness, watching as the unending barrage of snow fell. In a daze of weariness Joseph drifted out of time. He did not know how long they sat there—long enough that coldness became numbness. His mind felt detached from his body. He stared into Ben's eyes. The boy's limp head tilted back towards the black sky.

Joseph was not winning the struggle against the cold undertow that pulled him down. Yet, just as his head began to fall sideways and his clear vision slipped out of focus, a hand reached out and cradled his frozen cheek. Hands holding his face brought his eyes level with the gaze of another who called to him.

"Joseph, Joseph, I've found you. Joseph, what happened?" The voice was the gentle tone of a caring presence. It was the voice of Joseph's sole comfort in this world: Anna.

Hearing her voice from the distant place he was being pulled into, Anna's arrival was like a dream—the apparition of a divine being plucking him out of the dark.

Anna brushed her hand over Joseph's ghostly face. She looked down and felt Ben's face, "Joseph, what happened? Where are your coats? Nevermind, it doesn't matter," she said, throwing off all questions.

Joseph's head was limp, his eyes were open, but he stared blankly at her from within a daze of hypothermia. "Joseph, you have to wake up!" Anna ordered him, adding in a soften plea, "Please, wake up."

Joseph's legs were just mounds beneath the perfect blanket of newly fallen snow—a shroud that had been pulled halfway over him. She pulled Ben to the surface of the snow. "I've been looking for you both for weeks. I'm so glad to see you. I didn't think our reunion would be like this, but at least you found each other." These last words were strained as she heaved Ben up out of the snow encasing him. She laid him down, took off her coat, buttoned Ben into it, then turned back to Joseph.

"Joseph!" she said firmly. Joseph heard her voice as though it were an echo traveling through a void. He reached for it, trying to grasp hold of it—trying to wake. She was not a dream. She was real, and he needed to get up.

From within his frozen state, Joseph's eyes showed him the scene. The blurred figure moving around began to clear, until finally he could see her auburn hair and hazel eyes.

"Ben...sick," he said in a weak, vague, disconnected voice.

Anna stopped fussing with Ben and looked Joseph in the eyes—cradling his cheeks in her hands. "I've got him, but you have to help me," she stressed. "I won't leave you here. If you don't get up, I'm staying, and if that happens, we'll all freeze and Ben will surely die. So get up Joseph. Get—up!" Anna knew Joseph could not rise to save his own life, but he would find the strength to rise if it were to save Ben and her.

Jerking painfully, Anna began to move his legs and arms until at last he moved them on his own. The first movements felt like he was forced to break his very bones. Yet, the more he moved the easier it became.

Anna picked up Ben and helped Joseph to his feet, and the three of them moved slowly, shuffling out of the alleyway and down the street.

Through the night, through the storm, and through the blinding pain, Joseph just kept walking—step-by-step led by the sound of Anna's voice calling him forward

"Keep going, Joseph. I've got you. Just keep walking. We're almost there...."

CHAPTER 2
OLD FRIENDS

B EFORE JOSEPH EVEN FULLY WOKE, his senses began to absorb clues about his surroundings. There was no wind. He was not on the street and his wet clothes had dried. The darkness rolled back as he opened his eyes and there—sitting across from him—was Anna. She was running her fingers through Ben's thin hair. Wiping the sleep from his eyes, it took Joseph a moment to realize what he was seeing. One by one the faces of his loved ones came into view: Nicolaus, Rachel, Abbey, Beth, Davy, and dear Asa and Emma. They were all covered by what looked like a sea of canvas. Looking above them, Joseph noticed the same canvas overhead, held up by many bowed, wood slats shaped like an arched ribcage of a whale that might have swallowed them.

"Anna," Joseph whispered as he slowly sat up. "Where are we?"

Anna looked at him with a smile of relief. "We're safe," she answered softly, "Shhh now, everyone's sleeping. We're on the edges of the city in an abandoned wagon. I found it a few days ago."

"How?" he asked in a hoarse voice. "All this time, you've all been together here?" he went on, feeling relieved.

"No, we weren't together," she said regretfully. "I was alone. After that night we were chased out of the printing house, I searched the streets for weeks and couldn't find anyone. It was only two days ago that I found everyone.

"Nicolaus and Rachel managed to look after everyone these last few weeks. From what they told me, they returned to the printing house a few times, hoping they would find us but were chased away by some well-heeled business men."

"That's strange."

"Yes, well, they chanced a return when the latest blizzard started churning. It was there that I found them. They were all curled up in the basement."

"Basement?" Joseph asked. "We never go down there."

"Nicolaus thought it would be safer for them to be tucked away in one of the pantries. I tell you, I almost didn't find them. I checked the whole house. I went downstairs out of desperation but still didn't see anything. The window was broken, like all the rest in the house, but the boards covering it had been broken off during the storm. I was sitting in the basement defeated, watching the snow when I noticed there were footprints tracking through the patches of the snow covering the floor.

"Walking in those same steps, I followed the prints into the backroom, in the end coming face-to-face with a small pantry door. When the door swung back, I was gazing at seven small lumps huddled together sleeping on the floor. My heart stopped mid-beat."

Joseph smiled. Anna smiled back but her face quickly fell. "When you weren't there," she continued, recapping the story. "I feared..." she paused as tears filled her eyes.

There was a moment of silence, filled with intense heartache. "I've never been so afraid," she confessed.

"I know," Joseph assured her, "believe me...I know."

Anna cleared her throat, softly holding back tears.

"I was searching for you all when I found this wagon," she continued. "For weeks I'd been roaming the streets with no luck. I thought for sure that I'd run into you if I went to our usual places, but I didn't. So one day, I wandered to the outskirts, even though we never come out here. I suppose I was a bit desperate," she added with a little smile that resembled a twinge of pain. "While I was walking I saw a hulking shadow on the horizon. I walked toward it and found a wrecked wagon sitting in a barren lot. With the storm barreling in, I decided to stay out here. I climbed into the wagon bed and spent the night."

"No one has bothered you?" Joseph asked.

"No one ever showed up. I thought for sure someone would've claimed it, but no one really comes out here. There is dumped trash all around this lot, and by the looks of it when I found it, the wagon has been abandoned for months, if not years."

"Sure is different," Joseph looked around at the inside of the wagon. Something about the canvas walls were comforting—like a great tent made out of blankets.

"It's quiet out here," Anna's eyes went wide. "At first I was afraid of being out here alone. It was kinda spooky. I've gotten used to it," she added quickly.

Anna's red cheeks rounded into a smile. Joseph smiled back. The two old friends said nothing, they just basked in the happiness of having each other once more.

"And all this canvas…it was here too?"

"No. The wagon was naught but its wooden bones when I found it—no cover— nothing."

"You had all this stashed away somewhere without telling me?" Joseph asked jokingly. "I know you're resourceful but…"

"No," she said sticking out her tongue at him ever so slightly. "Before the first blizzard, I was down at the harbor looking for scraps from the fishing boats when I found this canvas piled up. It's the sail of a ship," she explained, wonder in her voice. "There are a lot of holes in it. I suppose they got a new one. I rolled it up and brought it here."

"All the way from the docks?"

"Yes. It was quite hard. It's heavy cloth. Like dragging a great big dead animal. You see, I divided it and brought it out piece by piece," she pointed to fraying edges. "I was actually glad for the snow on the ground—made it easy to slide. Thankfully, no one saw. I lashed down a piece to the frame. Then I put the rest of the sail in the wagon bed. I wrapped up in it…. I felt hidden away." Anna paused suddenly. A strained look crossed her face.

"I searched for you every day," she quickly added. "You must know how hard it was. I hated coming back here alone, knowing that I had blankets and would be sheltered, when all of you probably weren't. So many times, I just cried all the way through my walk back here…."

"Well, look at it this way, you got the wagon set up for us all," he said with a slight laugh. "I know you, and I have no doubt that you searched every day. You risked your life tonight staying out looking as long as you did. If you hadn't found us tonight, Ben and I would've certainly died."

They were quiet for a time. Both knew that Joseph was not exaggerating.

"The waiting is hard," Anna said in a solemn voice.

"I know," Joseph replied.

"Are you all right?" she asked, concerned by the worn face of her longtime friend.

Joseph hesitated.

"I'm just tired," he whispered in a strained voice. Shaking his head with a desperate look on his face, as if he feared he would go insane. He hesitated for a moment. "I'm so tired," he repeated. The fatigue settled not just in his bones but his soul.

Anna was quiet for a time. "I don't know what the answer is."

"I know," he absolved her, "I don't either. We need to find one—we have to."

"We'll find a way, together," she said strongly, leaving no room for a question or doubt.

Her words were like a healing bandage laid on his open wounds. Old friends, Joseph and Anna's bond had evolved, growing from the first moment they met at the age of seven. Now fourteen, neither of them were children anymore.

Sitting across from Anna, Joseph felt the tension pushing in on him begin to ease. In only a few moments she had managed to drive away the demons that had followed him for weeks.

Holding hands across the canvas, the two old friends looked warmly toward one another. His chestnut brown eyes met her hazel.

Ben let out a faint moan as he turned over.

"How is he? ...How's everyone?" Joseph asked.

Anna gently pulled her hand away from Joseph's to feel Ben's clammy brow. "He still feels warm. How long has he been like this?"

"I'm not sure. He already had the fever when I found him."

After looking at Ben for a long moment in silent contemplation, Joseph started moving his legs, pushing off the blankets as he tried to revive his stiff limbs and rise up.

"What are you doing?" Anna asked.

"I'm not sure when Ben last ate. By the looks of him, he hasn't eaten much of anything in weeks. I'm sure you could use some food as well and the others. I'm going to go find some. You stay with them, keep warm," Joseph said, determined. His will was returning, however his body was not. As he found his footing and pushed off to stand, he came back down to the wagon bed with a thump, as his legs gave out from under him. The sudden thud made Ben turn and moan again, but the sickly boy still did not wake. Nicolaus and Rachel stirred.

"Joseph," Nicolaus said in a loving voice, "we've been looking everywhere for you."

"I know. I've been looking for you too." Joseph smiled.

"What are you doing?" Rachel asked.

Joseph was trying to get up but his legs did not want to cooperate.

"He's trying to go out looking for some food," Anna said disapprovingly. Seeing Joseph's own weak state Anna immediately took charge. "How long has it been since you ate Joseph?" she inquired in a demanding yet concerned voice, knowing that Joseph had become too accustomed to putting his own needs last. "You should stay here where it's warm and watch the others. I'll go."

Joseph glanced through an opening between canvas flaps. "The snow seems to have stopped for now."

"It's probably just a pause in the storm. You should stay put," she reasoned.

"All the more reason I should go now," Joseph rebutted stubbornly. "I'll be fine," he stressed. "I can do it. I'll search Quincy and Faneuil and then come back."

"We'll go," Rachel and Nicolaus offered, finally getting a word in.

"No. I'm going and that's the end of it," Joseph said firmly.

Anna looked disapproving. Her eyes were stern. She knew that Joseph would go—even if he was bedridden, he still would have found the strength to go. "Fine, go, but let Nicolaus go with you. Rachel and I will stay here and watch the others."

Nicolaus smiled. Joseph agreed. He stood up, and this time he was able to remain steady on his legs. Joseph moved to the back of the wagon quietly, careful not to wake anyone else. Nicolaus and Anna followed behind him. He peeked through the canvas door that was draped over the back opening of the wagon.

"Before you go, I'm making you a new coat out of some canvas," she said firmly, "and you make sure you leave at the first hint of dark, no later! You promise me that, or so help me I won't let you out of this wagon! And believe me, with how weak you are right now, we could keep you here without much effort." Anna was being playful but, at the same time, Joseph knew that she was serious. "I know you Joseph—you have to promise me that you won't push the limit. You hear!"

They stared at one another, speaking volumes in the silence.

"All right, then," Anna pulled the massive canvas sail toward her and without hesitation began ripping it. With two hands she pulled the dusty, thick cloth apart until she had a large square about four feet by four feet.

She picked up her large square, cut a small slit—about eight inches—directly in the center of the material. She slipped it over Joseph letting his head come up through the hole. She wrapped a thin strip of cloth around his waist. It acted as a belt holding the tunic in place. She tore away another piece and wrapped his arms with the bindings. "There, that'll give you a bit of cover," she said, proceeding to cut off another length of the canvas.

Making sure that his sleeves and pant legs were wrapped securely under his canvas bindings, Anna knew that he was as ready as she could make him.

"Remember your promise, Joseph."

He nodded. Nicolaus jumped down from the wagon. Joseph was about to follow when Anna stopped him.

"Wait," she said as she turned back and ripped another square off the canvas sail that had already yielded so much fabric, yet still looked none the smaller as it filled the entire bed of the wagon.

Joseph laughed. "What else is there left on me to wrap?"

Anna looked stern. "It's not to use as a jacket, though I must admit I'd like to give you another layer or two. No, wrap everything you find up in this so it's easier for you to carry."

Taking the square, Joseph opened it out—both his arms extended to their fullest. Talking from behind the wall of cloth he muffled. "It would be nice if I found enough food to fill this. As it is, I probably could fit anything I find into my pocket. We'll hope for the best." Tucking the square into his new tunic-coat, Joseph lifted the wagon cover's flaps.

"Go quickly now before you wake the others." Anna urged. She looked over her shoulder to see Davy, Mary, Beth, Asa, Emma and Ben still resting.

She held his hand as he eased down to the snowy ground. Replying to all that went unspoken in her gaze, Joseph spoke in a firm tone, "I won't be long. I'll come back before night."

He smiled and continued to grip her hand, then slowly, hesitantly letting her hand slip from his, Joseph and Nicolaus began to make their way through the drifts. Turning around several times trying to see Anna and Rachel waving from the wagon, he knew they would not go back into the wagon until they were completely out of sight.

CHAPTER 3
THE SEARCH FOR WHAT IS VITAL

"**W**HAT HAPPENED TO YOUR HAT?" Joseph asked Nicolaus as they walked.

"I gave it to Davy. He lost his in the storm."

Nicolaus had a quiet reflective manner about him. Some people might think him a mute upon first meeting him, due to the fact that he seldom opened his mouth unless he had something truly important to say. Nicolaus had a long face, drawn and pinched like all the other children's. He had a long nose that rounded at the end. And on the ridge of that long nose, unlike the other children, Nicolaus wore spectacles—rectangular ones. The lenses were a little foggy where the wire frames wrapped around the glass, hiding his deep blue eyes behind them.

Most likely the son of Scandinavian immigrants, Nicolaus had sandy colored hair and stood taller than Joseph and a bit broader in the chest. Like all the other children, Nicolaus wore several layers of tattered clothing. His coat was nothing more than a brown waistcoat worn over his many voluminous shirts. In the place where the waistcoat ended around his arms, his sleeves puffed out, giving him the look of a Shakespearean peasant. For shoes, Nicolaus wore a ripped pair of cow-hide boots whose leather had cracked and peeled with age. The boots were obviously about two sizes too big for him, but too big was easier on the feet than too small, so Nicolaus did not complain.

"We'll search for food and then head back. That simple. The way I figure it, no carts will be moving down the streets. Our best bet would be the harbor. Let's try Long Wharf. Some ships might have made berth before the storms."

"All right." Nicolaus agreed.

Joseph threw an arm around his lost brother, and the two made their way into the city.

*   *   *   *   *

BOSTON WAS ONE OF THE GREAT PORTS of the East Coast, merchant ships, fishing schooners, and whaling boats—all made berth at Boston Harbor. Many smaller skiffs and sloops owned by native fisherman dotted the shoals of the Charles River. When the flounder schooners and other local fishing vessels came into port each day, they would pack all that they had caught into salt to preserve it or ferry it away to the city marketplaces. A few scraps were usually dropped during this process, allowing the children to gather up the bits and bobs once the fisherman had left. Old raw fish was not Joseph's favorite, but the children, like all the poor of the ages, had learned that good tasting food was a luxury, while filling the stomach itself was a necessity.

Boats came in and out almost every day, giving the children several opportunities to scavenge. Joseph was hoping that some ship might have come in between storms, taking the lull as an opportunity to put in, re-supply and drop their cargo. At which point they might have been in such a hurry they could have dropped a few scraps here and there. And it was with that hope he charged for Long Wharf.

Joseph and Nicolaus finally turned the last corner and the river came into view. His feet passed from the cobblestone street to the wooden dock. His steps rang out as he dashed across the wide, wooden planks of the landings. They searched the first three landings and found nothing. A few new boats had indeed come in to wait out the storm in a safe port, but there were still no scraps to be found. They started back down the docks to reach the streets when they came across a scattered pile of fish meat that had been preserved by their frozen surroundings. The small chunks were scattered around the gangway leading up to a fishing schooner that Joseph had seen many times before. The name scrolled across her stern read *The Dunton.*

Dropping to their knees, picking up those clearly visible first, Joseph found some of the chucks to be as big as his palm.

"You, there!" a rough voice exclaimed.

Startled, Joseph and Nicolaus looked up. A fisherman on watch aboard *The Dunton* had spotted them. He was a seasoned fisherman—a white-haired, round-faced old man. His wrinkles were like deep scars across his face. He stared with ice-blue eyes. His beard was gritty from the smoke drawn from the hand-carved pipe clenched in his few remaining teeth.

"Whatcha doin' there now?" he said, pulling the pipe from his mouth to release a puff of smoke into the cold evening air.

Joseph extended his hand, showing the man the scrap of cod he held.

"You're sack rats then?" the old man commented.

Joseph flinched. He hated the term. The homeless children

in the city were known as rats or "sack rats" because of their tendency to wear the old potato sacks as coats.

"If we don't take them, the gulls will fill their bellies come morning."

The old man considered the boys, "True enough."

Joseph was taken aback. He had expected a reprimand, not agreement.

"Still," the old man went on, "if the Cap'n done sees ya, he would say you're stealin'."

Joseph did not know whether they should stay or run.

"Do you think I'm stealin'?" he asked timidly.

The old man was quiet. His old, clouded eyes looked at Joseph. He stroked his scruffy beard. "You done take it all boy. But be quick about it though, else you'll get us both in trouble."

Joseph opened up the cloth Anna had given him. They packed the chunks of thick, preserved flounder and cod fish, scooping handfuls of snow in with it to keep it fresh.

Watching the boys the old man talked to them in a fatherly way, "You oughtta get yourself some papers boys. The sea can give a lad a fresh start."

"Um, we can't," Joseph answered, still gathering up the pieces.

"Are ya afraid then? …afraid of the water fillin' your lungs and takin' ya down with the selkies?"

"What are the *selkies*?" Nicolaus stopped and looked at the man.

"Souls that are part seal, part human. Spend enough time on the sea and you see your fair share of unbelievable beasts," the man answered to the boy's look of disbelief.

"I'd rather work the rigging than slave in the factories."

Nicolaus replied. "It's my family—if I went, they'd have nobody to care for them."

"Brothers and sisters then or you already find yourself a lady?"

Joseph laughed. "We have brothers and sisters—friends actually, who are like family," he awkwardly explained.

Gathering one piece after another, Joseph moved his hands through the shallow snow that covered the wooden slats of the dock, amazed at how much he was finding. Tying up the bundle of fish meat, he noticed that the large square, which Anna had given him to carry the food in—the one he remarked that he could never fill—was nearly full. He stood up.

"Did ya fill your bundle then?" The old man asked.

"Thanks to you," Joseph answered gratefully. Nicolaus nodded in thanks.

"You go on now, before you get us into trouble. I'm gettin' older by the day, and all those strapping lads are looking for a reason to see me go. I'm no longer as able-bodied as I once was, but more knowledgeable than the lot of 'em keeps me in good standin' with the Cap'n."

"You're a good man," Joseph said appreciatively.

"You don't know what I am boy," the old man answered back gruffly.

"Maybe not, but I know you let us take the fish, when others would've chased us away. For me, that shows you're a good man."

"Go on, now," the old man said, waving a withered hand in the air. "Storm's a-comin' back. Best get home."

Gathering his supplies, Joseph nodded in thanks and took off down the docks.

For the first time in memory he felt giddying inside. He was trembling with excitement. A smile spread over his face as he ran down the wharf towards the Common, and on to the wagon. He laughed out loud, rushing forward with a rising hope. The sheer force of which was enough to seemingly propel him into flight.

*　*　*　*　*

THE WIND WAS STARTING TO PICK UP. The snow was falling again. It was amazing how quickly the weather went from fine to fierce. Screaming against the wind, Joseph's voice still only barely cut through the thick gusts. "Did you hear anything about Duncan or Marie?"

Screaming back, Nicolaus answered him, "We looked everywhere. We went to all the usual spots but came up empty. Either we missed them each time, or they're at the hospital or reform or one of the orphanages out of our reach."

Nicolaus knew as well as Joseph did that some places in the city had to be avoided at all costs. If the authorities found the children, they would be split up. The older ones would be put into workhouses, while the little ones would be sent to the orphanages to sit in misery or worse shipped off across the great unknown on one of the orphan trains.

As they passed through the Common, Joseph glanced back toward the city as he continued walking. He felt a part of him seemed to be dragging behind—unwilling to leave without Duncan and Marie; however, the storm was driving them ever-onward. Joseph knew that, other than the printing house, he had absolutely no idea where else in the city to look. For weeks they had searched all the familiar places and every other corner of the city without finding them. It was as though they had vanished; only they had not. He knew that they were out there somewhere, trying to survive. *Had they been taken by the police? Were they still free but taking refuge in an unknown place? But if so, why hadn't they gone to any of their familiar places in the city where they knew they would look for them? Was one of them ill and unable to reach them or look for them?* These questions circled in the back of Joseph's mind throughout each day, tormenting him.

"We're almost there!" Nicolaus screamed, interrupting Joseph's internal reflection. "Look, there it is!" he motioned toward the horizon.

Looking at the wagon, Joseph then gazed back. The city was now but a looming gray shadow behind the heavy white veil.

He stopped mid-step, the snow swirling about him. "Take this," he handed Nicolaus the fish. "Tell Anna that I'm all right and that I went back into the city to search for Duncan and Marie."

Nicolaus looked horrified and shocked as he strained to hear Joseph's unbelievable declaration against the deafening winds.

"No!" he shouted, shaking his head firmly from side to side. "You won't find them. You'll die if you go back, you can't."

Joseph looked at Nicolaus. Their eyes met through the abrasive winds, and they stared at each other for a moment as the storm swirled around them.

"I have to," Joseph said in a deep solemn voice.

Nicolaus said nothing, part of him understanding.

"Let me go with you..." Nicolaus began to say in a plea. Joseph shook his head forcefully, and Nicolaus' words trailed off.

Then in a grim voice, as if he knew what this choice might cost him, Joseph said, "Take care of them."

Nicolaus looked scared. Joseph started to walk back down the trail they had cut through the snow.

Knowing that he was not going to change Joseph's mind, Nicolaus shouted, "Wait! Here, take my coat," as he removed the brown waistcoat.

The boys gave each other one last look, speaking without talking. Then Joseph nodded, turned, and marched back at a quick pace, so as not to be followed, disappearing into the whipping white sheets of snow-filled air.

Nicolaus' stomach wrenched. He pushed on to the wagon.

Anna heard footsteps and peeked out from the back of the wagon looking for the boys. A look of panic flooded her eyes as what little color she had left drained from her cheeks. "Where is he?"

"He went back to look for Duncan and Marie." Nicolaus tried to remain calm in front of the younger ones who were now watching the conversation with mounting concern.

Anna instinctively threw back the canvas curtain and leapt down, passing by Nicolaus without another word.

"No!" Nicolaus shouted at her, grabbing her arm. "He wanted you to stay. He's going to look for them in our usual places, then ride out the storm in the printing house."

She pulled herself away from Nicolaus and began following the path the boys had made.

"You can't, and you know it," Nicolaus reasoned. She pressed on.

"He's already gone, Anna," he said in a blunt tone. As the truth of his words sunk painfully into her, she came to a halt.

The blinding wind whipped over her. Her heart was breaking. She shouted against the roar of the storm, screaming Joseph's name—begging him and cursing him at the same time.

Nicolaus walked into the bitter winds, resting his hands on her shoulders. "He had to go," Nicolaus said plainly, "and he wanted you to stay and help take care of everyone."

Feeling Nicolaus' pull to come back, Anna still stood firm. "He always does this! He always puts himself last. He cares for all of us but never for himself." Raising her hands distraught and despairing, Anna screamed questions into the hostility raging around her—a storm within a storm. "Doesn't he realize that we need him here, alive? Doesn't he know that the best thing he can do to help us is to stay safe?" Anna stood in the snow oblivious to the blizzard whirling around her. She was indifferent to the burning pain of the icy snow blowing against her, when compared to the all-consuming worry now filling her. Pulling herself away, Anna finally surrendered to Nicolaus' tugging and went back to the wagon.

CHAPTER 4
THE FINAL BLOW

A S HE WALKED BACK INTO THE CITY, the winds were deafening but in his heart Joseph could hear Anna shouting at him, angry, and worried. He did not need to be within earshot of her voice to hear her words echoing in his heart. Nonetheless, going back in the face of the storm was a risk that he would allow only himself to take. As the torment, desperation and deep love he had for the others all collided in him, he found he was willing to do anything to protect them. Unfortunately, the only way he knew to protect them was by throwing himself in front of them.

Pushing on, Joseph moved up Boylston Street one grueling step at a time, wading through the frozen sea. Numbed to his very core, only two names repeated over and over again within the frozen caverns of his soul: *Duncan and Marie.*

For Joseph, Marie was different than the others. She was only two years older than Joseph, but she cared for him in a way no other could. Marie had awakened the hope that life could be better. When Joseph was younger he had been betrayed by those he called his *family.* Innocently he had opened his heart to them, as a child does, only to be forsaken, but Marie had saved him. She told him in the very beginning,

"Family is not made of the blood we share but by the love we feel. Family is not decided by who gave birth to you but by who *loves you*. One day you will find your real mother and father—the woman and man who would love you the way a mother and father should."

Blood had failed the castoff children; nonetheless they were able to survive each day by holding on to the belief that love would not fail them. Unlike the others, Marie had grown up not as an abandoned child, but as a true orphan. She once had a loving family so, she knew what family was. Taken by sickness, her mother and father had not been able to stay with her long, but they had loved her so deeply that in the short time they had with her they had imparted to her the knowledge of what true parents are. She in turn handed down that knowledge to Joseph, who tried to embody it.

*   *   *   *   *

JOSEPH FOUND HIMSELF BATTLING A WHIRLWIND OF SNOW. It was a solid whiteout. For hours he had searched all the familiar places in vain. He stood there—stopped dead in a thigh-high snow bank—trying to think of another place to search, any place that would provide him with the slightest chance of finding Duncan and Marie, but he could not think of one. Deep down Joseph knew that even if he could think of another place, he would be fooling himself to think that he could reach it.

Empowered by his love, he had entered the city with hope, but now his insides were withering. His heart was heavy. Defeated, he decided to retreat to the printing house. One begrudging step at a time, Joseph force-marched himself down the streets, making his way toward sanctuary, hating himself more with each passing moment for not having found them.

The journey to the printing house was a hard road. The bone-shattering winds were unrelenting, but Joseph could not feel them any longer. The thin scarf covering his face had slipped down, revealing that his lips and the tip of his nose had split open leaving trails of thick syrupy blood slowly dripping down his chin. His cheeks were past red. There were small purple cuts across his cheekbones made by the shards of flying ice riding the cold winds.

A few flakes of snow drifted down around him, falling to the ground. He looked up beyond the buildings and imagined Anna sitting in the wagon. The promise he made to her echoed within him. But he could not go back. He was not deliberately breaking his promise to Anna. (At least, that is what he reasoned to himself.) He did not have the option to keep it.

As Joseph rounded the last corner, the broken down printing house finally came into sight. It was a dilapidated wood framed building situated in the back of a neglected lot. The house had been overlooked as the city progressed into the industrial era. Boston had become one of the largest centers of industry in America. It was the cradle of liberty where the Revolution began. Appropriately enough, over the last five years, this neglected building had been a place for them—the overlooked children—to take refuge. Situated southeast of the Common near the harbor, the printing house was abandoned and unused by whoever owned it, allowing the children to find some small peace within its walls.

Looking at it from the outside, the house was a shack compared to the brownstone and brick mansions of Beacon

Hill. The white paint was peeling off the wooden siding, the dark forest-green shutters still remained on a few windows, though many had come unhinged and fallen off. Directly beneath the second floor windows there was a long rectangular spot where the paint was lighter than the surrounding area. Undoubtedly, this was where the long lost sign for the printing press had once hung. The only signs that remained were a very small, square sign near the front door that declared this building a historical landmark and another larger, rectangular sign stretched across the front of the door. The larger sign read in great bold, blood-red capital letters: CONDEMNED.

Shuffling down the walkway, Joseph did not even attempt to go through the front door. He moved across the snow-covered lawn and went around the side of the building. His pace slowed. He was cautious. As unlikely as it would be to find a policemen patrolling in this foul weather, Joseph did not want to take any chances. Lifting his aching legs high as he moved through the snowdrifts, he crept along the side of the old house. All the windows were boarded up. Joseph made his way down the length of the building towards a special window—one that only *appeared* to be boarded up but actually was not; he had fixed it to look that way. Boards had once been nailed into place to cover the now broken window. One night, years ago when the flooding rains came, Duncan had been looking for a place for the children to hole up when he found the abandoned house and pried up the boards with his own hands. Once the children started coming to the house on a regular basis, Joseph found some old, rusted hinges on an unhinged door inside the house. He attached them to the top of the boards covering the window, making a little hidden hatch-door for them to use.

No footprints, Joseph thought to himself. His heart dropped a little. If Duncan or Marie came to the house, they surely would have come this way and left a trail of footprints in the deep snow. He decided to go on and search the house all the same. After all, there was nowhere else to stay.

Joseph turned the corner trying to reach the makeshift door only to find his way blocked. A tall snow bank, reaching at least seven feet high, had blown against the entire length of the house. It was as if a slope of snow was now flowing down from the white siding of the house. The constant barrage of snow over the recent weeks had left the first floor windows completely covered.

Unable to get into the hatch, Joseph turned back down the path he had made across the front lot, thinking where else he could find a way through. As he looked around, he noticed that the other side of the building was not heavily blanketed at all, in fact, it had been sheltered from the wind. Only about two feet of snow covered the ground on that side. His gaze followed the snowline along the foundation. He saw a dip in the snow level and recalled the newly-broken window along the basement ceiling. He wondered if he was thin enough to squeeze through it. Putting a hand to his painfully-thin torso, Joseph gave a little ironic laugh at this thought then turned back towards the house and began cutting a path through the snow to the protected side of the building.

Making his way, Joseph was rounding the side of the building when one of his legs kicked something heavy in the snow, something that he could not push aside, something soft yet hard at the same time. All night Joseph had been walking without comprehending. He had just pushed himself forward like a machine, yet this unexpected obstacle had caused him to pause and actually look at what was before him. He saw a flap of dark, frosted cloth sticking up out of the snow. Following its whipping tail blowing in the wind, he saw a waxen face protruding from the crusted surface. It was a person partially buried by the gusting winds and piling snow. A familiar person. Joseph stood like a statue, not breathing. He had to be dreaming. There, half-buried in the snow bank in front of him, was Marie. The piece of thinning cloth flicking in the wind was her midnight-blue shawl. Her legs were completely buried. One arm was above the snow as was part of her chest and face, but the rest of her had been covered.

Joseph reached out a hand in disbelief, feeling her frozen cheek. *She's real,* he thought to himself.

He grabbed onto her hands, broke her free of the snow and dragged her around to the sheltered side of the house. Her lips were purple, and her cheeks were frosted and bleeding from cuts where the skin had split. Joseph hoped she would wake up, but she did not. She looked as though she had two black eyes, the shadows around them were so deep. Calling out her name over and over against the screaming winds, Marie did not wake. Though, to his relief, Joseph noticed her hand move—she was alive. That fact triggered a burst of intense strength, melting all coldness off him, cutting him free of the bonds of fatigue, flooding him with purpose. His glazed expression sharpened, his dull mind cleared, and his weakened body was renewed in an instant. He knew exactly what to do.

Joseph dropped down to the broken window and began franticly digging. The snow around it was only a foot or two deep. He clawed down until reaching the broken frame where his hand reached through the snow and broke through to the open basement on the other side. Holding her by her coat, Joseph pulled Marie across the surface of the snow towards him so that she was close to the window. Then, once he had her near the opening, he squeezed through the window.

Dropping down to the dirt floor of the dim, frozen basement, Joseph's eyes quickly swept the room. There was a wooden crate that he could stand on. He rushed towards it and pushed it underneath the window.

He climbed onto the crate. Taking her by the back of her coat, he slid her through the open frame, trying to ease her down into his arms. Yet, all of a sudden, Marie's unconscious body slid on the packed snow, causing her to come flying through the window toward Joseph. He managed to catch her but was pushed backwards off the tall crate. His bony back struck the cold, solid, dirt floor of the basement. In one sharp moment, all the air was forced from him.

His body had blocked Marie from striking the floor. He could see her lying next to him, unconscious. He tried to move but he could not. It was as though the impact on the floor had pushed him through time. In that violent instant, he was no longer a young man lying in the basement; he was a broken-hearted little boy newly cast into a terrifying world.

*　*　*　*　*

A SMALL BOY WAS SITTING on a long, wooden bench at the center of the Common. He was young, around six. His neatly trimmed hair recently had a wet comb run through it. His clothes were new. He wore a small knee-high pair of trousers. His best shoes had been shined to a glossy black. She had wrapped him in a long, secondhand, tweed coat that nearly came down past his knees, making him look very small, as though he was lost in it. The shadow of a woman passed in front of him. He sat on the bench and pushed himself back on the seat, leaving his feet dangling over the edge. Once situated, he looked at her. Her face was blurred, as though he was looking at her through a lens that was not quite clear.

"Sit here, Joseph, you just sit here," she instructed.

Assured that she was only going to shop and then would return for him, Joseph did as he was told. Innocent as a child is, he remained on the bench as the woman disappeared into the crowd, not even turning to look back.

Joseph stared out into the crowd, his deep brown eyes looking expectantly. As he sat with his hands in his lap, he was playing with one of the large, round buttons on his coat, swinging his feet back and forth in the air. His face had not yet been hollowed out and his eyes were the same wholesome chestnut brown but were not yet strained. He was still a boy—a true child—not yet aged by wear, not yet matured by circumstance. Completely trusting, his heart had yet to be broken. He still had a home, he still had a family, and he still had no idea that as he sat there faithfully waiting, one life was ending and another was beginning.

Hours passed. The Common was deserted. One by one all the people had left. All the shopkeepers had closed up. The stream of carts rumbling down Beacon Street, Park Street, and Common Street had thinned to a trickle, yet Joseph still sat upon his bench. The expectant look had faded as the sun had fallen. He was alone in the dark, clinging to the bench, begging in his heart for *his mother to return, searching the emptiness around him. His strained eyes showing the panic in him.*

Frightened by every noise, he jumped at every movement in the shadows. He had been left in the wildness of the city's savage night. He could sense the foulness. The unknown was terrifying. Empty tins, crumpled newspaper, trash, dirt, and soot blew through the pathways cutting through the park. The murmurings of drunkards echoed from the shadowed alleyways leading to the pubs and brothels. Night had fallen and with it the illusion of man's civility.

A light rain began to fall upon him. He brought his legs up to his chest, pulling them up under his overlarge coat, hugging them tightly as the unthinkable truth that he was alone began to sink in.

Days later, Joseph no longer sat upon the bench. Instead, he wandered the streets that haloed the park overshadowed by the crowds swarming around him in their busy commute. Joseph wandered through the engulfing crowds, looking anxiously at each face that passed by him. His clean clothes now were dirtying. He looked sickly and pale. He had not eaten for days. The skin around his eyes was red, swollen and beginning to bruise a little from the constant strain he was enduring. He remained on the constant verge of tears.

Throughout the daylight hours, he searched the faces in the crowds, and during the night, he returned to the bench in the Common near the corner of Park Street and Common Street where he sat until the morning. Lying on the bench, curled up with his knees pulled against his chest, Joseph did not sleep, he just cried. He just wanted to go home—that was all he knew. Yet it was the one thing he could not do. He did not know where his home was, not within a city so big, among so many buildings that looked so much alike. Thinking of his home, of his parents, Joseph hugged himself tighter as a harsh gust of cold wind blew against him like an unseen villain pushing his already crumbling self. And then, in the distance, he heard something. He stopped crying. He stared out into the darkness, straining to see the face of the approaching figure. He desperately hoped that it might be his mother but was deathly afraid that it might be someone else. The shape of another child appeared in the night. It was a girl. She was maybe eight or nine. Her head and shoulders were covered by a shawl. She was very thin and her face was smudged with dirt. She gave off a kindly aura as she came towards him from across the square, moving peacefully through the shadows and the beams of moonlight. Kneeling down beside the bench the girl reached out a hand to Joseph who was pulled up into the corner of the bench cowering.

"It's all right," the girl assured him. "I won't hurt you."

She was the first gentle person, one who had deemed to talk to him, in days. Pouring out all that he had held within him, Joseph told the nameless girl what had happened, stopping several times to cry.

Giving him her full attention, the girl listened to the same story she had heard told a dozen times before—the story that she knew the boy would tell her before she even approached him. She moved up to sit on the bench beside him. Taking him into her arms, she held him tight and let him cry against her, cradling him until he was done.

"It will be all right. I'm here now. You're not alone," she said reassuringly, rubbing the small boy's back as he cried.

"I want to go home," the boy sobbed, thinking that somehow

if he could go home the nightmare would end. But the girl knew there was no going home; there was no ending the nightmare. There was only helping one another to endure it until it was finally brought to its end.

"What is your name?" the girl asked in a kind voice.

"Joseph," the boy answered back, quivering. He wiped his eyes and sniffed loudly then leaned back close to the girl.

"My name is Marie. I'm going to take care of you now."

"But I want to go home," the boy said not understanding what had happened to him.

"I know you do. I want to as well, but I can't. I have not been able to go home for a long time. Something has happened Joseph and you can't go home, but you don't have to worry. I'm with you, and we will make it together. There are other children who can't go home, and we all have to stick together until we can find a new home. Why don't you come with me, and we can find a place to sleep for the night."

"No," Joseph answered quickly. "I can't go. My mother told me to wait here…and…and so I have to wait," he finished meekly.

"All right. It's all right," Marie said calming the boy. She did not force the hard truth upon him. Instead, she would wait with him, letting the boy come to the truth on his own.

"Well, then I guess we will just have to sleep here. Come on now," she said motioning for him to lay down.

Joseph still was crying, but his sobs were calming. His breathing was becoming steadier as he held tight to this girl—his one comfort in this foreign world. Just as he lay down, another sharp, chilled gust of wind blew. and he gripped her tighter as he shivered. Removing her shawl, Marie revealed her long brown hair, flowing with highlights of honey and auburn. Unfolding the great shawl, Marie draped it over Joseph, pulling it up over him like a blanket. Settling on the end of the bench, she let him rest his head on her lap as he lay down near her. She drew the shawl up close to his face, trying to make him feel as he had when he was wrapped up in his warm bed and life was still easy.

"I'm cold," he cried in a lonely voice.

"I know. You'll warm up in a minute. You should know that this shawl is very warm," she assured Joseph as she rubbed his back in an effort to try to get some heat into him. "You'll feel warmer. Just you wait," she said tucking the ends of the shawl under his legs and feet to hold it down in the wind. Her eyes swept over the paths running into the Common. Satisfied that they were safe, she leaned back slightly, still rubbing his back reassuringly. "Winter's coming, but don't worry, Joseph. I've got you."

CHAPTER 5
THE DREAM

THE TWO FIGURES LAY IN THE DARK BASEMENT, snow swirling in the air around them. The small boy was grown to a young man, and the girl who had once saved him now needed to be saved.

The musty, cold air of the basement refilled his flattened lungs. Joseph rolled onto his side as he gasped then curled up into a ball as he took a few difficult breaths. When at last he was breathing easier, he looked over to Marie. She was still unconscious. The hard blow had not woken her. Coming out of his memories, Joseph was back in the basement. The old park bench was long gone and now he had a new set of problems. Looking up, Joseph began pulling himself towards Marie, bringing himself to sit beside her.

"Marie?" He called to her, his voice echoing slightly within the empty stone-walled basement.

There was the rough grating of cloth on ice as Joseph dragged Marie through the snowy patches across the floor. He moved her into the small closet Anna had told him of.

Joseph lay down next to Marie, hugging her tightly in a desire to warm them both. *When she gets warmer she'll surely wake,* he thought to himself. He was utterly exhausted but did

not want to sleep. Calling her name as he pulled her in closer
to him, he tried to bring her back from wherever she had
gone; however, she would not come. It was like something had
cut her off from life. Her heart was still beating. She was not
dead, but she also was not alive. Her spirit was there within
her—some part of Joseph could sense it—but on the outside
she was lifeless. She was running a slight fever. Over his years
of surviving on the street, he had gathered some basic knowledge of treating illness, but he did not know what to do for
her. He nudged the closet door closed with his foot, leaving
them in darkness.

*   *   *   *   *

THE STORM RAGED for an unbelievable three days straight—
the snow never ceasing for longer than a few moments. And
for three days, Joseph and Marie stayed in the printing house.

Weakened by hunger and the strains of the last weeks,
Joseph had no choice but to lie still beside Marie and try to rest.
During the brief moments when he was awake and felt some
strength return to him, he left the closet and went upstairs to
the top-most floor of the house to see if it was night or day or
if the snow had finally stopped. He could barely tell, the snow
was so dense. It seemed neither night nor day. The clouds were
low and thick. The sky was the color of pearl marbled with a
lead gray.

Each time he woke, he checked the sky and then saw to
Marie. On the second day, he had begun gathering some snow
from outside, melted it in an old tin mug they had left behind
weeks ago so they both could have water to drink. For three
days, Joseph sat with Marie waiting for her to come back to

him, and for three days, she did not stir. He waited for some kind of assurance that he was not in fact losing her, but to his increasing sadness, she gave him no reason to hope that she would recover.

Over those three days, Joseph had nothing to eat, no one to talk to and only the icy water to drink. Lying on the dusty, dirt floor in the cupboard, he stared at the same round dark twisted knot in one of the old floorboards which composed the ceiling above him.

Throughout the third day of the storm, Joseph lay there in the semidarkness—the closet door open a crack to let some light in—racking his mind in-between the bouts of hunger for some way that he could save Marie. Pulling his thin arms back through the armholes of Nicolaus' coat, he wrapped them around his thin, boney rib cage, as if trying to cradle his empty, ailing stomach. Hugging himself as he lay curled up on the floor, his stomach writhed uncomfortably. He clenched his teeth, unable to breathe, unable to think…unable to make it stop.

"I can't do this anymore," he said in a strained voice. "It has been years, and nothing has happened to make it better for us. No one has come…no one has cared. I can't go on like this," he confessed to the barren room as he began to weep.

Joseph had always done his best to be a presence of hope, optimism, and steadiness. He had always kept his deepest doubts and heartache within, so as not to unload it upon one of the others. But this night he simply could not hold back any longer. There in the dark, Marie heard the confession of his doubts as he let his world-weary heart pour out its affliction.

"What are we supposed to do? Life's not supposed to be this way," he added in a tone of frustration, inwardly scolding himself for his bitterness but unable to help himself. "I feel like I'm losing myself," he confessed. "I have to do something, but I don't know what. All it would take is just one person to care enough to help us—just one. But there isn't even one, and I don't know how to save us myself. I know that without Duncan here everyone's looking to me, I can feel it every single day, but I'm doing all that I can. It simply isn't enough...*I'm not enough*," he said, cursing himself, revealing that, while he had indeed come to hate the people of the city for their inadequacies, he had come to hate himself for his own. "I don't know what else I can do," he finished in a pleading whisper, as if wanting forgiveness for failing Marie and the others, even though he had never let them down.

"You said that I would have to go and find my family...find my mother. But I already have. *You* found me, and you can't leave me now. You *have* to wake up."

On that thought, Joseph once again drifted off to sleep. His body slackened, yet his hand remained steadfast, holding onto Marie. And as he slept, his questions and pleas for help echoed throughout the cupboard.

∗   ∗   ∗   ∗   ∗

T*HE FIRST THING HE SAW WAS LIGHT. A gentle brightness of cream colored half-light filled the air around him, warming him, renewing him, comforting him, and carrying him. The coldness melted away. The torment was replaced with contentment. The fatigue was replaced by strength. This light encircled him, cradled him, and bound around him as if he were suspended* in a great renewing womb that was refortifying the fiber of his world-weary heart to restore him to the strong youth he always should have been and the idealist he once was.

As the light dimmed, a hazy shape began to emerge and sharpen in the distance. It was as though he were standing on the bow of a ship cutting through a bank of thick fog, drawing closer to a shore that was only now coming into view amid the parting mists.

The mist swirling in spirals around him settled at his feet. He noticed he was standing in a field of thick grass. The wide green blades hung heavy with morning dew. The vague, approaching image suddenly flooded with color, and Joseph saw before him a vast green land.

There was no city besmirching the land before him, no mobs of people, just a green, sloping horizon flourishing with trees, tall grasses and fields ready to yield a bountiful harvest. The deafening din of the city that he had been born into was gone, and in its absence Joseph could hear running streams—waterfalls flowing that could quench any thirst and wash clean all that dirt and blood that had built up upon him. He could hear the wind shifting the leaves that clung to the branches of the spiring oaks, which dotted the fields before him—trees so ancient their roots must have run down into the very core of the earth.

Turning in a circle, Joseph watched as the scene expanded— a wave of materializing land followed him as he moved. His eyes followed the graceful slopes of the scene then moved across a herd of brown jersey cows grazing in the lower pasture of a farm that appeared in the distance. Flocks of plump hens moved around the lawn, pecking and scratching for seeds to eat. As he watched the quaint movements of the small flock, a smell drifted to him on the westerly wind. It was the smell of a true home: a hearth burning thick, round logs of seasoned oak down to ash. He smelled bread baking and a meal stewing, all mixing with the salty crispness of a nearby ocean.

The aroma of the salty air, burning wood and cooking food profoundly soothed him. As he took in a breath, these scents acted as the vapor of a restorative tonic re-expanding his lungs, which had collapsed under the heavy weight of his hopelessness. It was the place of fruition, the place his heart had forever been seeking—the place where he would be free to flourish.

A flicker of something passed near him. Turning as he caught its movement out of the corner of his eye, he saw an old wooden post jutting up out of the lush hillside—a solitary remnant that must have once been part of a post fence—and upon that post had landed a brown sparrow. The bird sat on the old splintering post which still had a rusted nail driven into it. Charged with life, the bitty thing knew Joseph was staring at it only feet away. It was unafraid as it came to the very edge of the post and let out a warm tune that carried across the open fields. Repeating the same song three times, the bird then settled as though it had done what it came to do—this tiny herald of the great approaching spring.

Transfixed on this creature that seemed the embodiment of some spirit, Joseph's attention was drawn back to the farm again as some new sound rose in the distance. He heard laughter— the laughter of the others: Anna, Marie, Ben, Nicolaus, Rachel, Davy, Abbey, Beth, Emma, Asa, Duncan, and Marie. Everyone was there. He could see them moving towards the cottage as they crossed a distant field of tall, heavy-tipped barley. They were alive and healthy, smiling with a luminescent fullness so *complete that he felt sure he had never seen them so happy before in his life. Then in surreal slow motion, Joseph saw Marie come forward from the group. The others continued walking towards the house, but she turned towards the hills and began calling to Joseph to come join them—calling to him to come home.*

He reached out a hand to the vision of her, noticing for the first time that his hand was not bound with strips of canvas, it was not smeared with dirt, soot and dried blood as it usually was. Joseph's eyes pulled away from the farm, and he looked at himself. The rags were gone. He wore a pair of thick, new trousers; a single, cloud blue shirt that was soft against his skin; a plain, black, wool vest whose unbuttoned flaps blew in the warm wind; a matching, black, woolen cap tucked under his wide brown belt drawn tightly to hold his pants up; and a new pair of cowhide boots laced to his feet with thick, knitted socks underneath to cushion his every step. Closing his eyes, Joseph ran his hands in disbelief over his face. There were no wounds or dirt. Moving his hands across his cheeks towards the back of his neck, he noticed his hair was trimmed. He was clean, he was clothed, and for the first time in years, he felt human instead of some neglected animal covered in filth.

Rousing Joseph from his awe, Marie's voice carried across the rolling hills and broke over him once more, causing him to look up. He wanted to run to her. He made to step forward and descend the hillside, though found he was rooted to the spot upon which he stood. For some reason, he could not move. All he could do was stand upon that green slope calling back to her, wanting more than anything to walk into this perfect vision and dwell there forever. The smells in the air, the sound of laughter, Marie calling to him, the wind rolling across the waving fields,

one last glimpse of the small farmhouse, and then the dream was
heartbreakingly over.

The dream receded into the half-light, the warmth faded
away, and Joseph's senses gradually returned to the dark basement. Suspended between that golden scene and the empty
present, there were a few precious moments when he still felt
like he was living in that place of happiness.

The peace was abruptly broken by the cupboard door slam-
ming loudly against the stone wall, caught by a gust of strong
wind blowing through the broken window.

The tranquil moment shattered. Joseph's first instinctual
reaction upon hearing the harsh noise was to pull himself
back into the corner of the cupboard near Marie and throw his
hands up over his head, cowering. When nothing happened,
Joseph slowly let down his guard. His heart pounded in his
constricted throat. He simply sat there in the corner for a
moment, letting the fact that he was not in danger sink in.

After a few moments, what had occurred as he had slept
began to slowly rise in his clearing mind. When at last he
recalled the dream, his heart felt both grateful and mourn-
ful. While he knew he had glimpsed the place he belonged, he
could not help but think that such a life would forever remain
a dream.

Joseph sat up, looking immediately to Marie's face. His
heart was bursting with enthusiasm. All he wanted to do was
tell her what he'd just seen. "Marie," he whispered as he sat
in front of her taking up her hand once again. "Marie," he
repeated this time a little more desperately. "I"

To his surprise, suddenly, she stirred.

"Joseph … Joseph …"

"I'm here," he gasped.

"I'm cold," she shuddered. Her eyes stilled closed.

Joseph looked around frantically. His eye fell upon a group of decaying crates sitting in the far corner of the basement. He rose, marched over and began breaking them apart. Gathering up the pieces, he ascended the sagging stairs.

Confident and calm, he passed through the great room, dumping the wood in the old hearth. Going for another load, Joseph felt gusts of icy wind passing through the cracks around the dry, rotted windowsills. The persistent storm raged only inches away from him. Regardless of the volatility just beyond the glass, Joseph was strangely calm. After enduring the horrible years behind him, Joseph had come to fear everything—even the smallest of things—never realizing that he need not fear anything. He had already survived the worst. As he realized this, a line was drawn.

* * * * *

AROUND THE TIME JOSEPH WOKE FROM HIS DREAM, Anna, Nicolaus and Davy were setting out into the fading storm in search of him. Figuring their only way in was through the hatch window door, which was buried, they dug their way through the wall of snow towards the hidden door. Until finally, they clawed their way down to the boards, and one by one came tumbling into the printing house, taken aback by the scent of burning wood.

CHAPTER 6
A FIERY WILL

ICOLAUS PUT OUT HIS HAND, "Stop! Do you smell that?" Anna and Davy came to a halt behind the boney barrier. They had smelled the aroma of a burning hearth outside, though they had not considered it might actually be coming from inside the printing house.

"We should go," Davy whispered. "Joseph wouldn't make a fire. It brings too much attention."

He backed away from the hatch. Anna shook her head and prodded him through. She followed, Nicolaus bringing up the rear.

"Wait here, Nicolaus directed as he moved cautiously down the darkened hall, trying in vain to be quiet. His heavy legs were so wobbly with fatigue they hardly obeyed him. Jerky scuffs sounded on the gritty floor as he crept forward to peer around the corner, not knowing whom to expect. His eyes adjusted to the light of the great room, and he came to a standstill. He stared incredulously at the fire, unable to believe what he was seeing.

Anna and Davy watched from the back room. They saw Nicolaus' tense demeanor suddenly relax, then watched as he disappeared around the corner without fear, a signal to them that it was safe to come forward.

Rounding the corner themselves, Anna and Davy saw Nicolaus' scraggly silhouette lit against the bright fire burning in front of him. He was standing perfectly still, staring at Joseph and Marie sitting side-by-side.

"He did it," she whispered in breathless awe.

Anna and Davy came up behind Nicolaus. It felt like they were moving through a moment that could not possibly be real.

Suddenly aware of a presence in the room, Joseph spun around.

"You found her," Davy exclaimed, paying no attention to Joseph's bewilderment. "And you made a fire!" The boy rushed to sit hearthside beside Marie. He hugged her tightly, unwilling to let go.

"I don't believe it," Nicolaus added in shock.

"How did you all get here? …I mean, how did you make it?" Joseph asked, unable to conceive the three of them being able to walk through such high snows.

"All you need is a good reason, right?" Nicolaus said as if stating the obvious. "Besides, there was no way I was going to be able to keep this girl in the wagon any longer," he said motioning to Anna, whose worn face and shadowed eyes stood out starkly in the light cast by the fire. It was obvious the last four days had taken a heavy toll upon her. "Did you think we would let her go alone?"

"No…I just didn't expect any of you to be able to get through the snow," Joseph said with a dumbfounded look about him.

"We've been waiting for the snow to calm. Today was the first—" Nicolaus started.

"What's wrong?" Anna asked abruptly, without pretense, noticing that Marie wasn't her usual boisterous self.

Anna swept her long, wool skirt to the side as she knelt beside Marie.

"Dearest," Marie whispered. A weak smile crossed her cheeks. "I'll be fine. Just a bit under the weather," Marie assured in a weak voice.

"I found her here a few days ago. She was buried in a snow bank right outside here. She had a fever for the longest time. She came-to finally. We've been holed up here ever since."

Nicolaus stared through the square lens of his fogged spectacles, a look of concern creasing his brow.

After hanging their wet jackets and bindings near the fire, Anna, Nicolaus and Davy sat beside Marie, warming themselves as they spent time with the lost sister and adopted mother who had been miraculously returned to them. Joseph threw a few more pieces of wood upon the fire, poking at the blaze with the pointed end of a broken slat from one of the crates he had found in the basement. His prodding sent firefly sparks soaring up into the chimney as the flames rose higher.

Joseph melted more snow in the stout, tin mug they had kept hidden away in the house, letting the others drink and wash. Marie laid her head in Anna's lap and drifted off to sleep. As the three washed away the winter's wear, they listened to Joseph tell the story of what the last four days were like for him, starting at the beginning when he walked into the throat of the oncoming storm, through his long march and all the way up until the moment the three of them walked into the room. As he recounted the dream and the reflections to follow, the others said nothing, they just listened.

While Joseph spoke Anna was stern. She was relieved to have Joseph back and overjoyed to have Marie returned to them, even if she was in her sickly state. Nonetheless, as Joseph progressed through his story, she could not help but hold a little anger in her heart. For her, the last four days had not been filled with revelations and renewed hope; rather, she had experienced quite the opposite. To hear Joseph speak of his revelations after having lived through a breakdown of her own over these last days, made her feel distant from him for the first time in her life. It had been so long since she had seen him so full of confidence, which made her dearly wish she could give herself to his enthusiasm. All the same, she also knew the cycle of him endangering himself had to end.

*   *   *   *   *

W hEN JOSEPH WAS FINISHED TELLING HIS STORY he then moved into what he intended to do with his newfound hope. He told them the plans that he had made during the last hours as he lay in thought beside the warm fire. "…After seeing this vision of how life is meant to be, I realize how wrong our life is, and that it'll only get harder as the years come."

A look of deepest, tiring despair crossed Nicolaus and Davy's faces at the thought of such prospects. Anna simply stared without expression. She was waiting for what Joseph would say next, knowing that he would not bring forward such a hard truth unless he had a solution.

"We can't make it here. As time goes on, one by one we'll go into the factories or the docks—we'll have to. But even then we'll be wearing bare threads and eatin' broth. We'd end up in a one room apartment in some overcrowded slum. No, the only way for us to truly survive is to leave Boston. And so that's what we'll do," Joseph concluded dramatically, in a low toned resolute voice.

No one spoke for a long time.

"Leave?" Nicolaus said, breaking the silence. He could not have heard Joseph right.

Looking from Nicolaus who was confounded and then to Joseph who was wide-eyed and confident, Anna said nothing. She seemed content to let it all unfold.

"Leave." Joseph echoed back, letting Nicolaus know he had not been mistaken. "The only real chance at a life lies beyond the city, so we have to pull up our roots and go. We'll never be able to make it here; not when we need money in hand to have every little thing. We can't live here let alone flourish. So we have to leave. It's our only chance."

"I'm not arguing," Nicolaus said, not wanting to rip down Joseph's newly rebuilt hope. "I think that we would do brilliantly outside the city. But Joseph, how can we leave? We talked about this once before. We can't just walk out of the city on foot with nowhere to go and nothing to our name. And where will we go where we won't need money for every little thing? It's how things work.

"If we walked out of the city today there would be no place for us to stop and sleep. Without food, how many miles would we be able to walk in a day? Maybe five...if that. And what about Abbey, she would have a very rough time of it walking that far."

An image of Abbey hobbling along flashed into Joseph's mind. She had been born with one leg slightly shorter than the other, leaving her with a limp in her gait.

"I know—I know all this," Joseph interrupted. "And I know you don't think we'll make it, but we will. And I do," he added confidently. "Look, I'm not saying it'll be easy, but it's the only thing left to do. It's the chance we must take for a life. There's no hope here in Boston. We'll never have anything of our own here. But out there is something better." Joseph said raising his arm dramatically, not pointing to anything visible but rather to the far off horizon beyond the city. "Here we have no chance to make our own way. But if we could have a bit of land and could fill our bellies from the fields rather than the market, we'd be a damn sight more free than we are now," he said, pointing at the ground he stood on, speaking with passion.

"We don't know anything about farming or living off the land. How could we make it?" Nicolaus stated.

"Yeah, but we know about survival," Joseph reasoned. "Plus, I'm not proposing that we should walk out into the wild as we are now—starved and unprepared. We'll get the supplies we need and, when the time comes, we'll take the wagon."

Everyone just stared at Joseph, not knowing whether he had been inspired with a brilliant plan or had simply gone mad with some kind of fever.

"We'll get supplies…? We'll take the wagon…? Joseph?" Nicolaus said with a pain-filled laugh of bitter irony. "We can't buy a loaf of bread or a bottle of milk or a proper coat! How could we provision ourselves for such a journey?"

"We can't," Joseph said bluntly. Not at all angry with the others for their doubts, knowing full well how ridiculous his plan sounded. "You're right Nicolaus, we can't afford to buy any supplies. But I don't propose that we *buy* them, I propose that we *gather* them. We can scrounge for everything that we'll need and nip a few things here and there if needs be." Joseph started to pace the room as the pieces came together. There— in the dialogue—he was weaving together a plan. "I know the odds are against us, but I'm telling you we could do this. We can gather everything that we need into the wagon we can haul that thing up out of the mud and leave."

"If it will still even work…" Nicolaus interjected rationally. "How would we pull it? We don't have the money for a horse or an ox. And that's not something we can just find lying around in some alley."

"We'll gather wood and reinforce any parts of the wagon that seem weak. As for what will pull it…" he said, the tone of his voice going a little higher, as if he was trying to squeeze his argument through this tight spot, "I admit, I have no answer. You're right; we don't have the money to buy a horse or an ox. But I'm still certain that preparing to leave is the right course for us. It just feels like the right thing. We will just have to work in faith that…we'll be able to do it."

His voice leveled out. "I can't foresee everything that we'll need or how we'll go about getting it all. But what I do know is leaving the city is the right path for us. I know that we haven't survived all these years simply to live out our lives in some factory, squatting in abandoned buildings, eating moldy food. This is not life…life is out there," he said once more pointing a finger to the far off horizon, as if the shear fact that the land was out there somewhere waiting for them not only gave him hope but also drove him insane with an impatient yearning to reach it. "And we have to do everything we can to reach it."

He looked at the three of them. Davy seemed excited, but he could tell Nicolaus and Anna were still not convinced.

"Look," he said, speaking bluntly, his enthusiastic tone shifting to one of serious candor. "Since the day we were abandoned we've been living on the belief that one day we would be able to have a full life. Now we're going to put that belief to the test. We're going to dare to want things again. I know this journey is intimidating, but, between us all, we have spent over twenty years surviving what couldn't be survived. So, no matter how impossible this all may seem, I know we can make it. I know it'll be hard; I'm not blind to that. But when I look at how hard the journey could be, I also look back on how hard our life has been. I can't explain how every part of this will fall into place. All I know is this—I had a vision of the place where we can have a life, and I know that it's a real place. I can feel it in my heart. It's where we belong."

CHAPTER 7
TO WHAT LENGTHS

J OSEPH WAS STILL ON HIS FEET. The firelight highlighted half his face, leaving the other half in shadow. Yet through the darkness Anna could see that Joseph's eyes were fixed intently on her. She had not said a word throughout his whole speech. He had been so caught up in the moment that he had not noticed her complete silence until now, and it was deafening. Joseph watched and waited, willing her to voice what she thought, no matter what her opinion might be.

Marie lay sleeping. Anna stroked her hair while gazing at him. Nicolaus and Davy were so consumed in their own thoughts that they did not notice Joseph and Anna staring at each other from across the room—Anna hurt and Joseph sorry. In that moment, as he waited for her to speak, he felt the new belief that had risen in him tremble, as if its very survival teetered on a precipice. He knew if Anna said she did not believe, it would strike at him, and his newfound hope would drain like blood from a mortal wound.

Staring at her from across the room, a burning lump of emotion had lodged in his throat. His remorse for having left her, his renewed confidence, his desperation and the fear of falling from this high peak of possibility, all churned nauseously within him. Then, finally she put him out of his misery.

63

"He's right. We could do it," she said firmly.

Nicolaus and Davy looked over towards her, Joseph released the clenched breath he had been holding in his chest, and they all listened as she—the strongest will among them—took up the banner of Joseph's new belief and carried it forward. "If we aren't willing to believe that life will get better, we've given up—we've accepted this starvation is all we're ever going to have. Is that what we should tell Asa, Emma, Beth, and Ben— that this bleakness is all they're ever going to have? No. No matter how many fears we have, we still must reach."

Anna had cut right to the core of Nicolaus' and Davy's hesitations.

"I don't know how any of this will work," Nicolaus admitted. "But I believe in you, Joseph—in what you feel. And I can't deny that things have changed…finding each other. …finding Marie…it seems like a new time for us."

"Together we can do anything," Anna said, strongly declaring what she knew to be true, building up her own momentum of confidence. "We've been forsaken by everyone who should have cared for us. We've been held back and denied everything that we need to live, but we're not helpless. We have never known what it is to truly live, but that doesn't mean it ends there. We have to do this. In the end, no matter where we end up, we'll need to know that we did *everything* we could to escape this death."

The momentum of Joseph's and Anna's belief was so strong it was almost tangible. Joseph gave a look of deepest peace. He had finally managed to do what he had always wished he could. He had passed on a belief to those he loved that was going to keep them alive.

Anna and Joseph were united in their belief, and the force of that union was enough to silence every doubt and remove every hesitation in any of the other children. Nicolaus and Davy finally believed; it shone in their eyes. They sat there on the floor staring up at Anna and Joseph with looks of implicit trust. There were no others in the world in whom they had more confidence.

Exhausted after such a burst of emotion and excitement, Joseph sat down on the floor across from Nicolaus and Davy, listening to the two carry on about what should be done first to prepare for the journey. However, his moment of rest did not last long. Just as Nicolaus and Davy started to talk amongst themselves, Anna gingerly put Marie's head to rest on a balled up scarf and walked over to Joseph. "Can I speak to you alone?"

Entrusting the care of Marie to the boys, Joseph and Anna proceeded downstairs into the dimly lit basement.

Walking down the creaky stairs, Joseph stepped onto the dirt floor and walked over to a nearby crate where he sat down, leaving enough room for Anna to sit beside him. Yet she did not come over to join him. After stepping down from the bottom stair she simply paced a little silently, then stopped, arms crossed, staring at him. Joseph was not sure if she was waiting for him to speak or else trying to figure out whether she wanted to begin speaking herself.

Only moments ago she had been charged and full of conviction, but now she looked distraught.

"Are you all right?" he asked timidly. "Is it the plan? You do believe that it's possible, don't you? Or were you just being strong for them?" He began to reel.

"No...I believe that it's possible."

"But…?" he asked, proceeding cautiously into what he sensed to be dangerous ground.

Anna just stared at the floor, arms still crossed. "There's something I want to know. Over the last years, you haven't been willing to hope for anything unless you could see how every single step of it could be planned and carried out *by you*, so broken was your belief that good things could happen. Did that dream really change you that much? Or do you intend on killing yourself in the factories so we can save the money for the trip? I want to know now how you really plan on doing all this."

"Why are you talking like this Anna? Your words sound mean."

Anna knew he was right. She could feel the frustration of the last four days bubbling up as anger. She took a breath, trying to calm herself. "I'm sorry. I've just been so angry with you these last days," she said her voice straining a little. "I'm not trying to be mean," she added sincerely, continuing in a weary voice, "but I'm tired of being a witness to your self-destruction. I'm tired of not being included in your choices. I won't do it anymore, Joseph. I just can't. That's why, if you plan on getting us out of the city by sacrificing yourself in the factories, I want to know now."

Feeling guilty, Joseph hesitantly conceded that she was not entirely wrong, "I won't deny that the thought of the factories crossed my mind, just as a quick way to tuck a bit away, but as much as I hate to admit it, I could work at the factories for ten years and never save enough to buy a single horse."

Anna walked towards him, her voice wavering between pleading and frustration. "See, this is what I'm worried about. I'm more than willing to believe in this plan, but how long until you take everything into your own hands? If we're going to try to achieve this dream, we have to work hard and be resourceful, because, in the end, we simply can't escape this city on our own—we just can't. The exits are blocked, Joseph. We can gather most of what we'll need, but some things are beyond our reach. I'm not saying we should sit on our hands and wait for something to happen. We're going to have to work very hard. But even then, we'll need help, and either the help will come or it won't. You sacrificing yourself will only lead us all into more pain. You and Duncan tried to bring us out of poverty when you both went into the factories the first time, and we almost lost you."

A look of anguish crossed Joseph's face, one that someone who did not know him might mistake for frustration with Anna but, truly, was a sign that his own self-loathing was rearing its head.

"If I had to do it, I could do it," he firmly insisted.

Sitting down beside him on the dusty crate, Anna took hold of his arm, looking directly at him as his gaze remained downcast, willing the words to sink into him. "Yes, you could go back. But at what cost? You don't know how worried I was for you during that time. Working there nearly killed you, not just your body but in your heart," she said reaching out and placing her hand on his chest.

Knowing that at that very moment he was cursing himself for his weakness, Anna pressed on, wanting to make some-thing quite clear, trying to bring him back from the isolation of his self-loathing. "You have never failed us, Joseph," she said loudly and clearly. Her words resounded within the stone walls of the small basement. She hoped they would rise above the voice of Joseph's own self-disappointment. "You think that because you couldn't survive at the factories, you failed us. Deep down, you think if you were a stronger person, you could do something to save us…you think all our suffering is in some way due to your shortcomings. That's what you think, isn't it? Well, you couldn't be more wrong. No one could survive the factories, not I or Marie, not even Duncan. Your self-sacrifice isn't giving us an easier life. In fact, it is making our life harder because it was taking you away from us.

"Don't you realize how important you are to us? No…" she said with a humorless laugh, "obviously you don't know, which is why you're willing to take the chances you do. You think you failed us. But you're wrong Joseph. You have such a good heart, but sometimes you take too much upon yourself. Our circumstances aren't of your making. If it were not for you, we wouldn't survive each day. And not just because of what you give to us but because of what your presence brings to our lives.

"We would rather live in this unbearable way and have you, because to us having money and a home in exchange for you wouldn't be a fair trade. You're priceless to us. So please, Joseph, stop risking yourself and stop ignoring yourself, stop disregarding your health and well-being. Help us by staying strong and by staying near. We can survive without many things, but each other is one thing that we couldn't bear the loss of. This is what I need you to understand."

"I'm sorry," he whispered. He said it in such a way that Anna knew she had finally gotten through.

She hugged him tightly. And there in the semidarkness, they sat for a long while soaking in the stillness.

CHAPTER 8
NEW BELIEF

THE WARMTH OF THE HEARTH, the strain of the journey through the snow and the excitement of the new plan all seemed to wear out Nicolaus and Davy, who were passed out on the floor.

"None of us have slept well these last days," Anna commented in a hushed whisper, as she and Joseph sat on the other side of the fire across from the sleeping boys.

"Oh, here," she said as she rummaged through the small bundle she had brought. "We saved some food for you." She laid out a few pieces of icy fish and a wedge of stale bread.

Joseph placed the meat on a hot stone close to the flames. Sitting there in the flickering light, both of them stared at Marie, lost in their own thoughts as to what could be done to help her.

The water from the thawing fish had evaporated quickly near the blazing coals. What little fat there was in the skin had melted off. The fish began to sizzle. The smell of roasting fish came into the air. Finally, Joseph and Anna were called back to the fire from their thoughts by the sound of sizzling meat.

"Never have I smelled something so sweet. You have to have some of this. I won't sit here and eat a hot meal in front of you."

"There isn't that much there to begin with. Just eat it," Anna insisted.

"Oh no, you are having some. I mean it. When was the last time we had hot food?"

Exhaling a little short laugh as she thought back, Anna honestly could not recall.

"Exactly," he said gazing at her sternly, yet with a faint smile beginning to curve about his cheeks. "You're just lucky I'm not waking up the others and splitting it with them."

Burning his fingers as he picked up the cooked fish, Joseph pushed some of the flaking white meat into a pile for Anna.

"Careful, it's hot," he warned.

Scooping a mouthful into the palm of his hand, Joseph blew on the steaming hot meat a few times then inhaled it. Closing his eyes, he savored the taste and chewed it for a long while, knowing that it was the first mouthful of what would be a two-bite meal. The hot and juicy, white flesh of the cod fish was the best thing he had ever eaten in his life. The crispy grey skin, the lightly salted meaty flesh…

"Oh, my goodness." Anna said as she chewed the tender meat. "That's so good."

Reaching for their last bite at the same time with a mixture of excitement and disappointment, neither waited to blow on it. They each popped their small chunk into their mouths to experience the savory moment of happiness one more time.

When it was done and the meat was gone, Joseph sat there picking at the small flakes of fish burned to the stone with his finger.

"Ah!" Joseph said, letting out a little yelp as his finger slipped off the remnant of charred meat he was trying to scrape off and touched the searing hot stone.

"Careful." Anna said laughing a little. "You're going to burn yourself."

Having pulled off the few strands of burnt skin from the stone, he proceeded to lick his palm for any trace amounts of oil from the crispy skin.

Anna quietly giggled to herself as she watched him. She could not recall the last time they both had been so happy. They were together, they had just had hot food, there was a fire, the others were safe in the wagon and they had a plan. Life was good.

"Well that ought to keep the wolf from the door."

"At least for a little while, anyway," Anna added.

"We're doing that again," Joseph said eagerly, once he had lapped up the juices the fish had left upon his hand. "We're going to go down to the docks, gather all the fish we can find, bring it all back here and cook it. Everyone has to try this."

"Now the bread," Anna said handing him the warmed wedge of bread she had brought for him. It was stale, the crust had to be taken off and flecks of blooming mold had to be picked away, but it was still good. Taking a small hunk from the pie-slice wedge, Joseph ate and set the rest aside.

Anna set aside the extra bread for Marie.

Throwing another few pieces of wood on the fire, they lay down side by side on the dusty floor and stared up into the darkened loft ceiling.

"Tell me about your dream again," Anna whispered, closing her eyes.

Joseph called forward the images. Allowing himself to walk back into the calming scene, he described every single detail he could recall.

Moving closer, Anna eased her head down on his chest, letting out a deep exhale of relief and contentment. Putting his arm around her, they lay there together quietly, the fire light waving through the dim room, the burning wood popping and crackling, the slow steady breathing of the others sleeping not far away.

"We're leaving here, this city, very soon," Joseph said softly, knowing that Anna was so close to him he need not talk but in the faintest whisper. "I can feel it. As soon as we can gather what we need, we'll leave. And you'll be with me on this every step of the way, right?" Joseph asked wanting to calm even the faintest doubt.

Rolling back up onto her arm, staring into his deep brown eyes with blazing conviction and rock-solid certainty, Anna smiled broadly. "Where do we start?"

*   *   *   *   *

JOSEPH AND ANNA TALKED LATE INTO THE NIGHT. By the time they had finally closed their eyes, they had come up with a preliminary plan for the coming weeks. During the hours that passed while they slept, the fire had gradually died down until it was nothing more than smoldering ash sifting through the iron grate of the old hearth.

For the first time in days, the sun was actually shining. The gloom of the storm had passed, and rays of light beamed down through the thin cracks in the boarded up windows, illuminating the particles of dust that were gently swirling in the still air, glimmering as if someone had thrown a handful of fairy dust, which now gently descended to the floor where the children slept.

Upon opening his eyes, Joseph found he was lying on his back in the same position he had fallen asleep. He did not rise immediately, instead he stared up into the illuminated loft, watching the curled fingers of smoke flowing serenely through the air. He looked beside him expecting to see Anna fast asleep, but she was already awake and sitting beside Marie.

"Have you been up all night?" he asked softly, having no desire to wake Davy and Nicolaus.

Anna jumped a little at the sound of his voice. He noticed that she looked tired.

"She was up a short while ago. She just fell back asleep. She is very weak. We need to get her back to the wagon, but I am afraid she won't make the hike through the snow."

Groggily, Joseph drew himself up and sat across from her.

"I let the fire die out," she said on a side note, "seeing as it's light out, and the smoke will only serve to pique people's interest."

"I had intended to stay up and see to it, but I guess I dozed off."

"You needed it," Anna said in a serious voice.

"So do you," Joseph replied, staring at her puffy face.

Anna ignored this comment, continuing in a slow whisper. "I figured we'd wait until the boys wake, then we can decide what to do."

Usually it was the children's rule to leave the printing house during the daylight hours when it was more likely that the policemen might make their rounds. The printing house was far off the beaten path; however, over the last months, there had been an increase in the number of people coming in and out, so Duncan had judged it prudent for them to stop going to the printing house except for emergencies—a measure they ignored on the night the police burst in, and they were separated in the ensuing chaos.

"I was thinking about that actually," Joseph started, "I'd planned on trying to move her myself once the storm broke so I could return to the wagon. I think I can take one of the longer, sturdier crates, pry the lid off it, attach a length of rope, then pull the lid like a sled. We could sit Marie on the sled then pull it across the top of the snow. Like a dogsled in the Yukon," he added. "Of course it'll still be hard work pulling the sled all that way, but carrying her in this snow would simply be impossible."

"Perfect. We'll make the journey at night when there's less chance of being seen," suggested Anna. She looked tired.

"Seeing as we're going to be held up here all day, you should try to get some sleep. I mean, how often do we have a warm fire and a dry place to lie? You really should take advantage. Plus, it'll be hard work pulling the sled, and we'll all have to help. So please rest."

Joseph waited to see if his reasoning had sunk into her. She did not move. She just continued to stare at Marie, stroking the limp hair around the girl's brow. Beaten, Joseph knew he'd given his best argument, but in the end Anna would sit with Marie until she was done. Knowing there was nothing else he could do but leave her to do as she wished, he laid a consoling hand on Anna's leg then quietly rose to his feet. Stepping lightly across the wooden floorboards, placing each foot down delicately, then easing his weight slowly unto it, he made his way towards the basement staircase, trying not to cause any creaks or squeals that might wake Nicolaus and Davy.

*   *   *   *   *

THROUGHOUT THE AFTERNOON, JOSEPH WORKED on the
sled. Once Nicolaus and Davy woke, they went down into
the dim basement to help Joseph. It was not a big job. In no
time, Joseph was announcing that they were almost done.

As he finished tying the two lengths of rope onto the front
of the sled—one on the left side, one on the right side—the
three of them began talking about what was to come.

"I've been thinking it all over," Joseph started as he continued working to secure the rope, "and talking to Anna about it,
and I figure to do this journey we're going to need quite a few
things," Joseph said. Both Nicolaus and Davy looked up from
their work to give him their full attention. "The way I figure
it, these are some of the things we're going to need to find:
scraps of fabric that could be used for quilt squares, fabric for
clothing, and shoes—or at the very least durable cloth for foot
bindings. We'll need fishing line and hooks, small nets, and a
good hunting knife. For tools, we'll need: a hatchet, a broadax,
a saw, a mallet, a plane, and an auger if possible."

"What's an auger?" Davy interjected in a quizzical voice,
pushing back his hat to wipe the sweat from his brow.

"It's basically a hand drill used for making holes, which
we can hammer wooden pegs into instead of using iron nails.
We'll need it when time comes to make a house."

"All right then, I think I've seen one of them before,"
nodded Davy.

Davy was a brave boy. A truer heart had never been found.
He had ink black hair which only seemed to make his face
appear all the paler. He was a stout boy with a round face, short

nose, and heavy dark eyes. He had a boldness about him. His oily black hair grew thick and wild, though, as of late, it had been tamed by the charcoal colored sailor's cap Nicolaus had passed down to him. The constant wearing of the hat managed to hold down his thick hair and reshape his many cowlicks. Even when his hat was off, his hair stayed in the same pressed down shape, as if he spent the day with a bowl upon his head. The last two or three inches of his hair had taken to curling upward where the headband of the hat had ended.

While he knew little about his parents, it could be concluded that he was a second generation, Italian immigrant. He had no traces of an accent but had the look of a boy whose blood originated in the Mediterranean.

Davy wore a thin, dark green handkerchief wrapped around his throat three times then tied off to the side in a double knot, the short ends of which were tucked into the single-breasted, men's dinner jacket that he wore as a coat. Finally, tucked into an inside pocket, Davy kept a worn, long outdated book on husbandry that he had found discarded in a trash bin. Over the last few years, the boy flipped through the book so often the pages had begun ripping away from the binding.

Joseph went on, "then we'll need bits and bobs, like empty sacks, buckets, and barrels for storing things, matches, candles, and rope, as well as bandages in case someone's hurt. Anna tells me that the sewing kit will need scissors, thread, and needles, at the very least, and also pins if possible. For our kitchen, we'll need bowls, mugs, a soup pot, a skillet, and a kettle. Some of these things might be hard to come by, but they're pretty basic, so we really have to try to find them. Other things that would be useful later on would be a hoe, a shovel, and an ax. And finally," he said, taking a deep bracing breath, "we'll need food, as well as a horse, donkey or ox to pull the wagon. It's a small wagon so, it shouldn't take much to pull it. It's not one of those great prairie schooners that settlers are taking westward. We won't need a whole team of oxen just to get it moving. Finding the animal to pull the wagon will be the greatest challenge, but I'm sure that something will present itself. And if for some reason we don't find anything, we will take what's absolutely necessary and go on foot."

Nicolaus and Davy could not help but be a little stunned by the enormity of what Joseph was proposing. But, as always, when he spoke, building up examples and reasons why this implausible plan could actually work, the boys once again found their hearts swept-up in his enthusiasm.

"There," Joseph said in a satisfied voice as he finished securing the rope, "we're ready."

* * * * *

BACK AT THE WAGON, Rachel continued to sit sentry, keeping a weathered-eye fixed upon the city's edge. Hour after hour into the night and through the day, there had been no change until finally she heard noise in the distance.

Upon first hearing the commotion, Rachel was afraid, she had no idea of who was approaching. Looking out between the flaps of canvas, she saw the moonlit outlines of a group of people coming directly towards the wagon. She rose quickly and undid the flap ties. Everyone else in the wagon looked up, startled. Those asleep sat up just in time to see Rachel leap down into the snow and take off running towards the familiar silhouettes at a far.

"Abbey," she said on her way down, instructing her to hold down the fort.

Rachel dashed off into the night. She could see Anna, Joseph, Nicolaus, and Davy. They were back. Just then she noticed them pulling something behind them.

Abbey did her best to keep the others in the wagon calm, but once everyone came into view, the little ones erupted in excitement and started leaping down into the snow.

"Have you gone mad? Get back in here!" Abbey demanded, taking Ben by his scrawny arm, while Beth leapt down, trying to herd the little ones back into the wagon.

The two young girls did their best to hold the same order that Anna or Rachel were able to command, but it was in vain. They were not heard above the frenzy, and by the time Rachel noticed that she was being followed, she had already reached Joseph, Anna, Davy, and Nicolaus.

"Who is that?" Rachel said. A ghastly expression on her face, when she finally reached the worn out travelers. "Marie!" she shouted, but exuberance turned to fear. "What's wrong? Why aren't you walking?"

"She's fine," Joseph said, panting in exhaustion after the grueling trek. "Well she's not fine," he went on in-between hoarse ragged breaths. "She's sick. Help us," he added, motioning for her to take up the rope on the other side that Anna had been pulling. Anna was doubled over, trying to catch her breath.

Making their way the last hundred yards, the whole wagon had emptied as everyone rushed to see that Joseph was all right. All of them brought to a speechless halt when they saw Marie.

"Everyone, inside," Anna directed. "Davy, Abbey, get them inside."

Davy and Abbey pulled them away from their shock, answering what questions they could, as they kept them moving back into the warmth of the shelter.

Climbing in one by one, the little ones moved to the back of the wagon as Marie climbed up, aided by Nicolaus and Joseph into the waiting arms of Anna, Rachel, and Davy, who were already in the wagon. Once everyone was settled, Joseph and Nicolaus climbed in, the flaps were shut, and they settled in.

Marie sat at the center of the wagon, taking in the outpour of love from those who'd missed her. Once each one of the travelers were free of their wet jacket and bindings, they were wrapped in fold after fold of the great canvas blanket. Marie's pale face shone in the sea of ivory cotton. Asa and Emma were cuddled against her. A wide smile spread across each face.

Coats and shawls, socks and the long strips for hand and foot bindings were all removed, rung out, and strung from the rafters to dry, giving the children the feeling that they were camping out in the bottom of a huge closet—the occasional drip of water hitting one of them as they nestled.

After resting and warming themselves for an hour or so Joseph and Anna knew they had to tell Rachel and the others all that had happened in the few short days they had been apart. Joseph had brought that ripple of change to Anna, Nicolaus, and Davy, and now it was time to pass it on to all the others.

He started at the beginning, telling them all that had happened—the dream, the decision to leave the city, and the journey for which they were now to prepare.

Surprisingly, in the end, convincing Rachel was not as hard as it had been to convince Nicolaus or Davy. And when it came

to the younger ones—Ben, Abbey, Beth, Asa, and Emma—
they had no problem believing in the dream, for they were
still at that age where anything was possible. In fact, Asa and
Emma were so unspoiled in their absolute belief when they
heard Joseph's plan, they did not think it to be far-fetched or
even difficult for that matter. Rather, to them, it was an idea
they wanted to carry out right then, as if they both thought it
was as easy as simply going to find a horse, gathering all the
supplies in one morning, hitching up the wagon, and leaving
by the afternoon. Of course, it was going to be a little more
complicated than that.

CHAPTER 9
MOMENTUM

THE EARLY MORNING WAS TAKEN SLOWLY. Once the sun had risen, the excitement of the coming day began to take hold. Everyone was ready to get started.

Today was the day they would begin to gather supplies.

Everyone volunteered to make the trip into the city, however, the snow was still too deep for the little ones to walk through with ease. So it was decided that some would go into the city with Joseph, while others stayed at the wagon with Anna to watch over Marie and Ben, who was also still recovering. Beth did not have to stay, but she said she wanted to stay and help Anna. Abbey said she too would stay behind, though her heart was not truly in it. Inwardly she wanted to make the trip, but she was afraid of slowing everyone down, and so resigned herself to stay. In the end, this left Joseph, Nicolaus, Rachel, and Davy to make the trip.

Those who chose to stay behind at the wagon were given a few small jobs, among them were cleaning off the front bench of the wagon where the driver would sit and making a small tarp cover to be used as a temporary storage area for the supplies they would gather in the city.

As the group headed out, Anna handed Joseph the old, extra square of fabric that she had given him on his last journey into the city.

"Fill it up again if you can," she said encouragingly. "You could also use burlap sacks if you could find a few," Anna said as she handed Nicolaus another square she had torn off the voluminous canvas sail.

Bound up tight and warm, Joseph unlaced the canvas flap and jumped down onto the soggy, muddy ground.

"After a day of walking around in this, we're going to look lovely when we come back," he remarked, as he stood ankle deep in the thick mud made by the mounds of melting snow. "I'll try to find some kind of bucket or pail that we can use as a wash basin for our clothes." Waving an arm, Joseph motioned for Davy to jump down. Asa stuck his head out of the opening. He was eyeballing the mud. It was calling to be played in. Seeing his malevolent grin, Anna quickly took hold of the back of his shirt to prevent the inevitable.

Joseph reached his hand up to Davy, helped him down, then paused. Abbey was standing off to the side looking rather frustrated.

Anna had noticed her too. "Are you sure you didn't want to go?" She asked as Nicolaus and Rachel climbed down. "Go ahead, go. They'll go slow," Anna prodded. She laid a hand on Abbey's shoulder encouragingly, giving her a smile.

"Come on, Abbey," Davy called, waving her to join them.

Joseph reached up to take her hand, though she left his hand waiting in mid-air as an anguished look came over her face. Hand still in the air, Joseph motioned for her to take it. She did. Jumping down into the mud a little unsteadily, she slowly made her way toward Davy.

Rachel looked up to Anna. "Tomorrow, I'll stay and you can go."

"Oh, we'll be fine," Anna replied with a lightness in her voice.

"We'll return before nightfall. Look for us at dusk," Joseph assured her, his eyes still fixed on Abbey, watching until she cleared the patch of slippery mud. Once she was secure on Davy's arm, Joseph turned back and met Anna's eyes. In that moment, he expressed all the assurances they did not want to say aloud. Then, with a little nod, Anna encouraged him to go on without fear. Pulling his chestnut brown eyes away from her, he ran to catch up with Davy, Nicolaus, Rachel, and Abbey.

"I know what we should search for today," he said in a determined voice. "First, we're going to gather food—I don't think I have to tell you that.

"Other than that, I think today we should look for the makings of our clothes. A few of us will always have to be at the wagon, so we should find some things that will keep every-one busy there"

"Our best chance at having heavy clothes will be to make our own," Rachel added.

"I agree, which is why today we need to find as much raw cloth as we can. You and Anna are our best seamstresses. What else will you need to make proper clothing?"

Nicolaus, Davy, Abbey, and Joseph, all turned to Rachel who found herself a little tongue-tied under the spotlight.

"Um, well, thread and needles of course. Scissors wouldn't hurt, but they aren't necessary; we've been able to make do with your pocket knife, Joseph. I would say a tape measure, but we could use a length of string to take measurements. Really," she finished, "aside from fabric, we only need needles and thread. Thread we can probably find, but needles are going to be harder. How do you search for a needle?"

They all looked lost.

"Well, we'll find a haystack," Joseph said ironically. Trying to rebound and keep their momentum going. "We'll think of something, we always do," he concluded with a hopeful smile.

"Nicolaus, Rachel, Abbey, why don't you three go to the well-to-do tailors, dressmakers, and milliners down near the Common. Look through the scrap piles they've put out for the dump. You might find material scraps, buttons, threads, and who knows what else. We've had some luck there before. After you go there, spend the rest of the time looking for food. We'll meet at the printing house an hour or so before sunset."

"Where are you going? I didn't know you wanted to split up." Nicolaus said, a little taken aback.

"Davy and I will go down to the harbor and try to find some more canvas. Depending on how we do there, we'll try the cloth mill next. I don't know what they do with pieces that they can't use, but perhaps there'll be something we can scrounge." Joseph looked at Nicolaus sympathetically. "I don't like us splitting up either, but we'll cover more ground if we break into two groups."

They all came to a halt. The city streets lay just ahead.

Joseph and Davy hugged Rachel, Nicolaus, and Abbey. Then, taking him under his arm, Joseph brought Davy close and headed off toward the docks.

For years Joseph and the children had lived on the streets, having to pick through the thin, worn shirts and pants that were cast off trying to find something to keep them covered and warm. They never had found much of anything that felt like it was a real piece of clothing—thick, whole, clean, and durable. For all those years, they had mended the clothes they found and did their best to piece old shirts and jackets together, but they never had a secure place to work and store supplies until now.

✳   ✳   ✳   ✳   ✳

T HE STREETS WERE CHOKED WITH CARRIAGES: loaded down carts traveling to the harbor and empty carts heading toward the factories where they would be given their cargo.

Joseph and Davy made their way through the dirty chaos of the streets and down to the harbor. Most of the snow had been pushed off the wooden boards and into the sea where it melted. There were several dockages along the coastline of the city. One after the other, vessels were lined up along the shore. There were merchant ships, fishing schooners, wooden whalers, passenger ships, as well as the dories, cutters, and sloops owned by the local fishermen. And with each of these ships that put in, the children would have an opportunity to scavenge for supplies.

Given its size, the old sail Anna had found had most likely been from a whaler. It was a huge piece of canvas. Right now it was used for their blanket and wagon cover, but they still were going to need more cloth. The canvas was best suited for the heavy-duty clothing. Joseph knew that finding more canvas was vital, and he hoped they might find some to bring back today.

Davy and he went to the first dock where a merchant ship was anchored. They walked the whole length of the dock finding nothing of use.

Undeterred, they moved down the next dock where a passenger ship was moored and again found nothing.

They walked down a dozen docks, checking each and every one without a scrap to show for it. The entire time, Davy could sense Joseph begin to stress. He tried to keep saying encouraging things after they went down each dock only to walk back empty handed.

Davy was the first to see the pile of treasures. To anyone else it would look like a pile of rubbish heaped onto the dock by a crewman who no longer saw its use. Yet, Davy and Joseph's eyes could see the true worth and potential of this trash. "What's that?" Davy said holding his breath. He grabbed Joseph's arm and pulled him down the dock.

When they reached the pile, they started peeling back the layers of old nets, frayed ropes, and broken rigging. Joseph could think of a use for each thing his hand touched.

"Look Joseph!" Davy exclaimed. "Old fishing hooks and thick line. It's all knotted up, but we could still use some of it."

"Good, wind it up. We'll bring it. We can sort it out later. We can use it to fish. We could even use that heavy line to sew up our heavy jackets."

They dug through the pile of tangled line and netting, balling it up and tucking it into Joseph's canvas square. It was as they pulled back all the layers of matted netting and line that they found what they had been in search of: canvas. They saw the color of white canvas, as they peeled open the first fold. They saw that it was a large piece, not a whole sail, but at least half of one that had most likely been torn in the recent storm and then left when the crew was unable to salvage it.

"There are a few holes and tears, but we can cut around those," Joseph said cheerfully.

Joseph rolled the canvas up into a log, tied a length of rope around each end, then slung it around him as they moved on. When they reached the end of the docks, they looked down to another dock they had already searched, and they watched as a flounder schooner put in.

Joseph carefully watched as the men unloaded their catch. He saw smaller butterfish left on the dock. As the crew unloaded the bigger fish, they inadvertently dropped these little butter-fish that had been caught in the net. They were only about the size of a child's hand—golden scales with some meat on them, but not enough to tempt many people into buying them. They were of little or no value. But, as always, where many saw noth-ing of value Joseph, and the children saw treasure.

"Look, Davy, see the butterfish the floundermen are drop-ping? If we could find some salt, we could preserve the meat from those small fish and the other raw scraps we find."

Joseph watched the fishermen dropping more and more of the tiny fish. He was preoccupied as he thought back to the bit of fish he and Anna cooked on the hearth stones a few nights ago and all they could do with the dozens of butterfish now resting, uncared for, on the dock planks.

"We should wait here till they're done and gather up the fish. It'll be near impossible to find food elsewhere in the city with all this snow and mud."

Joseph and Davy lowered themselves onto the edge of a dock far enough away, so that the crew of the boat would not notice them waiting like a pair of hungry gulls. As they sat, Joseph took a length of the thick line and untangled it from the massive nest.

"What'll we do with that? Are we going to fish?" Davy asked, watching Joseph prepare the hook and line. The boy looked

down at the water with a questionable look upon his face. The
water beneath them was not that deep. It looked rather cold,
and Davy did not see any fish circling whatsoever. Just then
he saw a crab moving up the dockage post, while another was
moving horizontally and very quickly across the black seaweed
encrusted rocks that covered the bottom. It seemed as though
the creatures had realized they had been spotted.

"No, we aren't going to fish," Joseph said as he watched
Davy's eyes follow the fleeing crab and laughed to himself.
"Once the crew leaves, we'll go and collect all the tiny fish,
string them on this line through their gills, then tie the length
of line into a circle, so it's easier to carry them."

Joseph and Davy sat on the dock, their short legs swaying back and forth, all the while commenting on the strange
creatures that occasionally swam or crawled past them. They
waited for over an hour as the sun lowered in the sky and the
men hauled off their catch into the waiting wheelbarrows.
Davy swung his legs through the air back and forth as he
began counting the tiny fish he had seen the crew drop upon
the docks during their work. By the time the crew was done,
Davy had counted fifteen fish on top of those that had fallen
before the boredom drove them to start keeping track.

The crew finally finished. The fisherman set off towards the
nearest tavern to have a mug-up, while the boys walked fast
over to the dock to beat the circling birds to the bounty.

One by one they picked up the tiny silver and gold fish,
slipping them onto the line. Each time they slipped one on,
Davy would count the total aloud.

*　　*　　*　　*　　*

WHILE JOSEPH AND DAVY WERE COLLECTING FISH at the harbor, Nicolaus, Rachel, and Abbey moved closer to their first stop. All of the shops they chose served the well-heeled society who could afford to forgo practicality for the latest fashion. The children were not looking for fashion; they just wanted to be warm and dry. They would make practical clothing without ruffles or frills, wearing every stitch with genuine care.

The three of them roamed past the shops along the edges of the park. Droves of people walked the streets, dashing in and out of the stores. The children made their way into the alleys where the trash bins were kept.

So many times they had walked by thrift shops and admired the pairs of used boots, secondhand coats, sweaters, gloves, thick socks, and felted shawls. The older children could recall a time before they were abandoned when they gazed longingly at the new dolls, trains, and boats displayed in the toy store windows. But somewhere life had shifted, and one day they found themselves huddled before the paneled glass windows of the shops looking at a pair of warm socks.

Whereas once she longed for wondrous toys, Abbey now stood watching the baker pull sticky buns, steamy bread, and floury muffins from the oven. The smell always drew them. The aroma of hot, steaming loaves of butter brown bread or small, golden rolls topped with a powdery, white covering of flour was an excruciating tease.

"Come away, Abbey," Rachel said a little sad. "We'll search for food later, dearest," Rachel assured her. "First we have to see to this."

Abbey reluctantly left the delicious sights of the bakery, and they kept moving towards the clothing district. At the end of each project, the shops would throw out bundles of scraps they had no use for, which made for good scavenging for the children.

To avoid getting into a sticky situation with the shopkeepers, who were not keen on people taking from their trash, the children decided not to look through the bundles in the alley. The shops were humming as the well-heeled came in and out picking up orders that cost up to fifty dollars—a figure that most average workmen and able seamen made in a year. Rachel gaped at one particular woman who walked out of a nearby dress shop. Following the blizzards, the streets were flooded by snow, and there was a deathly chill in the air. But still this woman, like so many others, was dressed in thin cloth shoes, no thicker than slippers. The skirt of her green dress was donned with scalloped lace. The train and hems of this fashionable, expensive gown ironically dragged right through the mud as the woman walked. No matter though. The fox skin wrap she was wearing told Rachel she had many other gowns. When it came to the winter fashions of the socialites, there were two distinct classes: those who were wrapped in furs and those aspiring to be. To top off her absurd attire, this woman wore a hat with beads, feathers, and a shear little veil that left her ears and cheeks exposed to the biting wind. Upon her hands were thin cotton gloves stretched tight and buttoned up to her wrist.

As this peacock made her way from the store, she gave a little shudder as the wind hit her. She noticed Rachel staring at her. She turned up her nose with an indignant little sniff and strutted out into the busy sidewalk. Watching this spectacle, Rachel could not help but laugh to herself. She turned to Nicolaus and Abbey, both of whom had been watching the woman with some interest. Rachel threw back the ends of her tattered babushka as if it were a fur wrap. Then, taking up the fraying hem of her own wool skirt, she made a sweeping gesture at Nicolaus, cocked her head, turned it upward so high that she could barely see where she was walking, made a grand turn and strutted comically down into the alley towards the trash bins. "Well, " she said in a mock lofty tone, "she's frozen to the bone and will probably die of flu, but she's fashionable and that, as you know," she emphasized the words, batting her eyes as Nicolaus and Abbey laughed, "is the only thing that matters."

Tripping over her own feet as she did her imitation, Rachel broke into a little run, taking Abbey by the arm as Nicolaus followed behind them.

They passed down the alleyway quickly, their hearts pounding, expecting the side doors of the shops to open at any minute or a shout to come out of the crowd of shoppers questioning them as to what they are doing digging through trash that did not belong to them. Yet, they made it to the end of the alley without incident to find four huge bundles, wrapped in old thinning cotton and tied with a piece of twine like a package. Usually throw-aways were about the size of a loaf of bread filled with threads and cut-offs of fabric; however, today was different the bundles were the size of throw pillows.

"We can take them all!" Nicolaus urged. "Abbey, take this one," he said, handing Abbey the smallest. "Rachel," he said pointing urgently to another larger one. Finally picking up the other two himself.

"All right, now just walk out of the alley as if there's nothing wrong with us having these bundles."

Leading the way with Abbey and Rachel following behind.

Nicolaus walked from the alleyway, down the street in the direction of the printing house, he looked into the eyes of each person that stared at him as if daring them to say something. His intense blue eyes stared out from behind his tarnished glasses. For once his eyes were not downcast. Instead, he looked each person in the face, knowing that he had ingenuity and worth. They were doing what they had to do in order to provide for those they love. What was shameful in that?

Nicolaus helped guide them through the snow as they rounded the side of the printing house building. The snow had receded enough to reveal the hatch window. Dropping his bulky bundle in ahead of him, Nicolaus was the first to climb through, then Abbey and Rachel. One by one, they left the bright sunlight and stepped into the dimly lit rooms of the old, derelict building. Three wide, long boards were nailed across each window. Light shone in-between the wooden bars, casting its brightness on the dusty, chestnut floorboards that had long since dried. The children imagined the house in its heyday—the wood gleaming with a rich mahogany darkness. Over time, however, the once beautiful room had gone deathly pale. The life and purpose that once filled it had died out, leaving it in a state of quiet requiem. The children's voices echoed up through the empty room's vaulted ceiling, which was broken only by the wooden support beams that arched from side to side like small bridges.

Nicolaus, Rachel, and Abbey made their way into the great room. The snows had entered through every hole in the roof and every broken window. As they walked through the chilled house, the children's breath showed as white fog.

"Joseph should be here soon, it's nearly dark," Rachel said, her voice echoing around the chilled room. The cold winds whipping through the broken windows had frosted the walls with a glittering, white, crystalline dust. It was as though the old building had quite literally been frozen in time.

"Here, let's sit over here," Nicolaus said, finding a dry patch in a far-off corner of the room.

Situating themselves, the children peeled off their hand bindings and pulled the bundles toward them.

"Let's open this," Rachel said, pointing to Abbey's bundle.

"Here, Abbey, you carried it, you should open it," Nicolaus said, reaching out his hand to the bundle and placing it down upon Abbey's lap.

It felt like a birthday. Sitting before them were packages filled with treasures unknown. Anticipation filled them all as Abbey untied the twine then folded back the cotton wrapping to look inside.

"I think this is the bundle from the milliners," Rachel commented as Abbey started spreading out the contents to reveal cut offs of thicker materials, as well as lace and shear cotton.

"Some beads and wire. You're right, this must be the milliner's bundle." Abbey looked down into her bundle intently, still picking through the strips of cut offs. "I don't know what use they would be though," she said, continuing to sort through the jumbled contents. "Some felt," Abbey said hopefully. A moment later, she held up a few reasonably well-sized squares of brown felt. "And some other thread and bits of cloth."

Rachel set the larger bundle on her lap. She pulled away the twine and unfolded the cloth. "I think this is one from the dressmaker. Look," said Rachel immediately after the wrappings were opened. Her hand reached into the mounds of cut threads and frayed ends, grasping onto a tiny metal tab.

"Scissors!" Nicolaus announced in amazement, as Rachel held up a pair of scissors. "They're dull, and there's some rust on the bolt, but I can clean them up, sharpen them, and they'll be like new!"

Setting the scissors aside, they all resumed their hunt. The rest of the bundle from the dressmaker yielded nothing more than frayed ends of different color materials, which would be well-suited to a patchwork quilt but not much else.

Since the bundle that Abbey opened was so small, Nicolaus handed her one of the larger bundles to open, and Nicolaus opened his last bundle.

"Look," Abbey said pointing into her bundle, "at the bottom, there are a lot of buttons, none of them match, but there are a lot of them and in all different sizes too!"

"We can use them for coats, shirts, pants, pouches, and bags—everything," Rachel said as she looked through the handful of buttons Abbey had scooped from the bottom of her bundle.

"Look at this piece of velvet," Rachel pulled a length of heavy forest green velvet from the bottom of Nicolaus' pile that had to have been a yard long. "This might be big enough for something. A vest for Ben or maybe even a shirt for someone bitty like Asa."

Rachel held up the velvet for Nicolaus to look at, then passed it to Abbey who took it gently into her hands and rubbed its soft, smooth surface over her cheek.

"I think we should use it on Asa. It's really soft. He would like that," Abbey commented as she ran her hands over the cloth's brushed surface.

Rolling it up, Rachel put it into the pile reserved for those special unexpected finds.

"And look here," Nicolaus said pointing to something he saw tangled in the mess of thread. "Laces, really, really, really long, cotton laces." He was a little confused. "The ends are fraying a little, but we can bind them off," he said holding the ends up to the light of the window with an appraising look on his face. "These will have many uses, I bet."

"They're corset laces," Rachel commented matter-of-factly.

Nicolaus' face fell a little. His cheeks turned red. "Oh," he said awkwardly.

Laughing a little at Nicolaus' reaction, Rachel finished "But, you're right, they'll have many uses."

Nicolaus passed the laces to Rachel, his face growing redder. "You can roll them up." Flustered, he turned back to his bundle trying to focus, Abbey and Rachel laughing softly at him.

"Some of the threads are pretty long," Rachel said, changing the subject.

"Tie the lengths together and spool them onto this," Nicolaus said reaching behind him and pulling out a long, thick splinter of wood that had broken off the windowsill to use as a spool.

He picked up a clump of thread that he had been working to unknot. "Some of this simply is never going to come apart."

Nicolaus tried to follow his way through the maze of thread, noticing that Rachel and Abbey seemed to be flowing through the nests with more grace then he. The girls were untying massive entanglements with a few, simple flourishes of the hand, while he was growing steadily more frustrated with the same clump he had been working on for the past twenty minutes. Finally, thinking that he had found the key to unraveling the labyrinth before him, Nicolaus pulled a thread in triumph only to watch the loose clump compact into a very tightly wound ball of knotted confusion.

"The knot seems to be getting bigger," Nicolaus said at a loss. He grabbed either end of the ball and tried to stretch it back to the loosely knotted collection of threads it had been a minute ago.

After watching him helplessly wrestle with it, Rachel spoke up. "Maybe I should do that," she stared at Nicolaus' ball of knots and watched him pulling at it, his face screwed up in frustration, his eyebrows creased.

Moving to take it from him before it was made any worse, Rachel handed Nicolaus the piece of wood that acted as their spool. "Sweetie, why don't you just wind up what we untangle," Rachel said as politely as she could.

Holding the stick, Nicolaus watched as Rachel pulled on what seemed to be a magic thread, making the nest relax. She paused, looking closely at the mass of white threads until she seemed to find the specific thread she was searching for and handed the loose end to Nicolaus.

"Here," she said handing the cut end to Nicolaus so that he could tie it onto the last thread wound around the bobbin he held. Then, with ease and grace, Rachel pulled the strand of thread, and it seemed to unravel neatly in long, flowing lengths.

Confounded, Nicolaus stared at the knot as it unfurled indignantly before him. "Nicolaus, wind it up," Rachel said, nicely drawing to his attention the small pile of thread coiled on the floor waiting to be wound.

"Right," he replied, winding it up in haste as Rachel finished, and she and Abbey both moved on to the next thicket of thread.

CHAPTER 10
UNEXPECTED DISCOVERIES

W HILE NICOLAUS, ABBEY, AND RACHEL sat winding up the last of the thread, Joseph and Davy had long since left the harbor and were making their way down to the cloth mills.

The fabric mill was a towering block compared to some of the other buildings of the city. When Joseph and Davy reached the mill, the shifts had not let out yet. The streets were relatively quiet, allowing the boys to pass through quickly. Walking with bundles of rope, a roll of canvas, and a long strand of fish, the boys were quite the spectacle. Passing by one long brick building after another, Joseph and Davy came to this part of town looking for the fabric mills, where the machine-powered looms wove cottons to sell to the clothing makers. Rolls of cotton cloth from the regional mills were shipped to all parts of the country; however, even though cloth was milled in abundance here, it did not make it any easier to find.

"Perhaps we'll find some small bits in the bin that can be used toward patches or quilt squares," Joseph suggested. But after checking a few of the large trash bins near each mill and finding nothing, the boys were becoming a little doubtful.

"If we don't find anything here, we could try the furniture makers. We've done well there before finding large scraps of upholstery fabric," Joseph pitched.

"Don't be silly," Davy said, "we'll find something. Look at all we found at the harbor!"

"We've walked these streets for about an hour and haven't even found a scrap worth using. It was worth a try though," Joseph conceded.

Just then the boys jumped a little as they heard the sounds of gates crashing open. A stampede of over a hundred rung-out, melancholy workers poured out of the factories up the street as a new group of workers walked toward them. As the two groups of men passed one another, they called out, shouting to friends in low, lifeless voices. The fresh workers and the tired workers had the same defeated gaze.

"Hey, Joe, ya heard? They're letting go another dozen or so men." The boys overheard an older scruffy workman comment.

"That's over a hundred in the last six months!" a mid-aged workman replied in outrage.

"Well, if that's the way it's gonna be, they better get ready for a fight. Everyone is livin' on nothin' as it is. If we lose this job, we ain't gonna find another," the workman stated bluntly as the two of them walked through the gate together and onto the factory floor.

Watching the conversation with mild interest, Joseph and Davy remained on the curb off to the side, well clear of the droves of men. After the herd of weary workers had passed, the streets were eerily quiet again. They were about to leave when they heard a voice echo from around the corner. Peeking down to the alleyway, the boys saw two other men talking—one a worker from the old shift, the other a worker of the new shift.

"I don't know what happened. No one noticed it until there was already a roller full of the stuff. If the boss sees how much went to waste, it'll be our jobs. Blast it! You've gotta keep an eye on that machine. If this happens...."

With a thud, something dropped into the dump pile. The two men turned, walked back through the door leading into the factory, and shut it behind them. Curiously and cautiously, Joseph and Davy moved down the alley, hoping that no one else would come through the bay doors and catch them.

"What did they throw out?" Davy asked in a whisper.

"I'll lift you up into the cart, and you can try to find it," Joseph said, as Davy immediately started to climb up the wheel of the overflowing cart piled high with junk bound for the dump.

Climbing the great heap, Davy whispered back quietly, "I think it was this long sack." He was pulling off a long burlap sack that looked as though a rug had been rolled up and stuffed into it.

Waiting on edge, Joseph stared up at Davy, wishing he would say something more, anything. But he just stood there, staring in awe and knee deep in the pile of throw-aways.

"Well?" Joseph exclaimed in an attempt to get some news be it good or bad.

"You won't believe it. It's just impossible," Davy moved the long heavy sack across the pile and off the side of the wagon. Joseph pulled it into his arms, then Davy hopped back down onto the ground beside him, freeing himself of the engulfing mound.

"Open it! See for yourself," Davy said with a huge grin on his face.

Drawing back the end of the sack, Joseph, to his amazement, found himself staring at a huge piece of folded-up corduroy—one continuous, long flowing piece the color of darkest chocolate. Fold after fold, yard after yard filled the whole sack.

After staring in shock for a moment, Joseph and Davy were brought back to their senses by the sound of men coming towards the bay door from within the factory. "Quickly!" Davy said, picking up his bundles from the dock. Joseph flung the long sack over his right shoulder. Weighted down with their new treasures, the two boys made their way back up the alley.

Joseph and Davy softly giggled as the excitement and gratitude overflowed from them, wide grins stretching across their faces. They were in a wonderful state of euphoria as they went over all the things they had gathered that afternoon. The gathering had been easier than it ever had been in their whole life—easier than any of the children ever dreamed that it could be—as if it had been planned beforehand and all the things they found had been specifically put there for them to find. The children did not believe in luck. Simple coincidence, in their mind, was not something that existed. No, something greater was most definitely occurring. The tide was turning. It was becoming quite obvious that their feet had indeed been set upon a path. Leading where? They did not know.

*   *   *   *   *

THE BOYS MADE THEIR WAY to the printing house, their small backs loaded with secondhand treasures, joy beaming from their faces. "I feel like my heart's gonna burst," Davy laughed as they shuffled down the street. It did not take the two boys long to reach its end. On their way out, Joseph's eye was caught by something in a side alleyway.

"Davy, wait! I think we should look at those piles there outside that factory," Joseph said, as he tried to raise an arm and point while still balancing the load upon his shoulder.

Shuffling down the darkening alleyway, Joseph knew that they had very little time to make it to the printing house, meet with the others, and still get back to the wagon before dark.

"I think it's a wood mill," Davy said pointing to the older of the two brick buildings flanking them on the left.

"Well, I think it's worth a look anyway. There's a lot there, perhaps we'll find something useful—nails or rope or something."

"I don't think we can carry much more," Davy said as he peeked over the pile he was carrying.

"I know," Joseph said, adjusting the heavy sack resting on his back. "Here, you wait in that corner over there with all the supplies," Joseph suggested. "No need for you to haul everything over there. I'll go look through the crates. If I find something, I'll carry it. If my load's too heavy, I can always leave some of it at the printing house and come back for it tomorrow. Be back in a dash!"

Sitting Davy down in an isolated corner at the mouth of the alley, Joseph ran deeper into the alleyway. The sun was setting. Hues of red and gold splashed along the broad street.

The snow in the alleyway had been broken up and trampled down into a compacted layer by the passing carts and now was hardening to a choppy layer of ice. Joseph slipped a few times but held himself in balance—holding his arms out like a trapeze acrobat as he moved across the slicks, leaping from bald spot to bald spot wherever possible. Once he made it to the trash piles, he lifted up the crate lids and saw nothing but old, greasy machine parts, shavings of wood, blackened sticky rags, and empty tins. He went through all the sacks that were piled nearby but likewise found nothing. Moving down to the next set of crates, which were piled haphazardly against the high brick walls of the alleyway, he started rummaging, always keeping an ear open for any noises or footsteps. He peeled back broken crate after broken crate and underneath them all found an old worn box. It was in the shape of a long rectangle with a bar running from end to end for a handle. The box was splintered and dented, and the handle was very loose, but he did not care. To Joseph, the box's condition was perfect, and what was inside it went beyond what he ever imaged he would find. The long box was filled with tools—old battered tools, but tools all the same. Taking a quick glance through the box, Joseph saw the teeth of a short hand saw a little rusted but still sharp, a wooden mallet, a short handled hatchet with a few nicks taken out of its edge, and a wood plane.

He closed his eyes as an intensity flooded him and threatened to burst out. In that moment, he felt absolutely affirmed that a new time had indeed begun. For years they had scavenged for supplies and hardly found a scrap, but today had yielded a bounty. With his hand grasped firmly around the handle of his new tool box, he took one last glance towards the factory doors, then heaved up the chest and charged down the alleyway. He waved to Davy once he was in sight, holding the box as high as he could to show off the newfound prize.

*   *   *   *   *

A SHORT TIME LATER, after meeting up at the printing house, the small group of foragers hurried along the path laughing when finally they heard voices coming from the wagon that was buried in snow off in the distance.

"Anna! Anna, it's us. We're home!" Joseph called out, not wanting those in the wagon to be frightened by the sound of people approaching.

The canvas walls of the wagon rustled as those within stirred and began undoing the back flaps.

Anna was more relieved than excited, though she tried to hide it. Anna was still wrapped in worry as everyone climbed back in—worry that Joseph might not be with them. It was only after she had taken a deep breath once Joseph finally climbed in, that she fully realized the amount of supplies they had been able to gather.

In hurried, excited voices, Davy, Nicolaus, Rachel, and Abbey started telling the others in the wagon the stories of the day. As they did this, Joseph went to Anna who was still sitting in the far corner near the door, quietly watching the goings-on.

"I'm sorry we took so long," Joseph said, speaking in a soft tone that only she could hear as the others continued in their revelry.

"I was just worried because you had told me to look for you at dusk. I knew that you had probably just fallen a little behind and needed more time, but I still couldn't seem to hush my fears."

"Nothing bad happened. The trip just took longer than we expected," Joseph said simply and reassuringly. "Actually, it took longer because so many good things happened. You won't believe it." Joseph took Anna by the hand and brought her into the celebration. She had missed the telling of the stories, but it did not matter, those amazing stories would surely be told again and again throughout the night and over the years to come.

"...and we found some fabric," Abbey boasted holding up the yard of green velvet. "Here, Asa, feel this. We thought we would make you a shirt from that."

The soft material was placed in the small boys hands. He had never felt anything like it in his life; it was like having a pet with soft fur to snuggle against. Asa held it to his cheek, soothed by the comforting gentleness of it.

"Yeah, we found some fabric all right," Joseph said picking up the long sack and laying it in front of Anna who had yet to open a package. All watched as Anna untied the ropes that Joseph had attached to the sack and pulled out the unending folds of corduroy, like a magician pulling a long, thick handkerchief from his sleeve, draping yard after yard around the wagon.

"So what can you do with that?" Joseph said laughing as Anna, Rachel, and Abbey, all were covered by the solid piece of near perfect cloth as it stretched to the end of the wagon bed and back again several times.

Once they had the cloth opened and spread out, Joseph noticed there was a thinning bald spot that ran the length of the fabric. "I guess that's why they got rid of it," Joseph said, turning to Davy. "The machine must have messed up, and they knew they wouldn't be able to sell it like that. I mean, one of us would've bought it, but most other people wouldn't, which I suppose is good for us."

"There must be fifteen yards here, if not more," Anna said staring up at Joseph covered in the rolls of the thick brown material. "We can make every single one of us some real clothing."

"We'll all match, but at least we'll have new clothes," Rachel added with a laugh.

"There's only one problem," Joseph said not wanting to add a weight to the light atmosphere but needing to bring up the obvious. "We have thread, scissors, tape measure, fabric but we don't have a needle. I've been thinking all day where to find one, and short of buying one I just can't think of anything."

"I have the one needle," Rachel said bringing a small swatch of material out from within her coat into which a needle was anchored, woven in and out through it. "But we'll need more; one for each of us."

"I'm sure we'll come up with something," Anna said confidently.

"Now, you can get started on what you'll do for us. You and Rachel can work on our clothes during the days when you're here in the wagon, and I'm sure Emma, Asa, and Ben will find ways of helping too."

"And me, I want to learn how to sew," Beth said enthusiastically.

"Me, too," Abbey seconded.

Anna was so grateful. She appreciated everything, right down to the smallest button. She did not know what to say or how to thank Joseph, Rachel, Nicolaus, Abbey, and Davy for all that they had done.

Nicolaus and Joseph sat quietly watching the girls overflow with new possibilities and joy. The boys smiled at each other, knowing that they helped bring them that happiness. The whole wagon was filled with energy—Ben and Davy sat looking through the fishing line and nets, Abbey and Beth and tiny Emma sat beside Marie, listening to the different clothes Rachel and Anna would be making.

Emma was left outside an orphanage in the middle of the night during that previous winter. The doors to the orphanage were closed and Emma sat out front alone, crying in the cold as the snow began to fall. Wandering away from the steps, she went down the street in search of her mother. Confused and alone, the small child did not know what had happened to her, only that she wanted to be held, comforted, and made warm. It was then that Marie passed by the little one on her way to the printing house. Marie saw the young girl crying and went to see what was wrong. As Marie approached, she found a small note tucked in the little one's coat.

> *Please accept my sweet babe into your orphanage. I can't feed her no more and I can't work so long as I must care for her. Her name is Emma. Treat her kindly.*

Knowing all too well the fate that awaited the little one through the doors of the orphanage, Marie brought Emma back to the printing house where she could be cared for by loving hands.

Emma was the last child to join their close-knit group, Asa was found only two weeks before in the same fashion. Emma was small. She had lost some weight under winter's wear, but both she and Asa still had the full cheeks and glowing faces that very young children do. They had not endured the years of struggle that the other older children had, but they carried the scars upon their hearts that came with being abandoned and denied love. Both Emma and Asa were too young to understand the story of their life; however, they knew that the people they had once called mother and father were not coming back. They had not yet reached the point where they could ask why this had happened to them and actually understand the choices made by their parents. They knew, however, that love was present in the form of Duncan, Marie, Nicolaus, Rachel, Anna, Joseph, Ben, Davy, Abbey, and Beth. In their hearts, Asa and Emma knew that the one's they had called parents were gone, but they did have a mother and a father—several in fact—as well as brothers and sisters. Bonded at their young age, Emma and Asa were nearly inseparable—they spoke as one, thought as one, grew as one, and felt as one—after enduring the life altering changes as one.

Asa sat snuggling with his piece of velvet, worn out by the excitement. And it was as Joseph looked over the scene of the wagon that Anna's voice pulled him back from his thoughts.

"Wait, wait!" she exclaimed as an idea was so obviously striking her. "Joseph, hand me that mallet."

Puzzled and curious but loving the fact that he now had a mallet to give, Joseph reached into the toolbox lying near his feet and pulled the mallet from it, handing it to Anna.

"Teddy, give that to me," she said politely pointing to a piece of line that Ben was untangling. The whole wagon was now quiet, intently looking at Anna as she took the fishing hook that was tied to the end of the line in hand and began to bend it into a straight line. She took the mallet and banged down the barb that jetted out from the tip like a talon, turning her attention to the other end, she hammered down the large round eye of the hook, making it slimmer—only thread and not fishing line had to slip through it. Then she held it up for all to see. "We have our new, heavy-duty sewing needle."

Everyone laughed and shouted in excitement. The days gathering was now complete. Joseph just sat there staring at Anna in awe of her simple genius. He was proud to know her— always amazed at the things she could see that no other could.

Anna took a few hooks out of the dozens that were within the supplies gathered from the dock and made them into needles, which would very easily be able to pass through the thick corduroy and velvet. She was smiling ear to ear, proud of herself and happy she had been able to contribute something to the day, even if it was small.

"Wait!" Joseph said, wanting to hit himself over the head for having forgotten in all the commotion. "There's one more package. It's the reason why we were so late," he said as he brought forward one very small package. Anna took it from him.

"What's this?" she asked thinking at first there might be more sewing supplies but then changing her mind when she touched it and felt heat coming from it. "It's warm," she said in a suspicious voice unable to think what it could possibly be. Davy, Rachel, Abbey, Nicolaus, and Joseph, all sat with huge grins upon their pinched faces, absolutely beaming from within as they waited in silence for the others to see the treat.

Anna unwrapped the package, constantly glancing over to Joseph. And when the wrapping finally fell away, the small children erupted in shouts of excitement at the steaming pile of cooked fish. "You found all this?" Anna asked bewildered. Joseph and Davy nodded. "And you cooked it?" She said still holding the bottom of the package its heat seeping through to her hand. Joseph, Davy, Rachel, Nicolaus, and Abbey all nodded.

Bitty Asa started picking at one of the fish, eating small flakes of meat. Then the other tiny hands began to reach for the parcel.

"Wait now," Anna insisted, "let's do this proper."

Everyone sat next to one another and leaned up against the wagon's tall side panels to create a sort of oval within the square cloth-filled bed. Joseph and Anna passed out pieces of fish meat to the little ones and a whole fish to everyone else. They all ate as slowly as they could, given the hunger gnawing at them. The precautions they had to take with the bones was about the only thing that had stopped them from gulping down the meal in two bites.

They all sat rather quietly as they ate. They all needed to rest. They all had been exhilarated for so much of the day, but now that their stomachs had been given a warm meal, the heavy blankets rested on their weary bones, and a sense of accomplishment swelled in their heart. All the children felt rather sleepy.

One by one, they finished eating and began falling asleep. Anna cleaned up the fish, and Joseph took the bones a few yards away from the wagon and dumped them. When he returned, little Asa and Emma were already asleep. Asa was still snuggling with the yard of velvet, which was fast becoming his new blanket. Abbey and Beth lay side by side. They were not twin sisters, but they could have been. They were so close, with such a unique bond of understanding and deep affection for one another. Beth was quiet and might have been younger than Abbey. Ben was lying down and saying goodnight to Nicolaus and Davy. Everyone was tired, though not as worn as they usually were at the end of the day. This night, they were actually just sleepy rather than fatigued. And as foreign a feeling as it was, they were actually looking forward to the next day and what it might bring.

CHAPTER 11
LINGERING MYSTERIES

AS ANNA SAT QUIETLY PEEKING OUT the crack between the boards, she felt a hand rest on her arm. She turned back around to see that Joseph was awake. Like her, Joseph had not made a sound. From the moment he woke, the day had a gentleness about it, and he did not want to disturb this calm. Soon everyone would wake and start planning the day—but not yet.

Joseph looked at Anna through the dim light. In the stillness, they said nothing. Joseph smiled as Anna stared back at him—each of them with a look of relief and calm upon their worn faces.

As the warm hues of dawn brightened into the full light of morning, Joseph and Anna lay in the back of the wagon side by side talking to each other in soft voices. "I think today I'll just take Nicolaus with me. I'm sure Ben will want to go and so will Davy, but I want time to talk with Nicolaus alone. I figured that he and I would go into the city early this morning, find what we can, and bring it back to the wagon. Then, if any of the others want to come back for another trip, they can go back with us later on. I'll leave it to you to decide whether or not Ben's well enough to be out. I know he's eager to be out and of help, but that doesn't mean he should."

Tucked under the heavy blankets with her thin babushka drawn loosely around her head, she nodded softly. "I'll talk with Ben this morning and see how strong he is. I know he really wants to go with you today. Maybe since it'll just be a half day, he can go with you this afternoon."

"All right, that sounds fine. I'll make sure he doesn't carry a lot, and we go at an easy pace. I'll bring everyone home by dusk. And we truly will be home by dusk," he added firmly, still feeling bad for having made her worry the previous night. "What are you going to do today?" he asked, a soft smile now stretching across his face, as he rested against the soft blanket, his chestnut eyes gazing intently at her.

"I think I'll begin making some clothes. We all need a sturdy jacket. Rachel and Abbey can help me with the sewing, and I'll find other small projects for the little ones to do."

"I know it has been a while since Beth, Asa, and Emma have been out, as well as yourself."

"I'm fine. Everyone who isn't absolutely needed on your trips to the city should stay here with me, safe and warm. It's February, and the snow's melting. Spring should be coming soon, so that means that I could let the children play around the wagon. Davy or Ben could watch them. At least then they could get out and stretch their legs," Anna moved her hand under the blanket to find Joseph's hand squeezing it.

"We'll be fine," she smiled. "While you're gone this morning, I thought I would fit Asa and Emma for their new clothes first. I thought it was important to start with the smallest," she offered.

"Sounds about right. As far as shoes go, I have no idea where to start looking for them."

"It'll be easy to make clothes for the warmer weather, we can simply take the best clothes out of those we already have and patch all the holes, reinforce all the seams, and wear them as summer shirts," Anna looked focused, the concern she had for each person could be heard in her voice.

"You've been waiting for years, wishing that you had the materials to make us all the clothing we needed. Over the years, I've watched you take nought but scraps of material and string and make them into mittens. I've even seen you take apart a few old, worn shirts and put the pieces back together to make one good shirt. I've no doubt that with all the supplies we've gathered, you'll make each of us the best clothes we've ever had upon our backs."

Anna smiled, humbled by his confidence. Joseph slowly reached across the bed of the wagon and gently tapped Nicolaus on the shoulder to wake him. Nicolaus' eyes slowly opened. For a moment he looked panicked, but once he saw Joseph's smiling face he eased. Joseph motioned for him to rise and go with them. Nicolaus looked around and saw Rachel and the others all still asleep. Anna drew back the door flap, then Joseph quietly lowered himself outside, helping Anna down after. Very conscious not to step on or kick anyone, Nicolaus rose very slowly, placing his feet deliberately as he stepped across the wagon bed that was filled with deeply sleeping children. Finally, he made it close enough to Joseph that he could take that last step and leap down.

As always, Anna waited until they were out of sight, standing steady until they were absorbed into the horizon.

*   *   *   *   *

As Nicolaus and Joseph walked toward the city, the air was crisp with the winter morning cold, but hints of an approaching spring could also be felt. Their feet were soaked by the deep slush left by the receding snows, but they tried not to let it bother them. Their excitement at having another chance to go into the city and see what they would find made them impervious to the cold and damp.

Nicolaus wiped the sleep from his eyes as they walked towards the city limits. Joseph had asked Nicolaus to come with him that morning because he wanted to speak with him, and as Nicolaus started giving suggestions for places to search, Joseph gently eased the conversation.

"Nicolaus, I wanted you to come along with me this morning because I wanted some time to talk to you about Marie." Joseph paused in walking. "I was wondering when was the last time you saw her?"

"Weeks ago," he said in a regretful voice. "We didn't see her during the time we were split up. That night when the police broken in, Rachel and I grabbed Emma and rushed out. We went back to the printing house a few days later, after the police were gone, and we met up with Davy and Abbey. They had Beth and Asa with them. We looked everywhere for you and Anna, Ben, Duncan and Marie. But then those storms hit, one after the next, and that made it difficult just to walk, let alone search the whole of Boston.

"I'm worried for her."

With a solemn look on his face, Nicolaus reflected, "I know. In all these years, she has never been sick, even when all of us were."

"I know." Joseph heavily sighed.

PART TWO

CHAPTER 12
A SEASON OF CHANGE

THE COMING WEEKS AND MONTHS PASSED GENTLY. For the first time in their lives, the children had a purpose beyond day-to-day survival. They were filled with a sense of new momentum. Winter melted into spring, and with the return of warmth came ease. Outfitted in their newly made clothes, they spent their days gathering supplies that would be of use in their future journey. When scrap wood was found, the wagon was reinforced. For weeks, Joseph, Nicolaus, Anna, Rachel, Abbey, and Davy put in long hours to fix up their new home. Even the little ones were given odd jobs so they might feel their place in the great change sweeping through their lives. The hard work, while wearing, was a joy. For years, the children had wished for a home, only to be left wanting. But now, at long last, they had a roof—albeit a canvas one—and it was a labor of love to maintain that home.

Every inch of the wagon was appreciated, as was every stitch of cloth, scrap of fish or bread, and every battered tool they managed to collect. It was a season of hope after a lifetime of despair. At times, Joseph was frightened by just how full of expectation his heart had become. He was frightened because he knew none of the children, including himself, could bear going back into the hardship. Trusting a hope is not easy for a heart made fragile, yet, despite himself, he gave everything— every part of himself—to believing that they would indeed escape and settle upon a small foothold of land. They could not help themselves; it had to be true. That life of hardship, starvation, and wandering had to be over.

Riding that momentum of hope through the winter, into spring, and then into summer, the children continued to gather supplies and scavenge what they could. And from what bits and pieces they found, they made almost everything they needed. They did not need a purpose in mind for a found object. They simply gathered it into a bag and brought it home. "Sometimes the purpose of a thing comes later," Marie had taken to saying.

The summer became a season of creation. Every pair of hands in the wagon were busily building or sewing or mending or cleaning. After a brilliant idea from Joseph, they took to making weekly visits to the old trash dump where they found many a useful thing. On their first trip, Anna found an old, rusted iron pot that she was able to clean. From the sea of canvas cloth, they were able to pull out many things. Anna, Rachel, and Abbey cut and sewed canvas sacks for storing goods and an extra set of clothing to cover each frail body. Sewing away through the night, the three took the scraps of old cloth they found in the trash bins and made quilts, which were ingeniously lined with burlap to give the blankets a bit more heft.

There was laughter and lightness throughout the spring and summer. Those first days of gathering, when food, cloth, and tools had been so abundant, had launched the children into a strong belief that a new life was indeed beginning, and they had best start preparing for it. Nevertheless, as the fierce light of summer began to fade into the cool dim of autumn, Joseph felt the hope slowly begin to drain from him. One question haunted him: would they have to face another New England winter?

Through August, Joseph managed to keep his mounting fears secret from the others. He could not admit to himself what he was feeling, let alone share those fears with anyone else. After all, he had been the one to proclaim that the old life of suffering was over. How could he now admit that he might have been wrong—that he did not believe in his own dream?

Despite Joseph's efforts to spare the others his doubts, Anna sensed the growing stress he carried within him. There was a mounting tension around his eyes. More and more each day, Anna felt, within Joseph's silence, there were many words unspoken. A dense silence seemed to follow him. At night, when they all sat together in the wagon speaking of their hopes for the future—what the farmhouse would be like, what crops they would grow—what they would do for their professions, Joseph was quiet where once he was boisterous. No, he did not dash the dreams shared, but neither did he nourish them. He did not know what to believe, and so he did not know what to say.

Finally, when the pangs of cold wind began to blow at the end of October, Joseph's hope for change became even more brittle. The momentum driving them all had slowed. The food they had gathered early on was gone. Supplies in the city began to taper off. The gathering trips yielded less and less each week. The wagon was fixed as best as it could be, but it was still wrecked there in the field like an old ship upon the rocks—beset, just as their dreams were.

The image of what they wanted was fully-formed in their minds, but it seemed to Joseph that they had come to the end of how far they could take that dream on their own. The brightness that had burned months ago was now dimmed by the cold storm clouds mounting. For almost a year, they had worked, they had hoped, and they had believed in change, only to now be faced with another winter.

"A blizzard's coming," Davy announced as he and Nicolaus climbed back into the wagon after a long day of gathering.

Sitting propped up at the back of the wagon, Joseph heard the news and looked up. He was heartbroken. Anna watched as his face fell.

"But it's only the first of November," Rachel reasoned, as though maybe Old Man Winter might consider her appeal, come to his senses, and cancel the storm.

"I know, but there 'tis," said Nicolaus. "Better to hear the news and be prepared I suppose, than to be caught off guard."

Taking her watchful eye off Joseph, Anna turned to Nicolaus and Davy. "What were you able to find?"

"We searched everywhere. There's nothin'. We'll have to go into the stores," answered Davy.

Nicolaus looked at Anna, knowing what she was thinking. "All right, then," she said in a forced-reassuring voice, "we'll be fine. Come on now, get warm." She threw back the blankets so that Nicolaus and Davy could get tucked under.

"Of course, we'll be all right," Marie chimed, in a motherly voice as everyone got resettled. She sat in the middle of the wagon with Asa and Emma cozied up against her.

As Marie spoke, Anna noticed Joseph fidgeting, rubbing his palms with his fingers. So deep and violent were his frustrations, he looked as though he was about to come out of his skin. "I think I'll go for a walk," he announced abruptly. And before anyone could even turn to address him, he was gone, a canvas door left flapping in his wake.

"Joseph?" asked Marie.

"I'll go," said Anna. She laid a hand on Marie, shuffled to the back of the wagon and dropped down out of sight.

Joseph heard someone approaching behind him. He did not even have to turn around to know who it was. "I think it's best that I walk alone tonight," he said, not meanly.

"You don't have to hide your doubts from me. I already know what you're thinking. I do know you quite well after all," she reasoned, and crossed her arms as the wind blew.

Her words hit the floodgate.

He stared off into the darkening sky towards the outline of the city. "It's been months!" he stressed in a desperate voice. "And what do we have to show for it? We've been toiling away, believing in this impossible dream, but we're no closer to actually leaving this city and living it than we were last year. We have no food, no money, no horse to pull the blasted cart." He waved a damning hand in the direction of the wagon.

"You don't know how far we've come or haven't, because you don't know where we're going or how we're going to get there. All I know is, I've been happy these last months—happier than I've ever been. Doesn't that mean we've gotten closer to our dream? We have to hope," reasoned Anna.

Joseph let out a laugh that collapsed into a sob. "Hoping is drivin' me insane. We hope, and hope and hope, and nothin' ever happens."

"We got this wagon. Marie got better," Anna listed.

"Yes, but she is weak—so weak. And what can we do about it? We can't take her to a doctor. We can't fix her. It's like everything else in our blasted life. We're helpless.

"We found the wagon but can't pull it anywhere. We have the will but not the means, the need but not the aid. It's like some cruel joke, like being given a ship without a sail. All we can do is sit here and ache for all that we yearn for but can never have."

"But, your dream?" pleaded Anna.

"My dream," Joseph repeated despairingly to himself. "Maybe it was just that—some dream brought on by my fever. Maybe I was wrong to think it was anything deeper than some image passing through my mind. I probably saw some painting of some field while I was walking the streets, and it got stuck in my mind."

"No," Anna shook her head, "don't do that. Don't dismiss it. You knew when you had it that it was something more than a dream," she justified. "I remember how you felt—how you acted. It wasn't some memory of a painting. It was a reason to hope."

"What was it? Some flash of a life we're going to have?" he said attacking his own foolishness. "What was I thinking? What was I bloody thinking?" he banged his hand against his thick skull. "It was my own desperation that led me to believe that it was something deeper, nothin' more," his voice became very low as his heart sank. "I wish I never had it."

Anna moved closer to him. Her voice was still confident. "These last months have been the best in our lives. We have had hope and purpose. We've had a home. Everyone believes that life can and will be better. Your dream did that."

"Yes, and what happens when this winter passes and nothing happens, and next year rolls around and still nothing has happened. We're soaring high now, but the descent is coming. Tell me you can't sense it. And I'll have done that—my dream, which gave us so much hope, is going to cause a great deal of pain. Better if we had never begun this."

Joseph collapsed and sat on the ground in a hopeless heap. "I just can't do this anymore—I just can't. Every day I try to think of a way to make things better for us. Every day I try to think of a way to earn us money, or find us food, or get a mule, or make Marie her old, strong self," he reeled, eventually breaking down into tears. "It all drives me insane," he stressed, his fists clenched in frustration but unable to fight what was stopping them. "Every day that goes by when I can't find the answer, I hate myself that much more. I'm that much angrier with the world. No one is meant to live this way. Our dreams are so simple—so very simple. Why has it always been so bloody hard."

Anna walked over to him and sat down. She had no answers, no words of wisdom to stop the reeling. She no longer had a hope or belief strong enough to support both of them. All she could do was sit with him as he cried.

CHAPTER 13
UNFORESEEN EVENTS

T HE NEXT MORNING, Joseph found himself once more walking into the city—a forbidding sky looming before him.

"We'll check the docks and all the usual places," he said in a flat tone. He looked straight ahead, with a despondent stare.

"Maybe we'll find something," offered Nicolaus, hopefully.

Joseph did not respond. All the hope had left him. New questions of why they all had been given hope but no help to fulfill their dreams gnawed at him.

"Hey," Nicolaus' voice brightened, "I think we still have a pack of biscuits at the printing house." They had been keeping them there just in case one of them ever had to hold up there during bad weather.

"You assume they haven't been eaten?" Joseph responded in a questioning tone. "Fine then, we'll stop and get them." *Good, at least we'll have found something,* he thought to himself as they walked. *Probably the only thing, knowing our luck.*

Nicolaus didn't need to hear Joseph's thoughts to know what he was thinking.

"What's the harm in hoping we might find something?" said Nicolaus, interrupting Joseph's dark internal monologue.

Joseph considered him for a moment, wondering whether or not he should say what was on his mind. "The harm in hoping we might find something comes a few hours from now when we have to face the reality that we didn't."

Disturbed by this sad side of his adopted brother, Nicolaus said nothing. The boys walked on in silence towards the city.

*   *   *   *   *

J OSEPH AND NICOLAUS MADE IT INTO THE CITY. Winding through the long paths, they turned down the familiar street of the printing house. It was then that they saw it—the printing house being torn apart. The walls chopped into pieces, the roof torn away, the foundation laid bare.

Joseph and Nicolaus took off running down the center of the road towards the massacre of the only home they had ever known. Carried by the flow of their emotions, both boys pushed their way through the small crowd of emotionally detached onlookers gathered to watch the spectacle.

Usually the children moved quietly through the city, wanting to bring as little attention as possible to themselves. Yet, now, as Joseph approached the building, he could not help but draw every eye as he began yelling as loud as his voice would allow. "No, stop!" he vaulted over splintered debris making his way towards the main body of workmen hacking away at the remains of the gutted house.

The foreman saw the boy bounding toward the wreckage. He grabbed Joseph and pulled him back, allowing him to go no further.

Struggling against the strong man to no avail, Joseph rounded on him, helpless outrage in his voice. "What are you doing?"

Surprisingly, despite being yelled at, the foreman answered Joseph in a calm voice, seemingly wanting to ease the troubled boy as opposed to reprimanding him. There was a trace of an Irish accent mixed with the twang common among long-time Boston natives.

"This building has to come down, lad. There's nothing you can do," the man said in a calming voice.

"Why are you tearing down this house? Leave it be!" Joseph pleaded, defiance rising in the pit of his stomach. "You have no right!"

Both Nicolaus and Joseph stared helplessly as workers splintered away the walls that had protected them for the past eight years and loaded the scrap up onto a train of open bed carts that lined the street.

"The building has been abandoned a long time. Some men bought the deed almost a year ago. They got it in their heads to tear down all the small houses on that street to make way for a couple of Brownstone buildings. Talk is, the whole marsh is going to be filled over the next few years. People got it in their minds that the marsh can be turned into a new fashionable neighborhood. It'll make a lot of work for the lads coming off the boats. My boys and I were hired to make way for the new buildings. I'm sorry."

The children had no power to stop the workers; they could only look on, not knowing exactly what to do or how to feel as something that they loved so dearly was wiped from the earth—never to be visited again.

The foreman stopped talking to the boys and just stared at them sympathetically, a look of dawning comprehension on his face. He could see that the boys were homeless—anyone who looked at their clothes, the dirt upon their faces, their scraggly hair, and their thin bodies could see that they were homeless. And it did not take him a great deal of time to realize what the house had meant to the boys and piece it together with the story he had heard from the investors who had bought the building. On the night they acquired the title, they had chosen to inspect the house only to find a group of "vagrant children" sleeping within and chased them off.

Letting go of Joseph, the foreman reached down and picked up a nearby crate. "When the crew went into the house, they found this in a corner of the attic. I always tell the lads if they find anything in the old houses, no matter how worthless, they should bring it to me instead of just throwing it out."

The two boys had listened to the calm voice of the foreman; however, the entire time their eyes had remained fixed on the house. Yet, when the man held out the box for them to take, Joseph and Nicolaus turned towards him and finally put a face with the voice.

Taking in the man's appearance for the first time, Joseph saw before him a lean man of average height. Joseph was a few inches shorter than he was. Squinting in the sun, the light glinted on the man's light brown hair, which had a few streaks of gray even though the man was late-thirties. The man had an unkempt look. His clothes were clean for a carpenter. He did not look dirty, he simply looked forlorn—he was unshaved and had grown out hair. He had a heavy, brooding brow with a defined crease between his eyebrows, as though he had spent many years in prolonged pain, which had caused his face to fix in a permanent flinch.

Despondent, Joseph pulled his eyes away and looked to the crate. It was very old, the wood was a little gray, dry-rotted, and dented but still holding together. It was filled with a dozen or so blank, hardbound books. The leather covers were scuffed and parched by age and the elements. Many people would have considered these books worthless but to Joseph and Nicolaus they were priceless, simply because they had come from within the building they had called home.

Joseph silently took the box from the man. The look on the boy's face was one of bewilderment. There was obvious sadness as the tears welled up and trickled down, and yet there was a hint of gratitude that swept over him as the man placed the box into his arms. Joseph and Nicolaus did not know if the man had acted in care or out of pity, but the moment would always stand out to them as an act of kindness and caring during a cruel moment.

Care was common among the children. They constantly did thoughtful things for one another. However, it was rare to encounter compassion in the city, and as such it always stood out. As Joseph's eyes traveled over the leather bound books, his shock began to change from that of disbelief over what was happening to his old home into the disbelief that someone was actually trying to help ease him. He was no longer staring at the house in awe, he was staring at the man before him, helpless to convey what the moment meant to him.

Nicolaus stood behind Joseph looking into the box at the books with the same surging emotions of gratitude and disbelief.

Finally, someone had to speak. "We've never had anywhere to go," Nicolaus started shyly, speaking for the bewildered Joseph. "We felt safe here." Nicolaus wanted to be able to sum up what the last eight years had been so the man would know what the printing house had meant to them. He wanted the stranger to know the history of it all, but it was beyond his capability to tell.

After hearing Nicolaus's words, the foreman paused and stood up straight, having bent over slightly to listen to the boys over the noise of the wrecking crew behind them. He looked around at the wagon train, then turned back to the boys and said. "My workers are pilin' the pieces of the house over there." He pointed to the chain of carts in the distance. "I've already made plans for the scrap to be carted away and reused, but if you want anything else from the heap to take with you as a keepsake, you can have it. I'm afraid this is the only thing I can do for you."

In their silent shock, Joseph and Nicolaus followed the foreman to the carts.

The string of horse drawn carts were loaded with debris. Even torn apart, the pieces were familiar to the boys. They recognized the torn away chunks of the floorboards they had curled up upon, sections of the banisters they had held while climbing the stairs, and parts of the roof that had sheltered them. The old front door lay on the ground like a fallen shield, no longer able to keep the forces of change at bay.

Even with the dust and dirt that now covered it and the hack marks of axes, hammers, and pry bars that now riddled it, Joseph could place almost every piece—the faded ivy wallpaper from the largest office on the main floor, the wooden panels that lined the narrows halls of each passageway, the carved molding that ran along the ceiling edges. The children knew that house, every corner, every inch, every detail.

Joseph put down the box of dusty books to rest by his feet. He laid a hand on the wood in the cart before him. "This all had a lot of worth to us," he said, stressing the words. "We can take what we want?" he ended, meekly.

Rubbing his bearded cheek with a calloused hand, the foreman nodded. He seem moved by the boys reaction and wondered what they would take and to what use it would go. "Aye, take anything you want."

The foreman crossed his arms and stood back, watching Joseph and Nicolaus climb up onto the mountain of debris piled in the bed of the first cart. They started peeling up the different layers that had been tossed onto it as the workers' tools ate their way further into the house. For the boys, there was nothing more fitting than for this wood, which came from the house that had been their only sanctuary, to go to the wagon—their new home.

For Joseph and Nicolaus, going through the carts was not like rummaging through an old woodpile, it was like going through shards of reminders and fragments of memory. They peeled up layers of walls that had been torn down and, underneath they found the support beams that had once constructed the vaulted ceiling of the house's great room. Joseph could recall staring up at that ceiling countless times as the others had slept. To him, the way that the support beams had run were like small bridges from one side of the room to the other. The vaulted, beam ceiling of the great room had been one of the house's unique beauties. That room had always felt like home to him.

Staring at the unearthed support beams, Joseph was lost in the memory of what that room had meant to him. Nicolaus touched him, giving him a look that asked Joseph if he was all right. Joseph came back from his memories, he had been so immersed in them it had actually felt like he had been walking through the house again. Going through each piece of the dismantled house was like going through the pieces of a puzzle Joseph could put together in his heart, using his memories to rebuild what now lay in ruins behind him. Joseph came back to the present moment and wrapped his hands around one of the support beams and began pulling it free from the bed of rubble.

"This is it. This is what we'll use to reinforce the bottom of the wagon," he said in a strained voice as he slid the beams off the bed of the cart one at a time. Joseph found four beams, great in length and thickness, and while Nicolaus recognized the beams and agreed that they were suitable, he worried whether they could carry them back to the wagon without the others to help.

Almost as if he could read his mind, Nicolaus said in a slightly curious voice, "Joseph, how are you planning on us getting all of this back?"

"We'll manage, we'll take our time. We can bind all the beams together with some of the rope found here." He pointed to the front of the cart where piles of rope were tangled with rubble. "We'll bind them together, and each of us will carry an end."

Joseph and Nicolaus had rummaged through the carts, digging through other memories for nearly half an hour when they finally decided they had enough. They stood up knee-deep on top of the mountainous heaps after being hunched over and looked back to the house, which in those thirty minutes had been diminished even more. They watched the worker crew climbing all over the broken down house like termites eating away at everything.

"At least the old house was able to have a few more fires in the hearth before it was torn down," Nicolaus said trying to give some consolation, feeling now as though their fire had in a way given the house back its dignity and honor before it was ravaged. Long after the old building was gone and the new brick building towered in its place, the children would have their memories.

Joseph jumped down from the pile of debris, the wood sliding under his feet as he pushed off, then raised his hand up and steadied Nicolaus as his feet touched the ground next to him. Seeing that they were done, the foreman walked over to them.

"We're taking these beams, if that's all right," Joseph said as he and Nicolaus prepared to leave, binding both ends of the beams together with the lengths of rope they had managed to free from the entangled nest. They knew they would surely be late getting back to the wagon with this load, but it was a special circumstance.

"Are you two going to be able to pick up those beams yourselves?" The foreman asked watching Joseph and Nicolaus show a strength that some of his workers did not have, a strength that flowed from their heart and not their muscles.

"We'll manage," Nicolaus said, echoing the answer that Joseph had given to him.

The man rubbed his bearded cheek in contemplation as the character of the boys started to become clear to him. The man gave the boys a look of awe and pride. He reached out and patted Nicolaus firmly on the shoulder with a swell of respect. "How far do you lads plan on carrying those beams?"

Nicolaus and Joseph paused. Neither of them said anything. They looked rather sickened and suspicious when asked
the question. Neither of them wanted to tell the man where the
wagon was, even though he seemed trustworthy.

Stopping short of telling the foreman the full truth, Joseph
went as far as saying, "To the edge of the city," and left it at that.

Upon hearing Joseph's vague reply, the man also looked
saddened, as if he could sense how deeply his innocent question of concern had frightened the obviously traumatized boys.

"That's a long way to carry such a load alone," the foreman
said, expressing a sincere concern. "Lads, my name is Connor,
and my men will be breaking for lunch very shortly. While
they have a mug-up, I planned on going to a homestead just
beyond the city to bring out the first load of scrap lumber. If
you both climb onto the bed of the cart, you can come with me
on my rounds, and then I'll drop you off wherever you wish.
The homestead I'm going to is run by fine folk, they live just
beyond town. They're expecting me, so I best go there first. But
after I'm done, you boys can lead the way," he ended, trying to
assure them that there was no risk in letting him help them.

Joseph and Nicolaus looked at one another. Nicolaus was
stunned by the rare kindness, and Joseph felt the same gratitude at finding a seemingly kind heart. But, given all the
deceptive characters met over the years, he could not help
but be slightly apprehensive. The wounded part of Joseph was
wary, yet his heart told him there was nothing to fear. Heeding
that feeling in his heart above all else, Joseph replied kindly,
"We'd appreciate that very much," Joseph spoke in a voice that
let Connor know that neither of the boys had been offered
help in a very long time.

CHAPTER 14
ANOTHER LIFE

I T WAS ABOUT HALF AN HOUR LATER when Connor called his workers from the skeletal remains that once was the printing house and gave them all permission to take their lunch break. Then, with the exception of a few select men Connor had chosen to drive the other carts, all the workers climbed out of the rubble, wiped the sweat dripping from their brows, set aside their tools, and sat in the noon-day sun, eating rationed meals from steel pails. Joseph and Nicolaus watched as Connor walked over to one of the main piles of wood and stone around the old foundation of the house and dug through them for something that he finally found among the remains. The boys watched Connor as he pulled a board about a square foot in size from the ruins and tucked it under his arm as he walked toward the wagon train, which was ready to depart. Connor smiled at the boys as he hauled himself into the front of the cart and took hold of the reins. Joseph and Nicolaus put the beams and crate on the back of the cart then hopped on. With a flick of his wrist Connor snapped the reins on the old work horses and said, "Walk on." And off they went.

From the cart, Joseph and Nicolaus looked back at the sight of the printing house growing smaller behind them. It looked so strange to them to see only a mound of wood where the familiar house had once stood waiting for them. Sitting side by side on the back of the wagon, their feet dangling off the side of the cart, swaying back and forth as the wagon pushed on, the boys sat in silent remembrance feeling the grief for what was lost. But there was also a consolation: within their heart, they had gathered the spirit of the place, and within them, that spirit would be preserved.

From their new perspective plopped on the back of the moving wagon, the boys watched the people and buildings pass by. Neither of them could ever recall riding in a horse-drawn cart before. They both were grateful to have the burden of the walk taken off them, but, at the same time, riding instead of walking was a very odd experience. Walking was the lot of the poor man, while riding was the luxury of the gentleman. Being the poorest of the poor, the boys never thought they would ever be able to rest their feet, it was surreal to them.

"How are we going to tell the others about the printing house?" Nicolaus shouted to Joseph, speaking above the commotion of the city and the rattling of the carts along the bumpy streets. Each time the cart hit a muddy ditch, the stack of wood leapt up then slapped down against itself. The clapping noise the wood made was issued from all the carts as they made their way down the city streets.

"I think, after we tell them what we did—going through the wood, being given the books—they'll feel as though we have salvaged some part of the place. But it's going to be a shock," Joseph finished frankly.

Joseph's mind was still somewhat stunned and his thoughts were wandering, leaping from thought to thought like touching each piece of some greater puzzle—the finished picture of which he could not clearly distinguish. He was thinking about the moment he saw the building being torn down. He was reliving the memories made within the house and the dream he had while lying upon its floor. Then his mind came to Connor and what the seemingly caring man had done. Then, as the wagon jerked, he finally came back to the present fact that the two of them were in the back of a horse-drawn cart being given a ride through the heart of the city out onto its edges.

As the boys sat on the back of the cart talking to one another, Connor could not help but listen to snippets of the conversation he could hear above the din of the city streets. He said nothing of course to give away his open ear to the boys. He simply sat quietly, trying to piece together what the lad's story might be.

As the miles passed and the city faded, so did the boys' conversation. Connor took the pause to chime in. "You see, the city imports all of its foods," Connor explained, his voice shaking as the wagon passed over the rocky road. "They bring in cattle from this ranch and others that lie to the east. We're going further ahead to the edge of Roxbury, about two miles to the Scolfield farm. I've been delivering wood there for many years, a man named Jim Scolfield runs the farm where he lives with his wife and two children. The family uses the wood to fix the house and barn. In return for the wood, Jim has provided me with fresh vegetables and eggs from time to time.

"You see, when the grocers bring in the food from the farms, they double—sometimes even triple—the price of what it actually costs for them to ship the produce. The butcher does the same thing with his meats."

"That's not fair," Nicolaus commented a little bitterly.

"No, it's not," Connor agreed, adding in a resigned voice, "They have to make their money, I suppose.

"The grocers mark-up so high because they, like everyone following the hard years have deep debts which they need to pay off."

"Or they do it simply because they're greedy," Joseph interjected in a pitiless voice.

"Aye, that too," conceded Connor.

A little ways on, Connor turned off the main road onto a narrower dirt road that was bordered on each side by a rock wall. Watching the moving ribbon of the stone fence pass alongside them for a while, mesmerized by the blur of moving gray with the occasional speckling of green moss, Joseph finally turned his gaze upward when Nicolaus exclaimed, "Is that it?" He was pointing to the main farm house, silo, and barn. All the buildings looked weathered by the passing years. The patches of new brown shingles among the old cracking gray ones polka dotted the roof of the main house and barn. Without the luxury of paint, the replaced boards along the sides of the house stood out starkly against the peeling whitewash that covered the rest of the building. A new hole was forming in a far corner of the barn roof, which was perhaps what this latest shipment of wood was going to be set aside to mend.

Drawing closer, Nicolaus pointed to a small chicken coop and pen, which housed a flock of plump white chickens. A little further along there was a mucky pen in which four pigs were eating out of a trough.

"Don't they have a cow?" inquired Nicolaus out of the blue. He had never actually seen a cow in his whole life within the metropolitan city.

"The cow's in the barn." Connor explained, raising his hand, which still held one of the black leather reins, to point a callused finger in the direction of the barn.

The wagon continued rattling its way along the narrow slushy path until at last pulling up to the house, where Connor pulled back gently on the reins.

He turned around toward the boys. "Come on, now," he said cozily.

A solitary woman in a plain prairie dress, hauling a heavy wooden bucket across the mudded lawn, turned on her path toward the house and made her way towards Connor. A little smile crossed her thin, dirt-smeared face.

"No," Joseph and Nicolaus answered, shaking their head firmly, "we'll stay here."

"Come on now. These people ain't too proud."

"We can't," Joseph pleaded, "Look at us, we're—"

"They'll be no judgments made. Trust me now," he reassured.

The woman came upon them. Her fiery red hair had been drawn back into a bun but was coming loose after her day's work, leaving strands falling along the sides of her face and over her eyes. Her dress might have once been pretty with its floral-pattern print of lavender, but the colors of the fabric had faded, and there were several puckers and patches where holes had been mended. The woman herself looked worn, thin, and prematurely aged after surviving the lean times, but still there was something hardy about her, a fiery, wild spirit that would never quite leave her.

"Hello, love," she said, as brightly as she could under the strain of the load she hauled. She spoke with a thick Irish accent, not unlike Connor's own.

Joseph and Nicolaus stared at her. She was as different from the society wives as a woman could be. She was a country girl, salt of the earth and proud to be so. Some of the wealthier women of the city might have found her ill-mannered and been offended by her dirty appearance, but she was the embodiment of hospitality and warm-heartedness.

Putting down the heavy bucket, she took a moment to catch her breath, pushing the strands of hair out of her eyes with the back of her hand, which was likewise smeared with dirt.

"Good day, Clara," Connor replied kindly as he descended the wagon. "How did you fair the rains last week?"

"Oh, we weather all, don't we," she said in a weary voice, squinting a little as if looking into a bright sun, though actually trying to hold back the pain of her fatigue. "What else can we do?"

"I've brought a good load for you. Should make Jim happy."

"I reckon it will. He has been itching to patch the barn roof before the winter really starts a'howling. By the looks of it," she said, her gaze following Connor to the back of the wagon, "you have brought him enough to do just that.

"Got some new lads working for ya? Or are they part of the load you done brought us," she said ribbing the boys. She shifted her focus to Joseph and Nicolaus who were still sitting on the very end of the cart bed, trying very hard not to be noticed.

"This is Joseph and this is Nicolaus," he said, pointing to each boy in turn. "Boys, this is Mrs. Scolfield."

"Oh, Connor, enough with the Mrs, call me Clara boys." Moving around to the back of the wagon, she got a better look at the boys.

"Saints preserve us," she exclaimed upon seeing the state of the boys. "Would you look at 'em—I don't know where to start. Come on down boys."

Neither Joseph nor Nicolaus moved. They seemed lost.

"Come on, now, I won't bite." She reached out a hand to Nicolaus.

He timidly took her hand and climbed down from the wagon. Joseph following behind.

"They're not my workers. I'm just helping them. We're dropping off some lumber to their home after we finish up here."

Clara threw a disapproving look towards Connor. "Well, they ain't going nowhere until they been seen to. Come on now, boys, come in the house with me." Joseph and Nicolaus remained silent. They looked to Connor.

"Go with her, lads," he said laughing to himself.

"No reason to be nervous boys. Here, help me with my pail, and I'll take you into the house for some lunch. I have a lad about your age and girl who is a bit younger. They are inside finishing up their chores. We can all have a sit."

Clara made a little smile at Connor, then shepherded the boys towards the house. "Jim's in the barn," she called back over her shoulder. "We'll save ya both some lunch."

"Won't be but a minute," he called back, raising a hand to her as he tramped through the mud toward the old barn.

Upon entering the kitchen, Clara washed her hands in a wooden basin then took an old rose-colored apron from a hook on the back of a nearby closet door, pulled it around her, and tied it tightly in the back.

The boys moved through the house, looking rather lost. They were not used to seeing the day to day workings of those with a normal life—that is to say, a life of family, tea times, and aprons—of a mother and a father living in a house with dinner cooking on the hearth for their children. They simply did not know how to fit in—like wild animals that had been taken from the jungle and thrown in among civilized people—they simply felt out of place. Clara noticed that the boys were still standing in the doorframe, looking around, taking in every detail of the house and of her with a distinct longing in their eyes. Patting each boy on the back, she brought them forward, out of the threshold and into the kitchen.

"Here now boys have a seat at the table." Clara stoked the smoldering fire with the end of a split log. Then she swung the arm of an iron hook, which was anchored to the stone wall of the hearth, directly over the glowing heap of coals she had managed to rouse from the ashes and hung the handle of a heavy, soot-blackened iron pot upon its curled end.

"Tim! Meg!" she called, her voice echoing throughout the house.

Footsteps were suddenly heard directly overhead, moving across the floor above them. Then the creaking of old wooden stairs could be heard from down a distant hallway the boys had not come through.

"We were upstairs. I was going over the reader with her again, I think she—" the boy's voice trailed off. From the corner of his eye, he glimpsed Joseph and Nicolaus sitting at the table. His casual manner straightened up suddenly at the sight of the strangers. Then a little girl poked her head out from beside him.

"Now," Clara said, gathering up the front of her apron and wiping her hands upon it like a towel, even though she had already cleaned her hands when they first entered the kitchen. "This is Joseph and this is Nicolaus," she said politely. "They came in with Connor. Boys, this is my Tim and Meg."

"Hello," Tim said, nodding a little stiffly, clearly not use to having visitors.

A little more brazen, like her mother, the girl rushed forward to the table and sat down across from Joseph and Nicolaus, staring curiously at them. Nicolaus smiled uncomfortably as the little one examined him. She smiled back to reveal she had recently lost one of her front teeth. Meg seemed a funny creature dressed in the same style of prairie dress as her mother—a shade of faded plum with a bit of eyelet lace around her collar, which must have once been a pristine white, though had tinted to a beige color with wear. Her fine brown hair was pulled back into two braids, one on each side of her head, a navy blue ribbon tied at the end of each. She had a long face and had inherited a handful of her mother's freckles. She was a gangly little thing, but strong and inquisitive.

Her brother, Tim, had inherited his mother's red hair, though not her temperament. He was reserved, but polite, more like his father in personality. He wore a slate blue shirt with dark blue trousers that were pulled up a little past his waist by his suspenders to expose the peeling tops of his ankle-high, cowhide shoes.

"Tim, go help your Da and Connor unload the wagon. Meg, go fill up a pail from the well. It's time to wash up for lunch."

Meg stared unblinkingly at the boys, without any sense of manners, like young ones often do.

"Go on there, girl. And take Nicolaus and Joseph with you. Show 'em where the basin is so they can get cleaned up.

Joseph and Nicolaus shuffled behind her. Clara set about to cutting up some bread and setting out the dishes on the table. A few moments later the three returned—all a bit cleaner than they were when they left. The hair around their faces was wet.

"Meg, dear, go in and get a few extra bowls from the hutch." She turned to the boys, "Well, hands and faces clean. God knows, if we had the time, I would draw a bath for the both of ya. But I reckon I have to make sure that Connor keeps his job. Now then, take off your jackets. You're staying for lunch. Connor has to be getting back soon, but you're not leaving here until your stomachs have been fed."

The boys said nothing. Nicolaus looked at Joseph wanting to know what to do. Joseph made to untie his coat. Nicolaus followed.

Their coats off, the two stood in their hand-stitched clothes—skinny as scarecrows.

Tending to the stove, Clara turned around and was taken aback by the boys' ghastly appearance. She said nothing.

"Give me your coats. I'll hang 'em for you," Joseph and Nicolaus each reached out with their jackets.

She took them. "Well, they won't win any fashionable reviews will they, but I'll tell you, the stitching is strong. If I were in a storm and had to choose between some frilly coat or one of these jackets, you'd be making one in my size then."

The boys seemed to ease. The sense of shame bearing down on them lifted for a moment. They felt proud.

"Thank you," offered Joseph.

"Well then," Clara exclaimed in a teasing voice, "you do have a tongue. And what about you, do you speak as well?" She eyed Nicolaus. "No hats at the supper table then," she said kindly.

Nicolaus quickly removed his hat to reveal a band of missed dirt along his forehead. Clara gave a little shake of the head, then took up a wet cloth, and began wiping the dirt off his face. She talked as she worked, "You know, I'm only teasing you in good fun. It's my way. There's no need to be afraid or feel out of place."

Nicolaus listened to her, but her words seemed far away, as though he heard her from some distant place. He felt her hand upon his chin and the cool strokes of the cloth passing over his face. She moved the rag gently—with care. They were almost at the same eye-level. He had to look up at her slightly. His insides tensed as he held back the emotions that stirred. He looked at her from behind his broken spectacles—his eyes full of gratitude.

She finished. Her hands slowed. She looked at him in a motherly way. She could sense the loneliness in the boy. Never before had she seen a child so thankful for a moment's concern. Her heart bled for the boy.

"Thank you," he said as she pulled back her hand—still fixed on his eyes.

A scuffing noise sounded at the door. The sound of boots could be heard coming up the hall. In came Tim, Connor, and a man that must be Jim—Clara's husband. He looked a great deal like Connor, only he looked cared for—his cheeks were fuller. His clothes while dirty, were well-mended. He removed his hat to show a tuft of graying, ink-black hair.

After proper introductions, everyone sat down at the table. Empty bowls were placed in front of each chair. A platter of thickly sliced, wheat bread was laid out in the middle of the table.

"Well, it isn't much, but it's hot," said Clara as she took each bowl, brought it over to the hearth, and filled it with a ladle of steaming stew.

"Don't sell yourself short, love," replied Jim. "My girl is the best cook this side of town. No matter how little we got, she can make it a meal fit for a king. And that's the test of a true cook if you ask me. Any fool can make a slab of beef taste good, but give 'em a heart, a liver, and a stomach of a sheep and let's see what they can do with that."

Connor nodded in agreement. Joseph and Nicolaus looked ill. They were suddenly suspicious as to what was being placed in their bowls.

"Get those looks of dread off your faces. No sheep stomach today. It's lamb stew, dears, with some potatoes, parsnips, carrots, onions, and all manner of other root vegetables."

Clara set down a heavy earthenware bowl in front of Joseph and then Nicolaus. The broth was a deep mahogany brown. In the rich stock were big chunks of golden soft potatoes, nobs of chopped carrots, translucent leaves of an unfurled onion, and melting shreds of meat. A hot meal made with care and set down before them by a loving mother's hand—this was a first.

The boys did not move. They were starved, and there was a feast laid out before them: soup and bread and fresh clean water. So, why couldn't they eat?

"We can't," Joseph said with deep regret.

Nicolaus looked up from the bowl with a sad face. As hard it was, he agreed with Joseph.

"Why ever not?" asked Jim. "Don't tell me you're not hungry. You're naught but bones. Pick up those spoons and do right by your supper."

Joseph looked to Clara. "It's lovely, but we just can't. It wouldn't be fair."

"Fair to whom, love?" inquired Clara.

Connor spoke gently to them, "I think I understand. You have friends, don't ya? Friends that won't sit down to as fine a meal as this tonight, and you feel guilty for eating it without them."

Nicolaus nodded.

"If I promised you that we would see to your friends before the day is out, would you finish that bowl of stew without any guilt?" assured Connor.

Joseph's frown lifted slightly. The stress eased a bit. He believed in Connor—believed that he would see to it that everyone in their group ate well that day.

His hand moved towards his spoon. Nicolaus followed his lead. Everyone else at the table began to eat.

Joseph's mouth was watering as he slowly let the broth pool inside the deep spoon. He brought it to his lips—the vapors of the dark stock moistened the bottom of his nose as he held it there for a moment breathing it in. He slurped the spoon clean and held the warmth of the soup in his mouth for a time, wanting to taste every hour it had simmered before he let it go. He swallowed, then moved on to one of the soft potatoes gaining speed with each bite—the prolonged hunger took hold of him.

Nicolaus wasted no time. He did not have enough

self-restraint to savor the bites for more than a moment. Spoonful after spoonful, he scooped the stew into his mouth until finally the bottom of the bowl came into sight.

"It's bad manners to slurp, ya know," announced Meg as she watched the boys furiously eating.

"Hush, girl!" said Clara. "Here," she said to Nicolaus, bringing his bowl to the hearth then returning it to him full.

Nicolaus looked to Joseph as if for permission.

"Eat," argued Clara before Joseph could give an answer one way or the other. "And you'll be having another bowl as well. No arguments," she added sternly, looking at Joseph. "We've got plenty," she went on when it looked like Joseph was going to protest. "It's only autumn, and we still have a pantry full. Now, call on us come spring, and you'll be having more broth than anything else."

Done with their second bowls before everyone had finished the first, the boys sat there feeling full for the first time in memory.

"Thank you, Mrs. Scolfield," said both of them.

"Clara," she insisted "And you're welcome."

Meg and Tim both finished.

"Meg, dear, go to the hand-me-down bin and fetch some of the old clothes—shirts, trousers and anything else that might have some wear left and put 'em in one of the sacks. And Tim, dear, go fetch one of the blankets from the spare linens, will you."

Lunch eaten and the kitchen tidied, the boys were tying their coats back up by the door.

"Here now, you take this." Clara placed a stuffed sack in Joseph's hands. "Shirts and things, nothing to wear out to high tea but something to keep ya covered." She was trying to make light of a moment that was obviously causing her heartache. "Take this as well." She placed a folded wool blanket in Nicolaus' arms. "The flock has been sheared, and I'll be knitting away by the hearth all winter. We can spare it." Finally, she handed Nicolaus a wrapped, wax paper bundle the size of two bread loaves. "And this," she said sadly. She could not keep up her humor any longer. She had a good idea of the life they led. She did not want them to leave.

She moved toward the boys and gave them both a kiss on the head. She looked Joseph in the eye. "You promise me that, if you ever need a place, you'll come back here."

"Yes, ma'am."

"You boys go out to the cart. I'll be there in a moment," directed Connor.

Clara had to tear herself away. She watched them as they walked out the door. Never before had the two look so much like children—helplessly in need of love. Nicolaus looked back several times at her before finally turning out of sight.

"How can we let 'em go. You know they don't have nowhere to go," Clara argued. "Did you see Joseph? He tucked away pieces of bread into his shirt when we weren't looking. I'll bet you there are more with him, and he's the one taking care of them all. We have to do something." She turned away from the door to face Jim and Connor.

* * * * *

The entire ride back into town was quiet. The boys basked in the warmth of a perfect moment—soaking it in as the miles passed and it faded to a wonderful memory. While

Connor, troubled as he was, did not know what he should do.

Quite suddenly, a voice issued from the back of the cart. "This'll be fine, you can stop here," Joseph said, pulling Connor up from his thoughts abruptly.

Looking out across the open dump lots, Joseph could see the wagon—a small, box shaped dot on the horizon, looking like a massive boulder within the open lots. They were only about a quarter mile from the wagon.

Connor pulled back on the reins then jumped down to help the boys climb out and pull the beams down. Before picking up their load, Joseph and Nicolaus turned to Connor. The three of them stood there for a time not knowing exactly what to say. The boys knew they had to somehow convey the thanks of all the children for his kindness, but they did not know where to begin. Turning back to the cart, Connor grabbed a heavy, metal pail. "It's my lunch. A meal for your friends, as I promised." Connor smiled. His thick, brown beard covered his full cheeks. His gentle, kind eyes squinted in the sun. He placed the pail on the back of the cart.

"Thank you, Connor," said Joseph.

"You don't need to thank me, lads. I enjoyed meeting you both. I'm only sorry it had to be under such horrible circumstances." Connor looked over the pile now sitting on the back of the cart. "Between the wood, the crate of books, the pail, and all the supplies Clara sent you with, I don't think you boys can handle it all." Knowing the boys still did not trust him to come to their home, Connor had another suggestion. "Why don't you come back to the site?" he paused. "Come to the old house, tomorrow, and we can bring the wood in a separate trip. You should take this," Connor grabbed hold of the lunch pail placing the thin rounded handle in Joseph's outstretched palm. His hand dropped a little with the weight of the food inside it. "Along with the crate of books and Clara's things today."

"Sounds like the right thing to do," Joseph concluded. The speechlessness finally gave way to heartfelt thanks. Joseph stuttered a little as he spoke, overwhelmed by the man's kindness. "This could've been a horrible day to have to endure. But because of what you've done, it'll be a day remembered for its good things and not its bad."

"Aye," added Nicolaus timidly chiming in at the end.

Connor patted both boys on the back, then he helped them load their sacks.

"I hardly did anything. I wish I could do more. You both will be all right tonight?" Connor asked in concern. "There's a storm heading this way, rumored to swipe the city day after tomorrow."

Joseph nodded half-heartedly.

As they prepared to set off, Joseph's eyes met Connor's. There was a final moment of pause between them—the man and the boy. Pulling themselves away, the boys started walking. Connor slowly climbed back into his wagon and watched them go off across the empty lots. With a flick of the reins, the cart jerked forward.

CHAPTER 15
THE TURN IN THE TIDE

EARING A NOISE IN THE DISTANCE, Ben and Davy jumped up into the front of the wagon to see who was coming. "They're back!" they shouted as they leapt down.

Everyone shuffled out of the wagon to watch Joseph and Nicolaus' return. Anna, Ben, Davy, and Rachel took the load from them, not knowing yet what exactly they were carrying. Beth, Asa, and Emma began running toward them. Abbey, however, stayed in the wagon, not wanting to leave Marie alone.

"What's happening?" Marie asked.

"They have quite a load of stuff," Abbey explained.

"Good," Marie said in relief, "he needed a decent day."

Before Abbey could ask what she was talking about the crowd came back to the wagon and everyone climbed back up.

The walk from Connor's cart to the wagon was short, but still Joseph and Nicolaus were slightly out of breath when they finally climbed back inside. Joseph placed the crate of books and Clara's sack inside the wagon, then hauled himself through the opening in the back. Nicolaus handed up the pail and the blanket.

"You found this blanket in the trash?" asked Rachel in a tone of disbelief.

"No," he replied. "Actually, we didn't spend the day in the city."

The commotion settled. Each face had a puzzling look upon it.

Everyone was tucked away under the canvas blanket. Joseph brought the sack, pail, and blanket to the center of the wagon and began to tell the day's tale.

He started at the beginning. "The printing house is gone—torn down," as soon as the words left Joseph's lips there were looks of shock, outrage, and sadness—a speechless state of bewilderment. They were heartbroken. Joseph told them of the few sundries they were able to take from the house.

Trying to lessen the pain of the day, Joseph moved on from the sad fate of the printing house to meeting Connor, Clara, and Jim.

"Aye, you do look a bit cleaner," teased Davy after hearing the bit of the story about washing up.

"Shush now," said Anna, laughing a bit despite herself. "She gave you lunch?"

"Yes," replied Joseph. "Everyone was sitting down to lunch, and we were invited to stay."

Joseph stopped there. Nicolaus said nothing. "Well, was it good? What did they have?" Davy pushed.

"It was a stew. It was fine," he replied weakly. He said nothing more about it. He could not bring himself to let all his excitement show in front of the others, who had sat all day in the wagon without a scrap.

"We wouldn't have eaten without you, but Connor promised to send us back to the wagon with enough for you all. Here," he said reaching for the metal pail.

"What's in it?" asked Ben.

"Well, I don't rightly know. He just handed it to me. I think it's his lunch."

Joseph pulled out the tin lunch pail like a magician revealing his big finale.

Silent awe passed over the wagon as Joseph pulled back the cloth covering and began unwrapping the feast. It quickly became apparent that Connor didn't pack a light lunch, nor was he shy with the treats. Joseph revealed parcel after parcel of food all wrapped in parchment, wax paper, and cheese cloth. By the time the pail was empty, roughly a dozen small wrapped parcels lay before them.

"That's a big lunch," said Davy, matter-of-factly. "Was he a big man?" he asked curiously.

"Davy!" Anna said in a scolding, motherly voice.

"What?" answered Davy defensively.

"You know, it's not polite to ask such questions."

"Just curious," he finished weakly, wilting under Anna's disapproving glare.

Busily going through the packages and only half paying attention to the conversation, Joseph answered Davy's question offhandedly. "Not really, he looked rather fit to me, just a normal man."

"Well, either way," Anna said pointedly, bringing the gossip to a close, "he was a kind man for giving us all this food." Her stern stare turned from Davy to Joseph. Joseph gave her a strained, little smile in an effort to get Anna to lighten up.

"All right then, why don't we all open one, then we can lay the food out and break it into portions," Marie suggested.

Joseph nodded enthusiastically, wanting nothing more than to change topics.

Unwrapping the big bundle in front of him, Joseph uncovered a wide wedge of hearty rye bread. It had an unblemished, leathery brown crust wrapped around one side and a cross-section of spongy moist bread on the other.

"Look at that!" Joseph exclaimed as he laid it out for all to see. "Not a spec of mold on it, no dried out crusts, no stale foamy bits. It's perfect!"

As they tore the wedge into small portions, the soft bread smelled both sour and savory.

With a palm size chunk in front of each person, all eyes turned to Ben who had the second largest bundle.

"Looks like a wheel," Davy remarked, as Ben untied a length of butcher's twine wrapped around the package.

"Maybe it's a tin," guessed Abbey.

"Hard enough to be one," Ben said tapping the paper with his knuckles. As he peeled the brown waxed paper away, a small round of cheese lay before the meek boy.

"Wow, I've never had cheese," Ben said, looking at the waxy, buttery, golden wheel, holding it with the same awe a prospector would handle a nugget of gold.

"Are you joking, we've never had anything," Davy finished plainly. He sat next to Ben staring at the round of cheese. Joseph already had his knife out—poised to divide it.

The wagon was filled with a hushed anticipation as Anna unwrapped her waxed parchment bundle to find a cured hunk of salted pork. The hunk had deep crimson meat and was rimmed by a brown edge. It smelled salty and juicy. Hunger building, Nicolaus went next. His package was rather different from the others. His was like a little pouch and, whatever was inside, seemed broken up and soft. Opening the folded seams,

Nicolaus found a handful of dried apple chunks. Small slices of off-white, dried apple with dark red peel around its cut edges.

"What is it?" Asa asked looking at the little, white chunks.

"It's an apple," Nicolaus said kindly, passing the boy a piece for him to examine.

"No, its not, apples are round and red," Asa insisted, still wanting to know what the unidentified white pieces were.

"It's an apple that was cut and dried to preserve it through the winter," Marie explained. Remembering the taste from a tart her mother use to make. "Smell it," she encouraged. "It smells like an apple."

Placing the chunk to the tip of his nose, the boy inhaled deeply, then popped the small chunk into his mouth, and nodded in approval.

"Satisfied?" Joseph said as he laughed.

Next in turn was Davy, who had a rather odd shaped parcel as well. It was about five inches long, hard, and shaped like a carrot, which was what he guessed it must be. "Why would anyone wrap a carrot?" he asked. It was not until after he tore away the wrapper that he realized it was a large, pickled cucumber. It must had been pulled from a jar where it had been soaking in a salty, sour brine since the summer.

Next was Rachel, her bundle was light and long, but rather thick. Unwrapping it, she found long strips of smoked beef. The dark, coffee brown meat had been smoked and seasoned. The very smell of it flooded everyone's mouth.

"More meat," she said holding out the wrapper that held the stack of preserved strips of beef.

Turning to Joseph, Anna quietly asked. "Are you sure this was just his lunch and not his shopping?" She spoke in a dumbfounded tone as she watched Rachel place the preserved beef beside her salted pork.

"He said it was his lunch," he whispered back, just as lost for an explanation.

"How could one man eat all this?" she remarked quietly.

Leaning in Joseph whispered sarcastically, "I thought that was a rude question to ask?" A little wink and a grin passed over her face. They turned back to watch Abbey open her package.

Abbey pulled back her cheese cloth wrapping to reveal a thick hunk of wheat bread. The light brown crust was soft, and its meat was fluffy and had the smell of toasted nuts.

Holding it up for all to see, she placed it in front of Joseph to be divided.

At last, they came to the final two packages. Asa and Emma shared a rather large package, and Marie sat beside Beth with a smaller one.

"Well, go on you two," Anna said encouragingly, motioning to Asa and Emma.

The two small ones could not bear the wait any longer. They tore away the wax paper with such excitement that Anna knew the small shreds would be completely unusable afterward. However, once finished, they both looked at the contents of their package a little disappointed.

"Crackers?" Asa asked holding up one of the ten or so rounds stacked like coins then wrapped.

"No, not crackers," Rachel said reassuringly as she reached out to take the white, soft round Asa was examining.

"No, certainly not crackers," Anna said. Rachel handed it back to the slightly disappointed boy, who wanted something a little more special than crackers.

"You know what they are?" Rachel said, smiling from ear-to-ear. "They're what's called shortbread cookies. They are buttery, crumbly, sugary cookies. Not crackers."

At the word cookie, both Asa and Emma seemed to brighten, and the excitement re-inflated in their heart.

"Cookies, cookies, cookies," Emma and Asa chanted as they rocked back and forth.

"All right, last one," Joseph announced at which time all eyes turned to Beth, who was a little uncomfortable with the attention. Marie held her tightly. "Go on now."

Shyly and carefully, Beth unwrapped her gift, which was in the shape of a small brick and just as hard as one. Inside she found another sweet treat. It was a rather large square of dried fruit cake made with nuts and raisins. The entire cake was rich and gooey after soaking in a thick syrup glaze, making every piece sticky and moist. Beth grinned widely, clearly thrilled that she had gotten something so delicious to unwrap. Placing it tenderly in front of Joseph, all the food was unwrapped and they were ready to eat. Or so they thought.

Just when everyone thought that the pail was empty, Joseph burst out with something he had evidently been keeping as a final surprise. Reaching into the pail, he pulled out two glass liter bottles of fresh, thick, whole milk. He had seen the milk when he first pulled back the cheese cloth covering the pail's treasure. His heart had leapt at the sight of it. It had been years—many years—since any of them had tasted milk, and this, above so many things, had been what they craved the most.

Anna looked to Joseph, then motioned at all the food laid out before them. "I know we want to have a big feast, but we should save some and spread it out over the coming days."

Joseph thought about it for a moment, then said in a decided voice, "We're all hungry, and we haven't had the chance to eat such a meal. We'll set aside some, but we should all have at least one meat and one bread and one bit of vegetable."

"And the cookies!" Asa and Emma shouted, not wanting Joseph to forget.

"Yes, and a treat," he answered reassuringly.

"We're going to eat a feast in honor of our coming journey and also in remembrance of the printing house—the only home we've ever known. We're going to mark the journey we'll soon be taking to our new life and mark the end of the struggle we're finally able to leave behind."

Abbey and Beth gathered up all the brown, waxed parchment papers and handed one to each person, making a place for the food to be laid out for each of them. Anna passed out the bits of pork, hunks of cheese, sections of cucumber, chunks of apple, a small piece of the fruit cake, and a bit of the wedge of rye. The other food was saved for the coming days and weeks. But of course, the cookies, one for each of them, would be gone that very evening—without a trace.

The bottle of milk sat in the center of their circle, open, and waiting to be sipped on. "Here," Anna said, getting out the tin mugs they were able to salvage from the dump. A splash of milk was poured in each mug. Fuller cups went to the small ones and to Marie, who was still recovering.

Anna handed Marie her mug. "Are you all right?" Anna asked. "I'm fine," Marie assured her. "Now go and eat," she added in a motherly tone. Only Marie mothered Anna. She treasured her bond with Marie and the feeling that someone else was looking out for her while she was looking after the others.

Having eaten lunch, Joseph and Nicolaus put their portions with the other food being saved. Each child stared at the feast before them, deciding which morsel they wanted to try first.

"We should be thankful for Connor," Nicolaus declared before anyone began, "for all that he did to help us today. He's the first caring person we have met since—" His words trailed off as he tried to recall the last caring person the children had met, trying to put a face and date to an act of kindness, but his mind went blank.

"It's been a long time," Rachel said laying a hand on Nicolaus' leg. He could stop trying to remember, because no one was going to come to mind. But then he spoke up.

"—since we met each other," he finished with a smile, giving everyone something to think about.

And with that everyone turned to their food, trying to control their starvation and not gobble it all down too quickly. They rarely ate anything, let alone appetizing food. The first few chunks and bits were taken down rather quickly. However, after the first half of their food was gone, the initial burst of hunger seemed to ease a little, and they all calmed down, allowing the rest of the meal to be eaten steadily and easily, which was what they wanted. They never had such a feast, and they did not want it to be gone in seconds. They wanted the time to savor every bite and appreciate every taste.

It surprised no one that the first thing that Asa and Emma devoured on their papers was their shortbread cookies. The soft rounds were about the size of their little hands—thick and tender, moist with the butter folded into the dough before it was baked. There was a faint dusting of flour still on the bottom. The small boy took half the cookie with one bite. Asa smiled with happy satisfaction, tasting its butter and vanilla sweetness. And the other half was gone in one more enjoyable bite.

"Hmmm, not a cracker, is it Asa?" Joseph said in a merry voice as they all watched both Asa and Emma gobble up the sweet, soft treats.

"The sack!" Asa exclaimed, bits of cookie falling from his mouth. "What's in it?"

So preoccupied with the feast, Joseph had neglected the sack Clara had given them. He pulled open the drawstring and dumped out the contents on his lap.

"What is it?" asked Marie.

"New clothes," answered Rachel in voice reflecting a degree of awe.

Shirts, pants, a sweater or two, hats, mittens, scarves—the good woman had packed all manner of hand-me-downs into that small sack. There were holes and several patches, but it did not matter. The clothing had not been fished out of a trash bin in desperation; rather, it had been given in affection and out of concern, which made it a rare gift indeed.

It felt like Christmas morning—a feast to fill their bellies and presents that were all their own. A piece at a time the clothing was handed out. The sizes ran on the small side, as Clara and Jim's children were still quite young. Nevertheless, the clothing would ensure that Asa, Emma, Beth, Abbey, Ben, and Davy would be well-protected during the coming winter months.

Leaning back against the wagon, Joseph watched the scene before him—the little ones were putting on their new clothes, mouths still full, and faces beaming. He smiled. A warmth filled his heart. For a moment, however brief it might be, he felt no weights upon him.

CHAPTER 16
PARALLEL PATHS

IT WAS NIGHT IN THE CITY. The light the waning moon gave off was slight. He walked along the darkened streets of the North End with a hurried step, not wanting to pause and give a predator a chance to pounce. *Almost there,* Connor thought to himself as he turned down a narrow side street.

Sitting against the wall up ahead the shadow of a figure stirred, but there was no fear.

A hoarse tone issued from the heap of rags, "Something for a poor ol' man, lad?"

Pulling a small wrapped bundle from his tool box, Connor passed it into the old man's outstretched hands with a familiarity, as though he had done it every day for years. Connor walked on, rounded a corner, and entered a pair of narrow double doors that were painted a shade of dirty blue. Closing the doors behind him, he made his way up a narrow staircase. The floorboards creaked with each step taken. The halls were claustrophobic, cobwebs hug like bunting along the ceiling molding. Connor proceeded upward, carrying his tool box in front of him to narrow himself enough to make the tight turns. The corridor was dark, but it did not matter. He had climbed these stairs for the last eight years.

He rounded the first landing, passing by a door painted the same blue as the front entryway. He heard the voice of an embittered woman berating her disobedient children.

"You children ain't nothin' but a drain on my purse. Think of all the money I might've had if I never had you lot!"

Letting out a heavy sigh, Connor continued on until he came to the door of the second floor apartment behind which an incoherent muttering echoed. Pressing on still, Connor finally came to the door of the third floor apartment, where he proceeded to slide his old brass key into the rusted lock and turned the knob.

He entered the dark room, closed the door, and set the lock behind him with a metal click. He set down his tool box with a thump, removed his cloth hat, and hung it on a hook set into the wall beside the door.

The room was lit by moonlight only. He moved through the dim light. A small round table lay ahead of him. He pulled a thin strip of kindling from a tin and went toward the hearth. The fire was smoldering. Only a few fading embers still glowed on the burned remnants of a fat oak log. Connor let out a deep sigh as he knelt down and leaned into the hearth, placing the tip of the thin kindling on the embers and giving it a blow until a flame burst to life. Cradling the delicate flame burning on the end of the thin splinter of tinder, he moved across the room and transferred the light to a nearby candle. He pinched the tip of the kindling with his callused fingers, then fed it back into the tin with the others.

As the candle light fell around the room, one could see immediately the vast difference between the dark, dilapidated hallway and the new surroundings. The rest of the building was cold, dirty, and stark, but Connor's house was inviting, clean, and comfortable—a sanctuary from the harsh surroundings.

It was a small set of rooms to be sure. The front door opened into the main room. To his right was a tiny bedroom. To his left was a narrow pantry cupboard with a small table set in front. Upon the table, there was a basket of bread covered in cheesecloth and a few parchment-wrapped bundles.

Throwing a bit of kindling and a section of log upon the smoldering fire, Connor moved back to the door and peeled off his hide boots, placing them alongside his tool box. His heavy wool coat was still on his back and a pair of thinning socks on his feet, Connor shuffled half-heartedly across a worn, tan and brown, braided rug that lay out over the worn, wooden floorboards in the small main room. The edges of the old rug rolled up slightly against the walls as it stretched the length of the confined space.

The main room had one narrow four-pane window at the far end. Directly next to it sat an old upholstered arm chair, which Connor plopped down into wearily. Under the window, beside the chair, there was an end table. It had a pretty cloth drawn over it so only the legs showed through at the bottom. Atop the round table sat a solitary glass mason jar, which held a few dried out flowers. Next to that, there was a scrolled wood picture frame. The rest of the room was modest and poor, but the frame was elaborate. Vines of ivy and blooming flowers were hand-carved into the hard dark wood of the frame adorning the picture within. The frame had not a single speck of dust upon it. The glass had no streaks or smears. Behind the glass lay an image—a moment captured in time—of a happy family. There was an orange tint to the otherwise monochrome photograph. The looks upon the face of each person beamed brightly with intense affection. In the center of the photograph stood a young Connor with his arm around a longhaired woman beside him. Not a sign of tension or worry lay upon their faces. Both of them had an arm around each other—his around her back, hers around his waist. Their other hand rested on the shoulders of a small boy standing in front of them. The boy, no more than three or four, was dressed in dark trousers, a light white country shirt, and a rolled up cloth cap in his hands. The expression on his face beamed like that of his parents.

It was very late, and the loud city was quiet for once. He should have eaten something for supper, but he didn't. He should have gone to sleep after the bells of the nearby chapel tolled midnight, but he didn't. Ruminating in the dark, his thoughts slipped into the past, then back into the present. Every now and then his face twinged in the flickering candlelight as he recalled them—his family. He tried again and again to call up some happy thoughts, but he was unable to disconnect them from the grief.

His eyes stared pensively into the darkness. Countless unvoiced questions raced through the track of his mind—looping again and again without answers to halt them.

The moon arched across the sky. His eyes remained fixed. He looked at the window, gazing at the patterns of ice crystals forming along the corners of each pane. He was cold. A woolen blanket rested across the top of his chair, but he did not reach for it. The fire was smoldering—collapsing in upon itself—but he did not feed it. He just sat there. For hours, his thoughts kept him awake. Then, later, his acidic stomach and frosty feet kept him from finding comfort. Nonetheless, his fatigue eventually won, and he fell into a restless sleep.

A thick grove of trees encircled a small clearing where a white-washed cottage with a thatch roof stood. A steady stream of light smoke emanated from the house's chimney. A few scattered trees were left on the otherwise spotless rolling hills. The trees were all grouped around the house, as if huddling around the warmth of the home—drawing close to the life flourishing within. The air was filled with the smell of the churning brine of a nearby sea. Intermingled with the salty smell of the water was a fragrant burst of wildflowers. A sense of healing settled into the deep tissues of Connor's heart as he drank in the scene before him.

CHAPTER 17
A FRAGILE TRUST

UPON ARRIVING AT THE PRINTING HOUSE, Anna stood speechless before the barren plot of land where the only home they'd ever known had once stood.

"I believed you when you told me about it. But it didn't seem real until now." Anna gaped.

Joseph stood with Anna. His heart beating in sync with her own, sharing her shock.

The incredulous silence was broken by the voice of Connor.

"Decided to come back?" he inquired. "I thought I might see you again. I hoped I might anyway." He looked relieved.

"Anna and I came to bring you back your lunch pail," Joseph said, making a gesture towards Anna to introduce her to Connor.

"Good day to you, Anna." Connor smiled at the young girl who stood with the maturity of a woman and the face of a child.

"Empty, I see," Connor added as he took the pail from Joseph. "Good."

The three of them stood silently for a few moments.

"So, I was wondering, just how many mouths did this lunch pail have to feed?" Joseph and Anna said nothing to this. They looked scared and pressured. Any time they had ever taken an adult into their confidence, they had been betrayed and lived to know regret. However, after a moment, the tenseness in them softened. Joseph reminded himself that this man had proven himself to be different.

"Eleven." Joseph answered abruptly and with trembling voice. "There are eleven of us all together."

"Eleven!" Connor echoed in shock. "How old are the youngest?" he asked in concern, trying to pull his thoughts together.

"Asa and Emma are four," Anna said, as if speaking of her own children.

"Anna and I are the oldest. We care for everyone right now. There's another, Marie, she's like the mother of us all, but she —" Joseph trailed away.

"She is—?" Connor asked, wanting Joseph to finish his thought.

"She's unwell," Anna finished. "She hasn't been well for months now."

Anna recalled Marie's illness and semi-recovery, leading up to her present weakened state. Connor's face shown heartfelt concern. He took a breath and stared into a deep thought for a moment, then looked back up into Joseph's eyes.

"Yesterday, as I watched you and Nicolaus walk off, I knew you were not alone—that most likely you were caring for others. I didn't know how many others. I must admit that eleven is far more than I expected—but in the end it doesn't matter. I still have the same feelings."

"Feelings about what?" Anna asked, feeling lost.

"I want to help you—help you all," he added pulling the

two over to a quiet bench. "I knew from the first time I spoke with Joseph and Nicolaus that you are different. Don't worry," he clarified with the hint of a laugh. "I mean it in a good way. You are different here," he pointed to Joseph's heart. "You seem a great deal like my own family."

Joseph and Anna nodded. "We understand," Joseph replied, relieved that Connor was able to see some part of their true selves. "How are you going to help us?" he asked. He was hesitant to get his hopes up. This all seemed too good to be true.

"I don't know that yet. It depends on all of you, I suppose. We'll sit down and talk about what you all need. I don't have a fat savings. In fact, I have little more than good intentions, but we'll see what I can do."

Anna was quick to say, "Your intentions mean more to us than you'll ever know. Just your desire to help us has helped us, if that makes sense." She did not feel as though she was making herself clear. "I guess, I'm just in shock. It all means so much to us."

"I do know what it's like to have to live without anyone there to care for you. I know what it's like to wait a long time to find someone who feels kindred." Connor pulled himself back. It seemed as though he was preparing to tell some personal story but, at the last moment, brought the focus back to the children. Just then a worker called out for the foreman, and Connor's head turned to the site, then back to the children. "I have to be getting back. Can you meet me here in the late afternoon? I'll finish with my work around sundown, and we can speak then. Will it put you out to come back?"

Joseph shook his head. "No."

Connor went back to the worksite, leaving Anna and Joseph in his wake—shocked.

Anna turned to Joseph as they walked away. "He wants to help us." Her voice sounded disconnected as though what had just happened did not register in her mind yet. "This feels like a dream. It just can't be real." Her eyes filled.

Joseph laughed a little. "You—you always believed that people like Connor were out there. Why are you so shocked to find out you were right?"

"It wasn't a belief; it was a hope. Deep down, I thought it was just a delusion. I think," she said considering the situation, "I'm relieved actually. Not just because things might get better for us, but because, if he turns out to be real, I have reason to believe in other things that up until now were only hopes.

"I know that you have no belief left, Joseph," Anna went on, "and lately I simply haven't believed enough to carry us both, but now—today—I feel that life will come. I know I might be getting ahead of myself. Connor is still new to our lives, and we don't know what he's actually willing to do to help. All the same, I feel we are through the worst of it."

Joseph did not say anything. He took in Anna's words, and his heart timidly reached to them, wanting them to be true.

In the distance, Connor looked up from his work and turned to look at Joseph and Anna. He smiled at them and gave a little nod.

The two did not do any collecting in the city that morning, instead they hurried through the crowded streets, ignoring the people around them. They wanted to get back to the wagon and tell everyone the remarkable news.

They were walking the barren stretch along the outskirts when Joseph began voicing his concerns.

"Anna, I'm not so sure we should tell the others about Connor." Joseph was concerned.

"Why?" Anna inquired.

"Well, I don't want everyone to get their hopes up, that's all."

"You don't think Connor will do as he said and help us?" she asked.

"No," Joseph answered, "I think he'll be true to his word. But still, we don't know him all that well, and we haven't even really spoken to him about what he intends to do. I mean, if we go back and tell everyone that he promised to help us, they're going to get their hopes up—really high—and I just don't want to see them come crashing down. I think we need to be cautious in how much we allow ourselves to hope. We should wait to tell them until we actually speak with him."

"I understand your wanting to protect the others, but—" she trailed off.

"But what?" Joseph asked, picking up her thought.

"I think this is also about you not wanting to get your hopes up only to come crashing down. I think you're afraid," Anna said gently, not wanting to hurt him, "and rightfully so. I mean, we have been put through the wringer, but still I think Connor is genuine. I think we can trust him," she finished.

Joseph let out a heavy breath. "You're probably right. I do believe he'll help, but I'm not putting my full trust in him or anyone until they have proven themselves. And I don't want to play around with the hopes of the others until we are sure—beyond any doubt."

The pair walked on; the wagon was in view. Anna agreed to let it lie until they spoke with Connor.

When Joseph and Anna arrived back at the wagon the mood was rather awkward. It seemed Rachel, Nicolaus, and Marie had gotten their hopes up as they lay sleeping with a full stomach. A question had entered their mind: if the man was willing to give so much, was he willing to do more? When Anna and Joseph returned with no news, it was rather a blow to them.

"So, what did he say?" Rachel asked expectantly.

Anna and Joseph were settling into the canvas sea.

"He was grateful that we returned his pail," answered Joseph in a casual tone.

"Nothing more?" asked Nicolaus a little disappointed. He looked to Anna. She turned away, not wanting to lie.

"Nothing more," answered Joseph.

Marie spoke up, "Do you intend to see him again?"

"I think I might go back and speak to him later on this afternoon and talk to him about a few things."

"What?" Davy chimed in innocently.

"Just things," Joseph said at a loss. "He seems nice. Perhaps he has some thoughts on how we could make things better. We'll see," he said, trying to maintain his causal tone.

Joseph felt Marie looking through him. He knew she could feel him holding back.

"I think I'll work on the wagon for a bit today," said Joseph. The tactless change of subject did not go unnoticed by Rachel, Nicolaus, and Marie. The all looked to Anna for some kind of explanation as to what was going on.

"I'll help," announced Davy, getting Joseph out of the tight spot.

"All right then," Joseph rose, moved to the back flap, and dropped down out of sight.

Nicolaus looked around. He felt lost. "I'll go help as well, I suppose." His statement sounded like a question.

Anna nodded him onward.

Ben and Abbey followed the boys out.

"What's happening?" asked Marie.

Rachel was about to ask this herself.

"Nothing, everything's fine," Anna replied under the gaze of Beth, Asa, and Emma. "He's just working through some things, that's all."

Marie and Rachel were not satisfied, but the conversation was left there until a later time.

* * * * *

THE MORNING BECAME AFTERNOON. The children passed the time talking, resting, and working on various projects. Rachel was working on a patchwork quilt. Anna, Marie, and Beth saw to the little ones. The others worked on reinforcing the wagon with some spare wood gathered from the work site.

When the sun was waning in the sky and the bells of Kings Chapel and Old North Church chimed 4 o'clock in the distance, Joseph put aside his work and made his way back into the city alone. His eyes pointed down. He kept to himself among the crowds. He did not wish to provoke anyone around him. The children always did this. Their clothing and haggard appearance gave away that they were homeless. Most people simply overlooked them, others—like the police—tended to take notice. If caught, the children would face their worst fears: being thrown into a desperate, dark orphanage or being

locked away in one of the infamous reforms known for their
cruel methods or being split up and shipped off on one of the
orphan trains—never to see one another again. It was best to
move quickly and quietly through the busiest parts of the city
or to avoid them totally when possible.

When Joseph came to the printing house, all the workers
had already left, but Connor had stayed. He was sitting on an
old stone. Connor saw Joseph and rose to meet him.

"You came alone?" Connor asked immediately. "Is everyone all right?"

"Oh yes, Anna was going to come, but at the last minute
she felt she should stay with Marie and the others."

"Marie's the one who is ill?"

"Yes," Joseph replied. "I know what you are thinking, I
should take her to the hospital. But if we take her there, they'll
send her to an orphanage, and we'll never see her again. We
can't go there."

Noticing the fear rising in the boy, Connor realized that
Joseph was afraid of him—afraid of what he might do, now
that he knew of all the children. However, there was no ill-
intention in Connor's heart.

"You don't have to fear me, lad. I'm not going to force you
to do anything. I'm here to help you, not to bring more pain to
your life," Connor spoke in his own plea.

Joseph felt deeply assured by Connor's words. He exhaled
and felt an enormous weight lift off his heart. Not until that
moment did the boy realize how heavy the weight had been—
constricting his lungs, strangling his heart, bearing down on
his spirit. Anna had, of course. The words she had spoken on
their way back this morning rang all too true.

Joseph looked to Connor in a way that he had never looked to any other, as though just maybe this was a man he could look to as a father.

The cold wind gusted off the Charles River and through the narrow streets.

"Come on now. I think we should get off the streets and find someplace warm."

The boy and the man started walking.

"I don't have very many places within the city where I feel comfortable, so would you mind if we just went to my home and talked there?"

"Ummmmm," Joseph awkwardly shifted his weight from one side to another.

"I understand, lad. We'll go to an inn for a bite or some such place. You have no reason to trust me, but you will. No worries."

"No, I guess it's alright. We'll go to your house," agreed Joseph. He felt uncharacteristically comfortable. He just hoped his trust wasn't misplaced.

On the way to the house, JOSEPH and Connor passed through Quincy Market filled with foods that merchants were selling to the evening crowds. Stands and tables lined the sides of the massive brick and granite building. Behind them was Faneuil Hall and in the distance lay the harbor. The spiked sails of the ships dotted the shoals. Walking deeper into the market, Joseph was bombarded by the shouts of the bargain callers and the arguments of customers haggling. People weaved in and out of one another, their arms laden with parchment paper packages and full baskets. The smells of cooking meats and boiling soups filled the evening air.

"I never really come through here, you know," Joseph commented.

"Ah, I would imagine not. Hungry men seldom go to watch the king's banquet, now do they."

"Yes, exactly." replied Joseph. He was surprised that Connor understood. "Occasionally, one of us finds a bit or two on the streets, and we come here for a loaf of bread, but—" His voice tapered off. The pair walked by the tables of a local shopkeeper laid out heavy with foods. Joseph was transfixed—the smell of the bread and biscuits, wheels of cheese sliced into wedges then wrapped in thick waxy paper, cured hams with deep pink meat, coated in sweet glaze, being carved into hunks. Sausage links browned on open fires, liters of milk and juice, rows of flaky meat pies crimped around the edges, to seal in the torn chunks of tender meat in thick juices. Pots of soups and stews simmered over open flames, chicken and beef, creamy lamb broths with chunks of huge vegetables floating appetizingly, roasting chickens, duck and goose turned on spits brown and crisp dripping with golden juices and honey glazes.

Joseph had eaten one of the best meals of his life only yesterday, but the sight of the market was too much for him.

The children never came to the markets because they knew they could not have even a mouthful. They knew the merchants would give them nothing, not even the scraps, not even leftovers they could not sell. They would rather let the food rot than give it away for free to someone who needed it.

Joseph was thinking about all this as he and Connor passed through the maze of stands and the abundance of food that surrounded them on all sides. When they finally came to the middle of the long strip of tables, Connor stopped. "Here," he said placing a coin in Joseph's hand, "here's a bit. Pick out something that you want. You must be hungry."

Looking down at the tarnished coin in the middle of his open hand, Joseph was stunned. He could buy almost anything he wanted: a few wedges of cheese, few rounds of bread, two meat pies, five or six links of sausage, fresh apples. His stomach rumbled as he considered the near-infinite possibilities.

It was such a simple thing—to pull a coin from one's pocket and have the freedom to buy something, yet it was a joy the boy had seldom experienced. He didn't know what to buy. Joseph scanned the market. Meat was always a rare treat. However, bread was good as well—fresh bread. A big, round loaf would certainly fill all their stomachs.

Connor said nothing. He waited patiently while Joseph considered his options, then watched as Joseph walked to the meat stand and stopped in front of the huge, round, cured hams. The boy waited for the customer in front of him to get what she came for, then stepped forward, but he was ignored. The stocky man running the stand looked over him as if he were not there. A little bewildered that he had been overlooked when it was finally his turn, Joseph watched as the butcher took the order from the gentleman next to him. Joseph waited patiently and courteously. He brushed off the mistake and tried to decide how much ham to get. At last the gentleman left. But, again, the butcher did not attend to Joseph. He turned his back on the boy and did not turn around again until a lady approached the stand to buy some sausages. Connor watched all this play out only a few steps away. Joseph waited patiently, but Connor could not. He moved up to the stand and stood with the boy, and when the butcher approached Connor voiced his indignation. "This boy has been standing here waiting for you to help him," Connor said, not meanly but with obvious annoyance.

"This boy?" the butcher said, as though he thought Connor was making a joke about Joseph being a paying customer. "This boy can't afford anything here, look at him. I've seen him around here before with his friends—always begging, always looking for something for free. I have no scraps." Joseph looked beaten down, but said nothing. He did not want to have a confrontation with the man. He simply stood there quietly next to Connor, suddenly not hungry any more.

"He may not have been able to afford anything here, but I could, and now we'll take our business to another butcher," Connor said sharply, placing his hand on Joseph's shoulder and guiding him away from the stand back out into the market.

"I'm sorry, Joseph," Connor said from his heart, as if apologizing for his own fault.

"It's all right," Joseph said in a worn voice, as the excitement of the moment drained from him.

"What do you want to buy, Joseph? I'll go with you, we can do it together."

"It doesn't matter," Joseph said preferring to leave.

"Aye, it does. What do you want?" Connor asked, not wanting the boy to give up this treat, which had made him light up with possibility moments before.

"I just wanted something that we could all enjoy, something that would fill everyone's stomach. I was thinking of ham and bread, but now—I don't know."

"No, I think ham and bread are good. Come on, we'll go to another butcher, then to a baker. All right?"

Connor reached down and took Joseph by the hand, and the pair of them went to the next set of stands where they bought a pound of ham and two round loaves of fresh bread. Joseph offered the change to Connor.

"No, you keep that. There's nothing I need to buy with it. Perhaps you'll come across something you need, and now you'll have the means to get it. That always feels good to have that option sitting there in your pocket, doesn't it?"

Joseph cracked a little smile, though it was a worn one that was hard to keep convincingly upon his face.

The man and the boy walked on. Connor put his hand on the boy's shoulder and led him through the mob.

CHAPTER 18
SIMPLE ACTS

THE PAIR MOVED QUICKLY THROUGH THE STREETS. Joseph followed Connor along the paths until they made a turn into a small building off Hanover Street on the far side of the North End.

Connor led Joseph up the stairs to his small, third floor apartment and slid an old, brass key into the tarnished doorknob. The door was painted dark green. In the places where the paint was chipped, the white layers of the previous paint could be seen. With a click of metal locks, the door jerked, and Connor pushed it over a warped floorboard that apparently always gave him trouble.

"I've been meaning to fix that board, but the landlord won't let me make any improvements."

"But you want to fix it." Joseph replied, puzzled.

"I know. I've stopped trying to understand the people. I just work so I can get by, and then I come home to the one small place I've managed to make my own. It's my sanctuary," he finished, removing the key.

The old door opened into the small room. Joseph took a few steps into the room. The wooden floorboards creaked beneath his feet, but he hardly noticed he was so focused on

Connor's belongings. Joseph took another step in, passing by Connor who was watching him wander around like a stray cat exploring new surroundings.

"How long has it been?" asked Connor.

Joseph spun around with a questioning look.

"—since you've been in a proper home?" Connor clarified.

"When you took us to Clara's," replied Joseph. He moved toward the narrow window. He glanced through its clouded panes to the alleyway below. Connor had built a small wooden ledge off the window—a shallow tray box. It was covered with a mound of snow and ice after last night's storm. A few house sparrows were hopping around on the crust of the ice and trying to get to what lay below.

"And before that?"

Connor moved towards the window.

"The printing house," Joseph replied. "It was our home from time to time when the weather got bad."

"And now that it's gone, and winter is coming, things will be harder," Connor deduced.

"We've been holed up in a wagon for the last few seasons. It's better than nothing," Joseph confided, trying to sound optimistic rather than resigned. "This is the dream, of course."

Connor looked sideways at the boy.

"This—a small set of rooms somewhere. But no matter how hard we've tried, we can only get so far. This has always been out of reach."

"There's only so much one person can do to get to their dreams. A little help along the way is always needed." Connor moved towards the window. The sparrows scattered. He opened it, and a cold breeze flooded into the room. "In these hard times, so many people are focused on their own survival. Struggling day to day, we don't think about helpin' others." He grabbed a small sack from the pantry cupboard. "After all," his voice traveled across the room, "we barely have enough for ourselves let alone enough to help another." He returned from the pantry. "But sometimes it doesn't take as much as we might think."

He reached through the open window. With his bare hand he brushed away the snow and ice, clearing out the wooden tray. Then he poured out a pile of stale, broken-up bread crumbs from the small bag. He closed the window and backed away a bit. A few moments later, the sparrows returned. They dug through the stale bread, gobbling it up and flying away with their beaks full of fluff.

"Sometimes it takes very little effort—just one simple act— to change the life of another, and everyone needs help at some point. Sometimes, no matter how hard we try, there are some things we can't do for ourselves, and so we wait for some friend to see our plight and lend us a hand."

Both Connor and Joseph were silent in thought.

Joseph looked down at his feet awkwardly. His feet rested on a braided rug—tan with hints of brown.

"What are you thinking?" Connor asked trying to get into the boy's mind. "Can I get you anything?"

"No, I'm fine. Thank you," Joseph answered politely. "Will your family be home soon?" he asked timidly.

For a breath of a moment, Connor looked wounded—a twinge ran across his bearded face. He recovered quickly. "No. It'll just be us two."

"Oh," Joseph said. He felt sorry for the man. He could sense the weight of grief on him.

"Is your wife gone? I mean earlier you mentioned your family. I didn't know."

"I know what you mean," Connor cut in gently. "There's plenty of time to know my story. In this moment, what interests me is your life and what I can do to help improve it. I'm going to make some tea, and we can talk."

The two sat for a while sipping hot mugs of tea. Joseph did not know how to begin or how much he should say or how much he should hold back. This was a whole new situation. One part of him was telling him to let down his guard; another was telling him to play his cards close to the vest.

He put down his empty mug, careful not to make too much noise. The moment felt fragile or maybe it was they who were so. Joseph absent-mindedly flicked one of the ties to his canvas hand-wrappings sitting on his lap. Still looking at his lap, he began to speak.

"I'm only fifteen, but I've seen a great deal. Part of me wants to trust you."

"But another part of you is wary," Connor added. "That's normal, Joseph. I'm sure your life is a long tale of hardship. And I know it'll take time for me to prove that I'm not like those harsh people who came before me. Tell me as much or as little as you like. But, please, give me a chance to help you."

Joseph considered him. For the first time since they entered the house, Joseph met Connor's eyes directly. He held the gaze for a long, silent minute, then he began. "We were all left, you see—without warning or reason—just left behind. One moment I was living one life, and the next moment everything had changed. We've lived on hope our entire lives."

"I know how hard it is to live on hope. Sometimes it drives me mad—I have spent years hoping for impossible things, but things I can't live without," Connor offered.

Joseph gave a slight smile.

"We live on hope, and nothing comes, and all that hope turns bitter," his voice slowed. "I wasn't doing well before you came," he confessed. "There was another in our group, father to us all, he and Marie were very close. He has been missing since the night of the raid on the printing house, and after all these months I fear he is lost to us. I have tried to step up to fill the void—but haven't done that well. I was so afraid and so angry. For a short time, we had gotten our hopes up—high— that things would change and get better for us. And for a while they did, but it just seemed as though we were sliding back into the struggle. I didn't and still don't know what to do. Everyone has all these hopes now that we found the wagon, now that I told them things would get better. But I'm so afraid that I have just set us up for disappointment," Joseph finished desperately.

"Start at the beginning," Connor needed some context.

Joseph recounted the story of finding the wagon, his dream, and his idea to use the wagon to leave the city to start a new life.

"...and now I hate myself. I set them all up for a new life that isn't going to come. They all wait now—day after day— for something that isn't going to come. I can't bear to watch it any longer."

Connor let out a deep heavy sigh. "If you walk into my bedroom, you'll see a large, wooden trunk that I made many years ago. It's my hope chest. Over the years I filled it with little things that I found or bought or made that are meant to go towards a life that I don't even have yet. But I hope I one day will. You found a wagon and you made that wagon, your hope chest. You filled it to the brim with lil' bits and bobs that are meant for a life that you don't have yet but are reaching for. It wasn't wrong to hope," Connor repeated.

The tension hanging over Joseph cleared. "I never thought about it that way before." He smiled. He felt relieved. He had become so accustomed to figuring out life for himself; it was nice to have someone wiser he could look to.

"I don't know if I can give you all that you desire, but I can start by helping you have what you deserve. There are many things to talk about and many things that must be done. The first thing we must do is see to the basics: shelter, clothing, food, and health."

"You will help us then?" Joseph asked timidly.

"That's what I've wanted to do from the first time I saw you and Nicolaus chargin' down that street. Now, I don't have much. In fact, all that you see in this tiny set of rooms is about all I have, but it's something that I can share with you and your friends, if you trust me enough to accept it."

Joseph looked back up—directly into Connor's eyes— without blinking. "I want to trust you." His voice was strained.

"Joseph, I'm not taking control of your life or your friends' lives. I'm simply opening my door and my cupboards. You'll owe me nothing; you'll be independent—free to come and go as you please." Connor stared back, kindness reflected in his eyes. "I would never do anything to hurt you."

The verdict came in the form of a little nod from Joseph.

"All right then." Connor smiled, rising up from the table. "Let us pack up some things and go to the wagon. Everyone must be cold and hungry. You all can stay the night here, see if you feel comfortable, and we can take it from there. We'll go slow with the changes. Believe me, lad, I understand what it is to have wounds that make it hard to trust. This will all go at an even pace, and we'll see if we aren't kindred souls."

As Joseph wiped a few tears from his face, Connor opened his pantry cupboard and began filling a small, cloth sack.

"Can I help?" asked the boy.

"Aye, take that wool afghan from the chair in the living room and set it out near the door. Then go into the closet behind the front door."

"All right, what do you need?" Joseph said walking the length of the short room arriving at the front door with blanket in hand.

"On the topmost shelf, there should be four or five wool-knit sweaters. Pull 'em all down."

Stacked on the small shelf were five sweaters: a cream, a maroon, a brown, a deep green, and a navy blue. As Joseph reached up to pull them down he pulled the bottommost sweater in the stack and caught them all as the folded pile came tumbling out towards him—a woolen avalanche.

Connor moved from the pantry cupboard and set down the loaded cloth sack near the folded afghan and watched as Joseph juggled the mound of wool sweaters trying not to drop them.

Connor pulled an old pair of boots from the bottom of the closet along with two thick pairs of wool socks. He set these things down in his chair then made his way to his dresser in his bedroom that lay just beyond the main room.

"Put all those sweaters with the afghan, Joseph, then come in here." Connor walked into his bedroom. Joseph did as he was told then caught up with Connor, who was standing in front of a small, stout dresser. He was rifling through each drawer.

"Here, hold out your arms," Connor encouraged.

Into Joseph's outstretched arms, Connor laid a pair of heavy corduroy overalls, a pair of woolen long johns, and a navy blue flannel shirt. "So, I suppose you know this. Put on the long johns, then the flannel shirt, and then put on the overalls, and pull up the straps. Lastly, put these on." Connor handed Joseph two pairs of thick wool socks.

"The boots are probably a little big for you, but if you wear two pairs of thick socks, they should come close to fitting."

Joseph was dumbstruck—speechless. He stood there with his feet and hands bound in old canvas and burlap, two pairs of worn holey pants hanging off him, a thin piece of fraying rope for a belt and a cotton shirt under the canvas coat Anna made for him. He did not know what to say. He knew what he felt— gratitude—but he could not bring words to the depth of it.

The ragged boy stood there, his brown eyes set on the face of his savior.

"It's all right, lad. Go on now" Connor prodded. He began walking out of the bedroom. He turned back. "And before you start feeling guilty, by tomorrow morning all your friends will have fresh clothes upon their backs. So, don't start thinking you can't take these. There's water in the pitcher and basin." He nodded toward the washstand situated beside the dresser. "A proper bath will have to wait. I'm sure you want to get back to everyone waiting in the wagon." He gave a smile and closed the door so Joseph could have his privacy.

The door shut, and Joseph found himself alone in the small cozy room. A narrow bed covered by a worn, blue quilt stood in the center of the room. Situated against the wall beside the head of the bed was the trunk of which Connor had spoken. The wide, floor broads moaned as Joseph shifted his weight—shuffling toward the bed where he laid down the new clothes.

Joseph began to loosen the bindings on his feet. He felt out of his element, much like he did at the Scolfields. The ties holding the layers of cotton canvas and burlap were fastened tightly into double, even triple knots. He usually did not take them off until spring. He reached into a pouch Anna had sewed into his jacket—a pouch right over his stomach—and pulled out his pocket knife and cut the knots of his bindings. Slowly, Joseph peeled off layer after layer of the worn clothing, ridding himself of the rags he had worn throughout the hard winter of his life.

His bare feet stretched out upon the cool, wooden floor. He removed his few belongings that filled the patched pockets of his pants and set the precious items down near the pile of new clothes: the coins Connor had given him in the market, a polished purple and pearl-white mussel shell that Anna had found on the docks and given to him, a braided rope bracelet that Davy had made for him, and a little boat he had begun carving for Asa a few weeks earlier.

Joseph peeled off the muddy, worn pants and stained shirt and threw them on the heap of dirty bindings. He bellied up to the basin, picked up the heavy clay pitcher, and filled the deep bowl with water. Turning around to face the bed, Joseph's eye was caught by a flash of color on the wall. Mounted directly across from him was a small mirror only big enough for him to see his face. The person staring at him was unrecognizable. His cheeks had melted away; his brown eyes were lost in shadow; his lips had cuts; his nose was chapped; his hair was grown out thick, unbrushed, and tangled as it ran down the back of his neck, along the sides of his face, and into his eyes.

Joseph was startled by the reflection staring back at him from the mirror. Over the years he had caught faint reflections of himself in shop windows, but never before had he stood bare in the light and seen himself. He did not know himself. He was all teeth and eyes, gray skin and bones. He reached out toward the mirror as if to see if the specter in the looking glass were real or an illusion. What had these years done to him? Where had he gone? He hardly felt human, as gritty and malnourished as he was. But looking into his fragile reflection he also never felt more human—more vulnerable.

He reached out a trembling hand to the bar of waxy soap. He dipped his hands into the room temperature water. The warmth of it went through his skin and into his bones. Joseph had not realized how tense with cold he was until the warmth entered him, and his chest and muscles unclenched.

Joseph did not know exactly where to begin.

He looked closely at his hands and arms and chest and feet, now that they were uncovered from the rags and bindings, and saw dirt, mud, and patches of dried blood covering his skin. He picked up the thick, soft cotton rag that lay on the edge of the stand, placed it in the basin, and let it soak in the water. He rubbed the bar of pale yellow soap across its surface, rung it out, and cleaned off the caked on dirt.

The water stung his skin. Underneath the filth, his skin looked scaly, red, and raw. The cold, dry, winter air had sucked the moisture from his body causing it to become tender.

Joseph found that without the bindings to pad his feet, he could barely use them. Looking down at his bruised, red body, he could see his ribs sticking out as they spanned his chest. His bony arms and his knees looked like small, worn knots in the thin sticks that were his legs.

Joseph bent low and wet his head several times, watching as the basin filled with dirty water. He wrapped the towel around his head until his hair was just damp then tried to pat it down. The stubborn cowlick sprang back up. He saw a wide-toothed comb sitting on the dresser. His hand reached for it then stopped just short of it.

"Connor?" Joseph called from behind the door.

"Aye," Connor answered back from the sitting room.

"Can I use this comb here on the dresser?"

"Of course," Connor answered back in a tone that let the young boy know that he need not have asked permission.

Taking the wooden comb, to his hair Joseph tried to run it through, but it was anything but smooth. Again and again, Joseph made passes through his grown-out hair each time getting a little further down the length of it. Finally, he was able to make a complete pass and run the comb from the top of his head to the bottom tips of his hair. Several large clumps of hair gathered between the wide teeth of the comb when all was said and done.

Finished washing, he looked at himself once more in the mirror—still stunned by the stranger. His hair neatly combed, the ghost staring back looked slightly better than he did a few moments ago. Before turning away from the mirror, Joseph moved in closer—so close that his breath fogged the glass. He took in a deep breath and stared right into his own chestnut brown eyes. He remembered the last time he had looked into a proper mirror. It had been in his parent's bedroom just before he had been abandoned. The wear that he now saw on himself had not been there before. The eyes that stared back at him looked so very tired. In that moment, he felt himself a victim. Each day he had given his focus to caring for the wounds of the others and gave himself no chance to dwell on his own. However, in that moment the full weight of his past came to bear on him. He turned away, about to break down, when his eyes fell upon the pile of clothes Connor had given him. Strengthened by the new care present in his life, he took a deep breath and pushed onward.

Perched at the end of the bed, Joseph felt the cushion of the linens beneath him, which were soft against his bare skin. The bed sank in slightly as he sat down, cradling him. Joseph exhaled. He felt pulled to lie down, curl up, and drift to sleep. It took everything he had to fight the urge.

He grabbed a thick pair of hand knitted socks from the pile and slipped them onto his feet one at a time. He felt the knit of the wool pull as he slipped in his foot. He put on the second pair and stood up. He slid on the hardwood floors as if they were icy. Gaining his footing, he stepped into his long johns, one leg at a time. The suit stretched in one fluid piece from his ankles to his neck and down his arms to his wrists. Joseph did up one button at a time, he reached the final one at the base of his neck. Never did anything feel so good as the woolen suit. It felt as though soft bandages had been wrapped around his raw skin. A smile moved across his face; he imagined how Asa must feel when he hugged his velvet blanket.

Next, Joseph picked up the soft flannel shirt that lay folded on the bed covers. This was the most beautiful shirt he had ever seen. Like all the other clothes, it was huge on him. To

Joseph, wearing the soft flannel felt like being home—it was a warm embrace, a blanket-like tunic that he could take with him wherever he went.

Finally, Joseph took up the pair of corduroy overalls. One leg at a time, he climbed into them, pulled them over his shoulders and latched the buttons

Overalls buckled, flannel shirt buttoned, the boy emerged from the room unrecognizable. Connor gave a warm laugh when Joseph came into view. The boy was trying clumsily to roll up the overly-long sleeves of the shirt but could not get the cuffs to stay.

"Here," Connor said moving toward Joseph. He rolled back the long sleeves easily, making two thick folds until at last he saw Joseph's fingers. "All right," he said once everything was tucked, folded, and adjusted, "are you ready?"

"One moment," Joseph said going back into the bedroom where he picked up his few possessions and dropped them into the deep pockets of the overalls. "I couldn't pick them up until the sleeves were fixed," he explained. "I'm ready now."

Joseph stood there rubbing his hands over his thickly covered belly. With all the dense layers Joseph actually looked like he had some weight on him, though Connor knew it was just a woolen illusion.

Connor stood back. "Well, there was a boy underneath all that."

"I've never felt this good in my life." Joseph held the long ends of his pant cuffs up as he scooted across the floorboards.

"I'm glad," Connor said wholeheartedly.

"I still have to put on those boots you gave me," Joseph said as they moved toward the front door.

"All right," Connor said kindly as he began to gather bags. "You do that while I get one more thing."

Connor went to the pantry cupboard.

Joseph sat down, unlaced the boots, pointed his thickly padded toes into the mouth of the shoe and slid them in. With the double pair of wool socks, Joseph's foot did indeed fit the boots that were probably about two sizes too big. One by one, he drew the laces through the holes, crisscrossing them until he reached the very top where he pulled the laces tightly as he could and wrapped them around the tall leather tops.

He rose from the floor and cuffed his pants. He walked across the room. He tripped over himself a bit. He had not worn proper shoes since he was Asa's age. As he got his stride Joseph felt a strange sensation come over him—he felt like a young man, not a child. Fresh clothes, combed hair—he felt taller, stronger. He felt pride.

As Joseph came back into the main room, Connor was standing there holding a beautiful mossy green corduroy jacket for the boy.

"Here, lad, one final layer to keep you warm."

Joseph turned around and let Connor slip the jacket onto him. Then Connor came around to the front, adjusted the collar and sleeves, and buttoned up the jacket around Joseph. As Connor did this a swell of emotion filled Joseph and his eyes teared up. Joseph looked up at Connor. Only moments ago he felt like a man, but now the boy was back—the boy so hungry for care.

Connor saw all this on Joseph's face. A simple act of care touched the boy so deeply, Connor's heart near broke. Connor also knew there were ten more children waiting on them, and he knew he needed to carry on.

"You look much better," Connor commented. "Here take these, and it's done."

Connor placed a pair of dark gray mittens on Joseph hands. The wool of the mittens was just as thick as it had been on the sweaters. "And finally, this." Connor topped the boy off with a knitted, gray hat, rolling up the edge until he could see his brown eyes showing from underneath the heavy layers.

The boy shook his head. He looked up into Connor's eyes. "This is too much. The others—" Joseph said in a guilty voice, as if he were doing something wrong, taking more than he should have.

Connor cut in, "The others will get their own clothes. Over the next few days, we'll work on getting everyone together a decent outfit of clothes." Connor said with a hint of firmness, then a bit of laughter, but finishing in a very sincere and serious voice, "You need these things, Joseph, I want you to have them, and the others would want you to have them too—I feel sure of it.

"It'll be all right," Connor assured him. "You don't have to give up things so that no one goes cold. No one need do without any more. There'll be enough for all."

CHAPTER 19
BEYOND THE DARK HORIZON

JOSEPH AND CONNOR WALKED SIDE-BY-SIDE down the darkened streets. Connor carried two full sacks while Joseph walked with an afghan folded under his arm. It was night. As always, Joseph found the cold darkness intimidating. He walked quickly, keeping up with Connor and huddling alongside him. After the sunset, the city always seemed to sink lower. The most depraved of the population seemed to slink out into the night. Connor walked with his eyes straight ahead, his head up looking forward with determination. Joseph looked at Connor and saw strength and goodness emanating from him, as if his heart was giving off a shield to keep the beasts at bay.

"Sometimes, I feel like I'm going mad," confessed Joseph awkwardly.

Connor turned to Joseph, wordlessly asking the boy what he meant.

"What I mean is, have you ever seen something that made you feel that you were going insane—something you wish you could scrub from your mind because it's so vile, that you feel it pushing the limits of your sanity?"

Connor began to understand.

"Over my years in the alleys, I've seen things. And no matter how fast I was able to close my eyes—no matter how much I try to block it from my thoughts—it stays with me."

"You're not alone, Joseph. I've seen such things. I can't believe or even fathom some of the things I've seen the people do, mostly because I could never conceive of doing those things myself. And you're right: it is senseless, it's insanity, it's empty, and perverted. All I know for sure is life is not supposed to be this way. That's a feeling that has stayed with me every single day of my life. Life is not supposed to be this way. Life can be good, peaceful, and wholesome," assured Connor.

"I suppose, I'm just hoping that, when—if, I'm able to make a fresh start, these images will be wiped clean. I want to leave all the bad behind at the city limits. I don't want to carry them with me throughout my new life. I would give anything for them never to have happened in the first place." Joseph's tone was full of pain and, strangely, a touch of shame, as though having witnessed the disturbing moments and holding the memory of them in his mind made him feel as though he were a part of the evil that took place.

"We all have things we want to wipe away, lad. Believe me, I have my fair share. I can't tell you that all the horrible images won't revisit you in the night. But some of the memories fade. Right now, you simply have no distance between you and your time here—on the streets. As new experiences and joys come into your life, they'll create distance between your memory and the hard times. Until one day, you realize the pain of the past no longer holds sway over you—you've moved beyond it and your life has become more."

"Has it happened for you?" asked Joseph.

"No," replied Connor. "But then again, I haven't let it. What I want lies in the past, and so I cling to my past. People are always keen on telling ya how to live. Some would say my way isn't healthy, but I hold no illusions about myself. I know what most would tell me I should do. Thing is, I think they're wrong. But you aren't like me, lad. You have no love lost for the hard times you've known on these streets. When the good comes—and it will come—the distance will build easily, and the ill thoughts will fade."

"The good has already begun to come," added Joseph.

The pair rounded the corner, walking the narrow roads as they headed for the outskirts.

* * * * *

THE CITY WAS BEHIND THEM. The glow of the street lights dimmed, and there was peace. The crickets and the sound of the wind sweeping across the land rose as they left behind the stone walls and came into the open lots. The moon's light had shown their path to the wagon. The luminous crescent hung low on the horizon before them and in the distance, Joseph could see the shadow silhouette of their small home.

"There it is," he said pointing to an arched box shape in the distance. "Can you see it?"

Connor's weary eyes squinted through the night. He could see the rising arch of the top of the wagon, though, if Joseph had not pointed it out, he would have thought it nothing more than a large boulder or one of the many mounds of dumped trash that littered the outskirts, which is what most people from the city must have thought it was.

"Aye, I see it, but there are no lights, no fire."

"Fire makes people curious, and the last thing we want are visitors. Sometimes it's hurtful to be ignored, and other times it's a blessing."

"I know exactly what you mean," he quickly added. "But how do you all keep warm?"

"Staying warm, staying dry—these things make life a nightmare. We do what we can. Again, having the wagon has changed everything. It gets us up off the wet ground and holds back the wind in the winter. When Anna found the wagon, she also found a huge old sail. It makes for a great blanket. It's actually pretty warm in the wagon.

"Of course, before we found the wagon, we'd go to the printing house when the foul weather came. It was always a risk going there because we chanced being caught. Sometimes we'd have to stay away from it for months at a time because the police kept driving us out. They'd chase us, and, if one of us fell behind, they'd put us in an orphanage, a reform or even a prison for those of us who are older. We heard of children being taken to prison after being found in abandoned buildings. I don't know what the police would say the crime was…."

Connor listened as Joseph told him what life had been for the children. The wagon was coming closer as they walked, but there was still time to talk and time for Connor to tell Joseph how sorry he was that they had to lose the printing house.

"As a carpenter, I'd much rather build houses than tear them down. I never thought I'd be ripping down these brilliant, old buildings, but it was the only work I could find in the city. I try to do what I can to make up for the loss. Every day, I saw strong wood, made from the sacrifice of ancient trees, torn down to make way for granite and brick. I watched the old houses that generations of carpenters designed, maintained, and detailed with the knowledge handed down to them by the generations before. The wood was hauled to the dumps, fed to factory fires, or sold by the pound as scrap. I couldn't stand it. So I started gathering up the scraps and sent them elsewhere to be made into something new."

"You mean like sending them out to Clara and Jim?"

"Exactly," Connor nodded. "I gather up all the wood and stone and have it shipped to people on the outskirts who are building their homes. Aye, some of the wood is unsalvageable, but most of it can be kept intact and reused.

"You should know," Connor added, "all the pieces that could be reused from the printing house were gathered up, and they'll make homes for those who will appreciate that home every day. The printing house was neglected here in the city, and it fell into ruin. But it will rise as something that will again be filled with life."

Joseph looked at Connor through the dark. "Really? The printing house is going to become someone's home?"

"That's the way of things, you know."

"What's the way?" Joseph asked, at a loss.

"Everything that is torn into pieces or destroyed is put back together as something new. Sometimes, when something is torn apart, we can't see that it'll ever be put back together, because all we can see is the devastation. But there are no ends—we're always moving, always growing, always changing, always starting over."

Connor took Joseph by the shoulder, and they walked on together. Two devastated hearts waiting to be put back together—fresh and new.

*   *   *   *   *

ITH HER DEEP HOOD DRAWN UP OVER HER HEAD, Emma lay against Nicolaus, looking at the wagon's backdoor waiting for some sign that Joseph was coming. While next to her, Asa was snuggling with his small blanket that had been bound off on the raw edges, with his eyes likewise on the door. Both of the small children were losing their battle with sleepiness as their heavy eyelids drooped down.

Everyone was bundled and sitting up against the sides of the wagon's bed, and, every now and then, someone would whisper a question or a speculation about where Joseph and Connor might be. A solitary short candle burned as its wax pooled at the bottom of a short tin can the children had found to place it in. By the candlelight, Anna, Rachel, Abbey, and Beth continued to work on a quilt they had been piecing together. Davy and Ben sat next to each other talking in whispers about the printing house.

"What if something happened to him?" remarked Davy for the fourth time this evening.

"Nothing has happened to him, he'll be—" Anna stopped quite suddenly.

They heard the sound of shifting stones beneath boots outside. Someone was approaching. None of the children wore shoes, so the children were afraid when they heard the noise. A flood of what ifs raced through Anna's mind: *What if it was the police? What if it was vagabonds from the city come to force them out of the wagon? What if they had to leave before Joseph was back?*

Her heart stopped dead. Thankfully, Joseph's voice sounded, allowing her to take a breath.

"Anna," he gently called as they approached the wagon, "it's me. I've come back and Connor's with me."

The wagon was a flutter of noises, whispers, and the rustling of canvas. All the children were now wide awake. Anna began untying the back flap. At that moment, Connor pulled out a small lantern from his sack. Joseph swung around about to protest. "I know that light brings unwanted attention, but it'll be all right," Connor forestalled him. "We'll light it tonight, and I'll stay with you all to ensure no one comes."

Joseph nodded hesitantly and watched as Connor struck a match, slid it up the glass, and lit the wick within. The light radiated from the small lantern. It was not a great amount of light, but after being in total darkness, it seemed very bright. As the light came on, Anna, who was still untying the flaps stopped. "Joseph?" She held the same instinctive concerns that Joseph had about the light. "It's all right, Anna," Joseph answered back. The light passed through the heavy canvas and brought a soft glow to the inside of the wagon. Anna pulled back the flaps, illuminating the figures of the children who sat upright, still as stone, waiting to see who was coming.

Connor held the lantern in front of Joseph. With only a few more steps, he saw ten young, innocent faces, peering out from the wagon's open flaps. They looked at him with curiosity.

"This is Anna, and Nicolaus, who you already know. Then we have Rachel, Beth and Abbey, Ben and Davy, Emma and Asa and, of course, Marie," Joseph said, introducing his family.

Connor's eyes moved from Anna and Nicolaus to Rachel. Her long mousy brown hair was covered beneath a shawl that she had drawn up around her long face. Rachel's brown eyes narrowed with apprehension. Then his gaze moved to the two girls next to her. Beth and Abbey could have been sisters and were very near in age. Beth had black hair that came down to her shoulders, unguarded eyes, and a round, kind face that was worn but not as worn as the older children. Connor could tell that she had not been on the streets for long. Abbey was a little paler and leaner than Beth. Her curly, honey-colored hair was straggly but long, and her big brown eyes examined him in return. Next his eyes passed over two young boys sitting side by side, Ben and Davy, then the little faces of Emma and Asa, and finally, his gaze came to rest on Marie. She was ghostly pale. She had an innocent look to her, though a wise one of heartfelt genuineness. She had spirit about her, even in her diminished state.

All the children stared, at first the faces looking back at him were shocked and afraid. Then one at a time, faint smiles began to rise. Behind the wear and sickness, Connor could see the brightness peeking out from within their still-intact spirits.

The locked, silent stare was broken, however, as Ben's voice echoed out, "Look at Joseph! Look, he has new clothes."

The children had been staring so intently at Connor that they had not realized the change in Joseph until this moment. "Yeah, and he's all clean," Davy added, as the shocking events of this night went deeper.

Everyone's gaze turned to Joseph, and they saw him dressed in the clothes Connor had given him, without a speck of dirt upon his face.

"He's got boots," Asa exclaimed as he stood up in the bed of the wagon to get a better angle on Joseph's whole outfit.

"We've brought some for you all, as well," Joseph said quickly. He handed Nicolaus the sack Connor had packed. A heap of sweaters, hats, and scarves were pulled out. The wagon fell silent again as everyone stared at the pile of perfect clothing laid out in front of them. Connor stepped forward to the wagon, finding his voice at last.

"Aye, and we brought some supplies to keep here at the wagon, as well as a meal for tonight."

"He's got food!" Davy exclaimed. "Is that what's in that sack? Food?" He peered down at the bag in Connor's hand.

"Davy!" Anna scolded. She shuffled the little ones down toward the back of the wagon to make room for Joseph and Connor. "All right, let's all of us get inside before we freeze."

Connor placed his hands on the bed of the wagon and hoisted himself up. Suddenly a look came over him. He was half entranced and half sickened. He did not say anything. He just sat in a daze in the place where he had pulled himself. His eyes passed around the wagon, not so much staring at the children but, far off into his own thoughts, pulling away from that present moment into another place. Then, as suddenly as it happened, the strange moment seemed to pass, and Connor came back to them. The younger children had not sensed the shift in the man's demeanor, but the older children—Joseph, Anna, Rachel, Nicolaus, and Marie—saw a look of distress cross his face and did not know what to make of it.

Joseph drew the canvas flaps behind him securely, then turned back to the children.

Joseph told the others the story of how he met Connor and that the man could be trusted. It was always a big deal for another person to be brought into the circle, especially an adult.

At first the others had been uncomfortable with Connor in the wagon. Every adult had left them with scars. But as they spoke with the kind man, they all felt cradled for the first time in their lives. They felt protected. Connor pushed back all the threats pushing in on them, and in doing so, gave them a gift that was more precious to them than the food or the clothes. He gave them peace.

A calm passed over the wagon. Joseph felt a comradery with Connor. For the first time in a long time, he felt he had an ally. And Joseph sensed that Connor too was happy at the chance to care for those who truly appreciated what he had to give.

"I know you don't have a reason to trust me. You don't know me, and you don't have a reason to trust my good intentions. But I'd like to bring you all to my home. It's small, as Joseph can tell you, but there would be enough room. Joseph has told me what finding the wagon meant to you, and he told me that you all are making preparation for a journey. I know that you don't know me all that well and that you don't have many reasons to trust me. All the same, I'd like to bring you to my home tonight. I think ya all could use a good wash-up and a warm place to rest. If, come morning, you don't fancy my home, you can leave any time you wish. You are free to come and go as you please."

All the children looked to Joseph.

Joseph gave a little nod.

"What about the wagon? We can't just leave it," Ben said, sadly.

"Of course we can't," Connor answered. "My thought was, if you come, and you find that you are comfortable in my little home, I can get this old wagon travel-worthy again. We can bring it to the Scolfield's farm where it'll be kept safe and sound. I'd never ask you to leave the wagon behind. And you can bring all your belongings with you," he added warmly.

Joseph, Anna, Nicolaus, and Rachel were in agreement that they should go. Even Marie gave a little nod.

"All right then," Connor agreed, finalizing the plans. "Before we make this journey, you all should have a bit of food. The real meal will come when we get home, but Joseph has bought a little something for you all to nibble on now."

All eyes turned to Joseph and then to the food. "You bought something?" Anna said in a whisper of disbelief.

"Yeah, Connor gave me a few bits, and I bought some ham for us," Joseph answered back as he unwrapped the paper bundle holding the thick slice of cured ham. He cut it into pieces and passed it out.

"Remember, it's just to tide you over until we get back to my house," Connor assured, watching as the delicious, salty ham was gone in two seconds flat. "All right then, we've got something in our bellies, we've got a plan for the wagon, we've got everyone packed up, are we ready then?" He smiled, his brown beard glinting in the lamplight.

Everyone shuffled out. Anna and Joseph helped the little ones down from the wagon. Marie was the last one out. She slid over to the edge of the wagon and waited for someone to help her. Joseph moved quickly over to her.

"No, no," Connor said, beating Joseph to her. "How about you and I make the path together, love?" The man said, extending a gentle hand to greet her formally.

"All right," Marie consented, stepping down onto the sodden ground, her legs wobbly beneath her.

"It's all right, love. Lean on me now. We'll take it slow and steady."

Joseph watched as Connor took Marie under wing. A momentary look of relief passed over him.

CHAPTER 20
THE HEALING

"**D**AVY, BE A GOOD LAD. Would you reach into my coat pocket, take out the key, and open the front door?" Connor asked. His hands were full after carrying a tired Marie up the stairs.

Davy reached into Connor's deep pocket, slid the key into the thin slot of the iron door handle, and turned it. There was a hollow click as the bolt of the lock drew back. He turned the tarnished knob and opened the door—pulling back the curtain to reveal another life.

He moved aside for Connor to pass by with Marie. The rest of the children paused for a moment. They all looked rather lost.

"Can we go in?" asked Asa, the tiny boy voiced what all the children were thinking.

"Of course, ya can. Come on now, get in out of the cold," answered Connor. Trying to get them across the threshold was like coaxing stray cats in from the cold.

They came in slowly huddled together in a tight group.

"Hold on to me for a moment, love," Connor lowered Marie to the floor in front of the hearth. "It'll only take two shakes of a lamb's tail to bring these old coals back to life."

"Thank you," offered Marie.

He turned back to look at the others. All of them were still grouped together, as if afraid to touch anything.

"There now," he said to them in an assuring voice. "There ain't no wolves lurking. You're all safe and sound here." He moved over to Abbey, Asa, Emma, and Ben and knelt down. "There's only one thing I insist upon in my house." His voice was stern, but he spoke with a grin. Unable to recognize Connor's joshing tone, the little ones looked rather afraid for a moment. "You must clean your faces, change into fresh clothes, cuddle up with a thick blanket, and fill your belly. That," he announced, "is the order of the day—or evening as it were. Tomorrow is Sunday. No working, so we'll have the whole day to get things shipshape."

The fears seemed to fall away from the children. The tension in their small, tired faces eased into the warmth of Connor's care.

"Here now," he said lighting a lantern, "let's bring a little light to this dark room, so you can all see my humble set-a-rooms."

Light shone through the glass globe of the lantern, and a new world came forward from the darkness.

Joseph stood back near the front door and watched as the others took in the new surroundings. He had the faintest smile on his face. Connor met his stare and smiled back, giving the boy a little nod.

To some people in the city, it would appear, that Connor had very little. His home was small, and the furnishings were poor. The mismatched room was composed of whatever furniture could be found at the secondhand shop. There was an old, dusty braided rug laid down over the wooden floor, and a few handwoven blankets piled near a worn armchair. No paintings hung on the wall, no expensive knickknacks—simply some carvings that he had done himself.

The drapes that hung from the solitary window were not the heavy tapestry drapes that decorated most homes. They were tan cotton with a slight layer of dust along the ruffle at the top. Most of the furniture was made of old, battered wood, undoubtedly crafted by Connor himself. There was an end table and a tall, narrow bookshelf with a few dozen books, many of which looked older than the city itself.

The tight pack of children thinned. Each moved forward to acquaint themselves with a different nook and cranny in the room. Asa and Emma hoisted themselves into Connor's arm chair and stared—transfixed—at the fire. Beth sat down beside Marie on the floor, wanting a hug and a bit of warmth from the fire. She curled up on the rug like a cat—content and sleepy.

Davy and Ben walked the outer edge of the room and stopped at a cupboard.

"Boys, don't go pokin'," Anna followed the pair bringing a candle with her. Too late—Davy had already opened the cupboard doors, and the candle illuminated a pantry full of food. Ben and Davy stared at a sugary cake wrapped up in thin cheesecloth on a lower shelf. Curious as to what was going on, Nicolaus, Rachel, and Abbey came over.

Davy reached out a finger toward the sweet treat.

"Davy!" scolded Anna.

"What?" Davy snatched away his finger indignantly.

"It's all right," Connor reassured them. He had moved up behind them without hardly a sound. "I was given it for my birthday. I think Davy's right. A treat is indeed in order, but before we start our feastin' we need to wash up.

"I think I have some milk left from this morning there by the windowsill. It's the coldest place in the room," he explained. "Joseph, why don't you pour out some mugs to tide everyone over while I start some water on the hearth for the baths."

Joseph quickly started passing out mugs.

"Anna, if I showed you where and how to fill the tub, do you think you could see to it that everyone is washed and all tidy?"

"Yes," she happily replied.

"Good then. Nicholas, Davy, why don't you help Anna fetch water."

The boys nodded, both of them with thick mustaches of cream along their top lip. Anna laughed.

"Once you're squared away, I think I'll have to leave you all for just a little while. I need to dash down to the market. There are one or two little shops that stay open a bit later. We need some food and provisions and whatnot. Rachel, would you be willing to come with me to help?"

"Of course," she said, a bit taken aback that she was chosen.

"All right then, Anna, the boys will help you fill the tub. I'll show you where the cloths are, and we'll be on our way."

Connor pulled a wooden tub from a linen closet.

"Looks like a giant bucket," Davy exclaimed.

"Well, lad, that's what it is—a bucket big enough for you to sit in and be washed."

"Here," Connor moved into his small bedroom, "I'll lay out some of my shirts, and you can start giving the little ones baths. They can put on these shirts for nightgowns for the time being. Keep anything that's special to you of your old clothes and make a sack of all those clothes that are beyond saving, and we'll throw 'em away."

Connor walked into a small nook directly off his bedroom that was no more than the size of a small closet. He put the tub down. Everyone gathered around.

"We go from youngest to eldest here. Close the door to the bedroom, so everyone has their privacy."

"You heard him," Anna echoed with a smile. "I'll be careful not to let the water heat up too hot," Anna assured Connor.

"You're already ahead of me, dear girl. And be careful not to fill the buckets too high, or you'll have trouble carrying them from the hearth to the tub. Don't worry if you spill a little just mop it up with a towel. Here," Connor said as he laid down a towel around the tub, then handed Anna two more.

Connor reached into the wooden cabinet beneath the basin stand in his bedroom. "Here's a new bar of soap and some cloths, a comb, and a pair of scissors, if any of you decide you want to trim up your hair. If you don't feel comfortable cutting everyone's hair, I'll be happy to do it later.

"Unfortunately, those towels are the only ones I have. It has just been me after all. More will be needed—more of everything will be needed," he added, talking more to himself than her. "We'll have to make do for now."

"We're good at making do," Anna answered with a little smile.

"I'd imagine you are," his bearded face beamed.

Anna and Connor looked at each other. A swell of gratitude settled over them.

Joseph watched from the living room as Anna and Connor shared that moment together. In that moment, Joseph felt a weight lift. To his relief, he felt the happiness of those he loved was no longer solely resting upon his shoulders.

"Well then, I'll leave you all to it. We'll be back very soon." Connor announced. Joseph and Nicolaus busily filled the tub. "You all wash away that harsh winter," he said with a smile. But before turning to leave, another thought came to him. "No, wait here," he said as he walked into the bedroom and opened the small cupboard beneath the basin again. He pulled out a round tin and handed it to Anna.

"Put some of this in the water."

Anna opened the tin. It was filled with little, powdery flakes that she had never seen before.

"What's it for?" she asked, bewildered.

"It's a surprise." Connor smiled as he and Rachel slipped out the door, leaving Anna holding the tin and wondering about its contents.

"All right then," Anna turned away from the front door, which Connor and Rachel had just closed behind them, and looked back at the children who were still looking at the door. "Why doesn't Emma go first, then Asa." The young girl came bounding into Anna's outstretch arms. Anna carried Emma into the tiny bedroom, closed the door, and then moved into the small nook with the steaming tub.

Emma had not had a proper bath since she was a toddler, before she had been abandoned—none of the children had in fact. Anna prepared to slide Emma into the warm water of the tub. She reached her hand into the steaming water before she let Emma step in. "I think that's just right. We wouldn't want you to burn yourself, would we?"

Emma shook her head, her limp hair swinging side to side.

"Wait, I almost forgot," Anna took out the tin Connor had left with her. She poured a handful of the powdery flakes into the water, watched, and waited, but nothing happened.

"Well," she said rather anticlimactically, "no matter. Climb in now." She helped Emma into the tub, and Emma immediately began splashing the water. "Hey now!" Anna exclaimed trying to calm the little one. Then, she saw that Emma's splashing had caused a reaction in the flakes from the tin. Bubbles began to build, topping off the tub with great mounds of fluff floating atop the warm water.

Anna laughed out loud as Emma giggled and reached for the white, bubbly mounds. Emma splashed again, building the mounds of frothy snow. Anna shielded herself from the flying water. The others heard the commotion from the living room. Ben, Davy, Beth, and Abbey huddled outside the bedroom door listening to the laughter.

Afloat in a sea of bubbles, Emma laughed and played. Anna laughed along with her—her heart full of joy—without a care in the world.

CHAPTER 21
A GROWING HOUSEHOLD

ACHEL AND CONNOR WALKED DOWN HANOVER STREET and popped out at the market at Faneuil Hall.

"It'll be hard to get everything we need with the little coin that I have," Connor confessed to Rachel. "Clothes are very expensive, and the ones we'll find in the shops just aren't very practical for workin' and playin'. The fashionable clothes are made to be seen and not used. If we had the time, I wouldn't buy clothes at all. I'd buy material and yarn and make clothes for you all."

"We can sew you know," Rachel spoke up. "I mean, the stitching isn't nothing too fancy, and the patterns aren't fashionable, but they're good sturdy clothes."

Connor stopped. He had a change in plans. He stopped looking around the market and looked directly at Rachel. "Hold on just a minute. Now we got to be smart about this. All right then, so, if we bought what you needed—material, thread, needles and whatnot—then you all could make the clothing?"

"Oh, yes," Rachel answered without reservation. "Anna's very good at making the patterns." Rachel told Connor of Anna's efforts to make the children new clothes from the canvas sail and remnant fabrics they found.

They passed through the carts and wove in and out of the crowd making a path to the nearest fabric shop.

In the storefront's window there were many signs posted. **"1/2 Price Sale"** and **"Shop to Close"**.

"Well, a fabric sale means good news for us," Rachel said staring at the signs before they walked through the threshold of the shop door.

Connor walked deeper into the store. It took him a moment to realize that Rachel was no longer behind him.

Rachel had hardly walked through the door when a group of young ladies had started whispering and giggling. Rachel fidgeted with her ragged clothes, as if running her hands over them would somehow make them clean and new.

"Is that the new fashion?" one of the girls asked in a mocking tone. The puffed up looking girl was apparently the leader of the pack. She was dressed in a lavender, silken dress with lacy sleeves. "Very becoming," she added with a laugh.

Connor walked back over to Rachel who stood there looking very wounded. "Now then," Connor said very loudly, "don't you mind the peacocks. They may look pretty, but they haven't got a thought in their tiny, little heads." Connor took Rachel by the arm and led her into the back of the store. A little smile crossed her face when she saw the look of indignation on the girls' faces upon hearing Connor's defense.

"Never you mind those girls," he assured her. "Characters like that are just ornaments, as my mum would say. They may look pretty, but they have no real grit to 'em. You have a strength that other children your age don't, and you have a unique story."

"What good is our story going to do us? Rachel scoffed.

"Right now, you may hate that your life wasn't more

ordinary, but in time, you'll discover that all the hardships you've faced have left you with a singular soul."

Rachel nodded her head and blinked away the tears.

"There, there, lass." He patted her. "You still feel up to shopping? I'm counting on you to tell me what the others will like."

The pair made their way to the back of the shop. They walked past many empty tables and racks. Each section, once full of thick bolts of cloth, was cleared away by shoppers looking for a bargain.

Bypassing all the silks and linens, the two walked over to the sections of the heaviest fabric, looking for those cloths that would hold up the best to wear—wool, canvas, twill, and corduroy. There were a dozen or so bolts left, as well as piles of remnants. Some were as long as a few yards and others only amounting to a quarter yard or less.

In the wake of the sales, the shop had been reduced to only a handful of colors and choices.

"At these prices, I think we should buy a dress-length for each girl and a trouser length for each boy, then two bolts for work clothes and coats. We can buy all the other garments we need at the old secondhand shops. What do you think?"

Rachel nodded. She did not answer right away. She agreed with Connor, but she could not help standing in awe. She looked up at the bolts on the high shelves.

Rachel had been set free to get most of whatever she wanted. With Anna, Abbey, and Beth in mind, she ventured into the heavy cottons and draping twills

"How about these?" Rachel asked wanting both Connor's opinion and his consent on the price. She picked out a bolt of charcoal grey wool that was thick yet soft for pants and skirts or even heavier shirts, as well as a bolt of milk-chocolate twill that was softer than the canvas but nearly just as strong.

"I think they'll be good. Now, why don't we pick out one remnant package for each person? You know the colors that each person would like. They're pretty inexpensive, what with the sale," he said leading her to the end of the long table that had the remnant squares laid out upon them.

"Remnants?" she asked.

"Pieces from the end of the bolt—too small to make much of anything, but too large for any shopkeeper to throw away. They're a yard or two, which should be enough for a shirt or a vest or a skirt or a babushka."

As Rachel dug through the remnants, Connor brought the two bolts of fabric up to the counter where an older woman sat waiting for customers.

"We'll be taking these," Connor said as he set down the bolts of fabric upon the wooden counter. "If you please, how much are these?" Connor asked as he pointed to a large laundry basket of thread spools that sat on the counter.

"You can buy them individually or get them for half off, if you buy a dozen," the woman replied.

Without hesitation, Connor answered, "We'll definitely be needin' the dozen. And I'll take a box of those needles, please," he pointed to a small pile of matchbox sized containers sitting behind her against the back of the counter.

Connor saw Rachel making her way to the counter. Her arms were full of a rainbow of colored squares. Each was different, but all the colors somehow went together, as if they were part of a family set—all earth tones, natural shades, heathery, and gentle on the eye.

"And we'll be takin' all that, as well," he motioned toward Rachel. The older woman laughed.

One at a time, the woman added up the total, wrapping the squares together in packages of brown paper to protect them from the dust and dirt of the city streets. And one at a time, Connor slipped the packages into the baskets that he and Rachel were carrying.

Rachel watched Connor turn out his pockets for the grand total and could not help but feel bad. Connor, however, did not seem disappointed upon hearing the total. Rather, he looked satisfied. As they left the shop, baskets and bolts in hand, Rachel immediately thanked Connor.

"You should feel good about what we got. If we had gone into a normal shop to buy all the clothing we needed, we'd have spent ten times as much and still not gotten good quality. We're doing better than you think."

Baskets overflowing with fabric, thread, buttons and anything they might need to outfit themselves, Connor and Rachel headed back to the North End, sure to stop at the markets on the way home.

"Mind you, we'll need more fabric than what we have, but I think it's good we took advantage of that sale," commented Connor. "I want everyone to be able to pick out their own clothes. You all can make-do with the old clothes I have around the house until we can get to the secondhand shops."

Rachel nodded. They blazed a trail through the thick crowd of shoppers. Rachel stayed close to Connor's back, trying not to lose him in the hustle and bustle.

"Likewise, we'll pick up some basic supplies for our supper and breakfast and then come back and stock up properly."

"Are you're sure you have the money for all this?" Rachel inquired.

"We'll make do," he assured her. There was a little weight on his voice. "I don't think you all will be too fussy." He gave her a smile, and they pushed on.

*   *   *   *   *

T HEY'RE BACK!" shouted a bright and newly-cleaned Asa. Emma followed behind him.

"Hello there," Connor said looking down at the two little ones. He looked huge with his hands full of wrapped bolts of cloth and sacks of groceries. Asa and Emma looked frightened and backed away from Connor.

"I don't bite," Connor assured them.

The little ones look wary.

"Look at you two!" Rachel exclaimed as she made her way through the door. "You're all clean and trimmed."

Abbey and Anna came in from the bedroom. "Let them in, now. Let them in," Anna said, as she scooted Asa and Emma over near the fire. A freshly washed Marie sat on the rug near the hearth with Beth curled up by her side.

Davy and Ben had been tending to the fire.

All the children were dressed in Connor clothes. Asa, Emma, Beth, and Ben were wearing his wool work shirts, which fit them more like nightgowns. Davy, Marie, Anna, and Abbey had changed into one of his night shirts. Nicolaus had bathed but changed into a pair of Connor's trousers and a sweater. Likewise, Joseph had taken the time for a full, proper bath and then changed back into the clothes Connor had given to him earlier.

"Nicolaus and Joseph were just cleaning up the tub. Here, let us take some." Anna took some of the packages from Connor. Davy and Abbey came over to help.

"What did you get?" Davy asked enthusiastically.

"Davy!" Joseph sighed, as he and Nicolaus finished cleaning up the nook. "What?" he asked, wondering what he had said.

Joseph gave the boy a look warning him not to act ungrateful. Turning to Rachel, Joseph said, "Don't worry, I left the tub set out for you. We refilled it with fresh hot water near the end. It wasn't a pretty site after all the little ones finished up. How did your outing go?"

Rachel and Connor retold their adventure to the fabric store as they all unwrapped the bolts of fabric on the living room floor.

"Afterward, we went to the market and the secondhand shop," Rachel went on, "we got some nice food for supper and, Connor bought us new shoes and socks and long johns."

"I thought we were all going to do that together?" asked Anna.

"We noticed there were sales and Connor wanted to be smart with the money." Rachel explained.

"What's long johns?" Davy asked abruptly.

"These are." Rachel dug one of the suits out of her basket. She held it up. "See, it's like a wool suit to wear under your clothes. They keep you as warm as you would be sitting by the fire."

"And we all got one?" Ben asked in a soft hopeful voice.

"Aye, everyone has a pair. There'll be no flu in this house come winter," Connor declared.

"We got some soup makins' and some porridge makins' for the morning. Soup and porridge are really the only sensible things to make for this many mouths. Anything else and we'd spend a day's wage on dinner alone," Connor explained.

"Sounds like a feast to us," Marie spoke up. "We would be most grateful to have a lovely meal."

There was a general murmur of agreement.

"Well, let's get it cookin'. It'll take at least an hour to get good. We can use that time to make up some beds for everyone."

∗   ∗   ∗   ∗   ∗

THE EVENING PASSED GENTLY. At first, the living room was quiet. Connor was unfamiliar with the children, and the children were unaccustomed to having an adult around. Eventually, the silence started to ease, and everyone relaxed. Asa, Emma, Beth, and Ben lay fire-side curled up on the thick braided rug fast asleep. Bellies full of hot soup, faces clean, hair trimmed and combed, fresh clothes wrapped around them, the fire radiating a deep warmth, it did not take long for their exhaustion to get the better of them.

Connor stood at the pantry cupboard washing up the mugs and bowls. Joseph helped him.

"I was going to suggest that the girls take my bedroom and we lads take the living room. But being as this is your first time in a strange house with a strange man," he elbowed Joseph, "I think you all should sleep together, just as you have these last years. Change must come slow," Connor handed Joseph a mug to dry.

"Yes, I think that might be best at least for now," he added. "I mean," he went on awkwardly, "it isn't that we don't feel comfortable, we do. It's just—"

"No need to explain, lad," Connor assured. He gently put away the last bowl and wiped his hands on a cloth. "As I said, change must come slowly. You've been traumatized by what has happened to you. You may not have had much in your life, but you were used to it. This new time will be different for you—for all of us. While it's a good and needed change, it must be taken slowly."

Joseph nodded.

"You can have my bedroom."

"Don't be silly. You go sleep on your bed. This floor is the lap of luxury for us. A rug to lie on, a fire, blankets, a roof we'll sleep mighty soundly tonight. Besides the little ones are already asleep."

"All right," Connor begrudgingly agreed, "for now, at least." He smiled.

The pair walked into the living room.

"I'm turning in then," Connor whispered.

Anna, Rachel, and Abbey sat working away at their stitching by fire light while Davy and Nicolaus sat talking quietly. Marie had fallen asleep near the little ones.

"Good night," the children whispered in unison.

"All the blankets are there." He pointed to the baskets taken out of his closet. "Make sure everyone is tucked in good and tight tonight. There's another log there by the fire; last one to bed lays it on the coals. It'll keep us through the night."

Connor walked into his room and was about to close the door.

"Thank you, Connor," Joseph whispered. Deep gratitude resonated in his voice.

Connor nodded meaningfully and gently eased his door shut.

After talking for a while longer, one by one all the children turned in until only Joseph and Anna remained.

They lay buried in a mound of woolen blankets next to one another whispering in the dimly lit room.

"We don't have to worry tonight. We don't have to try to think where to find food in the morning or how to keep everyone safe," Joseph's voice was one of deepening realization. "I don't know what to do or to think. If someone had told me a fortnight ago that we'd be sleeping in a proper home, given a bath, clothes, food, blankets, and a fire, I wouldn't have believed them. In fact, I probably would've called them cruel for taunting us with the mere idea of it all. But here we are," Joseph finished, a touch of disbelief in this voice.

"It's all too much for me to take in. It's like a dream, isn't it? I mean, I'm here, and I'm awake, but it just hasn't sunk in yet. I'm in shock."

Anna lay on her side, looking out into the shadow of Joseph's face. She felt his hand take hers in the dark. After a while, the warmth of the fire and the softness of the blankets lulled them to sleep.

*   *   *   *   *

THE LIGHT FROM THE SWOLLEN MOON shone through the small window illuminating Connor's strained face. He sat on the edge of his bed. Reaching into his pocket, he pulled out a set of keys. He flipped through the ring until he found the right one. He slid the key in the old lock of the steam trunk in front of him and opened the heavy, bowed lid. A familiar, musty smell greeted him. After rummaging for a moment, he pulled out an old biscuit tin and dumped the contents on his bed—a few dozen coins and a thick fold of worn paper dollars. After counting this small savings several times, he scooped it all back into the tin and sat back against the headboard of the bed and let out a sigh.

He stared pensively out into the dark room, his mind working out how to care for eleven children on one meager income. No matter how he did the math everything came up short. He ran around in the same circles in his mind. At last, he had to turn in. Nestling the tin away, he gazed into the contents of the trunk longingly. For a long moment, he did not move or even breathe. He just stared into the trunk. Finally, he brought himself to close the battered lid, turned the key, and climbed into bed.

CHAPTER 22
FINDING A WAY

JOSEPH ROSE EARLY THE NEXT MORNING. When he sat up, he realized that everyone else was still asleep. The only one up was Connor. The bedroom door was open, and Joseph heard the slightest bit of noise issuing from his room.

Joseph crept across the room and hesitantly peered around the doorframe, not wanting to disturb Connor. He rounded the corner to see Connor doing sums on a piece of paper, counting invisible equations on his fingers.

"Everything all right?" Joseph whispered.

Connor turned toward the door. "Aye, things will be fine. Or, at least, they will be once I get things squared away."

"Anything I can help with?" Joseph approached Connor's bed and looked down at the sums. "I'm not good with numbers. I know my letters and can write and read a bit, but I can't do sums."

"Well, we will have to fix that. I think we'll have to start a little school right in the living room," Connor suggested, still distracted by the numbers scrawled across the paper.

Joseph laughed softly. "If we were to, Rachel should be the teacher. She knows the most of any of us when it comes to letters and sums. She picks it up easy as pie," Joseph stared down at the sums that were so obviously worrying Connor. He did not have to know his arithmetic to know what had Connor so concerned.

Looking up from his problem, Connor put down the pencil and turned his attention to Joseph. Joseph looked exhausted. His hair was ruffled, and shadowy circles darkened his eyes in the light from the solitary candle. He was wearing the suit of long underwear, which hung like a baggy sack on his thin body, and the blue, flannel shirt that Connor had given him from his own closet.

"You should be sleeping," he whispered back.

"I know, but I've been thinking of what I can do to help you," Joseph said sincerely.

"Help me?" Connor answered, as though he thought it was meant to be the other way around.

"Help you take care of everyone," Joseph supplied, giving a glance at the paper where Connor had evidently been trying to figure out a new budget. "I know that we're a burden and that you don't have the money to care for us all."

Connor corrected him, "Don't ever say that you are a burden."

"I just meant that I know. Taking care of us is going to be hard. It'll cost a lot to feed us and buy clothes and everything else we'll need. And I wanted to do something to help you. I've been trying to take care of everyone for a while. It's a duty best shared."

"What did you have in mind?" Connor inquired, understanding that Joseph, while only fifteen, had been seeing to all the children and still needed to feel as though he was doing his part to care for everyone.

"I thought that maybe I could come and work with you. Maybe you could hire me as one of your workers," he added. "I've tried to earn a wage all my life, but, short of the factories, I could never find a position. Since you're the foreman, you could hire me on as a worker—Nicolaus too. I spoke with him about this, and he wants to work, as well. The money we earn would go to you to help in buying all that we'll need. The way I figured it, three wages are better than one."

Connor considered him for a moment. "I didn't bring you here to work. You've been through enough. I wanted you all to be able to take some time to recover."

"I know, but I won't be going into the factories. I'd be working with you all day," Joseph reasoned.

Connor leaned back, his eyes shifting to the piece of paper with the calculations upon it. No matter how many different ways he tried to balance them, the problem just would not add up.

"If," he stressed the word, "if, we did this, the money wouldn't go to me. We'd start a household jar. We'd all put in the money we earned and take from it what we need each week for expenses. All the money earned in this house would be family money. Understand? We would earn it together and decide what to spend it on together."

"All right," Joseph said eagerly.

"Another thing," Connor interjected, "I'm the foreman of the workers, but I'm not the boss. The bosses are business men that work at a tall, brownstone, office building far removed from our suffering. If they find out that you're—" Connor hesitated.

"Sack rats?" Joseph supplied.

"Aye," Connor confirmed uncomfortably, "they will not allow you to work for them. So we'll have to keep that a secret. Don't let your heart be heavy. People who want to judge always find something to judge ya by. People look down on you because you are poor. People look down on me because I'm Irish."

"Some of them saw Nicolaus and me before, in our rags that day when we first met you."

Connor laughed softly. "Believe me when I say, the boys at the site will not recognize you. Now that we've cleaned up both of you I barely recognize you," Connor smiled. "So, tomorrow you and Nicolaus will come with me to the worksite. You can do odd jobs for the workmen and for me, and I should be able to justify to the bosses giving you a few bits a day. We'll start there, and, hopefully, it'll take. Second order of the day is getting clothes and linens squared away and getting our growing household in order. Third, we need to get the wagon sound enough to travel and bring it to Jim and Clara's for safekeeping. Finally," he said slowly, "Marie—we need to see to Marie."

"Shall I wake the others?" Joseph turned to go back into the living room.

"No, no." Connor grabbed Joseph's sleeve, "Let them sleep a bit longer. You should've slept a bit longer. You look tired."

Joseph had shared the weight of his worries with Anna, but he had always held something back—never wanting to put all his burdens on her warm spirit. For the first time in his life, he felt he was with someone who could shoulder the weight and bear it.

"It was never meant to be this way." He sat on the end of the bed and just began talking, "I'm so tired, Connor—so tired.

I'm tired of worrying—worrying about food, about finding money, about the people who might come for us, about where we could be locked away, about the bullies and brutes, about getting sick. I'm so tired of worrying. I'm so tired of being helpless. Why did it have to be this way? Out of all the ways that life could have turned out, why did it all end up this way?"

"Lad," Connor said wearily, "you're asking the questions a great many of us ask. You've simply come to your questions a bit earlier in life. The short answer is: I don't know why things had to be as they are—not with your life or with mine," he confessed in torment. "Some go through life sheltered from all harm, while others—" Connor stopped. "Joseph, there's no sense in asking yourself why all the bad happened. It happened because in your life you came across people who didn't care the way they should've. Your mum, your da, the people—they didn't care, and that lack of love impacted your life. But, by the same hand, meeting others—who do care and who do love— can impact your life just as deeply. Our life is shaped by the people who love us and by the people who don't.

"Joseph, I know you have questions—many will never have answers, but that doesn't mean your life can't be great. Those souls who endure a life such as yours, go on to do important things. You think that the heartache you've felt is all that you'll ever be, but it's not. It's not what the heartless people did to you that defines you; it's what you do afterward. You understand?" he laid a hand on the boy's arm. "It's not the wounds that make a man. It's how we hold ourselves and persevere while bearing them. It's over now Joseph," Connor assured him softly. "The time has come for you to be a boy, as you should've always been. Let me be the Da for a while. I can bear the worry."

Joseph gave a half-smile and then slumped over, his shoulders jerking in time with the sobs. The two sat there for a while.

*   *   *   *   *

B Y MID-AFTERNOON, EVERYONE WAS UP AND MOVING. It was terribly odd for the children to sleep so late. Then again, having a bed and food and warmth was odd for them, as well. They had a lifetime of rest to catch up on.

A proper trip to the market was the first chore that afternoon. Beyond the fabric and a few essentials that Connor and Rachel had picked up, the children had been living in Connor's clothes, which he was of course going to need back. Drawing some money from the savings in his trunk, Connor rallied the children, and they all got ready to set out for the shops.

"I want to stay," Emma pleaded, hanging on the hems of Rachel's sweater. The little one was still in her long johns and Asa was balled up in his nest of blankets looking content.

"Yes. All right," Anna said in an effort to calm her.

"I'm going to stay anyway," Marie said. She was curled up in the chair resting. "Emma can stay with me. I don't mind."

"I'll stay, too," volunteered Rachel. "I already went to the market last night. I don't mind missing the trip. Besides, it'll give me a chance to starting fitting the little ones for their clothes. We have all this fabric that Connor and I bought last night. It's time we put it to use."

"I'll stay," Beth added quietly. "I can help," she offered warmly.

"It's settled," Connor overheard the conversation from his bedroom while he readied himself. "You all stay here and start getting the household sorted. Rachel, why don't you see what you can scrape together for a soup. Just set it to simmer away on the hearth, and we can eat it tonight. Oh," he added as a side note, "I don't want you to think that I've forgotten about the wagon. I'm going to ask Jim to go out there with me tomorrow and haul it up out of the mud. We can keep it at his farm, and you can go out and work on it whenever you like. We still have those beams you chose from the wreckage. We can use those to reinforce the wagon bed," Connor suggested. "Is there anything left out in the wagon that we need?"

"The crate of books from the printing shop are still out there," Joseph chimed.

"Well, sometime today, you and Nicolaus and Davy should run out there and grab the rest of your things."

"Are we still going to make a journey in the wagon and leave the city as we planned?" Davy asked.

No one said anything. It seemed no one had the answer yet.

"I don't know," Joseph replied. "The wagon is important to us, and it's ours, and I think we should fix it up. And yes," he went on, mapping out the plan as he spoke, "I think that we'd do better outside of the city—where we can be free to grow our own food and live a better way. But right now, we're going to see how things go with Connor." All faces turned to Connor and he smiled. "And we'll think about what's the best next step." Joseph finished tying his boots and rose.

"What about all that planning and gathering—what was that for?" Davy sounded rather disappointed.

"The wagon was our hope chest," Joseph said, looking at Connor and smiling. "Everything we gathered will go toward our new life. We just have to wait and see how that life comes to us."

Everyone seemed comforted by this thought. They were all in agreement with what Joseph said. They grabbed the empty baskets, and they were off.

They quickly made their way down the street toward the markets.

"We're going to buy food, right?" Davy asked eagerly.

"Hush, Davy. Yes, we're going to buy food. Quit thinking with your stomach," Anna scolded.

"What?" he said indignantly. "I'm hungry."

"I'm hungry, too," Ben chimed in.

"We just ate," Anna said, exasperated.

"Don't change the fact that I'm hungry," Davy mumbled under his breath.

"So then, are we going to need a snack to get us through the market?" Connor offered.

"Oooooo, snack!" said Davy hungrily as they entered the market. There were food stands at every side.

Anna sighed. "Connor has spent enough of his money and is going to be spending more. No snacks."

"It's all right. Here we are," he stopped at a fruit stand.

After a quick stop, the children and Connor hurried to the secondhand shop. Each child with a juicy apple in hand.

"Now that we have fortified ourselves a bit more, it's time to do some shopping. Here," he said to Anna taking a worn bill from his pocket. "Here's a dollar. You and Joseph go to that fabric shop and get the rest of what we'll need to have a few sets of clothing for each person. Nicolaus, Abbey, Davy, Ben, and I will go into the secondhand shop. When we're done, we'll meet over there by that bench," he pointed across the square.

He placed the worn dollar in Anna's hand. She stood staring at it. She looked frightened to have so much money—more than she ever had in her life. She handed it immediately to Joseph, as if she didn't want the responsibility.

"You'll do fine, love. You know what you'll need, so just go and get it. Joseph will help." He laid an encouraging hand on Joseph's shoulder. "Off you go now," he finished, then ushered the younger ones into the shop.

Joseph and Anna made their way into the fabric store, both of them a little befuddled to have so much money. They both felt that, given how much they would be spending, it was important that they did well, got good quality, and were thrifty.

"What'll we do with all this money?" Anna asked in a stressed voice. She was surrounded by bolts of fabric. She did not know where to begin.

"All right, it's simple," reassured Joseph, "we just need lots of fabric and some thread and stuff," he finished meekly. He knew he was out of his element.

"Thanks," answered Anna, still utterly stressed out. "Very helpful."

"Here," he pointed, "let's start over in the sale bins and go from there."

She nodded.

After picking through the entire store twice, Anna finally narrowed down what she thought the best fabrics would be and shakily proceeded to spend almost all of the dollar that Connor had given her.

"I hope I did well," she said as they walked out of the shop, baskets overflowing. "It must have taken him months to earn that money, and I spent it in the space of a few minutes. I'm not a seamstress. I just do my best," she reeled in doubt.

"You did fine. I mean it. You have loads of commonsense, you just need to have more confidence in what you can do. So what if you are self-taught, You've kept clothes on our backs for years now using naught but scraps. That makes you a better seamstress than any of those women you'll find uptown making them fancy dresses."

Anna listened. She seemed roused by his words. "You're right," she agreed, still the sliver of doubt lingered.

After picking out undergarments and a few other sundries, Connor, Ben, Davy, Nicolaus, and Abbey marched out of the shop. They made their way toward the market where Joseph and Anna were already waiting, their arms weighed down with fabric. As always, Abbey was the slowest. She was following behind everyone when she suddenly stopped. She had seen a three-legged dog limping into the alley by the shop. She shuffled toward it, stepping in time with the dog's injured gait. Just as she reached the pup, she saw a boy make his way toward it. He was no more than eight years old, well-dressed, and obviously from a more well-to-do part of town.

Just as the boy made it close enough to pet the scrawny, disabled dog, a woman approached.

"Stop it! Don't touch that filthy thing! You don't know where it has been!" she scolded. The woman was clearly the boy's mother. She was dressed in the finest clothes—silks and lace, long white gloves, and a feathery hat.

"But, mother," the boy whined. "I want a dog. I can take him home."

"Don't even think about it. If you want a dog, we will get you a well-bred animal from the country. That dog can hardly walk. It won't be able to play with you or work. It will just be a drain on our money. It's best left on the street." The woman grabbed the boys hand and pulled him away. The dog limped down the street, scared off by the woman's shouting.

Connor came up behind Abbey to check on her. He arrived just in time to see the spectacle.

"Are you all right, love?" Connor asked. Abbey wouldn't move. She stood quietly staring at the place where the dog had disappeared.

"Abbey?" Connor said, as he bent down to her height.

"Is that why they left me on the street?" she asked, her heart in her throat. "Did they see me as a drain on their money— just a burden?" She was still staring at the place the sick dog had limped away.

Connor gently nudged her cheek until he could look her right in the eye. She welled up with tears. "I don't know what their reasons were, but I do know that they lost what could've been the deepest joy in their life. You have untold ability, dearest one. Your little limp does not take away from all that your heart has to give. Come on now, love." He took her gently under wing, and they turned back together to meet the others who had paused, waiting on the bench ahead.

CHAPTER 23
THE OLD WISDOM

RISING LATE and undertaking so many chores, their day went by in a blink of the eye.

Potatoes, carrots, onions, and a bit of leftover beef gathered together, Rachel managed to throw together a hearty little soup. Seeing as it was the first time Rachel had ever cooked on a proper hearth, she rushed to check the soup a little more often than was necessary. Nonetheless, in-between the cooking and checking, Rachel and Beth managed to cut out two complete sets of clothes for Asa and Emma. After dinner they planned to sew the pieces together.

When everyone was home and the time came to eat, the small table, which only sat two or three, was abandoned for another picnic-style meal eaten on the living room floor. Everyone filled their soup bowls. A round loaf of bread bought at the market made its way around the circle.

"This is very good, Rachel," complimented Joseph, as he soaked a wedge of bread in the rich brown broth.

Everyone nodded in agreement, mouths too full to speak.

"Next, you and Anna will have to learn how to make bread," Connor encouraged. "Since you'll be running the household, you'll have to know how to bake."

Anna and Rachel looked intimidated.

"I'm sure, Clara would be willing to give a lesson or two," Connor suggested. "I'll talk with her about it when I drop the next load of wood off this week."

"You'll like Clara," Joseph smiled.

"She's the best." Nicolaus spoke around a too-large lump of potato that he had to move to the side of his mouth. He looked like a chipmunk storing stew for winter.

"So, I have to go to my workshop for a little while tonight," Connor said in-between spoonfuls of stew. "I hope you will feel comfortable here without me for a time. Just keep the door locked, and try to be quiet. The old landlady doesn't like noise. If she found out all of you were here, she'd probably try to raise the rent."

"We'll be fine," Joseph assured.

"I'm sure, you will be. Oh," Connor added forgetfully, "in a little while, one of my friends will be stopping by—a woman by the name of Mrs. McCarthy."

Everyone stopped chewing and looked up from their dinner.

"There's nothing to worry about. Mrs. McCarthy's a dear soul from the homeland. Her kin have always been well-versed in sickness of the heart and body. Mrs. McCarthy is coming tonight to see you, Marie."

What little color Marie had drained from her. "What does she want with me?" Marie asked in a fearful voice.

"She's going to help you. And there's no need to worry," he added, in response to her uneasiness. "A gentler, kinder soul never walked the earth. No child, she's going to talk with you about what's been ailing you and see if she can't help you. I promise," he concluded, "by the end of this visit, you all will love her," Connor tore off a crust of bread and soaked up the last bit of broth lingering in his bowl. Despite his assurances, Marie still felt uneasy.

*   *   *   *   *

ABOUT AN HOUR AFTER THE SUN HAD SET, there was a knock at the door. Everyone stopped what they were doing. No one spoke. Joseph moved cautiously toward the door. "Who is it?" he asked in the manliest voice he could muster.

A kind voice issued from the other side. "Don't be daft. I know ya don't get that many visitors. It's me, boy. Now, let an old woman in by the fire before me old bones freeze up."

Joseph looked back at the others. Anna nodded encouragingly. Joseph clicked the lock and swung the door open. Mrs. McCarthy was a plump woman— not fat exactly, just a bit round—as people seemed to get later on in life when their bones start keeping them in their chairs. She wore a long skirt; an old, knitted sweater; and many, crocheted shawls wrapped about her shoulders and chest.

"Well, you're rather shorter company than I expected. I thought you were Connor." She came further in and saw all the children curled up in their beds.

"Well now," she said, taken aback. "Good evening, dear lambs. Now then, where's the man?"

The children stood in a kind of shock. They said nothing.

"Cat got ya tongue?" she said trying to pull a laugh from the quiet crowd.

"Ummm, Connor went out to his workshop for a while," Joseph said, finally breaking the silence.

"Well, he wanted me to come and pay a visit on a sick lass. I've brought me kit," she said raising up an old carpetbag.

"Marie," Anna spoke up, "You're here to see Marie." Anna helped Marie to her feet.

"I see," Mrs. McCarthy said kindly. "We're going to need a bit of privacy."

"You can go into Connor's bedroom. I'm sure he won't mind," Joseph motioned toward the room.

Mrs. McCarthy walked toward Anna and took Marie by the arm to guide her. "Don't look so fearful girl. I ain't got no claws. I'll do ya no harm. We're just going to sit and chat a bit. Do ya feel up to that? Would you like one of your sisters to come in with ya?"

"No," Marie answered softly.

Mrs. McCarthy led Marie to the doorway and turned back. "Could one of you sweet lambs fix me a kettle of hot water? Don't put no tea in it. Just bring the pot and a cup," she clarified.

"I'll bring some right in," replied Anna.

"Thank you, girl." And with that, she closed the door.

"How do we start?" asked Marie once they were alone. "I suppose you want to check me like a doctor would."

"Aye, I'll be checking ya. But we start with a gentle hello and a bit of a chat. You can call me Eliza." She reached out and took Marie's hand. "Come now, sit with me for a wee spell, and let's speak of when you first started feeling ill. We'll get ya back up to full strength in no time."

"Don't know if it will do any good," said Marie, a bit hopeless.

"Now then, what's all this?"

"I haven't had any strength for months now, and my heart isn't what it used to be. Once lost, I don't think they come back," she said sadly. She was listless and lost.

"They come back more than you might think. I've seen long-dead limbs come back, and those who've lived in the dark for many years, rise to see the sun. Nothing is ever lost, girl, unless you're willing to give it up. Are ya willing to give up?" she asked.

This seemed to strike Marie. For the first time all day, she had a bit of fire in her. "No. I want to be my ol' self. I want to watch my family grow."

"All right then. That's better. We're going to need some of that spirit back. I don't know ya all that well, but I know that your spirit is faint now compared to what it should be."

Marie gave a weary smile. Marie was tired, and her spirit was unsettled, but something about the old woman was calming.

"What do you think they are talking about?" asked Anna, pacing around the hearth, waiting on the kettle, feeling helpless.

"I don't know," replied Joseph. "She seems nice, though. I'm sure Marie will be fine."

Steam began to issue from the kettle's spout. Anna took hold of the kettle with a pair of thick mitts and filled a small teapot.

"Will you fetch me a cup, please, Joseph?"

Joseph dashed off to the pantry cupboard returning a moment later with a brown teacup and saucer. Anna placed everything on a tray and knocked on the bedroom door.

"Come in, dear," Mrs. McCarthy's voice echoed warmly. "Just set it down there." She pointed to the bedside table.

"Thank you, Anna," Marie offered with a little nod to let Anna know that she was all right.

Anna set the tray down and left, closing the door behind her.

"What are they doing?" Joseph asked, and dared not enter.

"They're just talking," she replied, at a loss. "Marie's all right. I could tell by her tone."

Joseph seemed eased though they both continued to pace. Nicolaus and Rachel looked on as they distracted the young ones with little games.

After God-knows-how-long, the knob to the bedroom door turned, and Mrs. McCarthy emerged.

"Marie is resting," Mrs. McCarthy closed the door behind her. "We had a bit of a chat, and I gave her some herbs that should help. I think ya should leave her be for now."

"Will she be all right?" asked Joseph.

"Aye, in time, I think she will be."

"Is there anything we can do to help her?" asked Anna.

"Aye, see to her heart. An ailing heart makes the body cry out."

"How do we help her heart?" asked Joseph, at a loss.

"Oh, my dear boy, everyone is different. You know her though, don't ya?"

He nodded slowly.

"Well then, you must know all that she's been struggling with?"

He nodded.

"Then help her with all that. Help her find the peace she needs. That's how you can help heal your sister."

"She's not truly my sister," Joseph clarified.

"Isn't she then?" replied Mrs. McCarthy affronted.

"Not by blood, I mean," he clarified.

"What's blood got to do with family? Family is about lovin' each other. Only fools will tell ya otherwise. If ya love that girl with all ya heart—unfailing—then she is ya sister. And as her kin, it's up to you all to help her spirit."

"So it isn't something she caught from being out in the cold?" asked Anna.

"Sometimes sickness ain't about what we catch; it's about what we lose, and the hurt we carry around inside. Heal the heart—then ya go after the root of it all," the old woman explained. "Connor still not home then?" she asked, looking around.

"No," Joseph answered, shaking his head.

"Well, I'm sure he'll be along at any moment. I must be off." She took a step toward the door.

"No, don't leave," came a timid voice from the sea of blankets. It was Asa. "Tell us a story," the tiny boy pleaded.

"What makes ya think I got stories, wee lad?" she questioned Asa with a smile.

"Asa, leave poor Mrs. McCarthy alone," reasoned Anna. "She's got to be making her way home."

"Oh, that's all right. It'll give me a chance to warm meself by the fire before I go." She moved toward the chair by the hearth. "You'll need to give up that chair, if you want me to stay, lad. Me legs just don't bend enough these days to get me down to the floor and back up."

Ben quickly jumped up and moved to the floor, teddy bear in hand. "Of course," he replied in a quick voice.

"My goodness, you're all so jumpy. Ya ain't got nothing to fear from me. Now then," she nodded in Ben's direction, "what's your name?"

"Ben. But everyone calls me Teddy."

"On account of ya bear then?"

He nodded.

"Well, Teddy, ya don't have to be fearful of this old woman. Ya could probably run rings around me."

She settled into the chair. All the children gathered around. "So, a story. I ain't never had any babes of me own to tell stories to. But back in the old country, when I was naught but a babe, I was told stories of the fairy folk."

"The fairy folk?" asked Ben.

"Aye, my mum would tell us of small little fairies that lived in the trees in the woodlands around our cottage. Fairies that could come late at night and wake children to lure 'em away from their homes."

"Do the fairies want to play with the children?" asked Asa, listening brightly.

"No, they want to carry the babes off to the spirit world," she replied, bending down to tickle Asa. Emma looked afraid.

"My mum told me to beware the fairies who come whispering in honeyed tones in the dark of night. She said the fairies try to tempt babes to go away with 'em. Telling 'em of the wonders that await 'em if they agree to go."

"What wonders?" asked Asa.

"Oh many glorious, tempting things—orchards of ripe apples and bushes of juicy berries, soft beds of hay and sheep skin to lie in, fires stoked high, burning logs that never die out, long days of sunlight and winters without the cutting cold, endless kettles of thick meaty stew, and tables of honey sweets—"

"I want to go!" Davy spoke up.

"Well then, lad. The fairies might've been able to carry ya off. Ya see, the fairies can't enter your house and take ya. You must agree to go with 'em if they're to have ya. And once you go with 'em, there's no comin' back. They'll say most anything to get ya to come away with 'em."

"You mean they lie?" asked Ben.

"I don't rightly know. Maybe the fairy world does have all those wondrous things. No, what the fairies are best at is making us forget the good things we have right here. They tell us of all the sweets and treasures they have to give and their words work a magic up here," she pointed to her head, "making ya forget the sweet joys that we have at home."

"What's it mean?" interrupted Joseph, speaking up for the first time. Mrs. McCarthy looked up. "Every story has a thread of truth to it. What's this one mean?"

"It means," she replied, "many a thing can come along to try to convince ya that there are greener pastures elsewhere, so much so that ya can become blind to the dearness of what surrounds ya. Many holy men will tell ya that the answers lie in the scripture, and maybe so, but I believe we find what is sacred when we learn to see the dearness in all the little things here at home. And some of us don't realize until after we've already left our homes behind, chasing grander things."

Just then, the front door clicked closed. So engrossed in Mrs. McCarthy's story, no one had noticed Connor's arrival.

"Indeed," Connor said solemnly, in agreement with the moral of the story.

"Indeed," Mrs. McCarthy echoed in agreement. "Well then, little lambs," she rose up off her weary bones, "it's time for me to be off."

A general cry of sadness issued from the children.

"Oh, hush now. It's time for ya all to be off to sleep, to dream of all that lies ahead." She moved across the room and gathered up her old carpetbag.

She approached Connor and pulled him aside. "Marie is sleeping in your bed. I'd leave her there for the night and curl up with the babes on the floor. I gave her a few herbs and a good talk. I fear that most of the weakness lies in her spirit. All the same, she should take this tea with her morning and evening meal." She gave him a parchment envelope of herbs and tea. "Her heart should improve over the coming days, but unless her heart is guided to peace, I fear some other illness will show its face. The body 'tis a mirror of the soul, and that young lass is in torment. She lost someone dear to her, and it has torn her in two."

Connor nodded sadly. "Aye, well, I know that pain."

"Aye," she agreed, "we all do. Life leaves us all rather lean in the end. Poor lass, she has just gone through too much, too soon. First losing her Mum and Da and then a boy who probably woulda been her husband," she shook her head and let out a deep sigh.

"Call on me if ya need anything, lad." With a kiss on the cheek and a wave to the children, she swept from the room.

Connor drew the bolt behind her and turned around to a lot of sad faces. "See now, I told you that you'd like her by the end."

"Everyone, ready for bed," Joseph said, trying to settle the little ones.

"Aye, it's late," Connor agreed. "But before we all turn in, we have time for one last thing. A gift for Abbey."

Abbey looked up, shocked to be singled out. "For me?" She asked, thinking she must have heard him wrong.

"Aye, for you, girl," Connor confirmed with a wide smile. "Here," he dropped a package in her lap.

She opened the brown paper. "The shoes I got in the market," she was at a loss

Connor laughed a little. "Aye, your shoes but with a few small changes. I noticed that limp you carry, on our first night we come out from the wagon. I used to work with a shoe smith when I was a boy. I replaced the soles of the shoes with new handmade soles. You see," he pointed out the new thick soles. "One is slightly thicker than the other. It'll help you when you walk," he explained. "Come on, now, try them on. Let's see if I got 'em right," he urged her.

She jumped up and slipped them on and took her first cautious steps. Instead of her usual limp, she walked smoothly from step to step, the special sole making up for her one short leg.

"They're great," Joseph and Anna both said at the same time, watching Abbey glide around the room beaming.

"These will make walking a bit easier on you," he began, but before he could finish, she rushed toward him with a deep embrace. She held the hug for a long time. "These will help you," he whispered so that only she could hear. "Even without them, you're no less than any of us. Your worth lies here," he said pointing to her heart, "and here alone. You must never let anyone or anything make you doubt your own self-worth."

PART THREE

CHAPTER 24
THE TIES THAT HOLD US

THE LAST WEEKS OF AUTUMN were spent in the warm glow of hearth and hope. The transition from the alleys to a home was surreal, like a sweet dream, and they were afraid to trust its reality. For many days, Joseph, Anna, Rachel, and Nicolaus waited for the other shoe to fall—for the flawless man to reveal his disingenuous motives. Nevertheless, the love that was given was never taken away. Connor gave everything and asked for nothing. Giving the children an example of a true parent for the first time in their lives.

Over the weeks that followed, Joseph and the children settled into a new life of warmth and fullness. Anna and Rachel slowly learned the workings of the household from Connor, and, after picking up a few tips from Clara, they had the daily routine running smoothly. Just as Mrs. McCarthy had predicted, Marie had started to strengthen in body, if not in spirit.

At sunrise, Connor, Joseph, and Nicolaus headed out to the worksite, lunch pails in hand while Anna and Rachel saw to the cooking, baking, and general upkeep of a household

of over ten people. With the boys earning wages alongside
Connor, it was easier to keep food on the table, but they were
by no means living comfortably. Connor, Joseph, Anna, and
Marie knew that their arrangement would only work for so
long. They could not go on sharing such a small set of rooms,
especially as the younger children grew.

More and more, Connor and Joseph realized their best
bet would be to take the wagon, which had been painstak-
ingly restored by Connor and the boys at the Scolfield farm,
and leave the city. Connor knew this to be the most practical
option, but his impractical heart was afraid to leave. Where
this fear was rooted, Joseph did not yet know.

*   *   *   *   *

I T WAS A WEEK BEFORE CHRISTMAS, and a new world of joy
and warmth was opening itself to the children. For the first
time in their lives, the Yuletide season was about celebrating
home and abundance.

"I'm telling you, this is going to be the best Christmas feast
in the whole city of Boston." Anna was up to her wrists knead-
ing dough. Beth and Abbey stood beside her rolling out their
own loaves on the table near the pantry cupboard. "I'm going
over to the Scolfield's for a bit tonight, and Clara is even going
to teach me how to make a Christmas pudding full of raisins
and honey and all sorts of good things," Anna continued while
Beth and Abbey listened with bright smiles.

Abbey's loaf was coming along, but Beth was having a few
problems. "Anna—" she said in a worried tone. Most of her
dough was spread in a thick, sticky layer across the table. "It

won't come together," Beth went on, looking at Abbey's perfect floury ball of dough and wondering what she did wrong.

"No worries, love," Anna moved over to Beth. "You just need a bit more flour, that's all. You see, bread is easy. If it's too dry, you add a bit of water. If it's too sticky, you add a bit of flour. You can't mess it up. You just keep working with it until it feels right."

With Connor and Clara as her teachers, Anna had come along quickly with her cookery. Her pastries and breads were now gobbled up as soon as she put them out. As Clara told her on the first day, "You have the gift of the hearth."

"All right then," Anna finished rolling up Beth's dough. "Let's put these loaves in the oven and finish the stew before the boys come home. It's almost dusk. We should be hearing their boots at the door any moment." Anna took the loaves and put them in the stone oven set into the hearth.

"We don't have anything else to put in the stew," Abbey echoed from the pantry cupboard, "and we've watered it down so many times, I don't even think we can call it a stew anymore. It's more like a soup," she held the empty vegetable basket in hand. Lately, the evening meal had consisted of a small bowl of stew and a large hunk of bread.

"We'll make do," Anna assured, grabbing a stack of bowls from the pantry cupboard and setting them out on the hearthstone.

"Of course, we will," Beth chimed in, following behind her with a pile of spoons.

In the weeks since being taken in by Connor, Beth had blossomed. As Davy pointed out, she said more words in the last few weeks than she did in her first eight years.

"Anna, I don't understand why won't the men at the dock let certain ships come in?" Abbey asked as she stirred the watered-down stew. "I mean, why would they want to turn away the boats bringing in food?"

Abbey was speaking of the recent blockades at the harbor where, over the past few weeks, crowds of unemployed men had fought off many of the immigrant boats trying to make port.

"Well," Anna tried to explain, "it isn't that they don't want the food unloaded. It's that, some of those ships are carrying immigrants who are coming to the city to make a new start, and the men don't want them to come into the city."

"Why?" Abbey asked, still stirring.

"Because the men think that the immigrants pouring into the city will make it harder for the people already living here to find work. A lot of the men getting off the boats are starting with nothing, and they will work for less wages. So the bosses have been firing the workers they have and hiring the men getting off the boats. That way the bosses can keep more money in their pockets. All the men who have been fired are gathering down at the docks, fending off the boats that bring in the families coming across the Atlantic."

"I don't understand." Abbey said, confused. She stood over the stew pot, looking down at the pale broth, still not sure why food had to be so expensive.

"It's all right, love." Anna said, checking on the bread in the oven "Just know that we will make do with food, just as we always have."

The wail of the hinges of the front door sounded. Connor, Nicolaus, and Joseph were home.

"All right then, that is it for the day." Rachel said. She had been sitting with Ben, Davy, Asa, and Emma teaching them their letters. When the boys came home, she knew she would not be able to hold their attention any longer.

"How was your day?" Rachel put away the piece of slate and chalk she had been using in their lessons.

"Yeah, how was the day?" Asa ran over to Joseph to give him a hug.

"Long." Joseph braced himself as the small boy grabbed him.

"It's starting to get colder." Nicolaus commented, already defrosting himself by the fire.

"Well, we got some hot bread and stew to warm you all up." Anna peered into the oven at the crisping bread.

"I can smell the bread from here." Connor left his mud-caked boots by the door.

* * * * *

W HEN DINNER WAS FINISHED, Joseph and Anna stood washing the bowls in a small basin of water.

"There is still a bit of sun left. I think I will head out when we finish." Anna rushed with the last dish.

"Head out where?" Joseph dried a bowl and looked confused.

"To the Scolfield's house, remember? Clara is giving me another cooking lesson tonight. Jim said he'd pick me up down by the Common. He is doing some business down there today."

"I can't have you walk out there alone near dark," Joseph reasoned.

"I'll be fine," she assured him. Her words drew out in a long exhale. "He's even going to drive me back when we're done."

"No, no, I'll come with you. I don't mind."

"All right, then, we'll head out in a few minutes." She handed him the last bowl, clean and ready to be dried.

"I'll go tell Connor." Joseph gave the bowl a half-wipe and put it on the stack still wet.

Anna sighed and grabbed the towel and the still-wet bowl.

A few moments later, they were bundled up and ready to set out.

"Should we get anything at the market?" asked Joseph.

Connor was sitting by the fire resting.

"I suppose. Get whatever is the cheapest," Connor suggested. "See what looks fair."

"Why don't we just move to the country, grow our food, and then we won't have to spend money buying it?" Davy argued as he sat playing with Ben.

"We will eventually go to the country. Connor just doesn't think it's the right time yet." Rachel replied. "He knows best."

Joseph could see the strain on Connor's face.

"We could buy some more from Clara and Jim?" Anna suggested.

"No, we can't take anymore off them, or they won't have enough for the winter." Connor answered in a tense voice. "No, we'll have to buy at the markets."

"We will find something," Joseph assured. Anna opened the door and started down the stairs. "Don't worry." And with that, Joseph hesitantly closed the door behind him. He wished more than anything that he knew what was troubling Connor, and why he was so afraid to leave the city.

It was a long but quiet walk out to the Common where they met Jim on Park Street. Joseph had gotten used to making the trip out on the wagon, and now every rock and bend in the road was familiar to him. It was a couple miles or so out to Clara and Jim's farm in Roxbury, but they went by quicky. Before they knew it, Joseph and Anna were standing in front of Clara's hearth. Anna was in her element; Joseph looked rather bemused.

"All right now," Clara began in her calm, encouraging tone. "Being able to make a good meal from all the bits that are left over is the mark of a good cook." Clara and Anna were huddled over a bowl chopping potatoes and kidneys, while Joseph sat at the table sipping on a cup of tea and looking horrified at the prospect of eating whatever the girls were cooking.

"I thought you were going to make a Christmas pudding?" he asked in an unsettled voice. He was watching Anna chop through the red, gelatinous kidney.

"Didn't you see us do the batter? It's already in the oven." Anna motioned toward the hearth with the tip of her knife. "Well, you were rather focused on that tart Clara gave you. Now, we are on to meat pies."

"Or rather, meat pies when you don't have any meat." Clara explained. "All right now, boy, you stop distracting my student," Clara said in a threatening tone, a little smirk on her face as she spoke.

Anna gave a little nod, as if to agree with Clara, and then kept chopping. "All right, you take your meat—whatever meat you have on hand. In this case, we have our kidneys. You take your sliced potatoes, onions, and carrots, and you wrap 'em up in your pastry like a little package." Clara rolled out a piece of the pastry on the floured counter and demonstrated as she spoke. "And you crimp the little edges nice and tight. If the juices escape, you have a dry pie and a dirty oven. Make a little slit in the top like a chimney. Then you slide 'em into the hearth and cook 'em 'til they are golden, and the gravy inside starts bubbling out the top."

Clara finished, a perfect pie sitting on the counter in front of her. "Now, you try," she encouraged Anna.

Intimidated at first, Anna plucked up the courage and started rolling out her pastry. After she was finished, she stood back and looked at it, her head tilted to one side. "It's not as pretty as yours," she commented. Her pastry dough was a bit thin in places, and the pie was a little misshapen when compared to Clara's perfect half circle.

"You just need to work on your crimpin' and your rollin'. You will get the hang of it. Please, girl, I have been making pies more years than you've been drawing breath.

"Now," she said as she slid the pies into the oven. "Last thing to learn for tonight, and then we'll have Jim run you two home: baked apples. I love doing them on Christmas morning with breakfast, and they're as easy as falling off a log." She picked up an apple from the bushel she had sitting on the counter and then a small knife. "You core out the apple, leave the skin on. Then set it in a pan." She pulled out an old cast iron pan. "Pack the hole with butter and cinnamon and raisins and put 'em in the oven till they're bubbling and soft and serve 'em with sausages—if you can get 'em—and bread and eggs. And trust me, they'll be gone before you can even set 'em out."

"I can't wait to try it." Anna beamed.

"Yeah, me neither." Joseph drooled. "I don't know if we'll be able to do them this year. Depends on the prices at the market. All the fruits have been very expensive lately."

"All the food, period, has been expensive." Anna added. "We

have been talking about going to the country where we can grow our own food, like you and Jim." Anna explained. "But—"

"But?" Clara prodded as she finished coring out a few more apples. "Connor doesn't want to leave the city," she finished.

"Exactly," Joseph said, shocked that Clara already had the answer. "But, why doesn't he want to leave?" Joseph asked. "I mean, I know he would prefer the country, so why would he want to stay in the city?"

"Joseph, what you have to understand is," she began, for once struggling to find her words, "Connor has things tying him to the city, and until he is done settling those things, those ties will stay, and so will he."

"What is tying him to the city?" Joseph asked, confused.

"Well, I don't reckon it's my place to say. I think you ought to ask Connor." She placed the finished pan of cored and stuffed apples into the oven. "Now, you both are going to wait until all this is done and take some with you back home—and I won't hear no buts about it," she went on, seeing that Joseph and Anna were both about to protest. "Joseph, why don't you go find Jim and Tim and see if they need any help putting the animals to rest. Find Meg, too, while you're at it. Lord knows what trouble that girl has gotten herself into. Anna and I will finish up, and then you two can be off. Oh," she added with a smile, "I almost forgot your Christmas present." She brought a basket to the table. Anna peeled back the cloth covering to reveal over a dozen apples, a dozen link sausages, and a dozen fresh eggs.

Anna turned to Clara, giving her a deep embrace. Laughter erupted in the small kitchen, echoing out into the lawn.

CHAPTER 25
YULETIDE GLOW

THE SHABBY APARTMENT WAS UNRECOGNIZABLE. The parched wood gleamed in the candlelight. Garlands and paper-chains were pinned throughout the room in abundance. In the far corner of the room stood a small pine Yule-tree. The surface of every table and windowsill was covered with evergreen cuttings and pine cones gathered from a lone pine growing on Clara and Jim's farm. Faded, flannel strips were tied in limp bows on all the doorknobs, latches, and posts. Finally, a pine branch wreath was set on the front door, where it received a signature flannel bow.

"When do we get presents?" Emma asked brightly, as she helped Anna tidy the living room.

"Two days. Then presents," Anna assured her.

"What are the presents going to be?" Emma asked. She was trying to mimic Anna as she folded an afghan, but the blanket was too heavy for her.

"You silly girl," Anna said with a laugh, taking the blanket from her, "if you knew what the presents were going to be, then it wouldn't be a surprise. You're just going to have to wait."

"And you two," Anna pointed at Asa and Davy. "No more sneakin' and tryin' to find the presents. You just have to wait."

267

"But—but Davy said he saw Connor come in with the presents," Asa reasoned, "and if he brought the presents inside, then they are hidden somewhere."

"Connor told you that the presents would be put out Christmas Eve. You're going to spoil Connor's surprise, if you keep pokin' your nose around."

Davy looked frustrated.

"You don't see Ben poking round," Anna motioned to Ben who was sitting with Rachel and Marie, working on his letters.

"I just don't know where to look. If I could think of a place, I might," Ben replied honestly.

Anna frowned. She was not winning the argument.

"Anna's right," Marie spoke up, "No snoopin'. This is our first Christmas together as a family. Let's not ruin it by being greedy."

Anna nodded in agreement, folded her last blanket, and went to fix lunch.

* * * * *

As Anna set out bread and cheese for their lunch, Joseph, Nicolaus, and Connor sat down at the worksite for the first time since rising at dawn and started eating the very same foods Anna packed that morning before they left for work.

Bundled in sweaters, hats, mittens, and thick work pants the boys sat next to Connor taking a moment of quiet amid the chaos of the worksite.

"What did this house used to be?" Joseph always asked the same questions with each new site.

"It was built by an old ship's captain for his wife. She used to sit up there on the widow's walk waiting for his ship to return—probably not seeing him for years at a time," Connor replied.

"How did you know that—?" asked Nicolaus.

All of a sudden a group of workmen approached Connor.

"Connor. We need to talk with ya," one of the scruffy work-men interjected.

Connor set aside his lunch and gave the man his attention. "Go on, Will."

"Well, me and the boys done heard that the bosses are givin' more of us our walkin' papers and taken on more of them men off the boat," the man, Will, motioned over to a group of workmen sitting off on their own. "I've done been workin' for you for goin' on four years, and, now, I'm gonna lose my place because some greenhorn off the ships will labor for a few pennies less than me? Don't loyalty count for nothin' to them bastards?"

"Will, I understand. I've not heard any such thing from the bosses. They don't tell me what's in their minds. If they did, I would tell you. All that said, every man here knows that there isn't any secure work in this town—not now. The walkin' papers will come. We all know it. Those businessmen never miss a chance to put two pennies into their pocket insteada one."

"All we lads have always had the highest respect for ya, Connor. You are a fair man. But I ain't gonna sit here like a fool and let me wages be taken from me. All the honest workin' men in Boston—we are gonna be heard. You should join us, Connor," Will rallied. The men behind him nodding in agree-ment, "We done need smart honest men."

Connor shook his head solemnly, "I've taken my stands. I've fought my fights. I don't think what's happening is right, but I won't join the blockade—I won't riot. I respect your right to do so, but I don't believe that's the way to be heard—humanity gets drowned out in the mobs. I've seen it before. I was once a lad off the boat, a long time ago. Many of us were. It isn't right to cast blame on our kin coming across the Atlantic. They want a better life, like we all do. It's just horrible how we've all been set against one another by a few greedy bastards." Connor let out a sigh. "Ain't no easy answer, lads."

"I know, Connor, I've seen the riots, too. I was here for the first riots, and I stood back while good men fought injustice—while the rich got richer, and the poor got poorer. I won't stand by again. These riots aren't gonna compare to those in the past. The whole city is gonna be takin' up arms. Make sure you and your boys are on the right side," Will warned. He and the others walked off, took up their hammers, and returned to work.

Connor stared as the group walked away, "A storm is a-coming, ain't no mistake."

"Are we going to be all right?" Joseph asked.

"We're going to be smart, and we aren't going to take any risks. First sign of riots, we pack up everything and go wait it out at Jim and Clara's. We could hole up in their barn. I've already talked it out with Jim. We should pack up a few things so we can leave at a moment's notice, if need be."

Joseph and Nicolaus looked worried.

"It'll be all right. All we're doing is preparing. Better to be prepared than taken unaware. Now, enough of that," he shook off the gloom, "tonight we're going to the markets to shop for our winter feast, then we'll drive out to Clara's and grab our goose. She said she picked a nice fat one 'specially for us. Did you boys bring your gift?"

"Yep," Joseph replied. "The girls finished it just last night. They wrapped it up tightly in some cotton from the rag bag. Rachel even put one of her little flannel bows on it," he said with a laugh.

Connor shook his head, "Bless Rachel and her flannel bows. Who would've known when we picked up that old faded bit of cloth that she would give it such a happy use."

The boys finished the last bits of their lunch and set off back into the half-demolished house, buckets and tools in hand.

* * * * *

Looks like snow is comin'," Nicolaus observed from the back of the wagon.

They were traveling the long, bumpy road out to the Scolfield farm, with a load of lumber and a special gift set aside for Clara and Jim.

"Oh, look, 'tis my two favorite boys," Clara welcomed them warmly as they entered the house. "Connor, Jim's got your goose all plucked and ready. Would you like a bit of tea and cake?"

"As good as that sounds, I don't want to be driving back through town too late. Things just are too uneasy these days," Connor replied with regret.

"Don't we know it. Even from way out here, we hear the ruckus. Them lads have the right on their side, but I don't think they're going to get their way through violence and blockadin'."

"I know. The workmen need to organize, choose representatives to put forth their grievances, and then act as one. But that isn't going to happen. Things have gone mad. Which reminds me, if things get too rough in the city, could we impose on you for a few days until things quiet down?"

"Of course ya, can. Ain't even a question. We got room for all," Clara replied without hesitation.

"Thanks, love," he bent in for a hug and a kiss on the cheek. "Now, I'll go see that husband of yours. Where is he?"

"He's out in the barn with Tim. The goose is out there as well," she replied.

Connor made his way toward the door. "You two, don't be too long. We need to be heading back soon."

"Won't be but a minute," Clara replied for the boys. "We just need to make up a little bundle of cake for the road, and they'll be out."

Joseph and Nicolaus smiled. The two were a great deal plumper than when Clara first met them, due in no small part to her cakes.

"'Tis oatmeal cake tonight. I'm sending you back with enough for everyone," she said as she cut up large wedges and wrapped everything in a cloth. "Here you are," she said, placing the cloth bundle in Nicolaus' hands. "And see to it that Davy eats his piece and only his piece," she said sternly. "I swear that boy's brain is in his stomach."

"Thank you," Nicolaus replied.

"You best be off now. No woolgathering. Connor will be waitin'." She wiped the cake crumbs from her hands with the ends of her apron and gave the boys a hug.

"We'll go, but first we have something to give you," Joseph said brightly. He dashed back to the door and grabbed a package that had been waiting outside. Nicolaus beamed with excitement. "Here you are. This is from all of us for you and your family for all you've done for us." Joseph placed the cloth wrapped bundle in Clara's arms.

"Well, what is this now?" she asked, completely surprised.

She untied the flannel bow and began folding back the wrappings to find a huge patchwork quilt made from all the remnants of the cloth Connor had bought them for clothes.

For once in her life, Clara was utterly speechless. The quilt unfolded as she held it—draping down across the floor. "I just don't know what to say," she finally replied. "What a beautiful gift and such delicate stitchin'."

"The girls did most of the stitchin'." Nicolaus explained.

"Yes, but we cut out a lot of the squares and such," Joseph added proudly.

"Well, cuttin' and stitchin' alike is just lovely. Thank you, my dearest boys." Still clutching the quilt in her arms, she gave each of them a long embrace, wiping tears away from her eyes as she pulled back.

"Oh, silly me, gettin' all watery-eyed. You'll be late now, go on, go on," she said shuffling them toward the door. "Tell the girls and all the others how much I like it," she shouted as they crossed the lawn and hopped into the wagon bed.

She raised a hand and waved from the porch as the wagon drove off. The quilt clutched tight against her chest.

* * * * *

CHORES DONE, DINNER EATEN, and the moon rising, everyone sat quietly relaxing in the living room. Connor was sitting in the chair by the fire reading. Joseph approached the tall, narrow bookshelf and started reading the titles.

"Joseph, why don't you put those blank books from the printing house on the bookshelf." Connor suggested, "No sense in them sitting in that old crate forever."

"What'll we do with empty books?" Davy asked.

"Why you'll fill them with your thoughts, of course," Connor replied, rubbing Davy's thick head of black hair as he walked by. "Here," Connor approached Joseph, "how many are there?"

"Not sure. Thirteen or fourteen. Why?" Joseph replied.

"That's perfect. Each of you are going to have one of these books to fill as you please. We'll write your name in your book and keep it here on the shelf." Connor got out the ink and pen, turned to the first page of each book, and scrolled one of the children's names. "Line up. Everyone take their book, as I finish, and put it away." One at a time, the children came when their name was called and took their book.

"Still don't know what we're supposed to do with 'em," Davy said as he took his.

"You have your letters about you now. You could write about your days. Write your dreams," Joseph approached Connor to claim his book. "Write your story," Connor said meaningfully.

Joseph opened his book and saw his name scrolled on the flyleaf. Not only that, he had seen that Connor had given each of the children his last name, Morgan, uniting all the castoffs under one banner.

As his eyes traced the letters, he felt something gathering in him. He wanted to write something. It just wasn't quite time yet.

The Journal of Joseph Morgan

"Look!" Asa exclaimed abruptly, "Snow. It's snowing!"

All the children rushed to the small window and watched the thick flakes descend, round faces beaming.

Joseph stood back from the window, still with his book in his hand. He didn't need to see the snow. What he needed to see was Anna, Rachel, Marie, Ben, and Asa—all his family watching the snow fall without a care or worry.

Finally, snow was as it always should have been: a magical event rather than a thing to be dreaded.

Anna turned back from the window, she laughed. The small sill was overtaken by the little ones all huddled in their long johns. Anna looked at Joseph, a wide grin spread across his face.

CHAPTER 26
MISSING PIECES

AFTER EVERYONE HAD GONE TO BED, Joseph crept over to the narrow window to peer through the thick, dingy glass down into the alley. Within the darkness, he saw bulky, shadowy figures shift around the trash bins. He tried to make out any details, but his warm breath fogged the window. The white vapor expanded and contracted across the glass. All of a sudden it struck him; he was on the other side of the glass now, and it felt odd. He turned around and stared down at his bed—an inviting nest of thick blankets. Then he turned back to the street. The wind shook the window in its loose frame. He shuddered and climbed back down into his bed and pulled the covers around him as he stared up at the ceiling. A deep sense of gratitude settled in his heart as he asked himself why some are saved and others aren't.

It was Christmas Eve morning, and the house was abuzz with anticipation. Connor had popped out to the market for last minute supplies while Anna, Marie, Rachel, Beth, and Abbey were busy preparing the evening feast of roasted goose, dressing, mince pies, and bread.

"Ready!" Abbey announced placing a floury loaf of bread onto the table.

Anna reached out a hand and felt the dough. "Well done!" she congratulated Abbey. "I'll go put it in the oven." She scooped the loaf onto a plate and walked out toward the hearth.

"Still tinkering?" she asked, as she watched Joseph, Nicolaus, Davy, Ben, and Emma standing around the little Yule-tree moving the decorations around.

"Just a bit," Joseph replied.

As Anna slid the loaf into the hearth, she heard a ruckus coming from Connor's room.

"What is that?" she spoke to herself.

She walked into the bedroom. "What are you doing?" There was shock in her voice. She had walked in to find Asa going through Connor's trunk. Keepsakes and papers were strewn across the floor. "Those are Connor's private things! How did you even get in there?" She rushed over to him and looked in the trunk to see what damage he had done.

"I was looking for the presents," Asa said timidly, knowing by Anna's tone that he had done something very bad.

"What's going on?" Joseph entered the bedroom.

"We had a bit of an incident," Anna replied gently.

"We'll put everything back as it was," Joseph said grabbing hold of the lid and shutting it.

"But what if he broke something?" Anna shouted. Joseph practically ran from the room, Anna hurried after him, Asa followed close behind her. "We have to tell Connor," she reasoned.

Everyone in the living room stopped and stared at them.

"What happened?" Marie asked, as she stirred the bowl of dressing.

Anna explained what had happened.

"Anna's right. We have to tell him," Marie agreed.

Joseph sighed a heavy sigh. He was nervous.

"He's going to know anyway. Best we tell him, and don't try to lie about it."

She was right, of course. Joseph knew as much.

A weight settled on his chest. "Fine," he agreed, however begrudgingly, "we'll tell him when he gets home."

Asa looked up at Joseph and Anna, eyes welling up with tears of remorse.

*   *   *   *   *

A FEW TORTUROUS HOURS LATER, Connor finally returned. "Everything all right?" he asked, taking notice of the dead silence.

For a moment, Joseph didn't say anything. He was afraid to. Finally, he forced himself to speak, "Today Asa was hunting for presents," Joseph began.

"Oh, what happened? Did he finally find a few?" Connor said casually as he took off his boots and coat.

"No," Joseph replied hesitantly, "he went looking for them in your trunk," Joseph confessed.

Connor slowed down a bit and began listening more intently as he untied his remaining boot.

"Anna found him right away," Joseph added quickly. "We don't think he hurt much of anything but we wanted to tell you. We thought it was the right thing to tell you," Joseph repeated anxiously.

Just then, Asa began to softly cry.

"What's a matter, then?" Connor approached the boy and knelt down to face him.

Very quickly, in-between sobs, Asa spoke, "I didn't mean to go in the trunk. I didn't know it was bad. I didn't break anything. I was careful. Please, don't make us leave."

"Oh." Connor said, comprehension dawning. "Don't be silly, now. No one's going anywhere. This is your home, and there's nothing that can change that," Connor consoled.

"I did find him pretty quickly," Anna spoke up, "I honestly don't think he hurt anything."

"I'm sure everything's fine. It's all right. None of you should be afraid. There's nothing you could do that would make me throw you out. I love each and every one of you," he assured. This was the first time he had ever told the children he loved them. For a long time, those words floated in the air, and the children soaked them in.

"In fact, because I love you, and because we're family, I should've shown you a few of the bits from my past that I keep in that trunk. After all, I know your stories. Time has come that you know mine." Connor walked into the bedroom. The children heard the squeak emanate from the trunk lid. He returned to the room with a carved picture frame.

He sat down in the chair by the fire. All the children gathered around.

"I'm not sure where to begin. This isn't a story I share with most people," he took a moment and gazed into the fire. "I suppose it all started back in the homeland—in Ireland. I came to this country some years ago, thirteen years ago, now that I think of it." His brow creased as he thought back. "The steamer sailed from England. The journey from Galway to Liverpool was the first time any of us had left the county, never mind the country."

"What made you leave?" Joseph asked.

"Years of hardship plagued the mainland, atop that, there were years of war, and then years of oppression behind that. The landlords were tyrants, and we were strong-headed lads. During the long stretch of hardship, there sprang a legend of a place of ease, equality, and opportunity: America.

"The Irish people have been starved for a place where we could have the freedom to live as we desired, instead of by class. During the hard times, the people needed hope for a better life, and many of us gripped onto the myth of this perfect land to get through the daily drudgery. For many, America was a reason to carry on—something to believe in. Families worked twenty hours out of each day just to save enough for passage.

"Ironically enough, when my brothers and I saved enough for our passage, things on the mainland had started to improve. My da had a bit of good luck and our family settled in a pleasant village on the western shore. Compared to the filth and injustice of the city, our village was paradise. Yet, blind as we were, we still went looking for the new life in America.

"Thinking back on the time, I'm always reminded of something my da used to tell my brothers and me when we started venturing out in our cutters to fish. He would say to us, 'Lads, 'tis alarming just how fast the current can catch ya up and pull ya out to sea. You must always have your wits about ya and know what direction your boat is being taken in.' He said these words to warn us of the treacherous nature of the sea, but 'tis a warning for life, as well. Colin, Liam, and I allowed ourselves to be swept up in the myth of America, and we gave up on our homeland."

"Colin and Liam are your brothers?" asked Anna.

Connor nodded his head. "Colin and I were already married men with children living in our own cottages on my parent's lands. Tara had given birth to our son three years before we set out. My da, mum, sisters, and my youngest brother stayed. When we told our mum and da that we were going, we asked them to come, but my da simply said, 'I was born on this island, I shall live on this island, and here my body shall rest.' My mum said, 'This is the place I know. It's my home.'

"We were all grown men, our parents let us make our own decisions. My da told all us lads before we left that even with all its faults and all the hardships that came with being an Irishman, a man must try to make his homeland better, if he can. 'When a man's family is threatened, there's no shame in leaving for another shore. But if a man has the choice to stay, he should.' He said, 'When a man leaves his home for a better place, he makes life better for himself. Yet when a man makes his homeland a better place, he makes a better life for all his countrymen.'

"We were too headstrong to hear the wisdom in his words. All we could hear were the promises of America; we were deaf to all else. Of course, in coming here, we simply traded one prejudice for another, one master for another. The only difference being that, at home, we at least had our friends and family who helped brighten our dark days. No, we were like the babes in Mrs. McCarthy's stories—carried off by the fairy folk, whispering in our ears of bright and shiny things, only to lose those who brought joy to our lives.

"What fools we were," he said in a harsh, bitter whisper. His mouth gapping a little, as though he was stunned by the stupidity of his past choices, now seeing how obviously wrong they were.

"When Liam got ill, we should've known the mistake we'd made. When he was dying all the boy wanted was to go home and be in his old bed. When someone comes to the end of their life, they have eyes clearer than any of us. In that moment, Liam could see what was important, and it was the place behind us, not the one that lay ahead."

"Did Liam die?" Ben asked with the brazenness only a child possesses.

Connor was wounded by the sharp question but held nothing against the boy's unfiltered nature.

"The conditions onboard ship were hard: close quarters, little food, filth, stagnant water. Hundreds of us, all kept in the hold of this wooden beast, living on prayers and hope, never questioning whether the stories of America would be true.

"Liam took ship's fever a few days into the journey. He fought for near a week. We all tended to him day and night. Tara had learnt to nurse the sick from her mum, who was a knowledgeable healer in the county, but even she couldn't keep him with us. He died ten days into the journey, and we buried him at sea and arrived at port one less. All tolled, thirty-two souls died during the eight week voyage, which I was told by the crew was not uncommon. We all thought we knew the perils when we set out. We all knew the stories of the 'coffin ships' that would bring us to the free land, if only we could survive the journey fraught with dysentery and death. But as I said, we were blinded by the myth of America, and we thought anything would be better than the humiliation and starvation ravaging Ireland.

"My mum wasn't blind, though. She had worried when Liam announced he was coming with us. He was only seventeen at the time—eager, bright-eyed, and innocent," Connor's voice trailed off, as his throat constricted.

"Colin and his wife Bridget had a boy of six and a girl of four. Colin and I thought we had it all figured. We'd make the voyage to America and travel to the West, where it was rumored that they were practically giving away land, and a man could be his own master. Liam heard our plans and pitched in with us. We never thought of telling him he couldn't come. We actually thought we were giving him the chance at a better life."

"What happened to Colin and Bridget?" Anna asked.

Taking a deep breath, Connor continued, "When the boat made berth in Boston, we stepped foot upon the fabled America only to be disillusioned. Our brother had died to reach these shores, which didn't live up to their legend. We were sick with regret. We knew then and there that we should've turned right around and got back on a boat headed home, but we didn't.

"We decided to go on. Colin, Bridget, Tara, and me, along with the little ones, were going to settle in the West. We bought a big ol' wagon and supplies for the 2,000 mile journey out into the Western territories, where we had heard stories of lands open for the taking. Yet the day we were due to set out, the riots started brewin'. The city was like a battlefield with fires and fightin'. We knew we had to get out. We set out with the wagon at dusk. I still remember—the night sky was ablaze with orange and red from the fires. It was hellish, like the devil himself had conjured up somethin'. Thankfully, we made it out of the boarding house we were stayin' in. I drove the wagon down the road. Our son sat on my wife's lap, while Colin and Bridget were in the bed of the wagon with their children.

"I drove the horses as fast as I could. I can still remember my bones shakin' as the wagon flew over the cobblestone streets." Connor's voice grew faint as he continued, "I remember, we were almost there—we were almost out of the city. My fear had even begun to lift, but then I saw it, and all breath left me. The streets ahead of us were choked with a loomin' mob. They were comin' toward us. I could feel the anger and spite about them. I pulled back hard on the reins, but there was no side street, no way to go around them, and no time to turn back. I sat in the cart watchin' the mob rushin' toward us like a dark wave.

"There was nothin' else to do. I grabbed Tara and our son and a bag holdin' our most precious bits including this picture," he held up the frame he had been clinging to, "and leapt down from the wagon. Colin stayed. He didn't want to give up the wagon. It had taken us years to save for those supplies, and he wasn't about to let them go without a fight. He and Bridget stayed and held their ground. Once I jumped out, Colin took the reins and tried to break through the crowd, but it was no use. The wave washed over the wagon leavin' nothin'. Colin and Bridget and their children were swept away into the chaos, and the wagon was picked clean by the vultures. I never saw them again.

"Tara and I stayed put in the alley. The mob just kept comin'. There was no end to the rioters. We hid our faces from them tryin' not to be seen, claspin' tight to one another, shieldin' each other. We held our son tightly between us.

"The mob eventually flooded into the alley we were hiding in. We were pushed and shoved to our feet. Anything of value was stripped from us—wallets, watches, coats, money, everything. And without any reason, the men started beatin' on me. I didn't fight back. I pushed them off and tried to move through the crowd. But the mob was too thick, and we couldn't get through. Tara was pulled in one direction with our boy and me in another. Our hands were ripped away from one another. I shoved and kicked and fought and clawed against the tide, tryin' to stay with her, but it didn't do any good. Through the rioters, I looked at her, and she looked at me. The men were roarin' and shoutin' and screamin', but all I could hear was her callin' my name, shoutin' to me.

"I raged against the crowd, but I was tangled in a sea of angry men. The light of the fires reflected in the men's eyes. The mob eventually spat me out. I lay on the side of the street hardly able to see, let alone stand. I tried to chase the crowds and find my family, but they were nowhere to be found. I continued to look—without food, without rest. There was no stoppin' until I found her. I went on like that for six days until, finally, I collapsed in an alleyway, sick from hunger and my wounds. I woke days later in the city jail."

"The jail?" Joseph echoed, "Why the jail?"

"I'd been arrested. The police had been roundin' up all the leaders of the riots, and I was taken by mistake. All the bosses of the city wanted the rioters locked up. The police were grabbin' anyone they could, not carin' if you were guilty or innocent. I was put on trial and sent to jail for a year. By the time I was released, there was no hope of finding my family. I searched, of course, but found nothing. All I had left was this photograph," Connor finished mournfully. "I managed to hang onto it."

"You never saw them again?"

"No, not dead or alive. I didn't see them lyin' in the wake of the mob the next day. I checked the bodies of all those who were killed during the night. They lined up the bodies for the carts to haul off to the cemetery beyond the city, and neither of them were there. So there's reason to think they may still be alive, but I've been in this city for twelve years, and I never found them."

"You never went out West?"

"No, here was the place I saw them last, so I stayed here looking for them. Here was where my wife could find me. I couldn't go on without them. As hard as this city is, I had to stay—I had to search for my family. And even now, I know it would be better for us all if we left, but I just can't go. I'm tied to this place until my heart finds a way to heal from it all."

A heavy sadness settled over everyone in the room. No one knew what to say.

"That's a photograph of your family?" Joseph asked gently trying to ease through a difficult moment.

Connor nodded, "We had the photograph taken when we docked in Boston. Colin and I both had photographs taken. We were going to have them sent back home to our mum and da on one of the boats."

Connor handed Joseph the frame, and he looked down at the tattered, faded photograph.

The frame was decorated with vines, flowers, and leaves all around the edges. Cut deep and sanded smooth, the flowers were beautifully carved into the dark, rich hardwood. Inside the frame, there was an old, faded photograph of three people standing together. One was Connor, though without the weight and wear of the years. His face shown with happiness and fullness. The second person stood beside him, a beautiful woman with a spirit so alive Joseph could feel her heart radiating from the picture. She held onto Connor's arm, standing at his side and looking at him with an expression of deepest love. The third person in the picture was a very young boy who had the look of both his mother and his father, a boy no more than three or four—healthy and happy.

Anna leaned in and looked at the photo. Joseph passed it down to her. She stared at it for a long time then passed it to Marie. No sooner did she take the frame than she dropped it, breaking the hand carved frame into pieces.

"Marie?" Anna spun around at the noise, horrified.

Marie was fixed on the photo. She didn't even care that she had broken the frame. It simply did not occur to her. No, all she saw was the photo.

"Marie?" Joseph said, looking at her.

"It's him." Marie said breathlessly.

"Who?" Anna asked.

All eyes were on Marie.

"It's Duncan," Marie replied, "Your son—is Duncan."

Connor stood up, eyes wide, the breath caught in his chest.

CHAPTER 27
THE SEARCH

"**M**Y SON'S NAME WAS DUNCAN," Connor replied. "You know him? You've seen him?" He stood up.

"Your son's name was Duncan?" Joseph and Anna asked simultaneously.

Anna and Joseph looked at the photograph. "I didn't even recognize him, but, yes, that's him. I can see it now."

"I knew him when he was younger. We met a few years after this was taken," Marie replied. For the first time in months, she felt alive.

"You met him? You were friends with him?" Connor asked, trying to catch up.

"Duncan and I met when we were both six years old, or so we figured. It was always hard to know. We helped one another get by," Marie explained.

"Duncan and Marie both cared for us when we were small," Joseph added. "Duncan was like my da for years."

"What happened? Where is he now?" Connor asked, frantic.

"We lost him." Marie frowned.

There was desperation in Connor's voice. "What do you mean, you lost him?"

"We were parted one night some months ago, actually," she

caught herself, "it must be near a year ago now. That night, we were all chased out of the printing house. We were never able to find him after that. We looked everywhere," Marie added sincerity in her voice.

"Where is 'everywhere'?" Connor inquired.

"We checked all our usual spots," Joseph replied.

"And we asked around for him. There was no word," Nicolaus added.

Connor started pacing. He moved towards the door and started putting on his boots.

"Where would he go? You know him. Where would he go to stay?" Connor asked.

"Like I said, we checked all those places, every day for months, and we couldn't find him," Joseph replied. "Chances are he was picked up and brought to an orphanage or a reform."

"Then, that's where we'll go. We'll check every orphanage and reform in the city, if we have to." Connor rose, his boots tied firmly on his feet. He put on his coat and hat. Marie quickly jumped up and started putting on her shoes, Joseph followed behind her. Just then, everyone started to rise.

"No, we can't all go," Connor raised a hand. "Anna, you stay put with the others. We'll come back when we find him."

"It's Christmas Eve. Will they even accept visitors?" Joseph finished buttoning up his Jacket.

"We'll wake them," Connor replied, determined.

*   *   *   *   *

EVERYTHING HAPPENED SO QUICKLY, IT WAS A BLUR. One minute Joseph had been afraid he was going to be turned from the house for Asa's prying, and the next minute he, Marie, and Connor were charging down the dark streets towards Jim and Clara's. The miles went faster than ever.

"Jim and the family will be sitting down to their supper about now," Connor said as they ran breathlessly up the walkway toward the house. "You go and fix up the wagon. I'll run in quickly and tell them what's happened. We'll borrow one of Jim's horses for the night."

Joseph and Marie ran toward the barn where their old wagon was kept.

"Grab those reins," Joseph pointed as they entered the barn.

Marie pulled the reins off a hook and brought them over to Joseph who was securing the canvas flaps on the wagon's cover.

Connor walked into the barn followed by Jim. Clara brought up the rear with a lantern, one child on either side.

"Here, we'll lash up ol' Cotton. He should be able to pull the wagon on his own no problem," Jim suggested, pulling a horse from one of the nearby stalls. "Cotton's a sturdy ol' fella. He'll get ya where you need to go."

Jim harnessed up Cotton, and before they knew it, they were climbing into the wagon.

"We'll bring him back tomorrow," Connor promised.

"Course you will," Jim shrugged.

Clara reached up and gave Joseph and Marie a hug. "You all be safe, now. Let us know any news. God be with ya in your search," she offered, giving Connor a bracing hug. "Now, go." She leapt down from the wagon. "Go."

With a flick of the reins, the wagon lurched, and the horse sped forward. They rounded the bend at the end of the drive and rushed down the lane.

"The orphanages and reforms are spread out all over the city. It'll be quicker with the wagon," Connor assured. "Where did you part ways with him?" he asked as the wagon raced toward the city.

"We lost him at the printing house," Joseph shouted over the ruckus of the wagon.

"All right then," Connor said with another flick of the reins, "we'll start with the orphanage in them parts first. Or did you already inquire there?"

"We didn't dare go near the orphanages," Joseph confessed, "we couldn't. They'd of kept us. Same with the reforms and hospitals. We wanted to go though," Joseph said, a bit of pleading in his voice.

"Don't fret. We'll go now. The important thing is that he is alive. Knowing that—knowing that he is indeed alive and in this city," Connor stressed. "We'll find him."

Before Joseph knew it, they were speeding through the city streets, down past the old harbor and the plot of land where the printing house once stood.

"There it is," Connor said as they rounded the corner and the orphanage came into sight.

Connor leapt from the wagon before it even stopped. He looped the reins around a post and dashed up to the double doors and started pounding. Joseph and Marie followed behind him and reached him just as the doors were flung open by a disgruntled old woman.

"Land sakes!" the disheveled old woman exclaimed, "what is this ruckus all about?" She turned to Connor demanding an explanation.

"We need to come in," Connor replied.

"What you need is to be quiet," the woman scolded.

"You don't understand," Connor pleaded, "I think you have my son here. Please, I need to meet all the boys you have around fourteen, fifteen, and sixteen."

Her eyes narrowed. She didn't seem convinced. "No, I really think you ought to go now. The children are resting, and we are closed. If you insist on coming in, return the day after tomorrow." She started to close the doors.

"This ain't no trick, and I ain't lying, please," he strained. "It's Christmas Eve. Take pity," he finished.

The woman stopped and considered him. She begrudgingly pulled the doors open.

"Follow me, the boy's hall is down here," she led them into the entryway. "Just you," she instructed, insisting that Joseph and Marie stay at the door. "Come on, let's get this over with. I've not got all day."

"It'll be fine," Connor assured the children as he followed the old woman.

Joseph watched as Connor disappeared down a gloomy narrow hallway.

"Don't like this place," Joseph said, rubbing his arms as a chill passed through his body.

"I don't reckon any children who have passed through those doors have much fancied the place," Marie pointed out. "Still, it feels good to be looking," she added.

"I'm in shock," Joseph said in a dumbfounded voice. "I just can't believe this is happening. It's like something out of a dream."

"I'll take this dream over the reality we have had," Marie replied.

Conversation died down. Both of them were anxious. At any moment, Connor could come back up that hallway with Duncan by his side.

They waited ten more minutes, or so they guessed, as they listened to the distant chimes of a clock. At last, they heard footsteps, a single pair of footsteps.

Connor emerged from the shadowed corridor alone. He shook his head. "None of them lads were my boy," he pulled open the doors, passed back into the cold air, and moved towards the wagon. "But it doesn't matter. This is the beginning of the search, not the end. There are still plenty of places to search."

Joseph, Marie, and Connor climbed into the wagon and dashed off into the night.

Each stop they made followed exactly like the first. And after each inquiry, yielded nothing. Connor would insist he wasn't finished. However, Joseph could see the toll each disappointment was taking on both Connor and Marie.

"Where would he have gone, if he couldn't go to the printing house? Was there a place that he would have gone to take shelter?"

"The printing house was our one safe place," Joseph replied, feeling helpless.

The wagon rattled along the cobblestone streets aimlessly.

"Wait!" Marie said suddenly, "there was a place he and I would take you when you were just little ones. An old, sheltered alley down by the factories."

Connor tugged the reins hard left, heading toward the factories. "There are two orphanages up that way. If he was snatched by the police there, they would have brought him to one of the homes in that part of town."

After a rattled ride, they found themselves in front of yet another set of doors. With a heavy sigh, Connor raised his hand to the door and dared to hope.

"Yes," a woman called. She swung the door open. She was middle aged, dressed in a schoolmarm's uniform, a long skirt, a blouse with puffed sleeves, and a small pocket watch hanging from her belt. "What can I do for you?" she asked curtly.

Connor made his request—the same request he made at the last six stops.

Thankfully, the woman let him through with a minimal amount of fuss and bother.

"We have a boy's hall, but few boys would fit the age you are seeking. Most boys that old have been adopted by farmers just outside the city looking for hands," she escorted the three of them down the halls to the common room. "You children stay here," she pointed to a stool in a far off corner. "You," she pointed to Connor, "the boy's hall is down there," she pointed to a door on the left. "Also, we have a few boys in the hospital ward," she added, nodding towards a door on the right.

His mind was tired and blank. He walked wordlessly toward the hospital ward, as though something invisible was leading him towards the door.

Connor rounded the doorframe and walked slowly down the room, rows of beds flanking him on either side. Then he saw him—A lone boy curled up on a thin cot. Connor didn't need Marie to tell him that it was his son. Without even knowing it, the boy was the spitting image of his lost mother with his auburn hair, round face, and a light spray of freckles about his cheeks.

Connor drew up to the foot of the bed. The boy in the cot didn't move. He lay there listlessly, knees pulled up tight to his chest, staring off into the dimly lit room.

"Duncan." Connor's voice was almost a whisper.

The boy stirred. Something about the voice was strangely familiar, like something out of a dream. He turned and lay flat on the bed, his dark eyes staring toward the man staring at him.

"Duncan, it's me," Connor said softly, as though he were afraid that, if he spoke too loudly, he might wake and discover this all to be a dream.

Duncan stared at him, trying to reach back in time to find a memory of his father's face undiminished by the intervening years. Connor could see his son trying to remember.

"We were all together in the wagon when the mob came. You were with your mum when we all were separated. I looked for you for a week before I collapsed. I have been looking for you for over ten years—never stopping, never giving up hope," Connor consoled. He stepped forward and sat down at the end of the bed.

"I never told anyone what happened that night. It was so long ago, sometimes it's like a dream—like you and mum were only a dream," Duncan said, scarcely willing to believe this to be true. The boy sat up, reaching out a hand toward his father.

"It's not a dream," Connor assured, tears running down his bearded cheeks.

Duncan laughed softly for the first time in what seemed liked ages.

The two embraced. Neither could pull away, so they just sat there for a time in the silence.

Joseph and Marie waited anxiously in the next room. Joseph sat on a stool in a dark corner while Marie stood impatiently, wrapped in her own thoughts.

"He's been in there a while. Do you think he has found him?" Joseph asked.

Marie shook her head, at a loss. She was not willing to get her hopes up.

While Marie went back and forth in her mind about what could be happening in the next room, Joseph wandered down the hall and poked his head into the boy's hall.

Here it was, Christmas Eve, but there was no trace of the season in the dank room. Never was there a more depressing place—gray walls, gray floor, stained and torn furniture that was undoubtedly salvaged from the dump. Far off, there was a small fire burning in the hearth with nowhere near enough wood to keep the whole place warm. And then there were the children. Joseph noticed that no one was talking to one another, no one was playing—everyone sat to themselves curled up on their beds or on the floor staring off with hopeless, lifeless looks on their faces.

In that moment, he felt profoundly guilty. It so easily could have been him in the moth-eaten clothes cloistered away in this dark place. But instead, here he was dressed in thick clothes, a feast at home waiting for him, a warm bed, surrounded by love and hope. Why? What made him so special that he should be singled out and lifted from his poverty? Why him and not these children? The question left a bitter taste in his mouth. He did not have an answer. It was all so senseless. He looked at the children—their lifeless faces—wondering how he would ever be worthy of the gifts he was given.

It was as he sat pondering these hard questions that the hospital ward doors burst open. Connor emerged supporting a weak Duncan on his arm.

Marie stopped, looked at him, and dashed toward him, throwing her arms around him with full force.

"I told you there was more waiting for you," Connor said with a smile on his face.

"But, how?" Duncan asked, utterly confused. Marie clutched him so tightly. He held her back, catching a glimpse of Joseph over Marie's shoulder. "I don't understand. I just don't understand," Duncan kept repeating in shock.

"We'll explain on the way home," Connor assured.

"Home," Duncan repeated. The word was a soothing balm on his heart.

Marie took one of Duncan's arms, while Connor took another. They moved through the hall and out toward the door.

Joseph watched the three of them disappear down the hall. He stood there for a time looking at the faces of those being left behind and wondered how to make a difference in such a sea of misery.

A small girl sitting alone gave him a broken expression. He smiled warmly back at her. She turned away from him as she rolled over on her bed. He tore himself away and walked solemnly down the hall, out into the cold night.

CHAPTER 28
BLESSINGS

"WE CAN KEEP ALL THE FOOD WARM and then serve it when they return." Rachel tended the coals. Anna nodded, only half-listening. No matter how hard she tried, all she could think about was Duncan and the oddness of how this had all come together.

She gazed deep into the fire.

"Was this all providence, then?" Davy asked. Along with all the other children, Davy was up far past his bedtime.

"What do you mean?" Rachel answered.

"You're always hearin' people talkin' of things happenin' by providence, like it was meant to be. Was this—us findin' Duncan's father and all—was that providence?" Davy asked.

Ben, Abbey, and Beth turned to see what Rachel would say. It seemed each of them had been pondering the same thoughts as Davy.

"I don't rightly know," Rachel replied in a tone of uncertainty, "but only a fool would chalk it all up to chance."

"Shhhh," Anna interjected, "I hear someone coming up the stairs."

All eyes turned toward the door. Breath caught in their chest, they all stared intently at the doorknob.

Joseph was the first through the door. Anna and the others looked to him expectantly, their faces begging for news, but Joseph gave anyway nothing. He held a straight face. Next came Marie, who likewise held steady, until the last moment when she stepped away from the threshold to reveal Duncan with Connor close behind him.

A general outcry echoed. The children ran toward Duncan jumping, shouting, embracing, and shaking his hand.

"I can't believe it," Anna and Rachel both exclaimed through tears, "I just can't believe it," they repeated in shock and gratitude.

Nicolaus came up to Duncan, grabbed his hand and started shaking it so hard his glasses slid right down his long nose.

"Let him through, now. We have to close the door, or the neighbors will complain," Connor shuffled all the children deeper into the living room and closed the door behind him.

The outpouring of emotion continued on, unrestrained for the better part of an hour before Connor and Joseph finally spoke up.

"Let poor Duncan have a moment," Joseph said, laughing as Emma, Asa, and Ben sat at Duncan's feet asking him question after question about all he had been through.

"First things first, Anna," Connor turned to her, "we need to put on the kettle and start filling the bath. Joseph, grab clothes from my dresser and lay them out on the bed."

Anna stood up and stoked the fire. "Davy, Ben, go fetch some water. The pails are by the door."

"After that, we need to get some food in you," Connor said, helping his frail son to his feet.

"The feast is ready," Anna said motioning to the roasted

goose sitting off to the side along the hearth staying warm. "We kept it all warm. We couldn't eat without you."

Joseph and Connor beamed, "Wonderful." Connor replied, "All right then—bath, clothes, and then feast. In the meantime, let's clean up the floor a bit so that we all have a place to sit.

A short time later, a clean and trim Duncan emerged from Connor's room dressed in his father's clothes. Everyone was gathered on the floor in a circle. The feast laid out on the floor in front of them.

Bowls of steaming food were passed around the circle. Duncan loaded his plate and cleaned it before the bread had even finished being passed. Seeing this, Connor swapped out his plate, which he had only just finished filling, for the empty one in front of Duncan.

"What about you?" Duncan asked, hesitant to dig into the plate.

"I'll refill this one for me. There's plenty to go around," Connor smiled warmly.

Duncan nodded and started eating. He took this plate a little slower than he did the first.

Busily eating, Duncan did not notice that everyone was staring at him. Connor sat on one side of him and Marie on the other, both of them hardly touching their plate, unable to take their eyes off him.

"So, how did you all meet?" Duncan asked through a mouthful of goose.

Connor looked at Joseph, "Well, that's a bit of a tale, isn't it?" Connor mused.

"Well, it all started when we met at the printing house…"

Joseph began, telling the whole story clean through to the moment when they found Duncan lying in his bed in the hospital ward.

"I'm just in shock, you know." Duncan concluded. "I never expected to find you again," he turned to his father, "let alone hope that you all would be with him when he found me," he smiled.

After eating dinner, Duncan seemed to grow tired. Everyone sat lazily in the living room, basking in the warmth of the fire and the contentment of the feast.

"If you want to sleep, you can go lie down in my bed," Connor offered.

"No," Duncan replied softly, "I want to stay out here and sit with everyone for a time. I've missed you all so," he added.

Duncan looked so frail, his auburn hair was thinning, his dark eyes were shadowed, and his skin was sallow. Connor was heartsick to see how worn away his son was. He consoled himself with the thought that now, having found him, he could fatten him up and try to heal the wounds caused by the world.

"So what of your story?" Marie asked. "What has happened since we saw you last?"

"Aye, I have wondered that, too," Connor turned to Duncan, "only, I want to hear your story from the last night I saw you— or at least as much of it as you can recall."

Duncan nodded. He stared down into his warm cup of brown tea and thought back, "Some things have stuck," he raised a hand to his head and tapped his temple, "while others haven't. I remember parts of our journey on the boat to come here. I remember the darkness of the ship below decks, and I remember the sea. I remember the night we were parted clearly," he went on, "that night stands out among others. I remember the riots. I remember you being taken," he turned to his father.

"Aye, what happened after we were parted?" Connor asked.

"I remember being with Mum," Duncan explained, "we were caught in the crowd. I remember her trying to get away from them, but she couldn't. She held on tight to my arm, so she wouldn't lose me," he struggled to recall what happened next. "A time later, I don't know how long, we broke loose and were in the streets and alleys looking for you. I remember walking until my legs hurt. Mum was hurt, I suppose it was from the fight with the crowd. Eventually, she couldn't walk any further either, and she took us to a chapel to take shelter. The minister took us in, fed us, and gave us a place to rest. We were there for a long time, many days, I think. I don't know what was wrong with her, but I remember her being confined to her bed for a long time."

"What happened next?" Connor asked, wondering how Duncan got separated from his mother.

"After some days there, the minster told me that Mum probably would not survive her wounds, so they let me say goodbye to her, and they sent me over to an orphanage where I stayed for a few years. Or there abouts, until I finally escaped. It was then, when I was on the streets, that I found Marie," he turned to Marie and laid a hand on her arm. "We saw each other through the years that came after," he finished.

"But what happened to your Mum?" Connor asked. "What did she say when you said goodbye to her?" There was desperation in his voice.

"When the minister took me into her to say goodbye, she was sleeping." Duncan replied.

"Sleeping?" Connor echoed, "She didn't wake when you came to her?"

"No, I reckon she was too sick to wake," Duncan concluded. "I was only given a minute. I kissed her on the cheek, and then I was carried off. I didn't want to go," he added, "I remember hugging her tight, and the men from the orphanage ripping me away from her."

"So you never saw her die?" Connor asked.

Duncan nodded, "No."

"Do you recall what chapel this was?" Connor asked.

Duncan nodded, "Um," He struggled. "I think it was downtown. I don't remember the name."

Connor was quiet for a time. Joseph sat there watching him, wondering just what he was thinking. Connor took out his pocket watch and looked at the time. It was past midnight.

"Tomorrow I want to go visit the chapels down there. Maybe they'll have some kind of record of what happened to your mum." Connor hoped.

Duncan nodded, "Not knowing what happened has been very hard."

"I know, son, for me too," Connor laid a hand on Duncan's shoulder.

Everyone sat solemnly together. The shadows cast by the smoldering fire flickered on the walls.

"I almost forgot," Anna announced in a bright voice, trying to fight the melancholy. She went to the table by the pantry cupboard. When she returned a moment later, she was carrying a plate upon which a Christmas pudding sat. The cake was rich and gooey. "It's chock-full of raisins, currants, plums, grated apple, and lots of dark brown sugar."

All the children, once tired, sat up and stared at the cake.

"Plus, Clara gave me some brandy to soak it in. Connor, would you do the honors?" She handed the plate to Connor. He set it on the hearthstone, took a thin piece of kindling, lit it, touched the flame to the cake, and a blue halo radiated from it.

"All right, everyone move in close," Connor said, gathering all the children around him. They all sat watching the small cake glow until, at last, all the alcohol was burned away, and the halo flickered and died out.

"Can we eat it now?" Davy asked, hungry as ever.

Duncan laughed, "Well, you haven't changed, have you," he said lovingly.

Laughter erupted from the small room. Connor threw a fat yule log on the fire, the cake was cut, everyone wrapped up snuggly in their blankets, and the next few hours passed in peace.

CHAPTER 29
THINGS FALL APART

IT WAS CLOSE TO DAWN. Everyone lay in a deep sleep, contented after the heavy meal and joyous news of Duncan's return. Joseph, however, slept lightly no matter how full his belly or light his heart. A creaking from Connor's room woke him. His brown eyes stared out into the darkness. He was sure Connor must be up.

Joseph eased up from his bed and over to Connor's door. He ever so slightly poked his head in and saw Connor sitting up in bed looking at the photograph of his family. Joseph shifted his weight. The old floorboards creaked underfoot.

Connor turned, "It seems, I'm not the only one who couldn't sleep."

Joseph walked toward the edge of the bed. "I heard noises coming from your room. I figured you were awake. I wanted to check on you."

"I'm fine, dear boy. I have my son back. I have waited many, long years for this day to come," Connor said reflectively. "God knows, it probably shouldn't have happened. It's unbelievable—the truest of blessings," he added, staring down at the faded image.

There was a long pause, Joseph could sense a "but" coming.

"—but," Connor went on, "I still don't know how to go on," he said sorrowfully. "Having Duncan back was more than I could've ever expected. He alone should fill the hole in me, but I still feel it. The city is falling apart around us, and we are bleeding money, but I still can't go," he confessed helplessly. "I can't leave this place and have peace until I know what happened to her—until I know what her days were like, and I either look into her face again or, God forbid, stand over her grave. Not until then, will it be done."

"Today, we'll go round to the city chapels. As you say, maybe one of them will have records of what happened to her. It's a place to start."

"If she died," Connor began, choking on the words, "they most likely dropped her in some nameless, pauper grave and, I'll never know where she lies."

"Well," Joseph replied, trying to maintain hope during this heavy time, "Duncan never saw her die. We don't know that she died," he reasoned. "She could have lived, and the minster just never reunited her with Duncan. I mean, once you go into one of them orphanages, you get lost in a sea of faces, moved from house to house, family to family—it's truly a miracle that we even found Duncan."

"Aye," Connor replied sadly, "we've already had one miracle—two actually, because we have to count you and yours finding me—so how then, can we expect a third?" he asked, looking for a reason to hope.

Joseph did not know what to say. He stood there at a loss. He put his hands in his pockets, not sure what to do with himself, knowing how badly Connor needed something to grasp onto.

"I don't know how miracles work," he began, "I don't know why some get them, and some don't. But I do know that this hasn't all happened because of chance. If life was ruled by chance, God knows we'd all be dead in some alley somewhere, but we're not. We have a place to go and search," he reminded, "and we will go today and see what answers we find. And we'll stay here, no matter what the cost, until you find what it is you need." Joseph smiled and laid a supportive hand on Connor's shoulder.

After a moment of silence, Connor got up and put the photograph back in his trunk.

"Well, if we don't do presents before we head off to the chapels, Davy and Asa will never forgive us."

"No, they probably won't," Joseph laughed silently.

"We'll get out the presents and have gift time and breakfast, and then we'll go," Connor suggested.

"Sounds like a good plan—" just then, Joseph was cut off mid-sentence by a loud bang and bedlam coming from the streets below.

Connor slid open the old, rickety window and stuck his head out into the chilly morning. He quickly came back in and shut it. "The riots are breakin' loose. I can hear the crowds. Should've known it would happen this morning. On Christmas, the poor always keenly feel the gap between themselves and the rich, I'm sure they feel it even more so this Christmas with so many losing their wages—" A noise erupted in the distance. Connor and Joseph rushed to the window. A few buildings just down the street had been set on fire and crowds had begun flooding into the street, where calls for violence were shouted by men.

"God, it's happening again," Connor said to himself in horror. "Quick, go wake everyone, grab everything that is precious, and we'll make our way down to the wagon. It's still hitched up in the alley alongside the house. We'll make our way out to the farm and hole up there till it's quieted down."

Joseph nodded and dashed back into the living room. Anna, Davy, Nicolaus, Duncan, Rachel, and Marie were all awake and looking out the window.

"We've gotta' leave," Duncan said without hesitation.

"I know," Joseph replied, "pack everything you can. We're going to go wait out the storm at Clara and Jim's."

No sooner had the words left his lips, than everyone set about to packing and getting the little ones up and moving.

"I'll pack a basket of food," Connor announced. He dashed to the pantry cupboard, and grabbed all the preserved foods. "Make sure you bundle up," he called into the living room, "it's cold out there."

"We can only bring one small bundle each," Joseph instructed as everyone gathered a few precious things to take with them.

"Will we be able to come back?" Ben asked innocently.

Joseph shook his head. No one had the answer to that question.

A few moments later, food packed, and little ones wrapped up warmly, they headed out the door. Connor was the last one out. He took his bundle containing the savings and the photograph of his family, tucked it inside his jacket, grabbed the basket of food, gave the room a once-over, and closed the door to the apartment behind him.

"Everyone into the wagon," Joseph directed.

Anna and Marie were lifting the little ones into the wagon one at a time. Duncan slid up onto the driver's seat and stared at the door to the building, chaos erupting around them.

A few seconds later, Connor bolted through the door, jumped up into the wagon, turned to make sure everyone was settled, flicked the reins, and pulled out into the packed street.

Connor tried to gain speed. The sea of people parted for the wagon as he forced his way through.

"Going past the harbor is the only way to the farm from here," Connor shouted back.

"Will it be safe?" Joseph shouted from the back of the wagon. "What about the blockade?"

"There's no other way without going miles around the other side of town, and that smoke," he motioned with his head, still staring straight ahead, "is coming from that part of town. No, best to get out quickly," he finished, flicking the reins again, causing the horse to step up his pace.

The wagon rattled towards the harbor, cutting through the hysteria around them. There was an ominous air hanging over the city. Connor was holding the reins so tightly, his finger-nails were digging into the aged leather. In the back of the wagon, Joseph, Anna, Marie, Nicolaus, and Rachel held the little ones tight, terror in their wide eyes.

"What about the chapels?" Joseph asked, shouting over the din.

"We can come back once things have died down," Connor replied.

The wagon raced forward. The harbor came into view. The scene was desperate. The blockade had swelled to a crowd of thousands. Two large steamers carrying immigrants from Ireland and Europe were trying to make dock.

The wagon rounded the bend, went barreling down the road, and came into view of the mob.

"Look!" a voice from the mob shouted, "the ships are unloadin'."

"Fresh off the boat!" Duncan shouted, pointing to the enraged mob moving towards them.

"They think we're coming off the boats!" Joseph shouted, pointing towards a steamer that had just pulled alongside the dock, its decks loaded with weary souls trying to disembark.

There wasn't any time—no time to change direction, no time to think, no time to reason with the hate-blinded mob. In the space of a breath, everything had changed. They all braced as the mob washed over the wagon.

To Joseph, it seemed that everything slowed and everything sped up at the same time. Angry, unfamiliar hands reached for them. Out of the corner of his eye, he saw Anna clinging tightly to Emma as she was pulled backward out of the wagon bed. He reached out to Asa. The small boy cried, overwhelmed and frightened. Joseph pulled him close. "Hang on to me!" he shouted above the crowd. He felt Asa's small hands grip his jacket for dear life. "Nicolaus!" he yelled, pointing to Beth and Abbey, both of whom had been yanked from their seats. Unable to reach them, Nicolaus looked panicked. Marie saw what was happening and followed the girls down into the crowd. Davy took Ben's arm and leapt down from the wagon. Nicolaus and Rachel followed after them.

Joseph looked helplessly to Connor. He was trying to spur the horse on through the crowd to no avail. "They're taking them!" Duncan shouted to his father as he leapt down into the crowd. One by one as the children were pulled from the wagon, they were huddled together with the crowd being pushed onto the freighter's gangplank.

"No!" Connor screamed as he saw the tails of Duncan's shirt trailing down into the crowd. Connor dropped the reins and stood up. Behind him, he saw the children shuffled through the crowd. In a surreal moment, he saw Joseph pulled backward out of the wagon, Asa still clinging to his jacket. He hit the ground hard. Connor leapt down. He crashed into several people as he landed.

The moment his boots touched the ground, the tide of the mob grabbed him and shoved him toward the steamer moored just yards away. Connor fought the forces that dragged him as he pushed his hand towards Joseph who was still lying on the ground gasping for breath. The boy had had the wind knocked out of him. "Joseph," he strained his arm as far as it would go. "Get up, Joseph!" he shouted as the tide pulled him away from the boy.

Joseph felt the mud caked to his back. The weight of Asa rested on his chest. The voices of the crowd and Asa's hysterical cries melded into one loud racket. The chaos swirled around him. Forbidding figures of outraged men hovered over him. Somewhere in the distance, he heard his name called, but he did not know what he was supposed to do. In that disoriented moment, he could not remember how to stand, how to walk. He just lay there, in a daze—lost.

"Send 'em back!" a man in the crowd shouted. He stood high on a tower of crates situated on the docks. "No room here! No jobs to give and no food to spare!" he screamed. The mob echoed his war cries.

"Joseph!" Anna shouted frantically into the mass of men sprawled out beneath her. She along with Nicolaus, Rachel, Emma, Duncan, Ben, Marie, Abbey, Davy, and Beth, and many unknown strangers were being shepherded up the gangplank onto the wide decks of the tramp steamer. "Joseph!" Anna screamed again, as loudly as her voice could manage. Her lungs crushed under the force of her wrenching heart.

Anna's call reached Joseph. It shattered off his haze as he lay there, broken in the mud. He wrapped his arms around Asa, and no sooner did he make to rise, than the crowd took him by the scruff of his jacket and pushed him down towards the docks. Ahead of him, he could see Connor reaching the steamer—his nose bloody and his face swelling. Duncan forced his way back down the gangplank to help his beaten father onboard.

The boat belched steam and the whistle pierced the air. Anna handed Emma to Marie and charged down the deck close to the railing, following Joseph and Asa's progress through the mob.

The crowd lost interest in Joseph and Asa as the boat prepared to depart. Once he was pushed toward the ship—unwilling to go—but now it was all he could do to fight his way toward the dock to board the ship loaded with his entire family.

"Where do you think you're going?" A stranger took hold of Anna. "There ain't no getting off this ship little girl," he scolded. A few dozen, burly men had taken over the ship, commissioned by the mob to see the boat out of native waters.

She raged against him but could not break his iron grip. The boat gave a lurch and the lines were cast off. Joseph saw her on the deck. For a moment their eyes met, and she could feel him saying a silent goodbye from across the distance between them—a goodbye Anna was unwilling to make.

In the distance, Connor and the others tried to push their way down the deck to help, but the crowds were too thick.

Knowing she was about to lose him, Anna fought against her captor with all her strength, kicking and pounding, striking a hard blow to the large man's shins and fat stomach. Breaking free, she charged down the gangplank. She could feel the ramp pulling away from the deck.

"Stop!" she pleaded, knowing that no one was listening. "Joseph!" she begged, her eyes wide and filled with tears.

Joseph saw her barreling down the ramp towards him. Driven by the sight of her, he forced himself through the crowd with new strength. In the very last moment, holding Asa tightly, he managed to leap onto the ramp. Anna heaved them up toward the deck, making it safely aboard, just as the steamer pulled away from the edge of Long Wharf and moved out into open water.

CHAPTER 30
THE VOYAGE

THE CITY GREW SMALLER IN THE DISTANCE. The deck was crowded with battered and distraught souls forced from their homes, parted from their families, bullied, accused, and sent steaming toward another shore.

"Stop the bloody ship! Stop dammit!" Connor screamed as the shoreline slipped away from them. He went thundering down the deck toward a man who was obviously a member of the crew. "I want to talk to the bleedin' Captain!" Connor demanded. He was distraught. He gripped the crewman with both hands—almost hanging on him. Joseph and Duncan dashed after him while Anna and Marie stayed with the shaken children.

"Calm down!" the crewman bellowed back, ripping himself away from Connor. "Ain't nothin' left of the captain but a puddle of blood on the floor. Them rioters saw to that," he cursed, pointing back at the shore. "The chief is in charge, now, and he won't be turnin' this ship around—not for nuttin'. This is the fourth time we've tried to put in, and the fourth time we've been turned away," the man waved a fist in the direction of the city. "Nah, we've had our fill. Chief's headin' back home."

"Where's home?" Connor asked, filled with dread.

"Galway Bay, then on to Liverpool. Same ways we dun come."

"But we have to go back," Connor pointed to the city growing still smaller on the horizon. "He can't take us against our will. Dammit, I'm a free man, and I'll do as I bloody-well please! And what about the passengers? They've paid their fare over; you can't just send them back! Plus," Connor went on, grasping at any reason as he reeled, "doesn't he have to take on fresh supplies? We must get off. We're not even supposed to be here!" Connor was frantic.

"I wish I could help ya, but there is nothin' to be done. Others have been forced on during the last runs we took at the city. The chief said you all can have passage down with the folk in steerage. It ain't much, but it's probably better than the ships you took over. As far as supplies done go, we'll put in at one of the islands to the north, take on fresh water and food, and trade for the remainder of what we'll need. Then we'll be on our way. You're welcome to step off there and stay, but there ain't no livin' to be had on them islands. And let me tell ya now, if ya stay and make trouble, the crew won't take kindly. You'll be put in the brig and wish you was dead," the crewman said bluntly. "Nah, goin' back ain't worth the trouble. What's back there for a man anyway but death, sickness, and drudgery," the man finished, walking away, leaving Connor in a state of shock.

Joseph approached Connor, and tried to lead him away by the arm. Connor, however, would not move. He stood there staring at the horizon. Boston was only a thin sliver floating on the horizon fading in the thickening fog.

"We had somewhere to go, somewhere to go and look," Connor stuttered, still in shock. "I would've had my answers. I would've known what happened to her—if she is alive."

"Come away," Joseph muttered, defeated. The first class passengers, already scandalized by the morning's goings-on had started to gawk. He tugged on Connor's arm, leading him back to the place along the rail where the others stood.

Joseph looked over all the children. By some miracle, all the children were accounted for and in one piece.

Connor slumped down the railing and stared out to sea towards Boston. All the children turned, staring silently as the city gently faded from sight before, finally, it dissolved completely.

It was done—the city was gone. They had spent the whole of their lives trying to claw their way out of it, and it was finally gone. Now, the great Atlantic lay between them and some unknown fate.

*   *   *   *   *

EIGHT FAMILIES HAD BEEN MISTAKEN FOR IMMIGRANTS that day and herded onto the ship. A steerage passenger by the name of Seamus had taken it upon himself to show the displaced souls the daily workings aboard the ship. Seamus was a young man of around twenty or so. He was tall and lean, a little too lean actually, with rumpled red hair and bright brown eyes.

Seamus had saved for the last six years to make the voyage, only to be sent back. One would think he would be in dark spirits, but he seemed willing to roll with the punches and pass on the insights he had gained over the first voyage he endured.

"Now, you see—" Seamus said, his thumbs looped around

the bottom of his suspenders, as he led the families down the corridors of the steerage level, "meals are usually served three times daily, but I've heard speak that the new captain is gonna ration us down to one meal and a mug up of tea and snacks," he explained. "The rations will probably be more of the same as we had comin' over: salt meal, rice, oats, potatoes—oh, Lord, potatoes by the bushel—" he exclaimed, "cabbage, some dried fruits, salted pork, and such."

"Joseph, Marie, Anna, and Duncan listened to Seamus intently, while Connor shuffled along despondently. He simply could not look beyond the loss he had suffered. Joseph had a sinking feeling that it was going to be up to him and the others to get everyone through the voyage in one piece.

They passed through the berthing hall where aisles of narrow bunks lined the walls, "Normally, they'll try to give each soul a cot, but we hardly had enough beds on the way over, so I don't know if everyone will get one now. The crew-men who help us down here told me to show ya to this far end," he entered the most forward berthing compartment, "where there be some beds left and a bit of space on the floor for those of ya who don't get a bunk. Look there," Seamus pointed to a far corner. "They did put out some mattresses for ya," he said happily. "They're filled with straw and seaweed, but they keep yer bones off the hard ground. Oh, and another thing", Seamus added, "basins for washing up are here and there near the beds. They ain't give us no soap, but all the same, you gotta do yer best to stay clean. It's gonna start to smell something fierce, once we get a few days into the journey. Keepin' clean is your best bet to ward off sickness. If you find ya need to know anything else, you'll find me here and there. Most of the passengers seem fair to me—we've gotta good lot here." And with that, he gave a little smile and a nod and left the weary souls to get sorted.

Just behind Joseph and the children, were other families who had likewise been forced aboard.

Duncan looked at the bunks. There were only thirty or so bunks open. He looked to his father for suggestions but Connor was still distracted. "Why don't you all take the bunks while me and mine curl up off in the corner," Duncan offered to the other families.

"Agreed," Joseph chimed in, "given how many there are of us, it's best we just huddle together, rather than take up all the bunks."

The families agreed and divided up the bunks while Joseph and the others moved towards the corner to settle in.

"Isn't any different than sleeping in the alleys," Joseph commented, "at least here we got a roof over our head, of sorts," he said looking around at the iron walls. "Still, we can do it. We've made it through worse," he added, trying to see the best in the situation.

"That's right," Anna agreed, trying to buck up the little ones who seemed overwhelmed by their new surroundings and unsettled by the ordeal they had been through. "It's no different than when we slept out in the wagon."

"Oh, it's different," Davy spoke up, looking around at their foreign surroundings.

They all turned to Connor expecting him to take part, but he didn't. He just stared listlessly down at the mattresses.

"Of course, we'll make it," Marie said warmly, "All right

then, let's get our supplies sorted. What do we have left from
the wagon. What was everyone able to hang on to?"

The children made a close circle and assessed their situation. Immediately, they noticed two of Rachel's hand-made
patchwork quilts. She had wrapped one around Asa and one
around Emma as an extra layer of warmth before they left the
house this morning. Beyond that, not much had been saved.
They hardly had time to save each other from the chaos, let
alone grab all the baskets of supplies they had packed. What
they had tucked away in their sweaters seemed to be all that
was left. Ben had managed to hold on to his precious button-
eyed teddy bear, Asa still had his soft bit of velvet, Rachel had
her sewing kit nestled inside her coat, Nicolaus had some
of the old tools rolled up in a canvas kit, and Joseph had his
battered old pocket knife, and his journal. Beyond these few
bits and bobs almost everything—all their supplies—had been
taken by the mob. The only thing that consoled them was the
photograph of Connor and Duncan's family and the money
kept safe in Connor's jacket pocket.

"Well, at least, we're all dressed warmly," Anna pointed out,
"in lots of layers." She pulled the collar of Asa's coat around his
neck. The boy was shivering.

"We never got our presents," pouted Asa.

"I know, sweet one," she consoled, "but we're still together.
Once we get settled somewhere, we can hold our own little
Christmas celebration. I promise."

"Oh, gosh," Rachel gasped, "what about Clara and Jim?
They'll never get Cotton back. They'll never know what
happened to us."

"They'll think we took him," Abbey feared.

"Clara and Jim would never think that of us. They'll hear of the riots and know something bad happened. We'll try to get a letter to them when we make port," Joseph consoled her.

"Where is Galway, anyways?" Davy asked trying to get comfortable on the mattress, which was no more than a canvas sack filled with molding straw.

"It's in Ireland," Connor replied, speaking for the first time in what seemed like ages. He still had a distracted look on his face. He had been staring off into his own thoughts—lost—until that moment. "'Tis a four day journey south to my mum and da's farm from Galway. We'll go there," he explained in a lifeless voice. "When we make port, we'll follow the coastline, and I'll take us all home." Cursing himself, he added, "Should of never left."

*   *   *   *   *

I T WAS A THREE WEEK JOURNEY ACROSS THE ATLANTIC, with winter setting in. Dwelling on their situation, Joseph quickly realized there was no lack of dangers aboard the ship. There were thick fogs, icebergs, sickness, starvation, thieves—the list went on. The few dozen first class passengers on board had the run of the ship and full freedom to walk about the decks. This left the third class steerage passengers—hundred or so—trapped in the poorly-ventilated lower decks.

Walking through the berthing decks, Joseph noticed the passengers had cloistered themselves in little communities. Passengers of German descent were in their own circle, the French were in their own—and so on. Joseph and the children seemed to have been adopted by the Irish group, mainly because Connor was Irish.

Each day, the steerage passengers were given a day's ration of food, raw. Normally, it would have been cooked. But the crew was mostly tending to the needs of the first class passengers, whose demands had gotten far more outrageous since the chief decided to make the voyage back to Ireland. The ration was divided among the communities, and each cooked what they pleased. Each evening, Joseph, Duncan, Anna, and Marie took small pails to be filled at the makeshift stove in the Irish circle.

Beyond meal time and a bit of exploring here and there, Joseph and the children mostly kept to themselves in their little corner. One of them always stayed in the living space just to ensure their belongings were safe. No one went anywhere alone.

Overall, it was a boring routine. Davy commented one evening, "I would think a sea voyage would be more excitin'. But it isn't." They spent their days penned up below deck like dirty, restless animals.

And so the days passed, and the massive propellers of the steamer churned. For the most part, it was a solemn, quiet trip—Duncan still recovering, Connor in a kind of mourning, everyone disoriented. There was little to be done about the lack of food, sunlight, and fresh air.

An aura of sluggish hopelessness hung over all the people in the lower decks. They all had spent years working to earn their passage to America, only to be turned away within sight of it. No one knew what to do next.

Strangely, there were still moments of joy shared over the voyage. The steerage passengers were people of hardship. They had long since learned how to make do with little and carve out a bit of happiness even in the darkest—most cramped—living situation.

"Can we go listen to the music tonight?" Abbey asked hopefully.

"Fiona said she'd be playin' her fiddle, Finn is gonna play his drum, and that man with the long beard said he'd be playin' his flute," Davy explained.

"All right then, but only if Duncan or Nicolaus go with you," Joseph agreed.

"I'll go," Nicolaus offered.

"So will I," Rachel said, "Duncan is resting. Let him sleep."

Joseph looked over at Duncan, who was indeed sleeping. It was hard to tell if he was getting any better. He had been pale and sickly before the voyage. The foul air and small rations weren't helping matters. Everyone had a sallow, queasy look about them.

"Come back by eleven. Don't be too late. Sometimes them parties have gone till dawn. And stay close to Mrs. Finnegan and her family, away from the drinkin' men." Joseph advised.

Abbey and Davy skittled off toward the Irish circle, Rachel and Nicolaus following behind.

Once they were gone, Ben asked. "What'll we do?"

"Yeah, what'll we do?" Asa echoed.

"Well, I just don't know," Joseph replied smiling at Anna, already knowing what the boys were hinting at.

Beth and Emma scooched closer. They knew what was coming. It even managed to bring the faintest of smiles to Connor, who was sitting propped against the wall resting near Duncan.

"Well, I suppose we could read more from the book of tales Mrs. Finnegan let us borrow," Joseph replied, taking the small leather-bound book from the inside of his jacket entitled,

Creatures of Lore by Angus Flynn.

"Where did we leave off?" he began, flipping through the pages.

"With the selkies," Marie provided. She sat mending socks using Rachel's sewing kit.

"Oh, yes, selkies, how silly of me to forget," Joseph replied.

"Very silly," Asa scolded with a serious face.

"The selkie," Joseph began reading. "It is a creature that is half human and half seal. For a selkie, the black skin of the seal peels back to reveal their human form. It is said that many a fisherman have been lured from their boats out unto the black rocks by beautiful dark-haired women—selkies—soaking in the warmth of the sun, free of their seal skins. These illusive creatures have been known to swim among the islands along the western shore of Éire—Ireland," Joseph clarified. "Some believe that selkies are the souls of those drown entwined with the beasts they met at their end in the deep, dark embrace of the sea. Both love and tragedy have followed the selkies down the generations of lore as they have been both a curse upon families as well as saviors…."

Joseph read on for some time, holding fully the attention of each and every child.

"I betcha that, if we could stay on deck all the time, day and night like the sailors, we'd see a selkie," Ben said with excitement As he watched Joseph close the book, the chapter on selkies finished.

"Maybe, but right now the only place you're going to see them is in your dreams tonight. Come on now," he herded the children into bed, "time to rest. It's near eleven."

"Maybe it's only ten," Asa argued, "and we can read another

story."

"Nope, those bells that just tolled were the men reporting the time, just like a clock." Joseph explained. "Nicolaus, Rachel, and the others will be back any moment. We all need our rest."

It was past midnight. Most everyone in the compartment was asleep. A few groups of men were huddled together here and there drinking grog and whiskey traded from the crew.

Joseph lay on his mattress, his head resting against the iron wall. As deep as they were in the ship, he could hear the churning of the propeller vibrating along the metal hull. Something about the noise was comforting, as if the slow, steady churning was a calming source of stability within the terror of the unknown.

His eyes passed over their small corner of the ship. Everyone was curled up as comfortable as they could get—fast asleep. The journey was taking its toll. Waking each morning to wash in a cold basin of sea water and eating the same salty foods day in and day out—left everyone looking rather ragged.

Through the dim light, his eyes focused on Anna, who was lying near him. He reached out and gently touched her arm. She slowly awoke.

"Shhhhh," he said in a whisper, holding a finger to his lips. He started to rise, and he motioned for her to follow. She gently crept from her bed, and the pair moved quietly through the compartment toward the main hallway.

The ship bells chimed one o'clock.

"What are we doing?" Anna whispered. Joseph had her by

the hand and was quickly moving down the hall.

"You'll see," he replied, still moving in a hurry.

A moment later, the end of the hallway came into view. Near the stairs that lead above deck, Seamus stood talking to a crewman who had been handed a small, unopened bottle of Irish whiskey.

"Go on," Seamus waved as they came to the stairs. "Go up. There are a few more up there."

Anna stopped. "No," she shook her head vigorously, "We'll get in trouble."

"It's all right, girl, but be quick about it," the crewman assured.

Joseph started up the stairs. Anna hesitantly followed.

"Smell that?" There was excitement in Joseph's voice, "I can smell the salt." They climbed the stairs—the closer to the top they got, the cleaner the air became.

"But what about the others?" Anna asked. "Everyone needs a bit of fresh air."

"I know. That crewman told Seamus that they are planning to let the steerage passengers walk about the lower deck tomorrow afternoon, while the first class passengers are having luncheon."

"Then, why not wait until tomorrow?" Anna begged. "No risk of trouble."

They continued to climb the stairwell, finally emerging at the top. "Because," he explained, "I wanted to see the stars out at sea."

She stepped out onto the hard, wooden deck and was overwhelmed by a vast night sky—ink black—dotted with sharp white stars.

She was stunned by the beauty of it. Joseph walked toward

the railing where a few other folk from steerage stood nearby taking in the crisp air. He pulled Anna along by the hand, her eyes still turned upward toward the stars.

"It's like a different sky. I never knew the world was so big," Anna said in awe.

"We only got glimpses of the sky between the buildings. We've never been out in the open. I wanted to see it." His chin was pointed up. His brown eyes were wide. With each exhale, a cloud of crystal vapor was dispersed into the crosswind swirling about the deck. So bewitched by the engulfing spray of stars, he hardly felt the frigid wind pushing against him.

"I heard men talk about the patterns the stars make. I never could see them through the smoky, city sky, but I can see them now. It's like some dark blanket, quilted with little patterns. You see it?" Anna asked.

"I see them," Joseph replied, following the invisible lines running between the stars. He turned back and looked at Anna. Her babushka was drawn over the crown of her head. A few loose strands of her hair whipped gently in the chilled wind. Her large, hazel eyes stared unblinking at the waning moon above them. He felt a swell of happiness expanding in his heart. He loved that he could give her this moment of wonder.

"It can't be real," he reflected, lost in the magical moment. "Some part of me is still in an alley somewhere. I suspect, part of me always will be. It's like something out of a dream.

"Yes, it is—out of your dreams, remember," she knocked him lovingly on the head.

"Yes, well, I know the struggle to reach a new place, all too well. As for what to do, once we get there, I am trying to get my bearings. I'm just waiting for it all to feel real." Joseph reflected.

The moonlight highlighted the whitecaps breaking along

the surface of the water.

"I know I'm the one who said we should find a way to leave the city, but I suppose I still never thought we'd actually make it. I never thought that you and I would be standing here on the deck of a ship, bound for some far-off land. The journey has its sadness, of course," he admitted, thinking back to Connor's plight, "but, regardless, I think Ireland will hold better things for us than Boston did."

"Do you think Connor's da and mum will like us enough to take us in?" Anna asked, voicing a concern that had been weighing on her.

"Well, I know we come with quite a lot of baggage, but I think they will. I mean, they are the people who raised Connor—who taught him to be the good man that he is. I don't see them turning us away."

"What'll we do?" Anna asked. "I don't know anything about living in Ireland."

"Living in Ireland is the same as living anywhere. We'll work the land, we'll grow our food, we'll find our way, and hopefully, we'll watch the seasons pass from a warm chair by the fire. No matter what," he finished, "we'll get through just as we always have, together." She smiled back at him. He wrapped an arm around her shoulder and pulled her close. Anna's teeth were chattering.

"We should head back in. You're chilled to the bone."

"No," she insisted, "just another few minutes. It may be freezing, but it's the loveliest night I can ever remember."

He gave a little smile and looked back out over the water. She leaned in and gave him a kiss on the cheek. He turned back to her. She smiled shyly and looked away—back toward the sharp starlit sky.

She had kissed him before, many times. But something about this kiss felt different—he felt different.

CHAPTER 31
THE HOMELAND

TWENTY-ONE DAYS AFTER LEAVING BOSTON, the steamer *Aurora* and the tired souls within drew near to the western coast of Ireland, and Connor found himself looking out over a familiar sight.

All the passengers aboard the ship disembarking in Ireland had gathered their belongings and waited with baited breath as the ship steamed into Galway Bay. The children stood huddled against the railing, watching as their new homeland came into view. Quite different from the shores of Boston, the Irish horizon was drenched in green with towering steep cliffs and small dark rocks scattered along the coast.

"My God," Joseph said above the din of the passengers around him, "it's beautiful! I never knew such a land existed."

"Aye, I had forgotten how lovely she is." Connor stared at the land of his childhood.

Most ships are greeted at port by crowds of natives awaiting their loved ones; however, no one knew of the forced return journey of the steamer *Aurora*, so there was no one to meet the ship other than the daily crews manning the docks.

The gangplank touched down on the wharf, and the tired passengers shuffled off.

Seamus gave a wave to the children as he walked toward the city. They had already said their goodbyes to the few friends they had made along the journey.

Firm-footed on dry land, they all turned to look at the massive ship that had taken them the distance, gathered themselves, and struck out into the city.

"The journey to the farm will take three or four days depending upon the weather. Given how cold it is," Connor said through clenched teeth, "I think we'll be moving with a quick step."

All the children nodded. Each of them had their chin and mouth tucked deep into their scarves, like turtles withdrawing into their shells.

"There should be inns scattered along the way, but we'll be on open ground for one or two nights. We'll need more blankets and some basic supplies and such. Come," he directed them into the heart of town, "if memory serves, there used to be a few markets down this way."

The children shuffled along the foreign streets. Galway was a city, for sure, but it wasn't half as loud and dirty as Boston had been. As they walked the streets, Joseph could feel a shift. In Galway, the ancient roots of the city ran deep. The older buildings had been maintained. The old ways, slowly being left behind in the States, endured here.

"Here we are," Connor said at last, "Delaney's, it's the same store Colin and I went to before we left on the ship. It's still here." He opened the door for the children and watched as they all rushed in to escape the biting wind.

Joseph was the first one through the door. He was greeted by a thin, middle-aged shop clerk.

"*Cén chaoi a bhfuil tú?*" the man said, leaving Joseph a bit lost.

"What?" Joseph replied, dumbfounded.

"Ah, an American," the clerk replied, speaking in English with a thick accent. "And fresh off the boat, if I had to guess. Don't worry lad, I was sayin' hello, not insultin' ya."

"Oh," Joseph stood awkwardly, not knowing what to say.

"Aye, fresh off the boat," Connor replied, to Joseph's relief. "But this is my homecoming. These are my kin I be bringing home with me."

The shopkeeper nodded. "Whatcha lookin' for then?"

"Well, we got a bit of a walk ahead of us. I'm thinking we need a few blankets and provisions to see us through."

"A few of these should do ya," the shopkeeper replied, pointing to a stack of thick wool blankets. "Wrap one of these around each of your dearest ones, and they'll be all right."

"Well, we already have a few blankets with us, so we'll take eight of them. We'll need some food, as well, and a pot," he finished.

Joseph stepped over near Connor. "We can't carry a heavy pot on the long walk," Joseph whispered, not wanting to contradict Connor, but also wondering how they could manage much more than what they had.

"We won't be carrying it," Connor assured him. "Which leads me to the last bit. We'll take one of those hand carts you got out in front of the shop." Connor pointed through the window. It was a small cart, four wheels with a handle to pull it along. He turned to Joseph, "The little ones won't be able to keep step with us. We can put them in the cart when they get tired. We can put the food and a small pot in there with them."

Joseph nodded.

"Anything else?" the shopkeeper asked, happily surprised by the amount of money Connor had already spent.

"No," Connor replied, "I think that's more than enough."

Connor paid the man, and everyone started collecting the supplies.

"You really should put your feet up by the fire for a night. 'Tis past midday; You won't get far now," the shopkeeper kindly suggested. "Go on over to the Ox and Plow, and tell Maggie that Delaney sent ya. She'll fix ya up good and proper," he nodded.

"Perhaps, we will," Connor thanked the man and herded them out the door.

"He is actually right," Joseph considered as they entered the street. He walked beside Connor so that only he could hear. "Duncan is terribly tired, as you probably know. What's more, we all could use a meal, a bath, and a roof over our heads for the night. Do you think we could afford to stay one night?"

"Well, it don't hurt to ask," Connor agreed. "We have our savings, but we also have a great many mouths to feed. I don't know what we'll meet at journey's end, so we need to be smart with what we have." A quaint, three-story building came into view. It was as white as cream with blue trim about the windows. A sign hung above the door with a carved pair of oxen pulling a plow. "Joseph," Connor paused, "head in, find this Maggie and see about a room for us. Ask how much it'll cost for beds and a meal. We'll be waiting here. Best not to cause a commotion and have all of us go bustling in and not be able to afford the rate."

Joseph nodded and took off for the inn. By the time Connor explained to everyone what they were doing, Joseph already had made it to the front door.

He entered the pub—a stone walled room with a blazing hearth, which nearly ran the length of the wall. There were four long, communal tables with benches lined up in the room where traveler and native alike sat sipping ale and slurping soup. Joseph walked across the wide floorboards to a bar where a woman stood washing glasses and mugs in a basin.

"Um," he began nervously, "I'm looking for Maggie."

"You got her," the woman replied. She had long ink-black hair, dark eyes, and a fair complexion. She had a way about her when she spoke that gave Joseph the impression that she could stand toe to toe with any man in the room and whip him.

"I was sent by Delany. I was wondering how much a room might be," he continued, still timid.

"Aye, Delany. Man's a fool," she replied bluntly. "Trying to get on me good side for God-only-knows what reason. But don't worry, lad," she said with a faint smile, "I won't hold that against ya. Well, how many are ya? Will it just be you then?" she asked, picking up a wet glass to dry from the basin.

"No, my family is outside. There are—well, there are thirteen," Joseph replied shyly.

"Thirteen?" she repeated in disbelief.

"Yes. But we don't all need beds. The floor would suit us fine. So quite a few of us could actually sleep in one room."

"All right, tell ya what I'll do. I have a pair of joined rooms. Only two small beds in each room, but you should all fit. We have a bathtub in the back. You fill it, you empty it, and you clean it at the end. Supper is hearty, but nothin' too fancy."

"That's fine. As long as it ain't salt meal, salt pork, or rice, we'll be pleased," Joseph assured.

"Well, you'll be pleased then. It's stew and bread and then a bowl of porridge come sunup."

Joseph smiled, "What'll we owe you for the night?" The moment of truth came.

"You'll be payin' with 'em American dollars then?" she asked, still drying the same glass.

He nodded.

"Aye," she considered the boy. "It'll be three dollars for the lot of ya'. It should be five, mind ya," she added quickly, pointing the glass at Joseph, "but I like ya. Ain't no nonsense about ya. I think you and your lot will be quiet. 'Sides, ya look like you're ready to fall over. What kinda woman would I be, if I sent you back out into the cold?"

"I think you have yourself a deal," Joseph replied warmly, "but I can't be sure. I'll be back. I gotta go tell the others."

"Do what ya gotta do, lad," she replied, picking up another glass to wipe clean.

A short time later, Joseph returned with his twelve companions. Before they knew it, everyone was bathed, settled in, and enjoying their bowl of stew by the hearth.

"Davy," Anna said sternly, "for heaven's sakes, would you please chew."

Everyone glanced down the table to see Davy inhaling his stew without the bother of chewing or even tasting it. He picked up the bowl and drank from the side of it. His mouth was too full of stew to respond but he hung his head a bit and started to actually use his spoon.

"It's really good," Abbey commented, spooning the thick

brown stew to her lips. It was loaded with chewy cubes of mutton, melted onions, and hearty chunks of potatoes.

Maggie had given their table two whole loaves of wheat bread, round and crusty with flour still dusting the deep golden surface.

Everyone nodded in agreement with Abbey, their full mouths a testament.

"Connor?" a voice suddenly erupted from the bar. "Connor Morgan? Why, that can't be you!" A wide-shouldered man around Connor's age approached their table, still grasping his pint in his hand. He had the look of a farmer—covered in a fine layer of dirt from his knees down to his boots.

Connor looked up, shocked to hear his name.

"Why, that is you. A bit older, a bit wider, a bit grayer, but it's you for sure." The man put out a hand. Connor wiped his mouth on his napkin, stood up—still chewing—and took the man's hand.

"Michael," Connor finally spoke, "how have you been keeping?"

"Been doin' pretty fair. What's it been? Goin' on what, ten years?" Michael said, straining to recollect.

"'Round abouts," Connor replied. Joseph noticed that, while Connor was being polite, he didn't seem all that excited to see Michael.

"How are my folks? How is the farm keepin'?" Connor asked with deep concern.

"Well, I don't rightly know. I left the islands shortly after you did. Couldn't take the smallness of it. Wanted bigger things, like you," Michael said, clapping Connor on the back. Connor smiled weakly. "I was actually gonna take a boat and follow right behind you, but when I got to Galway, well—" he came up short, "I met a girl and we decided to settle here."

"She make ya happy?" Connor asked.

"Happy enough. We got a mess of little ones running about. We live in a cottage just outside the city. I'm a farmhand and work on the boats from time to time when I must. Only thing I've ever known how to do," he finished.

"Only thing a lot of us island boys ever knew how to do," Connor replied. "Well, it was nice to see ya after all this—"

Just when Connor was so obviously about to bring the conversation to an end, Michael sat down at the end of the bench near Connor and pushed the reunion forward.

"All these little ones yours then? Where's Tara? I ain't seen that girl in ages." Michael asked, smiling wide, apparently oblivious to Connor's discomfort.

All the children looked to Connor and, with a heavy sigh, he proceeded to tell his story.

Hours later, once Michael had talked his fill, Connor, Joseph and the children retired back up to the rooms. The girls took one room and the boys the other.

Emma and Marie were tucked into one bed and Abbey and Beth in the other, while Rachel and Anna curled up on the floor in makeshift beds created by their new blankets and spare linens Maggie had provided. In the neighboring room, Asa and Nicolaus were tucked into a bed and Davy and Ben in another. Duncan, Joseph, and Connor used their blankets on the floor. Finally, in a proper bed and off the cramped ship, the children fell right to sleep. All, that is, except Joseph and Connor. Lying near him, Joseph noticed that Connor's eyes were still open.

"You didn't seem all that happy to see Michael. Did you not like him?" Joseph whispered.

Connor looked over at Joseph, "Should have known you'd be up. It's always we two who are last to sleep," Connor replied back in a soft whisper. "No, it isn't that I don't like him." Connor explained, "Actually, at one time, Michael, Colin, and I were very thick. It's just that time has passed and the lad Michael was looking for never returned to these shores. I may have his name and a shadow of his face but he's long since gone. And this isn't a sad thing, mind you," Connor added, watching as Joseph's face fell. "If I were the same man I was when I left, that would indeed be a sad thing because it would mean I hadn't grown. When we let ourselves grow as we should, there may come a day when we're strangers to those who knew us in the past. Part of us," he finished, pointing at Joseph's chest, "should always remain the same as it was when we were babes, but the rest of us should always be learnin', growin', and changin'."

Joseph smiled, "I'm not sure what I'm growing to be." He sounded lost. "I've been thinking about us settling with your family and that I'm getting to that age where I need to choose what I want to be doing in life. Only, I don't know. I mean," he explained, "what've I got worth anything to anyone? I ain't got no schooling, no standing, no lofty ideas, no trade, no money...what've I got of any value to offer this world?"

"You're right," Connor said plainly, "you ain't got no schoolin', you ain't got no trade, you ain't got no money, but you got the path behind you," he pointed out. "You've been through more in your short time than most will experience in the whole of their years. All that you have felt, and survived, and endured makes you unique. It gives you something that no schoolin' can teach and money can't buy," he stressed, trying to awaken Joseph to his self-worth. "Now," he went on, "what you choose to do with that story—how you choose to share all that you are with the world—is up to you. You'll find your way. What we each do in this life tends to just fall into place. It isn't always something that can be planned."

Joseph smiled. As ever, he was eased by Connor's words.

"Look at me, lad," Connor went on. "I learned how to be a fisherman and farmer at my da's knee. From the time I was old enough to listen, my da told me, 'The simple life can be hard but ain't no other livin' to be had that leaves the heart at peace.' I ignored him of course. I railed against the smallness of the farm and the island, dreamin' of America. But now I can see the wisdom of my da. I see the dearness found in the small things and I find simplicity is the tonic my mind and soul demand after so many years in that city. Tara would laugh to hear me say such things," Connor reflected.

"Why is that?" Joseph asked.

"Because she was like my da and mum, she was a farm girl and never wanted anything more than to raise our children and for us to pull our livin' from the sea and the soil," he smiled, a hint of pain about his mouth. "'Twas I who put the idea of America in her head and I know the only reason she stepped aboard that ship was cause she knew how much I wanted to go. ...more's the pity of it all," he finished, exhaustion weighing down his voice. "My point is, lad," he went on, not wanting the conversation to end on a sad note, "you have a great deal to give and you'll find your path or rather, your path will find you."

"Sometimes it seems like we've no say in our life, as though we're just swept along with the tide," Joseph reflected.

"Aye, make no mistake, part of your life is beyond all the plans you might have. Things will happen that you can't foresee, or prevent; nonetheless, even when swept up in the tide, you'll make the choices that determine who you are. You'll do fine," Connor stressed, knowing all too well of Joseph's worries. "Now, off to bed with ya. We've got a long day ahead." With a smile, Connor waved Joseph away. Joseph curled up in his bed and the room went silent but he couldn't sleep, his mind was still racing. He lay there for a long time, not even sure what he was thinking about. As tired as his mind was, his entire life seemed to merge into one large jumbled thought. Yet, within the chaos, something emerged: A few sentences that he suddenly felt compelled to write down. As though they might be important, the beginning of something larger.

He crawled from his bed over to a small desk off in the corner of the room, earlier he had noticed that a bottle of ink and a pen had been put out upon it, undoubtedly for lodgers to use to send post to their kin. Joseph grabbed it and slid quietly over to the window where a faint light filtered in, just enough light to write by. He took out his blank journal, flipped past the first few blank pages, dipped the tip of the pen in the thick, black ink and began to write:

When the winter has been long,
you can forget that there is a spring...

CHAPTER 32
AFOOT AMONG THE GREEN

I T WASN'T LONG BEFORE the hustle and bustle of the city
gave way to the calm road. They moved away from the
city and deeper into the green wild. Buildings, few and far
between, traded for a bleak rocky road. The landscape was
shrouded in mist from the fog rolling in off the shore.

They walked with the ocean at their right and the whole
of Ireland to their left. It was cold—below freezing, in fact. At
least any snow had held off. Marching at a good pace, the older
children helped the younger ones along, while Connor pulled
the cart behind them.

They found themselves entering a foreign realm of long
grasses, old trees, and open rolling hills.

Half a day's walk beyond Galway, the children saw their
first mystery of country life.

"There's a ship out there!" yelled Ben, pointing at a sail
emerging from behind a hill.

"Can't be a ship on the land," Davy said running up the hill
to investigate.

"Wait," Connor called, all the children running behind Davy.

The children quickly made it to the top of the hill and stood
in front of a towering stone building, a great wheel of sails
turning in the breeze.

Connor explained, "It's not a ship. It's a windmill. One of the oldest in the county, in fact. See," he pointed, "the sails catch the wind, the wind turns the wheel, and inside there's a mill. People from all around bring their wheat here to be milled. The sails turn a great mill stone inside that crushes the wheat until it's flour."

"Ain't never seen anything like it," Davy commented, his head tilted back as he watched the triangular sails turn.

They started back down the path. "You'll find there are a great many things you've never seen before. The city and the country are two different worlds, living at two different paces, with two different sets of priorities. The country will suit you," Connor assured them warmly. "Here you won't be outcasts for loving peace, quiet, and simplicity. Quite the contrary, you'll fit right in."

"What'll we do here?" Nicolaus asked timidly. "Will we continue to work with you, as we did in Boston?"

"Aye, if you like, but this time we won't be destroying things. We'll be tending things and building things. Work on a farm never stops. It's not easy, but it's meaningful. Now, as far as what you can be—" he went on, "you can be anything you wish. The little ones—Ben, Abbey, Asa, Emma, Beth, Davy— you'll all continue your learnin'. Maybe even attend school, if the Mallory's still have the school house they had when I was a lad. You'll be a great many things here, but, most importantly, you'll be children. And when you're grown and ready to find your place, you can go anywhere and be anything, as long as you're willing to work hard. Here, most men are farmers, fish- ermen, or carpenters. The women are mothers, wives, teachers or healers. Now, maybe one of those things will speak to you, or maybe you'll have to blaze your own trail. The world is open to you," Connor finished, strength in this voice.

Joseph walked the path, but his eyes were fixed on Connor as he spoke, wondering what he would do. It all seemed overwhelming. Hopefully, Connor would turn out to be right, and Joseph's path would open to him. Perhaps, it was right there in front of him—laid out as plain as could be—and he just didn't see it.

His pondering was interrupted by Nicolaus' voice. "Land's sake! Would you look at them cows!" He pointed to a nearby field. A farmer was herding his cows into the barn. They were round, spotted cows, far heavier than anything he had ever seen at Clara and Jim's farm.

"Just wait 'til they are fat with summer grass, they'll be even bigger. Oh, just wait 'til you taste fresh milk and butter. You'll taste the very grass the cows ate," Connor said, his mouth watering at the thought of it. "What I wouldn't give for one of my mum's cakes with creamy yellow butter spread across it."

"I'd heard in the papers that there's a famine here. I expected things to be more desperate," Joseph said, as they continued to walk down the lane.

"Times have been desperate since long before I was born. But aye, there's a terrible famine happening. It's why so many souls have been pouring into Boston. I dare say, you'll see the effects soon enough. It isn't as bad here along the shore villages where people can still fill their table from the sea. My parents had survived the worst and seen a lot of their kin die off in war and hardship. I hope they've made it through these lean times."

"You haven't spoken to them?" Joseph asked. "No letters?"

"I didn't know what to tell them even if I could get a letter across the distance," he squinted in the sun. "So much went wrong—" His voice tapered off.

"They wanted better for my brothers and me. Somehow, over time, America became that better place. We were wrong, of course. We only swapped out one set of hardships for another. It's true that a man has more liberties in America—the social structure is different from here in Ireland. While blood determines your status here, wealth determines it in America. Both sides of the Atlantic have it wrong. I would rather have my kin beside me to help me though this backward world than not."

"We know that lesson, don't we?" Marie spoke up.

"Yes, we do," Anna agreed.

"What lesson we be knowin'?" Davy asked, a bit lost.

"That you can face anything in this world, as long as you have loved ones steadfast at your side," Joseph replied.

"And we do have that, don't we," Connor said with a smile, albeit tensely, and brought Duncan close to him as they walked. "Regardless of all that we have endured, we have a great deal to be grateful for," Connor concluded, much to the surprise of Joseph who thought Connor would never start to come out of his grief over losing the chance to learn Tara's fate.

Turning toward the horizon, Joseph saw beams of sunlight falling upon an entirely new world—one that was still green and gold and good. Only a little over a year ago, he was crawling through the deepest despair—hunted by his demons and hopelessness—utterly alone. Had someone told him then of all that would happen, all that would be given, and all that would be possible, he would have cursed them for waving in front of him such a sweet dream. Everything—every single thing they have—was at one point impossible. From the shoes on their feet, to the coat on their backs, to the blankets wrapped around them, to the food filling their belly, to a parent to care for them, to Marie's healing, and to Duncan's reunion— all of it was impossible at some point, but now they had it. Thinking of all those things which seemed impossible, Joseph wondered how much more might come to pass and realized that nothing—not even the most seemingly far off possibility—is impossible. And in that thought he took deep comfort.

*   *   *   *   *

A FTER A FULL DAY'S WALK, they finally decided it was time to stop. They came to the shore's edge. The daylight was waning.

"We'll make a fire and sleep here for the night. We can mix up an old sea stew in the pot." Connor set the cart to rest.

"Shall we go find some firewood—some trees?" Joseph asked.

"No, we're looking for something a bit drier. Besides, finding trees that aren't on someone else's land will be hard. No, we'll collect some driftwood." He pointed down the shore. "Start walking the strand and pick up what you find."

The children paired off and started down the shoreline while Connor set out the extra blankets and the pot.

Joseph was the first to return with a bunch of parched, mangled driftwood under his arm. "There," he said, dropping it near Connor, "first batch. I'll go look for more."

"No, wait," Connor stopped him, "the others can see to that. You stay here with the camp. I need to go gather some bits for the stew." He picked up an empty basket and head off into the dusk.

A time later, Anna came up the beach with Abbey, Emma, and Asa—all of them carrying wood. Even the little ones managed to carry a few pieces.

"Where has Connor gone?" Anna asked as she put down her wood.

"Not sure. He said he needed to go get some things for the stew," he replied.

"Shall we get more wood?" she asked.

"No, we got quite a pile. Should last us the night," Joseph replied. "Well, I suppose I should set up the fire." He sat down and set about arranging the wood.

"I'll get some water from the cart and fill the pot," Anna offered. "I'm not sure what Connor has planned, but he'll need fresh water."

Duncan, Marie, Rachel, and Nicolaus came up the beach with Abbey, Ben, and Davy following behind. Each one dropping the wood they found onto the pile.

"It's freezin'," Davy said through chattering teeth. "It's even colder here on the shore. Why we sleepin' here?"

"Connor wanted to tuck us away against these cliffs and rocks. He thought it would be safe," Joseph replied. "Once we get the fire going, you'll be better."

"Nicolaus," Rachel said, "let's get everyone settled." She started wrapping everyone in their heavy blankets and gathering them around Joseph.

"There," Joseph said in a voice of satisfaction. The fire sparked and the flames crept up the dry wood.

The light from the fire illuminated the face of each child, as well as Connor who walked toward them with a basketfull of green seaweed, mussels, crabs, and a small fish. "Well, haven't lost me touch. I'm still my father's son. I can pull a supper out of the sea."

Connor passed the basket off to Anna.

"Can we eat this?" Anna asked, puzzling over the seaweed.

"Some seaweed can be eaten but not all. This is sea lettuce. It'll add some flavor to our stock, and we can eat it. We'll cook all the shell fish then pull the meat out and put it in the stock. We can throw in some of the potatoes and such we have in the cart."

Plan in place, Anna and Marie set about to helping Connor. They watched him as he went about making the stew and learned as they went.

Tummies full, wrapped tightly in a blanket by the fire, all the children rested contently. Connor sat up, leaning against one of the cart's tall wheels keeping watch.

"You should turn in," Connor suggested to Joseph, Anna, Rachel, and Nicolaus, all of whom were staring deeply into the fire—exhaustion on each face.

"I'm going to wait up for Marie and Duncan," Joseph replied. A little while after dinner, the pair had decided to go for a walk down the shore.

"Oh, I reckon they'll be awhile," Connor replied. "Between the rush at the city and then the cramped ship, they've hardly had two seconds to catch up. I'm sure they have lots to talk about. I'll wait up for them," he nodded encouragingly. "Get some sleep. We have another big day of walking ahead of us."

"How much further to the farm?" Anna asked.

"Well, we did pretty well today. If bad weather holds off and we're able to keep a good pace, we should be there in about a day and a bit," Connor replied.

"How do you know your family will still be on the land?" Joseph asked. "What if they were thrown off it or—" he hesitated, "what if they passed?"

"They can't have been evicted from the land. Unlike so many in this country, we own our land. My da and his five brothers worked and saved their money and bought it together. As for them having passed on, it's possible, but I dare say, they are still living. My sisters, Molly and Nessa stayed with them, as did my youngest brother, Cian. If, God forbid, something has happened to Mum and Da, they'd stay on the land no matter what."

Joseph smiled but then jumped as he heard footsteps in the sand behind him.

"No worries," Marie whispered from within the darkness, "it's only us," she assured.

She and Duncan emerged into the firelight.

"Cold out there," Duncan said with a shiver. He wrapped his blanket around his shoulders and drew closer to the fire.

Watching Marie and Duncan settle in, Joseph seemed to relax. The next thing he knew it was morning. He woke groggily. The fire was still smoldering. The sun was rising.

CHAPTER 33
WHERE THE STORY BEGINS

T HE MISTY MORNING YIELDED ITS MYSTERY, and the last leg of the path home was laid out before them. Connor led the children up steep hills and onto the shore, following a trail along black cliffs that overlooked the sea. The farm was drawing close.

"I never thought I'd walk these paths again," he reflected, in spite of his inner pain, there was a growing affection in his voice.

Joseph followed behind Connor and Duncan. Tall, limp strands of lush grass draped along the edges of the path.

"Saints preserve us!" a woman cried from a distance, "Connor! My little brother? Could that be you?" She threw down the bushel of herbs she had been picking and ran to him breathless, embracing him.

"Hello, dearest girl," he laughed warmly as she squeezed the life from him.

She let him go when she saw the children.

"Molly, you remember Duncan." He pulled Duncan forward.

"Oh, dear boy," she said grabbing him and pulling him close, "when last I saw you, you were naught but a babe."

She pulled back, staring silently at the others.

"Molly, these are my friends—now family. Not mine by

blood but certainly by bond." One at a time, Connor intro-
duced the children. Molly was very gracious. She gave each a
warm welcome in turn.

"This is like a dream—we never thought we'd see you
again," she said in shock. They'd all started walking toward the
cottage where the rest of Connor's family was waiting.

"I know," he replied, looking over the familiar horizon, "I
never thought I'd return."

"No, no," she shook her head, "you don't understand. We
thought you dead. We were told you were dead," she explained.

"What?" he asked, only to be cut off mid-sentence by an
outcry.

"Connor? Connor!" The voice was that of an old woman,
short and a bit round with a kind face and gentle manner.

"Mum!" he said, rushing forward.

"I was just bringing Molly a bit of lunch when—Connor?"
she said, not believing her eyes. "God be praised," she said,
tears in her eyes, holding his face in her aged hands, "your da
ain't going to believe it could be true. Your return will pull him
from his darkness. It'll heal us all."

"What darkness?"

"'Tis the farm," Molly provided. "It's failin'. The years have
been hard. The sea isn't yielding what it once did, and Da
is getting too old for the work. Cian does his best but he is
lost—doesn't know what to do to get us all back on our feet.
But this—you," Molly said, the tears returning, "it'll change
everything."

"What's this about you thinking I was dead?" Connor
asked.

His Mum looked pained, "We'd heard you passed some years ago. Both you and Duncan," she explained. "It came as a terrible blow."

"Aye, well, until just a few weeks ago, I thought Duncan lost to me forever, so I know what has weighed on your heart. I only wish," he finished meekly, "that Tara, Colin, and Brigit were at my side and this reunion was complete."

"Connor," Molly said in disbelief, "Tara's alive."

"What?" Connor said in shock. All eyes turned to Molly.

"She's alive, Connor. Colin and Brigit, they found her after the riots."

"I don't understand," Connor gaped. Duncan stepped up alongside him. "Tara is dead. Colin and Bridget too. I never saw them or heard anything of them—nothing."

"Aye, Colin and Brigit were caught up in the riots," his mum explained, "but they took shelter in some chapel after the smoke cleared. It was there that they found Tara. She was near death. The ministers said she was going to meet her Maker, but Colin wouldn't accept it. He took her from the chapel and found an old woman who believed in the old ways who was able to bring her back. Tara, Colin and Brigit were told Duncan was dead by one of the minsters."

"Why would they say that?" Duncan demanded.

"Who knows," Connor replied, still trying to get his bearings with all the new information. "I'm sure there were a lot of orphans after that night. Perhaps there was some kind of horrible mix up."

"Tara wasn't the same after losing Duncan. She, along with Colin and Bridget, searched for you for a year but never found you—even heard rumors of someone by your name and face having passed."

"I wasn't free to be found!" Connor cursed. He explained the mock-trial and his imprisonment.

"After the year of searchin' and hearin' that you was dead, Colin and Brigit moved on into the West as you all had planned. They settled on a farm out West with their sweet babes," Molly explained, agonized for her brother.

"And Tara—" he went on, frantically putting together the pieces, "she went with them West?"

"No," Molly shook her head, "she didn't want to go after all that had happened. Colin took some of the money he had left and booked her passage back home. She's here, Connor," she finished.

The words stunned Connor. For a few moments, he couldn't think, he couldn't speak—he just stood there.

All the children huddled close. Joseph looked to Connor, watching the tension that had ever-surrounded him begin to fade as the news of his wife soaked deeper and deeper into him.

"Where?" Connor asked. "Where is she?" Looking back and forth between his sister and mother, needing one of them to speak.

"This time of the mornin' she often takes to the hills," his mother replied.

"Aye, I know where she goes." Molly jumped in. "She walks to the western-most cliffs—the ones right on our land, on the hills overlooking the whole of the farm."

Connor nodded, dropped all his bags and started running. The children—all twelve of them—followed behind him.

As they ran, Joseph met Anna's gaze. She was smiling brightly. There was a momentum building in the heart of each child—a new beginning was at hand.

*   *   *   *   *

SHE HAD HER BACK TO THE HILLS as she stood looking out mournfully over the sea—part of her heart buried on a distant shore. The curls of her long auburn hair, now streaked with light touches of gray, were whipping in the winds. The hem of her long, striped skirt gathered up by the gusts coming off the water. She was clutching the familiar shawl she had wrapped around her, as though its wrappings were the only thing holding her fragile heart together.

It was then, standing there alone upon the cliff's edge, that Connor saw her. Some yards ahead of the children, he made it to her first. The sight of her—her silhouette on the horizon—made him stop. For a moment, he just stared. His hungry soul at last quelled.

As she stood there, her heart stretched out to loved ones she thought long since lost—she heard the voice of a ghost call out her name. Wishing with every fiber of her being for it not to be a mere product of her grief, she slowly turned. Tara's legs gave out from under her. She fell to the ground as she watched Connor approach with her grown son charging up quickly behind him.

Joseph, Anna, Marie, and all the other children, finally, made it to the crest of the hill to see Connor standing beside Tara. Tara gripped tightly to Duncan as the tears streamed from her eyes.

"Wait," Joseph said, holding out his arms to stop everyone, "give them a moment."

There upon the hilltop some yards away from Connor and his family, the children stood witnessing a scene of overflowing love and gratitude. Marie, Anna, Rachel, and Nicolaus held tears in their eyes—there was no more touching scene than that of a family reunited.

Joseph stepped up beside Anna and took her hand. She kept her eyes set on Connor, Tara, and Duncan but squeezed back tightly.

A low, flying bird flickered past him and drew his gaze for the span of a moment, and it was as his eyes turned that he saw a hauntingly familiar sight.

He turned his back on the shore, let go of Anna's hand, and walked forward in a haze. On the edge of the hill he stopped—transfixed on the site before him.

Laid out before him was a green sloping horizon flourishing with trees, tall grasses, and fields ready to yield a bountiful harvest. The deafening din of the city was gone—never to plague him again. His eyes followed the graceful slopes of the scene then moved across a herd of brown cows grazing in the lower pasture of a farm that appeared in the distance. Flocks of plump hens moved around the lawn, pecking and scratching for seeds to eat. Then the smell came to him riding on the wind: that of the hearth as smoke rose from a set of whitewashed, thatched-roof cottages dotting the green field.

Somewhere in the distance behind him, he heard laughter—the laughter of the others. He turned back. Tara, Connor, and Duncan had come. Tara knelt down to meet Emma and Asa. The others moved closer, hungry for the love of their new mother. Joseph's eyes met Anna's. She smiled widely and laughed warmly, reaching out a hand for him. He stepped forward into his new life. The dawn of spring finally broke after the long winter.

With gratitude to those friends and colleagues whose encouragement made this book possible and whose kindness continues to strengthen my work with each passing year: LaRue and Marie Owen, Amy Nawrocki, Eric D. Lehman, David K. Leff, Gunilla Norris, Tomm Moore, Gary Whited, Gail Collins-Ranadive, Jason Kirkey, Theodore Richards, James McDowell, Frank Owen, and others who go unnamed but not forgotten.

Thank you to the staff at the Boston Public Library Central Branch for all their assistance digging through the archives. Many thanks to the staff at The Last Hurrah and the Omni Parker House Hotel for keeping me in good food and clean sheets during my many stays. Finally, a tip of the hat to the "Saturday Club" for giving this New England girl something to aspire to.

Thank you.

————

ABOUT THE AUTHOR

L.M. Browning is an award-winning author of nine books. In her writing, Browning explores the confluence of the natural landscape and the interior landscape. In 2010, she debuted with a three-title contemplative poetry series. These three books went on to garner several accolades including a total of 3 pushcart-prize nominations, the Nautilus Gold Medal for Poetry and *Forward Reviews*' Book of the Year Award. Balancing her passion for writing with her love of learning, Browning sits on the Board of Directors for the Independent Book Publishers' Association, she is a graduate of the University of London, and a Fellow with the International League of Conservation Writers. She is partner at Hiraeth Press as well as Founder and Editor-in-Chief of *The Wayfarer*. In 2011, Browning opened Homebound Publications, an independent publishing house based in Connecticut. She is currently working to complete a B.A. at Harvard University's Extension School in Cambridge, Massachusetts.

www.lmbrowning.com

HOMEBOUND PUBLICATIONS

Ensuring that the mainstream isn't the only stream.

At Homebound Publications, we publish books written by independent voices for independent minds. Our books focus on a return to simplicity and balance, connection to the earth and each other, and the search for meaning and authenticity. Founded in 2011, Homebound Publications is one of the rising independent publishers in the country. Collectively through our imprints, we publish between fifteen to twenty offerings each year. Our authors have received dozens of awards, including: Foreword Review Book of the Year, Nautilus Book Award, Benjamin Franklin Book Awards, and Saltire Literary Awards. Highly-respected among bookstores, readers and authors alike, Homebound Publications has a proven devotion to quality, originality and integrity.

We are a small press with big ideas. As an independent publisher we strive to ensure that the mainstream is not the only stream. It is our intention at Homebound Publications to preserve contemplative storytelling. We publish full-length introspective works of creative non-fiction as well as essay collections, travel writing, poetry, and novels. In all our titles, our intention is to introduce new perspectives that will directly aid humankind in the trials we face at present as a global village.

WWW.HOMEBOUNDPUBLICATIONS.COM

CPSIA information can be obtained
at www.ICGtesting.com
Printed in the USA
BVOW04s0319091216

470300BV00002B/4/P